THE MINNESOTA KINGSTONS | BOOK THREE

DOYLE

THE MINNESOTA KINGSTONS | BOOK THREE

DOYLE

SUSAN MAY WARREN

Doyle

The Minnesota Kingstons, Book 3

Published by SDG Publishing

Print ISBN: 978-1-962036-33-7

For more information about Susan May Warren, please access the author's website at the following address: www.susanmaywarren.com.

Published in the United States of America.

Cover design by Emilie Haney, eahcreative.com

For Your glory, Lord

ONE

THREE MONTHS ON A CARIBBEAN ISLAND helped a man find clarity. Sunshine, sand, and most of all, the children of Hope House orphanage had loosened the grip that grief had on Doyle Kingston.

He might actually be ready for a fresh start.

At the very least, he felt in the best shape of his life.

"Over here, Jamal—I'm open!" He gestured at the eight-year-old as he ran down the rutted, weedy, semi-dirt soccer field, the sun fighting through low-hanging clouds that were turning the field to shadow. Salt and brine hung in the air, waves crashing against the high cliffs where the former-monastery-turned-Hope-House-orphanage sat, and it might be the perfect day to tell the boys the good news.

But not yet.

Jamal dodged a player from the other team—a nine-year-old named Lionel—and then glanced over at Doyle. Jamal wore the yellow-and-white jersey of the Mariposa Wings, the number nine from his favorite player—Ronaldo Vieira, another striker.

Ronaldo and the entire team had donated the jerseys to Hope.

A move Doyle could only blame on Tia Pepper, his new . . . what, codirector?

Annoying wannabe boss?

Doyle kept pace, running at center field. A glance in his periphery said that Aliyah had found a spot in midfield, her brown-eyed gaze on him, ready to intercept. And at goal, sixteen-year-old Kemar wore the gloves Doyle had received in a recent donor package.

Again, Tia's doing. It had been more than a little awkward when she shown up a month after he'd arrived on the island, her only explanation being that she'd been hired by the founder of Hope House, Declan Stone, to "get the orphanage on financial track and head up fundraising."

He'd been hired—by Declan—to reorganize and help the kids find a solid future. Whatever that meant. He was still trying to do that for himself.

Jamal kicked the ball, and Doyle ran to intercept, caught it, and sidestepped Taj, one of the RAs in the boys' dorm, a big guy, wide hands, wider smile. Taj laughed. "Yow, Big D, you drink jet fuel this mornin'?"

Something like that.

Doyle raced down the field and spotted twelve-year-old Fiona waving her arms, open. With her hair bound in tufts on her head, and a generous smile, she'd been easy to spot. He kicked the ball to her.

Aw, it shot past her, out of bounds.

He stopped running, grabbed his knees for a breath.

Andre, another RA, ran to retrieve the ball, blowing his whistle. Lionel set up to throw it in, and his team lined up.

Under the early-afternoon heat, sweat poured down Doyle's face, saturating the back of his shirt, and he was tempted to pull it off. Except he'd already managed a wicked sunburn his first week here. He didn't need a reminder of the way he stood out against the population of the island.

Outsider, from his skin to his mannerisms to his expectations for the kids. Like being on time for, well, *anything*.

So, yeah, he needed to loosen up, live and let live, breathe.

So far, the plan was working—start over, leave the grief behind, focus on something new.

Like finding permanent homes for these children in his care.

He stood up, moving to guard Lionel, the nine-year-old laughing as he pushed Doyle out of his way, stepped in front of him, then grabbed the ball and maneuvered it around him.

"Hey, that's illegal."

"Keep up, old man."

Doyle took off after him and as if to steal the ball, although of course he'd let him win. The entire team had improved since their last game with nearby Sint Eustatius, and now Lionel shot the ball off to Aliyah.

Jamal intercepted and the game turned. Doyle again switched directions, heading toward the goal as Jamal passed it off to Gabriella, a playmaker, lean and tall and fourteen years old. He hadn't found a home for her yet, but maybe she would age out of Hope House, go on to college.

She had the makings of a doctor, the way she helped out in the medical clinic.

Gabriella kicked the ball through the legs of an opponent and raced toward the goal.

She passed it over.

He ran to intercept—

Bam! The collision hit him so hard it hurtled him into the air, and he flew, thudding into the weedy grass.

His head bounced off the ground, and he lay, dazed. Blood erupted from his nose, his face on fire.

"Gotcha."

He held his nose—grimaced and looked up.

Kemar stood over him, holding the ball in his gloves, the sun against his dark head, no smile.

Right.

He sat up, and Kemar stepped away as Andre crouched beside Doyle. "You okay? Let's get you to the clinic."

"I'm fine," Doyle said, even as Gabriella ran up, holding a towel. He shoved it against his nose, then got to his feet.

The world spun.

Kemar stepped away, smirking.

"Why'd you do that, Key?" Jamal had run up, now stood in front of his brother. "You didn't have to hit him." His voice shook.

Doyle held up a hand. "It's just a game, Jamal. We're all good."

Kemar laughed as he grabbed Jamal, his arm around his neck. "See, bro? Don't worry about it."

Jamal pushed away from him. "You good, Mr. D?"

Doyle touched the boy's shoulder. "I'm good. Get back in there." But he didn't miss Kemar's glower. Or the clench in his own gut.

Kemar would hate him if the Jamesons refused to adopt both boys.

Doyle sank onto a bench on the side as Andre blew the whistle. Andre had run to get the out-of-bounds ball that had fallen into an old grotto, now overgrown at the edge of the field. Another project on Doyle's long fix-up list.

Kemar threw the ball back into play.

"Doyle. I've been looking all over for you. I thought you were going to meet me—"

He turned, still holding the towel, now soaked, to his face.

Tia, her long brown hair up, a few hairs falling out of the bun, wearing a sage canvas shirt that pulled the green from her hazel eyes and a pair of black cargo pants and KEENs, strode over to him.

The look in those pretty eyes said *oops,* he'd landed in the doghouse.

Again. Seemed like a regular occurrence over the past two months.

She frowned at the towel, one perfect brown eyebrow dipping, and then shook her head. "You can't go like that."

"Like what?" He took the towel away, glanced at his shirt. Sweaty, blue, and, *oy*—covered in his own blood. Checking his nose—the bleeding had stopped, so maybe not broken—he stood up, trying to wipe the blood off. "Where are we going?"

"Seriously?" She sighed.

Oh, right. "The X-ray machine."

"Yes. It came into the port in Esperanza yesterday." She braced her hands on her hips. "Never mind. I'll take Keon again."

He threw the towel over his shoulder. "No, I'm in. Just give me five to get changed."

"Ten, and you shower first. The harbormaster is new, and . . ." She gave him the once-over. "We don't need you looking like you're a member of the S-7 crew."

"Thanks. First thing I check in the mirror every morning—do I look like a gang member?"

She rolled her eyes. "Just change your shirt."

Of course. Sheesh. Clearly she hadn't gotten their first meeting out of her head.

Talk about needing a fresh start. He sighed as he started walking toward the former monastery's back entrance, where an arched door hung open and led to the interior of the compound.

She followed him, glancing at the game, the kids. "Do they know yet?"

"No. I'm planning to save it. We still have a few days left."

"Scared about what Kemar is going to do?"

He glanced at her, his mouth tight, and didn't answer as he walked through the entrance into the cool embrace of the eighteenth-century building. Freshly whitewashed, the thick walls kept heat from invading, and a long, shaded corridor aproned the complex. The middle courtyard, repaved with black limestone that had turned slick and shiny over the years, held a granite fountain with a statue of the Holy Mother holding baby Jesus in the center.

Beyond that, gates—now closed—opened to a dirt road and a view of the harbor town of Esperanza, the capital of tiny Mariposa and home to some four thousand inhabitants. The town was a postcard—red-roofed stone homes, a few three-story, arched-veranda hotels overlooking the pristine turquoise sea. Fishing boats cluttered the port, evidence of their main source of income—conch, snapper, and mahi-mahi.

The smells from the kitchen—located in the remodeled wing—suggested jerk chicken on tonight's menu, a blend of allspice, Scotch bonnet peppers, and ginger over grilled chicken, and Doyle's stomach growled.

"You sure you don't want to stay?"

"No. I just skipped lunch. I was working on the chapel, then I got roped into the soccer game." He glanced at the open wooden doors to the building across the courtyard. "Had to brace one of the beams—it felt loose."

"I poked my head in. The kids did a great job on the murals."

Was that praise?

"It's a good way to show their talents, as well as the focus of faith we have here." He reached the stairs. "I think the donors will be impressed."

"Impressed? Maybe amused."

For all her beauty, she had a way of dropping a stone into his soul. He reached the stairs. Turned. "I know you think this is a waste of time, but having the donors on-site just might get a few of these kids adopted. And that could change their lives."

She held up a hand, the wind catching her hair, whisking it across her face. "It's not that I don't think it's a good idea, but let's not get your hopes up, Doyle—we need them to donate to the medical clinic, get some real equipment here. The clinic isn't just for the orphanage, it's for the entire community, and it desperately needs equipment and supplies. That's why they're here. The only souvenir these donors want to take home is a conch shell."

Nice.

"I'll meet you at the garage in ten." She walked away.

He bit back a growl and headed up to his room in the center area. The boys' dorms extended down one wing, the girls' along the other. He unlocked his room and opened it to a small but tidy room with an adjacent bath, a single bed, desk, standing wardrobe, and a glorious view of the sea below. Looming over it all was the Cumbre de Luz, the dormant volcano that lumbered along the north side of the island.

The smells from the surf and the lush rainforest vegetation that swept down from the volcano filtered into his room, and he breathed them in as he stripped off his shirt.

If he wanted a fresh start, he'd have to let Tia's cynical words roll off him.

He stepped into the shower, braced his hands on the tile walls, and let the cool water revive him. Who knew what Tia might be trying to escape in the States? He knew very little about her.

Except that she could drive him to his last nerve.

He stepped out, toweled off, pulled on a clean pair of jeans, boots, and a white oxford, rolling up the sleeves. He didn't bother to shave—most of the men on the island wore scruff, many of them fishermen. Others worked in the fledgling tourist industry, hosting divers who came to the island in search of the fabled gold treasures located in the thirteen wrecks caught in the coral reefs offshore.

He raked a hand through his short hair—*good enough*—and headed down to the garage, a building outside the monastery that Declan had added when he'd upgraded security. The garage also housed small security offices, with monitors that captured all corners of the building, as well as a corridor and the main hall.

Thank you to the S-7 crew, whose terrorizing of the locals had only increased after the hurricane five years ago that had left so many of these kids without parents.

Not anymore.

He didn't care what Tia said. He planned on finding homes for every one of these kids. It was the least he could do for the woman he'd once loved. Still loved, but . . . he was moving on.

Trying.

Tia leaned against a lime-green 1960 F-100 pickup, the straps a jumble in the middle. She glanced at her watch. "Twelve minutes."

He shook his head. "Let me drive, and we'll make it up."

She rolled her eyes and walked around to the driver's side.

He took a breath. Exhaled.

Maybe it wasn't so much trying to start over as it was focusing on something new.

He forced a smile and got in.

Like not strangling his codirector.

She refused to listen to fear.

No. fear.

It helped to have Doyle sitting beside her. For all his annoying, too-easygoing, charming ways, Doyle was built, and she'd seen him pop back up after Kemar had slammed into him.

Not a guy who stayed down easily.

Even if he should back away from his big, unrealistic dreams.

But if Sebold and his S-7 crew showed up at the port, having Doyle around might . . . what?

Yeah, she should have brought Keon. Their security guard had about fifty pounds on Doyle, and sure, he possessed the personality of a Brahman bull, but maybe that's what she needed.

Power over personality.

Tia blew out a breath as she bumped down the dirt road on the way to Esperanza, the town at the base of the massive volcano, dormant for centuries now, just a few ridges of black lava that spilled into the sea.

The village sat in a pocket between ridges, largely protected from hurricanes—although they'd taken a direct hit some five years ago, according to her research.

It had devastated not only the village but also the sugar and cocoa plantations northeast of town. And birthed the S-7 gang.

Namely, its leader Sebold Grimes.

She blew out a breath, gripping the steering wheel of the old Ford. Hope House needed a fleet of new vehicles, starting with a supply truck that didn't have gears that slipped and fought her as she downshifted.

"Easy on the clutch—"

She shot Doyle a look. He'd put out his foot, held on to the handle over the door. There were no seatbelt laws in Mariposa, but she guessed he wouldn't wear one anyway.

Doyle Kingston followed his own rules. Like playing soccer with the kids when they needed to prepare the grounds for the upcoming Hope House fundraising weekend. It wasn't every day that twenty or so multimillionaires showed up to tour their facilities and consider taking on their tiny project.

"Listen, this weekend has to go well. Just a few big donors could change the entire outlook for these kids. Give them education beyond what the nuns at the school can provide."

"The nuns are fantastic."

"They are. But they also teach in giant one-room classrooms. They can't possibly prepare these kids for colleges like St. George's

University in Grenada or even the School of Medicine in Sint Maarten."

He sighed. "I know. Gabriella has the smarts to go to medical school. Did you know that Dr. Julia Tremblay, our local doctor, attended there?"

"I do." In fact, Tia's head was too full of ideas that ran through her mind every night as she lay on her bed, staring at the whirring fan, the sounds of the sea outside her window.

Yes, here maybe she could shake off the last three years, find herself again. She just needed to stay focused.

Doyle held up his hands. "I'm not saying they're not smart enough, but kids have a much better chance of success with a loving family behind them."

She refused to argue with him. Yes, family helped. But so did determination. Edward had taught her that.

And in the end, his connection to her family had gotten him killed. So, there was that.

They came into town, passing a fruit stand with fresh mangoes, papayas, passion fruit, and guava.

"Let's stop there on the way home," Doyle said, clearly reading her mind.

"Yeah, if we're not on the run from a gang of thieves."

"Wow. And me without my machete. Listen, it's going to be fine." He looked over at her. "You brought some cheddar, right?"

She frowned at him. "What?"

"A bribe?"

Her mouth opened.

He shook his head. "You've been here nearly two months and you haven't figured that out yet?"

"I don't bribe people."

"For the love—it's the culture. Think of it as a *tip*."

"It's dishonest."

"Yeah, we're not getting that X-ray machine."

She nearly slammed on the brakes and told him to get out. She drew in a breath. "If we don't try, then it'll end up in the hands of the S-7 crew, and buh-bye any more donations."

"I thought they only worked on the other side of the island."

"According to Dr. Julia, they stole an entire pallet of medical supplies from the harbor—and then offered to sell it to her for a ransom." She looked at him. "Or should we call it a *tip*?"

"That's different." He folded his arms. "Okay, we'll get the X-ray machine. Don't worry."

Oh, she was plenty worried. "Just . . . let me handle it."

He quirked an eyebrow. "Okay, *boss*."

For the love, as he would say.

They entered a neighborhood, and after a moment he said, "Is Declan coming to the fundraiser?"

"I don't know." It was hard not to glance at Declan's home, settled above the town, a sentry. If it hadn't been for his generosity after the storm, the monastery would have stayed destroyed, the children homeless. He'd put hope back on the map, literally.

She'd discovered that back in Minnesota after he'd offered her the job. Did her research and decided this could be her chance.

No more murder, no more grief, no more wishing she'd listened to her head instead of her heart years ago.

Never again.

Which was why it didn't matter how handsome, or charming, Doyle Kingston might be with those deep-blue, nearly hypnotizing eyes, that short dark-brown hair, all tousled on his head, the thin layer of dark whiskers, the white oxford that showed off his tanned forearms, and the smell that drifted off him—the fresh shower, the soap, a hint of sandalwood, and maybe a little ocean breeze—

Stop.

Why Declan Stone had hired him—well, he certainly hadn't

told her. And it had felt a little like a slap when she arrived to find Doyle wondering the same thing.

Codirector. She didn't codirect anything. *Hello.* Why Declan had left that tidbit of information out of his offer, she didn't know.

But she wasn't turning around, thanks.

Boss was right.

Now, Doyle nodded, his elbow out the window. "I think Declan's back on the island. My brother Stein works for him—personal security—and sent me a text saying he was here."

"I send Declan a weekly report, and he mentioned that." She lifted a shoulder.

"You send him a weekly report?" He looked at her.

"Don't you?"

He raised an eyebrow.

She refrained from shaking her head.

"Maybe Declan will get smart and give the entire operation to me." Words she'd said to her sister Penelope, back in Minnesota, a couple weeks ago on the phone.

"I don't know, sis. Conrad says his brother is pretty good at these humanitarian gigs. Spent a lot of his time on a disaster-relief team over the years, raising money and working with the locals."

At the time, Tia had pictured her sister in her cute remodeled bungalow in Minneapolis, probably poring over research for her newest murder podcast. No doubt wearing the hockey jersey of her boyfriend, Conrad Kingston, who inconveniently had to be the older brother of said Doyle.

That was an unlucky coincidence. The last thing Tia wanted was for her complaint to make it to Doyle via her sister, via her boyfriend, via . . . whomever. His family seemed closer than most. You never knew when a Kingston would pop up—case in point, his brother Stein working for Declan.

She seemed to be surrounded by Kingstons.

"Just try to not be so bossy. Get along with him. You'll find that he has more in common with you than you think."

Doubtful.

At best, he would charm the donors, prime them for her big ask—to upgrade the medical clinic with a three-million-dollar renovation and equipment donation.

They bumped along on the coral-encrusted roads, past reconstructed neighborhoods, all the way to the city center, also rebuilt, with new two-story, Louisiana-style storefronts, metal roofing, and charming galleries with pillars supporting the long second-story balconies. Freshly planted palm trees edged the boardwalk, from which stretched the black sand beach. Hand-painted store signs gave the village a quaint feel, and with so few cars on the island, the cobblestone streets held mostly scooters, a few bicyclists, and a number of food carts.

Out in the harbor, sailboats attached to mooring balls stretched into a blue sky, and farther out, a cruise ship sailed south, probably on the way to St. Kitts.

She spotted the shipping harbor, a deep-water harbor, dredged out after the hurricane, that allowed for yachts and supply ships.

"There's the *Invictus*," Doyle said. "Whoa, she's pretty."

"Where?"

He pointed to the one-hundred-and-fifty-foot yacht owned by Stone, moored at his private dock in a channel cut out into the harbor.

"Wow. It's three stories."

"And has a helicopter. Holy cannoli. I can't even imagine being that wealthy."

Right. She glanced at him, said nothing. But yes, even her father, billionaire owner of the Pepper fortune, didn't have his own helicopter, although he did own a nice chunk of a Caribbean island and a small yacht. And sure, she could ask her father for the money for the hospital. But he had his own charitable organization he was trying to keep funded, and frankly . . .

Frankly, she wanted to shake off everything that had to do with the Pepper name. Not forever . . . but . . . reasons.

She was lucky to have made it out without a cadre of security agents.

So she kept her mouth shut and pulled up to the gates guarding the harbor. A man emerged from the security booth.

"Tia Pepper, with Hope House. I'm here to see the harbormaster."

He stepped back, called in clearance on his radio, and in a moment, the gate shuddered open.

She drove in, up to the three-story building-slash-warehouse. Got out. "I'll go talk to the harbormaster"

"I'll check on the shipment."

She glanced at Doyle, a chill brushing through her.

No fear. She could handle Mr. Harbormaster.

"Please don't get us in trouble," she said to Doyle.

"Oh ye of little faith." He held up his fist.

She looked at it. "What's this?"

"A fist bump."

She shook her head. "No, I don't . . . Doyle, we're not *buddies*. We're workmates." Or really, maybe rivals, but she wouldn't go that far because in truth, he stayed out of the financial running of the orphanage. But he did have a different agenda for the week with the donors, so maybe.

"We'll fix that." He pointed at her, then headed around the building.

She didn't need fixing, and she nearly shouted that, but the door opened, and a large man, clearly a descendant of the island inhabitants, smiled at her.

"Miss Pepper, right?" He stuck out a beefy hand.

Seemed nice enough. "That's right. I'm here to pick up our shipment."

"Mr. Nevo Baptiste. Come in, then. Let's get the paperwork started."

See? Nothing to fear. She'd overthought everything until she tied herself into a knot.

She walked inside, past an empty reception desk, into an office, all windows except for the back wall, which held shipping schedules and mapped routes. He motioned to a rolling chair, then leaned against the front of his desk, arms folded. "So, unfortunately, there are fees attached to the storage of your pallet."

"It just got here yesterday." She sank into the chair. A metal fan hummed from the top of a filing cabinet, stirring stale air, the lingering memory of a cigarette, lifting a couple of papers on the desk.

He sighed, his barrel body rising and falling. "Yes, but we had to unload it and store it in the warehouse, and . . . so much trouble."

"Right. I thought those fees were covered in the shipping costs. And were prepaid."

He made a tsking noise and got up, shut the door.

She didn't know why the click sent ice through her.

He pressed a hand on her shoulder, leaned down behind her, spoke into her ear. "These are island fees, Miss Pepper."

She stilled. "How much?"

He paused. "Twenty thousand dollars."

Okay, breathe. "That wasn't . . . I don't—"

"Then perhaps we could negotiate." He put the other hand on her shoulder. His low voice into her other ear. "Let me bring in my negotiator."

Behind her, the door opened.

No fear. No—

As someone closed the blinds, they shook, and she along with them. She jerked away from Nevo and turned.

A man stood behind him. Dark hair, bearded, dressed in white pants, a Hawaiian shirt, and flip-flops. He cocked his head at her, smiled. "Hello, Miss Pepper."

Sebold. Just a guess, but by the way he glanced at Nevo and smirked—

"What do you want?"

"I think you know. Baptiste told me about your new toy." He put a hand on Nevo's shoulder. "We think probably you need some insurance to keep it safe."

Insurance?

"On top of the fees, we're going to need some . . . monthly attention."

He turned her chair, crouched in front of her, his hands on hers, on the armrests. Ran his thumb over the back of her hand.

Don't scream.

His unwashed odor swept over her.

A knock at the door, and then, suddenly, it burst open.

Doyle stuck his head in. "Hey, guys. So, I think we're done here, Tia. Let's go."

She stood up.

The motion knocked Sebold onto his backside, and she stepped over him and nearly lunged for Doyle's outstretched hand.

"Thanks, guys," Doyle said and shut the door.

She turned to him—

"Keep moving." He nearly pushed her out the main door.

The truck was gone. "Where—"

"Just keep moving." He pushed her across the parking lot, around the back to the warehouse, where her truck sat, the X-ray machine in a box in the back, strapped in.

"My grandfather had a Ford like this. Easy to hotwire." He clamped a hand on a skinny man, maybe early twenties. "Thanks, Ricky."

Doyle got into the driver's side of the still-running truck, and ahead, someone had opened another gate.

Shouts fell behind them, and Doyle floored it. Tia spotted Sebold running across the yard toward the truck.

They cleared the gate, and dust kicked up as drove up the road.

What just happened? She'd suddenly landed in a rerun of *MacGyver*.

Doyle gripped the wheel, glanced back, then at her.

"What did you just do?" She too shot a look behind them.

Sebold stood, gesturing, yelling at one of the guards. She winced when he hit the younger man.

"I got your X-ray machine out of hock. And I'm not sure what was going down back there in the office, but from the looks of it, it didn't look like you were making friends."

She gripped the overhead handle, still shaking. "They wanted twenty thousand dollars."

"Yipe. My Seiko was considerably less, so I guess it was a deal."

"You traded your watch? A dive watch?"

He lifted a shoulder. "Gut move. I figured, write-off, you know?" He shrugged. "Now we just have to make sure that Sebold and his boys don't decide to pay us a visit."

Her eyes widened, and she looked away, her heart still a hammer, her throat thick. Heaven save her from a man who led with his *gut*. "I don't do impulsive, Doyle. I had a *plan*."

"Which was?"

She swallowed. "I was going to negotiate."

He raised an eyebrow. "Yeah. So that's what that was." He turned onto the road back to Hope House. "Sorry to mess with your negotiation, but my gut said you weren't going to win."

And now he'd probably ignited a small war with the local gang. And the timing couldn't be worse.

Still, he *had* saved her. Sort of. Probably. She sighed. "How much trouble are we in?"

"Calm down. We have security." He lifted his hand from the

steering wheel, and for a second he looked like he might reach out to her, and maybe—touch her arm? In reassurance?

"Thanks." She sighed. "Keon usually handled that before. I just wanted . . . That was a dumb idea."

And now he did reach out, pat her arm. "No problem, partner. We're in this together." Then he looked at her and winked.

Oh boy. That's what she was afraid of. Another person in her life that just might get himself—and maybe even her—killed.

TWO

DOYLE MIGHT NEVER FORGET THE TERROR written on Tia's face when he'd opened the door to the harbormaster's office.

For two nights that image had filled his mind before he fell asleep. And of course, in his dreams, he marched inside, grabbed Sebold by his skinny throat and—

And then he usually woke up, shaking, because the fury in his veins couldn't live there. He'd worked so hard to expel it from his body . . .

It helped that Tia seemed unfazed by the incident. They'd spent the past three days installing the X-ray machine, and Dr. Julia had even used it to check Aliyah's arm after a collision with Lionel on the soccer pitch.

Doyle had asked Keon to add a night guard to the building, and so far no issues, but he'd seen the look on Sebold's face.

Trouble. Doyle had been lucky to only lose his watch.

Now he wished for said watch as he entered one of the classrooms, clearly already late. Taj sat with a few of the boys—Jaden,

Elias, and Rohan, along with Kemar and Jamal, who were waging a brotherly thumb war.

Pictures hung on the walls—self-portraits done in what he'd call cubism style—along with a multiplication chart, an alphabet, including diphthongs, and the periodic table. So yes, a mishmash of ages. Maybe Tia was right about upping their education.

The kids seemed pretty smart, however. Jaden had walloped him in a game of chess, and they devoured the books in the library. So this was what a life without e-devices looked like.

Jaden grinned at him, wearing a clean white dress shirt and black pants. "Heya, Mr. D. You like us now?"

"I always liked you, JJ." Doyle grabbed a chair and turned it around, leaning his arms on the back. The cute Parnell twins looked up at him from where they sat on the floor driving cars around a road mat. With their gap-toothed six-year-old smiles and bright eyes, he dared anyone not to fall in love with them.

The girls had come in too, Aliyah, with her arm in a sling, wearing a dress that she'd picked out from the clothing sent by his mother's church. Cottage style, he thought they called it in the States—gingham with a ruffle. A few other girls also wore that style, a number in pants and blouses.

A hint of hope hung in the air. And he didn't want to pop it, but . . .

"Okay, ladies and gents, it's a big night. These people are . . . well, they care about Hope House. And we're going to be on our best behavior just in case God nudges some of them to—"

"Adopt us!" This from Lionel, who turned and pumped his fist.

"Yes." Doyle let out a sigh, nodded. "I know you heard the rumors that a few of the donors have inquired about adoption. Do not ask them. And remember, you are already loved, by the staff here and by your Father in heaven. Maybe some of you will go to new homes. But others might stay, and that is exactly where you're supposed to be. And to be fair, I'd miss you all terribly."

He got a smile from Gabriella, who stood back, one arm clutched to her elbow, a wary expression in her eyes.

Tia's words about sending some of the older teens to university pinged inside him. She might be exactly—

"What if they want one of us and not the other?" Kemar asked, his arm around Jamal's neck, his eyes hard on Doyle's.

"Let's not get ahead of ourselves—"

"Ain't nobody taking Jamal." Kemar found his feet.

Doyle held up a hand. "Nobody is taking anyone. This is your choice too, Kemar. You say no and it's done. But . . ." He drew in a breath. "You might consider that families matter—"

"We have a family!" This from Jaden, who glanced at Kemar.

"Yes. But some of these people need a child like . . . well, like you, Elias, to love."

Elias lifted a shoulder, looked away.

"Let's just go to the party, and please—be on your best behavior, okay?" Doyle stood up and set the chair back at the table.

"Like you were down at the docks?" Again, Kemar, and Doyle frowned.

Kemar surveyed the group. "I heard that Mr. D went all beast mode against the S-7 crew. Grabbed the X-ray machine right out of their hands, bam! Took them down!" He'd stood up, made a few hand gestures.

Aw. Doyle held up a hand. "I did not *take anyone down*, Kemar. I . . ." All eyes were on him. "I . . . um, persuaded them to work with me."

Shoot. Sort of a lie. Sort of not.

"That's the way to do it. '*Persuade*.'" Kemar finger quoted the words. He grinned at Doyle, held up his fist. "That's savage, Mr. D. Don't let nobody tell you what you can't do. C'mon, Jamal. Let's go eat something."

Jamal scooted off the desk he sat on and followed Kemar out the door.

Taj came up to Doyle. "Sorry, man. I should have shut that down. I heard one of the guards talking to Kemar and Jaden a couple days ago. Clearly the story got bigger."

Not much, but Doyle nodded. "It was more God's providence than anything."

"Heard you traded your sweet wrist candy to liberate Mr. X-ray. Tragic."

"It's okay, Taj." He had liked the watch—his sister Austen had given it to him last Christmas. "I had to think of something."

"Betcha Miss Tia was happy." Taj winked, walked out the door.

Not that he could tell. Seemed like she wanted to wallop him. At least, five minutes *after* the look of terror.

He followed Taj out of the room into the glittery evening. A local band played soca music, a blend of soul and calypso, the energy smooth and infectious as it lifted around the courtyard. Twinkle lights hung along the upper-floor balustrades, and in the center of the yard, food tables held the best of Hope House's kitchen—roti, flatbread filled with curried vegetables; callaloo, leaves filled with coconut milk and crab patties; baked pasta shells with spicy seasoned meat; and of course, conch fritters. And the nuns had crafted a batch of nonalcoholic rum punch.

Fire blazed in floating containers in the fountain, and guests strolled through the front gate, greeted by Andre and the female residence director, a twenty-something woman named Anita.

Most of the guests wore flip-flops or sandals, some in bright island colors, others in fancy summer dresses, most of them talking in their own groups. Doyle had the sense that many of them already knew each other before they walked in the doors.

His gaze found Tia and stuck there. She wore her dark brown hair down in a loose braid, the wind twining a few fallen tendrils through its fingers. Her white cottage-style dress showed off her tan, and she wore it off the shoulder, with puffy sleeves and hem ruffles that fell just above her toes, which poked out from the bottom.

One of the little girls came up and gave her a side hug. Tia grinned down at her, said something that made the little girl laugh.

He shouldn't be so hard on her. Tia cared about their well-being. She simply did it in a different way.

By the time he made it downstairs, she stood by the hors d'oeuvres table with a tiny square plate, adding conch fritters and grilled shrimp on a skewer.

"Impressive spread," he said.

"Thanks." She picked up a napkin, blew out a breath. "Most of it was Rosa, but it was my idea to do the floating fire in the fountain. Did that once for an EmPowerPlay event."

He chose a conch. "That's right—you ran your family's charitable organization."

Her eyebrow quirked. "You know that?"

Now his eyebrow rose. "My brother is dating your sister."

She popped the conch into her mouth, nodding, then choked, covering her mouth.

"Hey, you okay?" He stepped back, and she managed to swallow, took a drink.

"Yes." She coughed again. "Sorry."

"I have Heimlich skills, and I know how to use them."

Was that a hint of a smile?

"We should mingle," she said, setting down her plate at a discard table. "When does the program start?"

"Program?"

She stared at him, her eyes wide. "I thought you . . . Aren't the kids going to sing?"

Oh . . . "Aw, you were serious?"

"Of course I was serious. I thought . . ." She turned away, shook her head. Turned back. "Okay. No problem. Maybe I could interview a couple of them."

"Sure. I'll ask Aliyah and . . . maybe Jamal." Get them in front of the audience. And he had it on his list to meet Elise and Hunter Jameson, who'd asked him about adopting Jamal . . . and hopefully Kemar.

"I see Declan." She raised her hand, and he turned.

Not only Declan Stone, who walked through the crowd wearing a linen shirt, dress pants, and loafers, but beside him, similarly dressed, although probably hiding an armory, Doyle's brother Stein.

Stein had cut his dark-blond hair shorter, shaved, and wore a hint of a tan. No smile, though, so he hadn't changed that much. Doyle followed Tia over to the pair.

Tia gave Declan a hug. "Thanks for bringing in so many potential donors."

"Aw, Tia, you're the brains behind this. I knew I could count on you." He turned to Doyle. "And there's my other director. Thanks for whipping this place into shape. Rumor in town is that you're training up a coed soccer team to compete in the tri-island competition this fall."

"We have some great kids, sir." Doyle shook his hand, then nodded to his brother, who gestured to him to step away for a private chat. "How are you doing?"

"Me?" Stein asked. "I don't have a BOLO out with my face on it from a local gang."

Oh.

Stein's mouth pinched. "If you needed backup, you should have called me."

"I didn't need—" Doyle sighed. "I had it under control."

"Bro—"

"Stein. Listen. Small altercation. It'll blow over."

"Doyle. These S-7 guys are dangerous. Yes, they mostly live on the other side of the island, but they've been creeping over into Esperanza, and we think they're trying to gain control of the port.

And if they do that, they get control of the fishing, and then local businesses are affected and . . ." He ran a hand across his mouth. "Just watch your back. This Sebold character is . . . There are stories."

"What kind of stories?"

The voice came from behind them, and even Stein jolted, turning.

Doyle had no words at the sight of his big sister Austen standing in the glow of the firelight. Her hair had grown since Boo's wedding last winter, and brightened under the sun, the red in it sparkling against the flicker of light. With her deep green-blue eyes and slim build, she always reminded him a little of a mermaid, given her love of the sea.

Now, she wore a black sundress and sandals and held a rum punch. "Hey, bros. 'Sup?"

"Austen, what the—" Stein started.

Doyle leaned in for a hug.

She one-arm hugged him, then Stein. "Declan brought me for some tourist dive he's putting together. They need a guide down to the *Trident*."

"Which is?" Doyle said.

"A pirate ship that went down in the late seventeen hundreds. The thing is, they had just looted a Dutch ship, so apparently she was full of gold bullion and all sorts of riches." She leaned in. "There's lore that the gold is somewhere at the bottom of the sea."

"And you're going to find it?"

"No, I'm going to find myself with some good tips after I bring Declan's guests sixty feet down and back up again, safely." She lifted her glass. "Please tell me you're both coming with me. I can't remember the last time we went diving, Stein."

"Me either."

"I went with Doyle two years ago—remember when you came down to visit me?"

He did, and made a grim nod.

She sighed.

"I'll do what I can, Tennie," Doyle said. "I get pretty busy with the kids. Speaking of . . ." He'd spotted Kemar filling up a plate with patties. "Excuse me." He walked over to the kid and Jamal, who held a handful of olives plucked from a bowl on the table.

He took the plate from Kemar's hand.

"What?"

"You had dinner. This is for the guests."

"C'mon—that's not fair. I'm a guest." He picked up the plate, grabbed a patty, and shoved it into his mouth.

The sauce spilled down his shirt.

"Nice, Kemar." Doyle looked down at Jamal. He'd finished the last of his olives and wiped his hand on his pants.

Perfect. "Would you like to meet some nice people?" He held out his hand.

Jamal took it, glanced at Kemar.

"We're having baked plantain and custard for dessert. I'll make sure you get some." Doyle addressed his words to Jamal, then looked at Kemar. "Please. We are trying to make a good impression here. Try to . . . just . . ." He drew in a breath. "Would you like to—"

"No. I'm outta here." Kemar turned to Jamal. "You with him or me?"

Jamal's eyes widened.

"Give me five minutes, Kemar," Doyle said. "Please."

Kemar shrugged and walked away. Maybe he was a lost cause. Kemar was eight years older than Jamal. But Jamal still needed a father, a mother, a chance.

He recognized Elise and Hunter Jameson from the photos they'd sent—both from North Carolina. She was petite and pretty, dark hair down to her shoulders. He had darker skin, dark hair and eyes, a warm smile. They both wore pink shirts and white pants and held rum punch.

They talked with a couple—the woman shorter, blonde, fit, and possessing a hint of a trophy-wife vibe as she stood next to an older man, tall, white hair, tanned.

Doyle came up to the group. "Everybody having fun?"

"This is groovy music," said the blonde, swaying a little.

"It's called soca. It's local. You must be Elise and Hunter." He stuck his hand out to the couple, and they shook it.

"I'm Dr. Scott, and this is my wife, Heather," said the older man as he crouched down to Jamal's level. "And who is this?" He looked at Jamal.

"I'm Jamal." He held out his hand, smiled.

"Glad to meet you, Jamal. I'm a dentist. You know what dentists do?"

"Sure. They fix teeph."

Dr. Scott ruffled his hair, grinned. Stood up. "I heard that Declan got a new orphanage manager," he said. "Last time we came, the place was in a little disarray."

Heather put her hand to the side of her mouth. "Riffraff."

Right. Doyle turned to Elise and Hunter. "Would you like a tour? Jamal and the other kids have painted murals in the chapel."

"Really? I'd love to see them." Elise held out her hand to Jamal.

He hesitated and Doyle grabbed his hand instead. "We'll walk with you."

Elise nodded, kept her smile, and he wove through the crowd.

Oh good, Anita and Aliyah were chatting with the Roses, a couple from Tennessee, and Taj had introduced Lionel to the Stuckeys, from Texas.

Maybe this would work. At least for a few of the kids.

They headed to the chapel. The place had been a wreck when Doyle arrived, the ceiling beams caved in, the floor chipped, the windows broken, the altar in shambles. He'd debated rebuilding it as a church, but the nuns had long ago rebuilt the monastery church, with the stained-glass windows and domed nave, and the priest from town came up to hold Mass every Sunday.

So this he'd made into an escape. When he'd restored the altar, he'd found a small room behind the gated area of the altar, down a stairway in the back, filled with wine. The priests' secret wine room.

He'd repaired the stairs, then restored the altar, but he'd removed the crucifix and hung a cross. Then he'd installed leaded windows, created at a shop in town, and whitewashed the walls. Retiled the floor in stone. Added simple prayer pews. Started taking his morning coffee in here, reading his Bible, praying.

And now, murals from the children painted the walls—waves and shorelines dotted with palm trees, the dark volcano. In one rendition, it erupted, with yellow lava flowing down its slopes. Coconut trees and pictures of the sugar-cane plantation and a flowing sea with octopuses and dolphins and crabs and sharks . . . The chapel had come alive with color.

As he stepped inside the room, lit with flickering candles, the place felt nearly magical. A few other donors followed them in.

"These are amazing," said Elise. "Which one is yours, Jamal?"

He pointed to a whale floating on the sea.

"That's a big whale," said Hunter.

"I can see them sometimes, from my window!" Jamal squeezed Doyle's hand.

"Wow." Elise crouched in front of him. "I've never seen a whale."

Doyle leaned over. "My guess is that they're dolphins."

Elise looked up at him, her face alight. Back to Jamal. "What else can you see from your window?"

"The ocean. Big waves. Sometimes Kemar is outside, riding his motorbike."

Kemar had a motorbike?

Doyle said nothing, and Jamal let go of his hand.

"Want to see my elephant?" He grabbed Elise's hand.

"Absolutely."

She walked away with Jamal, toward his depiction of the jungle. Okay, so Jamal had a wild imagination.

But Kemar, outside the orphanage?

It didn't feel made up.

Doyle walked out of the chapel, passing a few of the other guests, then stood in the courtyard, scanning for Kemar.

His gaze landed on Tia. She stood holding a cup of rum punch, listening, nodding, something sparking in her beautiful eyes.

Oh, for Pete's sake. Eyes. Just eyes.

But she seemed mesmerized by the conversation. Or maybe just by the man.

Doyle didn't know him. Blond, tall, built. A Hemsworth-style guy with round glasses, wearing a suitcoat and jeans, loafers.

And then she laughed, and a spear went through him.

C'mon, Doyle.

He turned away, not caring.

Not caring at all.

This night had all the earmarks of success. *Unless* . . . He turned away and headed up to the boys' dorm, a fist in his gut.

This was not some sort of competition. So what that Doyle had hugged some beautiful, tanned—and had Tia mentioned beautiful?—donor with long blondish hair and reddish highlights. Not that she was looking! And of course he'd laughed with her and the man who'd walked in with Declan. Tia guessed that might be his former SEAL brother, given the dark and intense once-over he'd given the orphanage compound, and then the tight-lipped nod to Doyle's story about the altercation at the harbor.

She had to stop thinking about the way Doyle had popped his head into the office and saved her.

From what, she didn't want to guess, but she knew it in her bones.

Doyle Kingston had used his stupid, annoying charm, not to mention his fancy watch, to get her that X-ray machine and get her to safety, and she owed him.

She hated owing people.

More, she'd been stuck here for the better part of fifteen minutes talking with Ethan Pine, who, albeit handsome, had spun some crazy story about a sunken treasure, and all the while, her stupid gaze kept drifting over to Doyle, sweetly holding Jamal's hand, then walking into the chapel and—

Just. stop.

"So, if there's a way I could spend some time in your library, I might be able to uncover the story."

Aw. "Um. Remind me again—the story?"

Ethan took a sip of punch, then lowered his voice. "The one about the pirate."

The pirate.

"I wanna hear about the pirate."

She glanced over and spotted Jaden standing nearby, dressed in his best shirt, a splotch of curry on the front. Elias stood with him. "Tell us about the pirate."

Ethan smiled. He walked over to the edge of the fountain, sat.

Please don't get burned. She wanted to say it, but he moved away from the flame as Elias sat down.

Little Soraya sat on Elias's lap, and his arms went around her. *Sweet.* Next to them sat Lani, so young when she'd come to the orphanage that she didn't remember her parents. Doyle wasn't wrong to find them homes, but they needed so much in the meantime. And what about those who didn't find families? Didn't get the happy ending that others got?

She stepped back, a chill brushing through her, something in the wind, and she looked up, hoping a rain gust wasn't moving in.

The air hung thick with the scent of the sea, and the glow of the flames rippled on the water. The soca players had taken a break, leaving just the murmur of conversation.

"Are you sure you're ready?" Ethan asked, grinning.

"Tell uth!" This from Lando, one of the seven-year-olds. He had gotten his cleft lip corrected a year ago, during a Mercy Ships docking.

"This is the tale of Raging Rodrigo and the Dutch merchantman." He looked at Tia and winked.

She should find Doyle, see how it was going. Her gaze went to the chapel, but it seemed that it had emptied, the children joining the rest of the listeners.

"It was a night much like this, dark as a crow's feather, and windy enough to sweep the devil off his course."

Giggles, and even she smiled.

"Raging Rodrigo was a fearsome pirate, notorious across the Caribbean for his cunning and greed. It was the golden age of piracy, and he aimed to carve his name alongside the likes of Blackbeard and Calico Jack. But that night, his eyes were bigger than his belly, you might say. He set his sights on a Dutch ship, heavy-laden and slow from its long voyage, just entering the harbor . . ."

"And filled with gold, right?" This from Jaden.

"Yes. Gold and spices, enough to make any man's heart quicken. Rodrigo took it all, but his greed was his undoing. He loaded his ship with the Dutchman's gold, hoping to escape, but as soon as he sailed out of the harbor, the gale hit. He tried to make off with the gold in the chaos of the storm. His ship, the *Trident,* didn't stand a chance against those rocks." He pointed northwest, toward the cliffs. "Dashed against the rocks, it went down, into the depths." He lowered his voice. "To Davy Jones's locker."

Tia laughed and looked across the crowd that had formed. Declan Stone stood with the woman Doyle had greeted. He leaned over, said something to her. She smiled.

So maybe . . . Aw, what was her problem? She'd been so very blind for years, maybe now she'd overcorrected. It didn't matter—Doyle was her coworker. Er, codirector, rather . . .

Aw, whatever. Dating a co*director* could only get complicated. She was over complicated, *thank you.*

"What happened to Rodrigo?" one of the donors, a blonde, asked Ethan.

"They say he washed overboard, swallowed by the sea. Never found his body, nor the gold. But"—he held up his hand—"someone did survive."

A beat.

"Who?" Lionel, now, standing in the back. "Who lived?"

"The only soul who made it to shore was a young Dutch sailor, name of Henry van der Meer. The monks found him half dead on the beach come morning, clutching a piece of the wreck."

"What about the gold?"

Tia looked up, tried to find the source of the question. Ethan did too. He looked around, then leaned back toward the children.

"Henry never spoke a word about the gold. Claimed he knew nothing. But folks around here? They say he found it and hid it away, fearing Rodrigo's ghost and greedy eyes alike."

"On the island?" Jaden whispered.

Tia rolled her eyes. *Great. Just super.* Now she'd have children sneaking out to find lost gold.

Ethan shrugged. "Many have looked. But this island's got secrets as deep as the ocean."

"I'd hide something in the crypt under the chapel. No one goes there," Rohan said.

What crypt? She gave him a look, shook her head. They didn't need treasure hunters, or even the kids trying to find a secret passageway under the monastery.

Rohan shrugged. "Just saying. I heard bootleggers used to hide whiskey in caskets."

"That's enough, Ro."

He grinned at her.

"Yes, maybe it's just waiting for someone brave enough to look for it," said Ethan. "Or maybe it's cursed, just like Rodrigo and his ill-fated plunder."

"Nothing is cursed," Tia said, giving him a look. "There's no such thing as curses."

Ethan pushed his glasses up his nose. "Curses or no, it's a good pirate story. And maybe, just maybe, we'll find it, eh, kids?"

A few clapped, and *oh, see,* that's why he wanted to visit the library.

Ethan Pine was a treasure hunter.

The musicians came back, and the music revived, and in a minute she'd have to host the program, although the kids had already seemed to make friends with the adults. Gabriella and Fiona had started to dance with little Soraya, and a couple women joined in. Andre had found a female donor in her mid-fifties to dance with, and Anita danced with another donor, a man.

So, maybe . . . relax.

Ethan came back to her. "What do you say? Let me into the library?"

She pressed a hand against her growling stomach. "Why do you think you'll find any information there?"

"Because our boy Henry was rescued by these very monks and lived here for ten years before he went back to Holland." He raised an eyebrow. "My research tells me that the library has books dating all the way back to before the shipwreck. And Henry was a journaler." He touched his chest. "Give a guy a break?"

She sighed. "Who are you again?"

He held out his hand. "Ethan Pine. Stellartech."

"Wait. You design satellites."

"Yes. And we launch them into orbit. Our grid is nearly worldwide. We're setting up Declan Stone's new communications system. And in the meantime—" He held out his hands. "It's just for fun."

"Okay. Sure. But you also have to let me give you a tour of our medical clinic so I can show you what we're hoping to accomplish."

"Absolutely." He lifted his now-empty rum-punch glass.

"Declan mentioned your clinic." This from a taller, older man, attached to a blonde woman. "Do you have any dentistry?"

"Not yet, but we'd love that. We just got an X-ray machine, and a few weeks ago, a portable ultrasound machine. The clinic in town was destroyed by the hurricane, so we're the only place people can go for care. Our resident physician is a local, and she makes house calls and works out of our clinic. The ultrasound machine has been a game changer. I don't know that we've met—" She held out her hand.

"Dr. Greg Scott, and my wife, Heather." He gripped her hand. "We're old friends of the family, back when the Stones had property in Miami." He gestured to Declan's house on the hill in the distance, all lit up and white. "He's upgraded." He laughed at his own joke.

She smiled. "Would you like to see the clinic?"

"Tomorrow, maybe. We're jet-lagged." He put his arm around his wife. "Besides, I promised my wife a view of the stars from the hot tub in our room."

Tia raised an eyebrow. "Okay. Um . . ."

"Great party, though. Love the seafood." He grabbed his wife's hand, did a Travolta move to pull her onto the dance floor.

As Tia finished her drink she spotted movement on the second story.

Doyle, coming out of one of the boys' rooms. *Weird.* She set her glass on a tray, then headed toward the stairs. She met him at the top of the staircase. "Everything okay?"

He looked drawn. "I think so. Jamal said that he saw Kemar

with a motorbike outside the orphanage and . . . I don't know. The way Kemar left earlier—"

"He left?"

"Got mad at me. I told him to stop eating all the patties."

She folded her arms against the wind. Why she'd worn this flimsy dress, she had no idea. It felt practically see-through. "We have plenty of food left. Some of the guests are already leaving." As she spoke, the dentist and his wife walked out of the gate. Beyond the gate, a driver with a golf cart waited to ferry them back to Declan's house.

Some of the others were staying in town, at a hotel Declan owned, the Stone Harbor.

"It's okay, Tia. They're here for a week. We'll get our chance."

And now the man read minds?

"We just have so much riding on this."

He stuck his hands in his pockets, as if trying to force himself not to reach out to her, and nodded.

And for a second, she had to try not to step closer.

Aw, what was wrong with her? Now she needed a *hug*?

"It's too late to give our little talk." She sighed.

"It's fine. The kids met the right people. The donors saw the artwork, and they had a good time. And, most important, nothing tragic happened, right?"

She took a step away because he smelled good, too, and the firelight was picking up the blue-gold in his eyes. "Yeah. I guess so."

"Listen, glass-half-empty woman. We have an entire week to impress these people. I promise you that by the end of the week, we'll be so far into the black you'll be able to buy a fleet of X-ray machines."

She laughed. "I don't need a fleet."

"You need a fleet. An armada." His eyes twinkled.

Trouble. She headed back down the stairs. "I think I'll go help clean up."

"I'm drying."

"What?"

"Oh, in our home growing up, whenever someone said it was time for dishes, someone always called dryer. No one liked washing."

He lifted a hand to someone, and her gaze followed the gesture to the . . . *Oh, the woman.* She grinned up at him, warmth in her expression.

See. Calm. down. The guy was taken. And frankly, she'd been there, done that. Had no desire to be the second choice.

She headed over to the tables, where the nuns had already started packing up the food. So much callaloo left. Maybe that had been a bad choice. The patties had vanished, as had the conch fritters and the flatbread. But the cou-cou and flying fish had hardly been touched, along with the curried goat stew.

Even though she'd omitted the word *goat* from the placard.

Oh well.

"We can clean up, Miss Tia," said Rosa, putting plastic over the rice-and-pea dish—rice, coconut milk, allspice, peppers, and pigeon peas.

"Sorry no one ate your delicious food."

"Oh, honey, more for the children. And now I don't have to cook tomorrow." She grinned, her eyes shiny. "You go on now."

Fine.

Doyle was walking the woman, along with Declan and Stein, out the front gate. The music played, and a few of the girls twirled on the dance floor. Some of the boys threw twigs into the fires, still alive in the fountain. That hadn't been a terrible idea.

Still, they shouldn't play with the fire—oil filled the floating containers, and it could splash on them—

"Stop. Lionel, Jaden—" She headed over to the two. They ignored her, and she stepped up to them, hands out. "Stop!"

Jaden held a skewer from the olives and tried to flick it past her, into the flames. She reached out to grab it—

Tripped.

Her hand splashed into the water, upset the container, and of course, it spilled onto the water. She bit back a scream as the oily flame touched the arm of her dress. She yanked her arm from the water.

Flame licked it and she shook it.

Oil and flame spat out from her arm, and now she *did* scream, dancing around. "Off, off!"

"Hold still!" A napkin landed on her burned sleeve, snuffed out the flames, but the heat sat on her skin. She reached up and ripped the napkin and charred sleeve away from her, yanking them down, pulling her arm free.

She stared at the burn, breathing hard. The sleeve had offered some protection, but the burn had already seared the skin, and her violence had skidded off the top layer of epidermis.

"You need water!"

She looked up just as Doyle grabbed a water pitcher and doused her entire arm, her body, and—*perfect*—now she stood in the courtyard in a see-through dress.

Sopping, dripping, and bearing a second-degree burn.

She met Doyle's eyes.

He breathed hard, swallowed, glanced over her. "It's not that bad."

"Which part?" She turned to Jaden. "I told you to stop!"

He stood, his mouth tight, eyes filling.

Doyle set a hand on her shoulder. "I got this."

"Great. Because I'm going to the medical clinic."

"Wait—let me look at the burn—"

But she ignored him, turned, and did a super job of not running, not crying, as she stalked to the clinic. Out the side gate and into the two-story building attached to the monastery. Stone walls, arched doors, and tile roof, it was once the refectory, with an expansive garden out back. Now, the main floor included the reception area and the exam and treatment rooms, with the upper rooms used as a birthing center, including the ultrasound suite, an X-ray room *(thank you, Doyle),* and a surgical suite for minor issues.

The small pharmacy sat in the back of the building on the main floor. She punched in the code and let herself in, her arm pulsing.

Maybe she'd overreacted. Fifteen-year-old boys hardly had impulse control. *Still.*

She flicked on a light, and it illuminated the hallway.

A crash and she stilled. *What—*

And maybe she should have turned around. *Definitely should have turned around,* maybe fled from the building. But her arm hurt, and the idea of someone stealing from them just ignited her. "Who's there?" She started down the hallway.

Quiet.

"I know you're there."

"No. I'm *here.*" Someone's hand clamped onto her mouth, jerked her up against his body, and a voice said. "Miss me?"

THREE

"JUST CALM DOWN, JADEN." DOYLE SAT ON THE edge of the fountain—after dousing the fiery containers—and pulled him over. "It's okay."

"Miss Tia's really hurt." Jaden's voice emerged small, broken, and Doyle remembered the trauma these children had suffered five years ago. Inside, Jaden might be about ten years old.

Doyle felt about ten years old the way his insides shook.

He'd heard the girls screaming even before Tia had shouted, was on his way back inside the compound—leaving Austen and Declan and Stein in the yard—and his EMT training just kicked in.

Oil burn. Towel. Then water.

The poor woman got drenched. So much for the teamwork moment on the balcony earlier when he'd almost made her laugh.

Doyle patted the stone next to him for Jaden to sit. "She'll be okay. Burns aren't fun, but she'll heal. But . . . you do know that when an adult asks you to stop, you should listen. We're not trying to wreck your fun. We're trying to keep you safe, right?"

Jaden nodded.

Some of the other boys—Lionel and the Parnell twins and Rohan—stood with stricken looks on their faces.

Except, they weren't looking at him.

He followed their gaze and—*oh no*.

Kemar had Jamal by the back of the shirt, pushing him down the stairs, a backpack in his hand.

"Kemar!" Doyle stood up, headed across the courtyard, and planted himself at the bottom.

Jamal was crying, tears streaking down his face. "I don't wanna go!"

"You're going." Kemar shook him.

Breathe. "Where are you going, Kemar?"

"Away from here!" Kemar spat at him, and Doyle dodged to the side.

"Hey—calm down."

Kemar pushed Jamal the rest of the way. "You're not giving my brother away to . . . to anyone. He belongs with me." He dragged Jamal across the yard by the shirt, toward the side door.

"No, Kemar. The orphanage has custody of your brother. And you. You can't leave!" Doyle took off after them, ran to the gate, slammed his hand on it before Kemar could open it. "You can't leave."

"I'm sixteen. By island law, I can leave."

Doyle clenched his jaw. "Okay. Yes. But Jamal can't."

"He can. With me."

"No. You're not his legal guardian—"

A scream lifted from the medical clinic, just outside the gate. Even Kemar's eyes widened.

Doyle pushed through the gate, running to the building. He slammed through the open door into the lit hallway and stopped.

Sebold held Tia by the neck, her back against the wall, a knife pressed against the hollow of her throat. His mouth bled at the edges.

"Let her go!" Doyle advanced on him, but Sebold turned, aimed the point at him.

"You won't get to me before I slice her." He pushed the knife to her neck again.

Doyle stopped, held up his hands. "Let her go. Take what you want—"

"I want what's mine. I came for my machine."

He sighed. "It's not your machine,."

"I want what she owes me. Twenty thousand dollars."

Sebold wasn't watching her, and suddenly Tia slapped his hand away, kneed him hard, and spun away.

The knife clattered against the far doorway.

Tia scrabbled farther away from Sebold, and Doyle reached for her.

Sebold landed on her, hauled her up, and found his knife. He pressed it to her neck again. "Stop! Stop!"

Doyle's hands went into the air. "I'm stopping!"

Kemar picked right then to come in behind him. "Kemar, run!"

Sebold motioned to Kemar. "Pick that up, kid."

A suitcase lay on the floor in the hallway.

"No—no. Please. You have no use for an ultrasound machine—" Tia's voice seemed more angry than afraid.

Sebold slapped her, and Doyle shouted. "C'mon!"

Blood darkened her blouse, the tip of the knife finding flesh.

"Listen. Take the machine," Doyle said. "Take whatever you want!"

Tia spat at him. "You're a sick man."

C'mon, Tia! Don't make him angrier!

Blood dripped down her collarbone, her eyes fierce.

Kemar picked up the suitcase. Outside, shots sounded.

Sebold didn't even flinch. Oh no—maybe he had S-7 guys here.

Jamal hadn't moved from where he stood by the door, and now he looked at Doyle, his brown eyes wide.

"Get out of here, Jamal."

"No!" Kemar turned to Jamal. "Come to me."

Jamal shook his head.

"Come *here.*"

"No!"

Kemar lost it. He shouted, threw the ultrasound machine at Doyle, then rushed him.

Doyle hit the suitcase away from him, but Kemar had him. He slammed Doyle against the door, outside into the yard. Got his knee on his chest and punched him.

Doyle didn't hit kids but this was *enough*.

He grabbed Kemar, rolled, and pushed him face down in the dirt, his arm in a submission hold.

Kemar screamed—maybe rage, or pain, or even frustration.

"Don't, Mr. D! Don't hurt my brother!" Jamal bounced around them, crying. "Don't hurt him."

And right then it occurred to Doyle—where was Keon? Or any of the other security they'd hired?

He needed help. "Taj! Andre!" *Shoot—*

Kemar started screaming.

"Stop it. Nothing's broken." However, Jamal started screaming too. Aw. Doyle rolled off Kemar just as the clinic lights flicked off.

Then, more gunshots and shouting from around the compound, and Sebold barreled out of the building, holding the suitcase.

Tia! Doyle couldn't move.

Not even when Kemar got up, grabbed Jamal, and tried to hit Doyle as he ran by.

Doyle came to life, dodged him, pushed him away—and ran for the building. "Tia!" He slapped on the lights by the door.

Tia sat on the floor, blood on her face, her chest. A man—no, *his brother Stein*—crouched over her, holding a cloth to her neck.

What—?

Stein looked up, a grim expression on his face. "I heard the screaming, and I told Declan and Austen to go back to the house. When I came back, you were gone—and that's when I heard the shot. I found one of your guards out by the edge of the wall, and I figured . . . maybe I'd try to flank whoever was in here. Sorry he got away, but it was him or her."

Her.

Tia sat holding the towel, her jaw tight, eyes dry despite the tear stains down her cheeks. "He took my machine."

Doyle swallowed, looked at Stein, back at her. "Yeah. Yes, he did. Um . . . I think we can get another one."

She stilled. Shook her head. "No. He took the X-ray machine."

"What?"

"Yeah. While he held me, a couple of his guys carried it down and loaded it on our truck. It's gone."

He really liked that truck, too.

"I'm sorry."

"Declan will buy you a new machine," said Stein. "And a new truck."

She pushed Stein's hand away and stood up.

Doyle knew that look. "Tia—"

"Declan doesn't need to know. The last thing—the *very* last thing—I need is for him to think I can't handle this job. I don't need any favors."

"We were *robbed.* That's hardly your fault."

"I agree with him—" Stein started.

"You don't get a say." Her eyes sparked, hard on Stein. "You should have gone after him. I was fine—"

"You looked a lot worse. I thought he'd slit your neck."

"So now he's gone, with our ultrasound and our X-ray machine—"

"And Kemar and Jamal," Doyle said, hanging a hand on the back of his neck. The conch stirred in his gut, foul.

"What?" Tia looked at him. She'd removed the towel. Nothing

a stitch or two couldn't handle. Maybe a butterfly. "He took the boys?"

"To be accurate, Kemar took Jamal."

Her mouth tightened. She shook her head, then looked at Stein. "I think Kemar was in on it."

"Feels like it, the way Sebold ordered him around."

"He loves Jamal. He'll protect him." She looked away, a sort of fury in her expression. "We need to call the authorities."

"I don't know what they can do," Doyle said. "S-7 is heavily armed, and the small police force is afraid of them. We could try to get some outside help, but . . ."

"What about you, Mr. Navy SEAL. Can't you help?"

Stein cocked his head. "You heard the heavily-armed part, right? I will try to figure out something, but I am not a one-man army. I was part of a team." He glanced at Doyle, his mouth tight, and looked away.

Huh.

Clearly, Stein had thoughts he wasn't sharing.

"We can't just let them steal from us and kidnap—or coerce—our children. If we don't stop them, who will?"

And maybe it was her words—almost the same ones that Juliet had spoken so many years ago: *"If we don't go, who will?"*—or possibly the look on her face, the anger, desperation, horror—

But just like that, the swell of grief rifted over him and his knees buckled. Doyle turned, covered his face with his hands.

Deep breaths.

Silence.

"Bro?" Stein said.

"Yep," Doyle said.

The waves hit him less often these days, but when they did, they could still take him down.

He put his hand on the wall, trying to find himself. Looked

at Tia. "Let's get you cleaned up, and then we'll figure this out." He glanced at Stein. "You think Declan and his guests are safe?"

"They're locked inside his compound. I can check everything on my phone."

"You mind hanging out at the monastery?"

"No problem."

He opened an exam-room door and flicked on the light. A metal table sat in the middle of the room. He helped Tia onto it.

Stein stuck his head in. "Quick patrol, then I'm locking down the convent."

"Monastery. Go."

Tia wore what an expression of what looked like relief on her face.

Oh. Yeah. Stein had that SEAL charisma that women seemed to like. *Whatever.* If they really knew the man . . .

Aw, that wasn't fair. Stein was a great guy. Just came with baggage.

Shoot, so did he.

He found gauze and butterfly bandages and chlorhexidine in a cabinet, put them on a tray, and snapped on gloves. Then he found a swab and started to clean her wound.

Just a nick on her throat, but an inch higher and . . .

"I'm okay, Doyle." She caught his wrist. "If it weren't for—"

"Stein, I know. He's Superman."

"You. You distracted Sebold. I was already getting away when Stein came in."

"I don't care how you got away. Just that you did."

She winced, one eye closing as he dabbed the wound.

"You're pretty tough, Tia Pepper. What's your secret?"

Her eye opened. "I don't like to lose."

Interesting.

"And I refuse to be afraid."

"A little sting," he said as he added the chlorhexidine to the wound, and she drew in a breath. "Sorry."

He unpeeled one butterfly bandage, then the other, and closed the wound. Added antibiotic to a gauze pad and pressed it over the injury. Pulled out tape and bit it off.

"You're pretty good at this doctor thing."

"Thanks. Two years of medical school." He put the tape over the gauze.

"Really?"

He moved over to the burn on her arm. "How's it feeling?"

"Hurts like a bear."

He smirked. "Let me see if I can find any silver sulfadiazine cream."

"It's in the pharmacy, across the hall."

Leaving her, he headed into the pharmacy.

Oh no.

Glass was scattered across the floor around the narcotics chest, the lower door ripped open.

"Did you find it?" Her voice lifted from the next room.

"Looking. Stay there." He searched the shelves and found the cream in a box, returned to the exam room.

She'd actually obeyed him, stayed sitting on the table. He examined the burn. "It doesn't look too deep. I'm just going to put the cream on for now and cover it. We'll take another look tomorrow." He used a wooden spatula to apply the cream, then covered it and again taped gauze into place.

"Why'd you quit?"

He looked up at her. "Quit?"

"Medical school."

"Oh." He sighed. Shook his head. "It's a long story. I guess the short of it is that I . . . I just lost the desire to go."

She frowned.

"It wasn't a calling?"

He met her eyes, not sure, and then, for some reason: "I was called to be a missionary. Being a doctor was how I was going to get there."

"Wow. A missionary, huh?"

He had gathered up the debris and now dropped everything into a canister. "Yep." He took off the gloves, dropped those in too. "All set?" He found a smile.

But inside, a hole had opened up, and along with it, the strangest urge to . . . *No.* She didn't need to know the sordid, broken past.

He'd come here to start over. Not weep over what could have been.

When he turned back, she'd slid off the table, headed out into the hallway. *Wait—*

"Tia—"

"Oh!"

Shoot.

He swung into the hallway, spotted her staring into the wreckage of the room. She shook her head, looked at him. "When were you going to tell me?"

He lifted a shoulder. "Now?"

Her mouth tightened. "I'm going to get everything back." Her eyes found his. "Including Jamal."

"No, you're not."

She gaped at him.

He stepped toward her. "Sebold is an evil, ruthless man. He will kill you."

She blinked at him. "I'm sorry to tell you this, Doyle, but . . . you're not the boss of me."

Aw.

She pushed past him, out into the reception area, then into the night.

He closed the door, then locked up the clinic.

And as he watched her disappear into the monastery, he knew he couldn't watch another woman he cared about die.

He wouldn't sleep anyway.

Stein checked the lock on the gate of the compound, having walked the perimeter and checked the two other entrances—one by the kitchen and one at the church.

Now he folded his arms and leaned against the building, one foot on the wall, looking out to where Declan's house perched on the hill.

He had already texted the security lead there—a man named Zeus—and updated him on his overnight stay at Hope House, as well as secured reinforcements.

In the valley, along the harbor, the homes of Esperanza lit, tiny lights against the curve of the sea, under the vault of night. He liked it here—the salt in the wind, the smell of the sea, the heat on his skin—and he'd started to unwind, finally, from the chaos in Barcelona, where he'd nearly, inadvertently, let his boss get run over by a Vespa.

A Vespa ridden by a woman he thought he'd forgotten.

Okay, in truth, he'd never really forget Code Name Phoenix, if that had truly been her back in Caledonia. Hard to forget someone who saved your life.

Then left you for dead.

Maybe it wasn't her. He'd started to think he'd dreamed up the entire thing—the girl named Avery who possessed the same mysterious green eyes as Phoenix, who'd made friends with Declan. A woman who looked very much like someone he'd met at his sister's wedding.

His brain was playing tricks with him. Especially in the wee hours of the night.

So, better to not sleep. Tomorrow, he'd reach out to Jones, Inc., a private security team in Minnesota that his cousin worked for, and see if they could send down support. At least until Stein figured out how to get the S-7 crew off the backs of Hope House.

Tia had stormed into the monastery, hot about something, and now Doyle came walking over, blowing out a breath.

"You good?" Stein asked.

Doyle nodded. "Yeah, she's fine."

"You, bro—*you*."

Doyle raised an eyebrow, then sighed. "Yeah. Sebold left with a couple kids from the orphanage, not to mention some expensive medical equipment, so there's that—"

"And nearly stabbed Tia."

Doyle's mouth tightened.

"Stay away from that guy."

Doyle held up his hands. "You don't have to convince me. I'm not signing up to get into a battle. Tell it to my codirector."

Stein tamped down a smile. Still, "Seems that you two have an interesting relationship."

"If you mean she can't stand me, and that maybe I feel like I'm getting in way over my head every time she walks into the room—yes."

"You get in way over your head all by yourself, little bro."

Doyle gave him a look.

Stein lifted a shoulder. "Just saying . . . Ever since . . ." *Oh . . . well,* "Just, it seems for the last few years you've been all jump-in-and-then-figure-out-where-you're-going. Like this gig. Did you even know where Mariposa was on a map before you jumped on a plane?"

Doyle frowned. "Did you?"

Right.

His brother met his gaze, hard. "We're both just trying to figure out what's next. You do it your way, I'll do it mine."

Stein nodded. "You're right. Sorry."

Doyle sighed. "No, I'm sorry. Thanks for circling back around tonight."

"Something didn't feel right."

"Good thing you still have those SEAL instincts." Doyle thumped Stein's arm as he headed past him into the compound. "Tomorrow we'll buy a security system. You can't sit outside all night every night."

"No worries." Because, again, he wouldn't sleep anyway. He checked his smartwatch. Zeus had said he'd send relief in a couple hours.

Now Stein walked over to the steps of the medical clinic and sat down in the shadows. Ran a hand over his knees. They still swelled sometimes, especially after a hard workout.

"You do it your way, I'll do it mine."

He wasn't sure what his way was, really. For a long time, he'd hoped it meant getting back in the game, rejoining his team.

He just hoped to keep one step ahead of whoever wanted a piece of Declan Stone.

"I think someone is after you, sir."

The conversation he'd had with Declan after he'd been released from the Hospital of Barcelona, as they'd been packing to leave, returned to him as he sat in the cool of the Mariposa night, the wind stirring the grasses.

"It was an accident, Stein," Declan had said as he limped around his room, packing, his nose in a bandage, his hands wrapped in gauze.

"Sit down, sir," Stein had said, and taken the clothing from Declan's hands. He'd turned into a valet, but after spending over a month with Declan, he liked the guy. Which frankly, was a perk of the job.

That and the fact that Declan treated him more like a friend than a bodyguard, giving Stein a chance to get close enough to really watch his back. And speak the truth. "I don't think it was an accident."

"Then what?" Declan had sat in a nearby overstuffed chair, leaned forward, looking at his hands. Probably considering taking off the bandages. Stein would have taken them off already if it were him, and it seemed his boss might be cut from the same cloth despite his wealth and, frankly, IQ. He'd learned a lot watching the man teach at the AI symposium in Barcelona.

Declan Stone was some version of Elon Musk, complete with patents and world-changing technology. Which meant, "I think someone is after something—like your bio-encrypted vault." He'd then gone on to describe how Avery had swiped Declan's bloody gauze. "Probably enough to synthesize a bio key."

That had sat Declan upright, and he'd gotten on his phone, and suddenly, their flight plans changed to Montelena, a small country north of Italy, nestled in the Dolomites, the location of the world's most secure cryptocurrency and digital-tech hard-storage vault.

Whatever Declan had retrieved, he'd brought to his estate in Mariposa and locked in a hard-storage, off-the-grid vault located under his home, deep in the lava rock.

So maybe he'd turned a little Howard Hughes in that moment as he'd locked the vault with his bio key. Stein hadn't asked.

And Declan hadn't offered any information as to what he might have been securing.

Not Stein's business. His job was to keep Declan alive, and so far, so good. Especially since his sister Austen had shown up, just like that, to guide a dive to a sunken ship for Declan's high-end friends.

High-end potential donors to Hope House, the orphanage founded and funded by Declan, which made Stein like him even more.

They were safe. Surrounded by a town that treated Declan like the local hero. And in his concrete, built-in-the-rock fortress with house security—no one was getting in.

Relax.

Still, ever since arriving, and especially over the past week, a feeling had woken him in the middle of the night. As if he was being watched. Which was crazy because his room was on the third floor, just down the hall from Declan's, with a view of the estate, and nobody could get up those sheer walls. Or, for that matter, peer into the room from outside, as the estate sat on the highest point of the island, not counting Cumbre de Luz, the sleeping giant, so . . .

Calm down.

Last night he'd gotten up and walked through the darkness to the balcony. Stared out over the ocean. And yes, if anyone had wanted to take a shot at him, they could have. But as he stood there, Phoenix had walked into his brain and sat down.

Looked at him, a spark in her green eyes, and said, *"Are you going to get in my way, Frogman?"*

A memory, one he'd tried to ignore, or bury, and now it dislodged and floated to the top, and for a long moment, he was back in Krakow, Poland, at a safe house, trying to figure out if he had to shoot the woman who'd saved his life.

After all, she had stolen the asset he'd sneaked in to grab. The asset who, at that very moment in his mind's eye, sat in the back room, probably freaking out. But that seemed right, given their under-siege escape through the embassy tunnels and out into the back alleys of Old Town Krakow to a house built like a fortress with a secure back entrance.

She still wore the canvas pants, the tech vest, and shirt—looking very commando—but she put down her gun and opened a fridge and tossed him a water bottle.

He caught it and looked at her. "Not sure yet."

And then she smiled, something of playfulness in it, or perhaps challenge. And it just sparked something in him.

Stop.

The voice had thundered through him then, just like now, and Stein brought himself out of the memories and back to the darkness. To the humid Caribbean night, the stars bright, the moonlight on the silvery grasses.

No one had been watching him. And the woman in Barcelona couldn't have been Phoenix.

Really.

He'd watched her die. Or at least, disappear into an explosion, so . . .

Light glinted out in the grass. Or maybe not light, but . . .

A reflection of light. Like field glasses.

Or a scope.

He pulled out his own binoculars and searched the road, the field, his heart thumping. Nothing.

Stood up.

Searched again.

There. Another glint of light near the edge of the property where it dropped down into the valley.

The hairs rose on his skin. He pocketed the glasses, then walked over to the compound and let himself inside, locked the gate, and then pulled up his radio and called Zeus as he climbed to the second floor of the monastery.

"Control, this is Patrol One. How're we doing on that relief crew? I have a visual on a potential optical reflection from the road to the house."

Zeus's voice came over the walkie, deep and low, his island accent thick. "Copy, Patrol One. Can you confirm the source?"

"Negative on source confirmation. The reflection was brief but distinct. I am adjusting position for better observation and cover. Requesting support. Maybe drone deployment?"

"Acknowledged, Patrol One. We'll get remote surveillance in the air. And relief is on the way. Maintain your position and keep visual cover. Stand by for further instructions."

Fine.

He lowered the walkie, clipped it to his belt.

Stood, arms folded, staring into the darkness.

And maybe it was crazy, this feeling like . . .

No. Crazy or not, she was out there. He knew it in his gut.

And the answer was yes—yes, he was going to get in the way.

The knife pricked her throat, and that's when Tia shot straight up, out of a sound sleep-slash-nightmare, a scream in her throat.

Her heart pounded against her chest, and she put a hand to it.

Overhead, in the semidarkness, her fan churned the early-morning breeze, and light filtered in through the gauzy curtains at the window.

So, no more sleep for her. Tia got up, brushed her teeth, braided her hair, then pulled on a pair of shorts and a top, flip-flops, grabbed her phone, and headed down to the kitchen.

Rosa stood at the stove, stirring a pot of cornmeal porridge in coconut milk. Fresh papaya lay on a board, the deep orange-red juices puddling under slices. "You're up early, Miss Tia." The woman, mid-forties, wore an apron around her ample middle, her hair up in a do-rag. "How are you?" She indicated Tia's bandages.

"Better than I look." *Maybe.* Because Tia had woken with a plan.

She'd pay Sebold out of her own money. She just needed to wait for the bank to open.

Stealing a slice of papaya, she helped herself to the fresh coffee, brewed in a tall metal coffee maker. She added some cream, then took another slice of papaya and headed out the side door to the rising sun.

A small stone patio jutted off the kitchen, and she sank into one of the metal bistro chairs, setting her cup on the round table. Dew glistened on the garden—crisp green cucumbers, bright red tomatoes, yellow squash, still small on the vine—and the scent of freshly furrowed earth imbued the air.

Beyond that, the chickens in the yard clucked, a few still in the roost.

Tia sipped her coffee, trying not to sink into fury, her gaze on the back door of the medical clinic. Her own words rumbled inside: *"Declan doesn't need to know. The last thing—the very last thing—I need is for him to think I can't handle this job."*

Okay, she knew that pride seeded those words, but . . .

"I don't like to lose." Not quite accurate, really. She didn't like injustice. Or fear.

Didn't like being controlled by emotions that caused her to make stupid decisions. Like saying yes to marrying a man who didn't love her.

She took another sip of her coffee, then pulled out her phone. Sent a text to her sister.

Tia

You up, Pen?

Dots, and then they vanished. The phone buzzed and Tia pressed speaker. "Hey."

"How'd the party go?"

She imagined Penelope dressed in a fuzzy robe, at her kitchen table, maybe nursing a coffee too and reading through the latest murder headlines on her tablet. Her dark hair would be tangled and messy—and of course, her little sister wouldn't care in the least because she possessed a sort of easy beauty, although she knew how to glam up too.

Tia was more practical, utilitarian with her approach. But being on the island had sort of given her the easy beauty of her sister—she'd cultivated a tan, raised a few freckles, and added a glow to her skin.

"It was good, I think. I have a couple donors coming by later today to tour the clinic. And it's an all-week event. Declan invited them for both fun and fundraising, so we'll have more chances to talk." She glanced at the clinic. "I did have another run-in with Sebold."

"What?"

"Yeah. He broke into the clinic, took the X-ray and the ultrasound machines." She touched the wound at her neck, glad she wasn't on video.

"You're kidding. What did the police say?"

"I haven't talked to them. Stein said they wouldn't be a big help—they're afraid of the S-7 gang."

"Stein—as in Conrad's older brother?"

"Yes. He's here with Declan Stone—I think working security."

"Where was Doyle?"

The question stirred the image of Doyle, horrified, desperate, standing in the reception area, a look of fury in his blue eyes.

The man just fueled something in her.

Like, frustration. "He was there. Told Sebold to take the ultrasound and go." She still couldn't believe he'd said that.

Then again, Doyle didn't have his entire future riding on this gig. Sure, she could return home, take over running the family's charitable organization, EmPowerPlay, but the truth was . . . she needed to break free of the trauma hovering over her life in Minneapolis. Even the stigma of being a Pepper. She wanted a career that she made on her own, without the favor of her family connection.

Although, clearly Doyle knew who she was. However, maybe he didn't know about Edward.

"How well do you know Doyle?"

"He was at Boo's wedding in January, but we didn't really talk. The family sort of drew a circle around him. They're pretty protective."

"Why?"

"I don't know. Maybe it has something to do with his fiancée dying a few years ago. Conrad told me that she was in an accident on the way to the wedding."

"You're kidding."

"That's all I know. Conrad doesn't talk much about it."

She sat back, drew up one knee. "Doyle said he was going to be a doctor. And a missionary. Do you think the accident is why he dropped out of medical school?"

"I don't know. But you certainly put your life on hold after Edward was murdered."

Her entire body jolted at that word—*murdered*. Especially since, for the better part of the last three years, she'd believed his death to be an accident in a fire.

"Yes, but I'd broken up with him before that," she said quietly.

"I know. But it was still devastating. You loved him."

Had she? Of course, yes, but three years had given her clarity. Maybe she'd loved him because he was the sensible, convenient *yes*. The *yes* that had made her feel safe.

But maybe true love wasn't *safe*.

She had Penny to blame for that thought, but she didn't want to stir up the past, so she made a sound of agreement. "Mm-hmm."

"So, what are you going to do about the lost equipment?"

"I'm going to buy it back."

A beat. "Really?"

"What's a trust fund for if you can't use it to ransom medical equipment from the local brutes?"

She though Penelope might chuckle, agree with her, but—

"This Sebold guy sounds dangerous."

"He just wants money. And I have money. Maybe it's time to start using it."

"I just think you need to let Stein—or even Doyle—handle this, Tia."

"Listen. Doyle is . . . he's a little impulsive. Follows his 'gut.'"

She finger quoted the last word, even though Penelope couldn't see her. "I need someone who can keep their cool."

In the chicken yard, the rooster crowed.

"Just don't get in over your head."

"I've got this," Tia said, and finished her coffee. "How's the new podcast season going?"

"I'm working on the story of a serial killer in Alaska. Boo gave me the deets—he's been at it for about twenty years, and they just recently caught him."

"So, no more unsolved mysteries for you?"

"Trying to figure out if Conrad is going to propose now that the Blue Ox season is over is enough mystery for me."

Tia laughed. "And?"

"He's acting a little weird. And he's about the worst secret keeper. But you'll be the first to know." Her voice changed as if she'd just picked up the phone. "Be careful, Tia. You don't have anything to prove."

Tia refused to argue with her. But indeed, she had everything to prove, probably mostly to herself.

She wasn't going to be a woman who let fear rule her life.

"Love you, Pen." Tia hung up, finished her coffee, then returned her mug to the kitchen. It smelled of the cinnamon and nutmeg Rosa had added to the porridge. Now Rosa poured johnnycakes onto a griddle, the oil sizzling.

"Those smell good."

"I pulled fresh honey from the bees out back." She pointed to a jar with a honeycomb inside. "Have a cake."

Tia slathered a hot johnnycake with the honey, folded it, and came over to Rosa, wrapping an arm around her shoulders. "You spoil us."

Rosa patted her arm. "Don't do anything rash, Miss Tia. Remember, the Lord will fight for you."

Oh. Clearly her voice had carried. "Maybe he already has." *Hello, trust fund.* She gave Rosa a squeeze, let her go, and headed upstairs. She grabbed her fanny pack and passport, sunglasses, then went to the garage.

Grabbing one of the old dented scooters, she wheeled it out and took off for town.

The wharf woke early, fishermen heading out to sea in the predawn hours, and now a few already unloaded their catch onto the docks, spraying off the decks of their small fishing trawlers, others weighing their haul. The scent of fish and brine rose, along with the salt of the sea. She motored down the cobblestones of Main Street. A few shops had opened, and the scent of accras—salted cod made into fritters and fried—stirred in the breeze. She parked in the shade of a palm tree and went across the street to the bank.

Knocking, she spotted Neville Moreau, bank president, inside. She waved, and he came over and unlocked the door.

"Miss Tia. How can I help you?"

"I need to make a withdrawal from my account."

He nodded and brought her to his office.

She'd started the account when she first arrived, just in case.

This was *just in case.*

Neville accessed her trust account, then sent the money to Mariposa Trust and Commerce.

An hour later, she had the cash, tucked into her fanny pack and secured to her body. As she drove back to Hope House, it occurred to her that she'd need a driver for the truck once she liberated it. Or she'd simply exchange it for the scooter.

It didn't have to be complicated. Pay off Sebold, get her equipment back, and yes, she'd bargain for Jamal too. Doyle had filed a report with the local authorities, but they didn't seem to share her sense of outrage.

Or maybe they just knew that the hope of getting Jamal back was slim. Besides, she'd seen Kemar. She knew what she'd do if the threat of losing her sibling grabbed hold of her heart. Frankly, she'd been there, done that, so yeah, she got it.

But the X-ray machine saved lives. And it would take months to redo the paperwork for a new one. Even if she did buy it herself.

Pulling up to the side gate outside the clinic, Tia took off her helmet, set it on the bike. The sun had crested the far horizon, casting Hope House into shadow under the rise of Cumbre de Luz. The ocean roared just over the cliffside, the waves thundering against the rocks. A gorgeous day in the Caribbean.

She could do this. She keyed in the gate's code, opened it, and walked through the thick walled entrance.

"Seriously?"

She jerked, turned.

Doyle stood, his arms folded, wearing a denim shirt with the sleeves rolled up and a pair of faded jeans, hiking boots. As if he might be going for a trek through the rainforest. His hair hadn't been combed, and the swath of whiskers on his jaw seemed darker.

He seemed darker. No smile, just a tight purse of his lips as he cocked his head. Didn't move.

"What?"

"For one, you're not pregnant, so my guess is that's a fanny pack full of cash." He gestured to her midsection.

"What of it?"

He gave her a grim shake of his head. "Why, why, *why* are you so intent on getting yourself killed?"

She stared at him, her mouth open.

He shook his head, his hand up in surrender. "Okay, fine. If that's the way you want to play this, let's go."

"I can do this by myself. Or I can take Keon."

"Keon is working for them."

"What?"

"Yeah, he disappeared last night—left his post and probably let them into the clinic. Stein found his room emptied out. The guard who was injured was one of the temporaries I hired, recommended by the local magistrate, so *not* on the take."

"Keon betrayed us?" She pressed a hand to her mouth. "He was—"

"Bought off? Maybe. Scared? Probably. I don't know. But Stein is working on getting us a new security crew. Meanwhile . . . for the record, this is a bad idea."

"It's the *only* idea."

"*Tia!* For the love of Pete—do you have no recollection of what happened last night?"

"Are you serious? I have *every* recollection! I hardly slept—"

He winced, just a little, around the eyes.

"But I refuse to let Sebold win—"

"Isn't that what paying him off is? I happen to remember a certain conversation as we drove down to the harbor. One that cost me my thousand-dollar dive watch."

"I'll buy you a new one."

"That's not the point." He took a step toward her. "You give in to bullies and they keep coming back." He lowered his voice. "Let's hire security, and use that cash to get us a new X-ray machine."

"It's the principle."

"Your principles could get you hurt. Or killed."

"Without principles, we have nothing."

He raised an eyebrow. "Okay. Yeah, I get that. But . . . maybe a higher principle is *don't get killed*."

"You want Jamal back?"

He crossed his arms. "Stein and I have a plan."

"What, you're a Navy SEAL now? Please." She unstrapped her money belt. "There's fifty thousand dollars in here. Enough for both of our machines *and* Jamal."

A flicker of surprise, and he looked at the bag. Back at her.

"It's just a dive watch," she said and lifted her shoulder.

He sighed. "He's going to want more. Give a mouse a cookie—"

"Right now, I just want the X-ray machine. We'll cross the 'more' bridge later."

He sighed. "Fine. But let Stein and me handle this."

She strapped the pack back on. "No. I'm the director, I should do this. Show Sebold that I'm not afraid of him."

"Codirector, and he won't care."

"I will."

He considered her for a moment. "Right. You refuse to be afraid."

She nodded.

"A little fear might be a good idea," he said.

Silence as her jaw tightened.

"Okay, fine. Let me tell Stein what we're doing."

Aw. But the idea of him going with her sort of grabbed her, settled into her bones. Still, "If either of you try to tie me up and duct tape me to a wall or something, I'll come after you."

He seemed to hide a smile. "Fresh out of duct tape."

"Hurry up."

She headed back outside and sat on the scooter. The road out of town circled the small island, only twelve miles in circumference, and ran right into the S-7 camp, located on the eastern side of the island at a former resort destroyed by the hurricane.

Doyle came out of the gate, a dark look on his face, carrying a backpack. He stopped at the scooter. "I'm driving."

"You think so. Get on."

His eyes narrowed for a second; then he shook his head and got on. Didn't put his hands on her waist but held the bar behind the seat.

"What's in the backpack?"

"Something I hope we don't need."

Perfect. More secrets. Just like last night's cryptic conversation about being a missionary, about the death of his fiancée.

It hit her then that maybe he had a reason for his fears. Beyond Sebold.

But they weren't engaged, and she wasn't going to break his heart. She turned on the bike. "Just don't do something nuts and get us killed."

"Oh, I think you're already there, Lara Croft. Let's go."

Lara Croft. She bit back a smile despite the fury radiating off him.

And for a second, as she took off, she had to ignore the crazy sense that once again, Doyle Kingston was not at all the man she thought him to be.

But exactly the partner she needed.

FOUR

"TELL ME AGAIN WHY WE'RE NOT JUST BUYING a new machine?" Doyle held the back of the scooter, the ocean splashing against the shoreline as they drove east along the coastline.

He had to shout it, although she wasn't driving fast, and who knew if she could actually hear him through her helmet?

She said nothing, so clearly not. Or maybe she just didn't want to answer questions, like how did she come up with the fifty thousand dollars in her fanny pack? Yes, he knew she was a Pepper, and according to his brother Conrad, who was dating her younger sister, they had money.

But what was she doing *here*, working with him, raising support, if she already had enough to buy them an entire suite of medical equipment?

Ever since he'd gotten up this morning and gone down to the kitchen to find Rosa praying under her breath about something Tia might be getting into, the words *if you give a mouse a cookie* had been going through his mind.

This couldn't end well, he knew it in his coiled gut, but apparently there was no talking Miss You're-Not-the-Boss-of-Me out of her escapade.

So he hung on to the back of the scooter, his gut tightening with every mile closer to the S-7 complex.

He probably should have alerted Stein, but his brother had gone to town to talk to the local police about last night's break-in. Which felt like the *right* move.

Doyle did have the diversion in the backpack that Stein had given him, so that might help too.

Tia seemed to know where she was going—and the HQ of S-7 wasn't exactly hidden. Even now, he spotted it, a resort seated at the foot of the volcano, the tropical forest rising behind it, a smooth black-sand beach in front, spilling out to the ocean. The resort still bore the debris of the hurricane—palm trees, roofing material, sand and dirt spilling out of lower-story windows of the two main buildings, both two stories, balconies fronting every room. Shirts and pants hung, stirred by the breeze, vehicles parked on the former tiled pool deck, and the stone wall surrounding the complex now hosted barbed wire.

Book him a weekend in paradise ASAP. Doyle shook his head as she stopped, still a distance from the complex. He put his feet down to hold the bike as she turned to him.

"Let's not get creative. We'll ask to speak to Sebold, offer him the money, ask him to release Jamal. And hopefully he'll also release the truck and the machines."

"Tia—again, maybe we should leave this to the police."

She cocked her head at him.

"Just . . . my gut says this isn't going to go well. Sebold isn't a man to reason with. First sign that your little plan is backfiring, we leave."

She hesitated for a moment, then nodded. "But on my signal—not your *gut*."

He raised an eyebrow, but she turned back around and hit the gas. He held on to the back, his legs tightening around her.

Listen, he'd gotten her out of trouble before by listening to his gut.

A guard stood at the gate, an AR-15 over his shoulder, and Doyle's instincts rose up and called this thing stupid. But she drove right up, stopped, and raised her hands in surrender.

"I'd like to speak to Sebold." She took off her helmet.

Doyle got off the bike and did the same. "And Kemar."

The guard looked about sixteen, skinny, wearing cutoff jeans, ratty tennis shoes, and an oversized faded black shirt, some band name written on the front. He shouted to someone inside the gate. "Get the boss."

Vines had crawled up the outside of the stone wall, tangling with the old bougainvillea, overgrown and spilling over the side. The scent of a campfire, meat cooking in the yard, lifted on the breeze.

Doyle spotted the Ford sitting outside the gate, parked near another entrance. *Don't worry, Duke, I'm coming for you.*

The old Ford had reminded him of a vintage John Wayne movie his father loved.

Sebold showed up at the gate, holding what looked like a turkey leg. He wore a suit coat, ratty and open, no shirt underneath, and a pair of black suit pants, his bare feet in slides.

"You got my money?" He called her a name, but Tia didn't flinch, just walked up to the gate, now opened by the guard.

"I do," she said. "But I want Jamal. And my truck, my X-ray machine, and my ultrasound machine,"

He laughed and threw the turkey leg, and a couple of dogs pounced on it. Then he wiped his mouth with the back of his arm and walked out to her.

"Lemme see." He extended his hand, flexing his fingers in a *give it to me* way.

She unstrapped her fanny pack. "Not until I see that Jamal is okay. And that my X-ray machine isn't destroyed."

He smiled with one side of his mouth, then glanced back at the guard and a few others who had gathered to watch.

Doyle spotted Keon standing with them, out of uniform, wearing a black T-shirt, the arms ripped off, jeans.

Sebold gestured to him. "Get me the kid."

Doyle had stayed behind Tia and now glanced at the truck, back at Sebold. He'd dropped his pack off one shoulder, the front pouch unzipped. Just in case.

"Let him go!" Kemar's voice preceded him as Keon dragged Jamal by the shirt to the entrance. Kemar stumbled, running after them.

Jamal clawed at Keon's grip, fighting, then froze when he spotted Doyle. He stood, wiped his face with his hands. "Mr. D!"

"Shut up, kid!" Sebold said and reached out for him, dragging him by one arm.

"Please, Sebold!" Kemar ran up behind him, grabbed Jamal's other arm.

Doyle saw it coming before it happened. *Run, Kemar!* But he couldn't get the words out before Sebold turned and hit the kid.

Kemar fell to the dirt, bleeding, backing away, his face wrecked.

Stay down, Kemar. But Doyle jerked, ready to launch at Sebold.

His hand closed on the canister in the outer pocket of the pack.

"Show me my money," Sebold growled to Tia.

"Not without Jamal."

Keon had backed away, his gaze hard on Tia's. Then he looked at Doyle, and weirdly, gave the smallest shake of his head.

Yeah, Doyle thought she was brazen too, but right now, he was team Tia, *thank you*.

"Take the kid." Sebold shoved Jamal toward Tia.

Kemar shouted, scrambled to his feet. "No—no—"

Sebold turned, and Kemar caught his breath, held up his hands, stepped back. But his expression twisted—fury, helplessness, pain—

Despite his stupidity, he clearly loved his brother.

Tia caught Jamal, put him behind her, then held out the fanny pack.

No—Tia—don't—

Sebold swiped it, opened it, and the hope on Tia's face could made Doyle ill.

The man nodded, zipped the pack shut, smiled. "Price just went up."

It took a second, a long, brutal second, for Tia to gasp, to shake her head. "That's . . . that's all I have."

Interesting.

"I don't want your money," Sebold said, hanging the fanny pack over his shoulder. "I want my gold."

Gold?

He turned to Kemar, laughed, turned back to Tia. "The kid told me you're hunting a pirate treasure—" He thumped his chest. "My treasure."

"I don't have a treasure," Tia said, and Doyle had to give her credit for not letting her voice break.

"Then find it," Sebold said. He leaned in. "It belongs to me, and I want it back."

Doyle pulled the pin from the canister and depressed the lever.

"I don't know—I don't have any idea where—"

"Find it, or Jamal isn't going anywhere!"

The skinny guard raised the AR-15.

Nope, nobody was getting killed today. Not on his watch—

Doyle threw the smoke grenade.

The place exploded, a cloud of dark fog bursting from the grenade. Sebold shouted and Doyle grabbed Jamal.

"C'mon!" He sprinted to the Ford, half-carrying Jamal. Please let Tia be behind him—"Get in!" Shoving Jamal into the center, he leaned down and pried open the steering column case, still loose from his first go-round at the harbor.

Tia barreled into the passenger side. "This is crazy! You're going to get us killed!"

He found the dangling ignition wires he'd stripped, touched them together. Sparks, and the motor churned, then turned over. He twisted the wires together.

More gunfire, and he pushed Jamal down, shouted at Tia—"Get down!"

Then he hit the gas. The truck shot out of the shade, toward the road, and he deliberately hit the scooter, disabling it as he spat dirt down the driveway.

"What are you *doing*?"

He glanced at her. "Saving lives." He grabbed up Jamal, wishing this old rig had a seatbelt. "Hang on to him."

Tia put her arm around the boy, her hand on the dashboard. "Slow down!"

He'd hit the main road, glanced in the rearview mirror. No tail, and he let out a breath and eased off the gas.

Beside him, she said nothing, her jaw tight.

"What?"

"I just think—maybe you should be less . . . I don't know—"

"Brave? Daring? Heroic?"

"Impulsive! Are you kidding me? I could have *negotiated*—"

"With *what*? He had your money. And in a second, he was about to grab Jamal again. We got the truck—and Jamal. And that's enough. We'll buy an X-ray machine, Tia. Sheesh, if you can't afford it, Declan will—"

"No!" She looked at him, and were those tears glazing her eyes? "Don't. I'll figure this out—"

He turned onto the highway and picked up speed. "What is *wrong* with you? This is not on you, Tia. For crying in the sink, we were robbed. At the very least, our insurance—"

"We don't have insurance." She gritted her teeth, looked away. "The policy lapsed over a year ago. I should have checked when we ordered the machine. Anyway, yeah. That's on me. And so is this entire fiasco. I should have done this myself, like I planned. Alone. I could have paid them off at the harbor—"

"Are you even listening to yourself? I walked in on them nearly going to—" He glanced at Jamal, who had sat up, staring at them like they were squabbling parents, horror in his brown eyes. Doyle sighed. "They weren't going to stop at extortion."

She swallowed, and again looked away.

"You know that, right?"

Her hand went to her cheek, and she wiped away a tear. "I shouldn't be here. This was a bad idea."

Oh. "Yes. We should have let Stein handle—"

"No. I mean here. On this island. Doing this job. I'm . . ." She shook her head. "I made another bad decision."

"Another? As in . . . what? Yes, you shouldn't have gone to Sebold, but that was . . . okay, it might have worked, maybe—"

"No." She looked at Jamal, smiled. "I shouldn't have thought I could do this. I believed something about myself that"—sighing—"clearly isn't true. And now I'm putting everyone in jeopardy."

And he so wanted to reach out, take her hand, track down what on earth she meant. But Jamal turned to her. "I'm glad you're here, Miss T. I was really scared."

"Me too, Jamal," she said, and then looked over at Doyle. "But Doyle wasn't, was he?"

Oh really? That's what she thought?

"Mr. D is sick."

He raised an eyebrow.

"I think that means good," she said, and offered a slight smile.

"You're sick too, Miss T."

She wrinkled her nose at him.

What did she believe about herself that wasn't true? The question sat inside him as they turned onto the road above the village, toward Hope House. Even after they pulled up and spotted Stein standing near the gate with a couple other men and Declan Stone, along with his sister and even Rosa. They stood in a circle, Austen with her hands on her hips, Stein's arms folded, Declan looking out toward the sea. One man wore a uniform, and as Doyle got out and closed the door, he recognized the other as Indiana Hemsworth Jones, the bespectacled archaeologist from the party, the man with the pirate story. He'd overheard him telling the story while he'd been searching the boys' dormitory.

And then he got it. Kemar had probably heard the story too and brought it to Sebold. Hence the crazy demand for some legendary gold.

Jamal ran into the courtyard, and Rosa caught the boy into her embrace and led him inside, probably ready to fill him with corn porridge.

Doyle glanced at Tia, who had shoved her hands into her pockets, walking over to Declan, her mouth a grim line.

And the sudden, brutal thought hit him—*wait,* was she going to resign?

He caught up to her, walked beside her, his voice cut low. "Just take a breath. Everything is going to be fine."

She frowned at him but pursed her lips, nodded.

He retracted the urge to take her hand and followed her up to the powwow. "Stein. Declan." He gave Austen a side hug in greeting. "What's going on?"

"You tell us," said Stein, his arms still folded. "This is Chief Renault DuCasse. He says you were at the S-7 compound."

Doyle said nothing, the words falling through him like a stone.

"We have a man embedded in the crew," the chief said. "And he nearly had to blow his cover because of you."

Oh.

"My fault," said Tia. "I . . . had this stupid idea to . . ." She drew in a breath, looked at Declan. "They broke into the clinic last night and kidnapped two of our kids—"

"One. Kemar went willingly," Doyle said, his mouth tight. "Or it looked like it."

"He stole our new X-ray machine, along with narcotics and the portable ultrasound machine," Tia continued, not looking at Doyle. "I'm sorry. I—"

"This is not your fault, Tia," Declan said. "We can replace the machines. I can't replace you." He put a hand on her shoulder.

Funny how his words crested over her, the way she swallowed, a strange vulnerability flashing across her face. Then it vanished, and You're Not the Boss of Me resettled on her face. Or at least, she faked it well when she said, "I have a plan. Don't worry—I got this."

Declan raised an eyebrow. "You let me know how I can help." He looked at Doyle. "I'm bringing a small private security team in, just for now, until the local police can take down S-7. Next time something like this happens, don't deal with it yourself—I don't need to lose you either."

Funny, the words affected him too, landing in unfamiliar soft soil. "Yes, sir."

"Good. I'll see you at the dive this afternoon? And both of you at tonight's dinner, for the presentation?"

Doyle nodded. Austen walked over to him, put her hands on his shoulders. "Stein is supposed to be the one who scares us." Then she kissed his cheek and followed Declan to his golf cart.

Tia was looking at him, her expression almost shaken. Then she turned to Indiana Jones. "Can we talk?"

And Doyle didn't know why, but the words simply grabbed him up and tightened his gut, and he knew, just knew, this wasn't over.

"Are you sure you're okay?"

Ethan Pine gave Tia a searching look as she opened the monastery's library door. The light filtered in through two tall windows that overlooked the rising volcano, and a slight breeze sifted the gathering humidity of the day, along with the scent of jungle and ocean.

Okay? She'd left *okay* somewhere in the dust back at the S-7 compound. But maybe she would be. She just had to stay strong. "Are you sure that you can find something about the *Trident* treasure in here?"

The library contained books donated to the children over the years. She had already found a few of her favorites, a time-travel book called *Ghosts* that had ignited her love of history, and of course all of the Walter Farley Black Stallion books, which had prompted her to beg her father (unsuccessfully) for a horse.

Along one wall, old books sat behind glass, the history of the island—and the monastery—bound in cracked leather volumes, along with Bibles and scholarly texts that Hope House had inherited. At least according to Rosa and Anita.

"According to the biography of Henry van der Meer, he kept a journal during his time here and left it behind when he returned to Holland and bought a haberdashery. The haberdashery grew, and today it's one of Holland's biggest department-store chains. His family says he started it with a gold-laden azure locket that he said he found during his travels."

Ethan was a good-looking man, had an adventurer's aura, save for the round professor glasses, which he pushed up on his nose before reaching for his phone. In a moment, he flashed her a picture of an oval locket. It seemed crafted from a solid piece of burnished gold in a delicate filigree, something she might have seen in a historical photograph. Set in the center was a deep blue stone with veins of light blue, encircled by diamonds. The locket might take up the entire palm of her hand.

"This is called the Duchess's Locket. It belonged to the Duchess Eleanora Maria of Valmont, a noblewoman from the 1700s, in Prussia. She was the only daughter of the Duke of Valmont and his wife, Duchess Isabella, and was given this on the day of her marriage to Duke Frederic of Middleburg, Holland."

"It's gorgeous."

He pocketed the phone. "The locket was stolen during a trip to New Holland—now Brazil—when their East Indian ship was sacked by the *Trident*. Henry was a sailor on that ship."

"And that's why you think the pirate loot survived . . . Because the locket resurfaced when Henry van der Meer returned to Holland."

He touched his nose. "Why he didn't bring the entire treasure back is the question."

"Maybe he feared getting caught?"

"Perhaps." He had gone to the bookcase, looking at the titles. "Or, and this is my theory, the pirate who sacked the ship, the one that vanished, actually lived. And Henry had to hide the treasure from him. Maybe the locket was the only thing he could safely recover and steal." He pointed to a book, the leather worn and broken along the spine. "Can I see that one?"

She unlocked the door and pulled it out. Small, the size of a mass-market novel, the pages were thick, watermarked, and uneven. She should probably be wearing gloves.

Ethan pulled out a pair of black fabric gloves and put them on. He took the book and set it on the table.

Inked writing, cursive and small. She leaned over him. "Can you read that?"

"Barely, but yes." He pulled out his phone and opened the camera. "This is better. And, yes, I believe this is from the hand of Henry van der Meer." He handed her the phone. "Look at this."

She centered the camera where he pointed. At the bottom of the page, initials—*H.V.D.M.* "How did you know—"

He closed the book and showed her the spine, where a stamp had been pressed into the leather. "My guess is that this is homemade. It's probable that Henry carried a stamp with him to emboss letters. Which made him not a crewmate but someone of importance. From my records, a lawyer. And you know how lawyers are."

"They like to keep track of events."

He pulled out a chair. "Let's see what I can find out."

"We," she said.

He looked up at her.

"Mr. Pine, to be clear, if you do find anything, it's not your property." She hated to sound prickly, but she needed the leverage.

His mouth tightened at the edges.

"You can't seriously think that you can come in here, use our resources to find the gold, then cart it away as if it's finders keepers."

"I'll be invoking the Treasure Trove Law."

"Yes, but if it's found on monastery land, it belongs to Hope House."

"Not if I've filed a THRC permit."

She hadn't seen that in her online search. "A what?"

"Treasure Hunters' Rights and Compensation Act permit. It gives me permission to search and, if a treasure is found, to realize a portion of it. In the case of Mariposa law, it's fifty percent."

He pulled out a chair. "I did the math on this, and it's in the tens of millions. I'll be happy to take my fifty percent."

Oh.

He looked at her. "However, the THRC does say that if it's found on private land, the owner of that land can claim up to thirty percent. The rest after that goes to the country where it's found, unless, of course, Holland sues Mariposa." He offered a smile. "So . . ." He patted the chair next to her.

She pulled it out. "I'll hold the phone. You read."

He opened the book. "That's what I was hoping you'd say." He read aloud: "'August 12, 1702. Today marks a month since the tempest that shattered our vessel against the rocks. I, Henry van der Meer, once a lawyer in the bustling streets of Amsterdam, find myself captive to fate's terrible decree. The pirates who seized our cargo intended for the New World took me prisoner, only to meet their doom in Neptune's wrath. Amidst the chaos, I clung to a splintered plank, praying for deliverance. By some miracle, amongst the ruin and despair, a chest from the ship's hold—filled with gold meant for the New World—washed up beside me. Morning light brought salvation ashore, though I lay at death's door, the chest hidden beneath seaweed and stone.'"

Ethan looked over at her. "I knew it."

She smiled, but weirdly the words seeped into her.

He turned more pages, skimming, then, "'October 3, 1702. The brothers of Saint Augustine's cloister discovered me, nearly dead, on their rocky beach. They knew nothing of the chest, now secreted away, as they nursed me back to health. These weeks, enveloped in monastic calm, have revealed a treasure I had not anticipated—the peace of a quiet mind. The simple rhythms of prayer and labor soothe the tempests within. I am healing, nurtured not only by broth and bread but by a serenity that the world beyond these walls seems to lack.'"

She seemed to lack. Her own words slunk back to her. *"I shouldn't have thought I could do this. I believed something about myself that clearly isn't true."*

Like that she could start over, become a woman who didn't make terrible decisions that ended up hurting the people she loved.

"Here's one from June 15, 1705. 'Three years have woven me into the fabric of monastic life, a tapestry rich with contemplation and brotherhood. All the same, beneath this cloth of peace rests a weight, a shadow that haunts me. Rumors from occasional traders whisper that the pirate captain, thought drowned, yet lives. I shudder to think what pursuit might ensue should he learn of my refuge and the gold's hiding place, now deep within the monastery's seldom-used storerooms.'"

Ethan made a sound of triumph, looked at her. "I knew it."

Tia shook her head. "Sorry, but the storerooms were redone after the earthquake. Refrigeration added, new shelving. I can guarantee that there is no eighteenth-century chest of gold in our pantry."

"Listen to this," Ethan said. "'March 29, 1707. Curiosity led me today through an ancient, overgrown path the monks seldom wander, and I happened upon a hidden tunnel, its walls weeping with sulfur. With this discovery, I've moved the chest into the depths of the sulfur tunnel, secured in a narrow shaft.'"

Ethan looked at her, then out the window at the volcano, and he blinked, startled. "Of course. The sulfur mines. For years the island operated a sulfur-mining operation. It's defunct now—but the mountain is cut with lava-made tunnels filled with sulfur."

"Sulfur? Why mine sulfur?"

"Otherwise known as brimstone." He was paging through the book. "Used for gunpowder, and today, fertilizer and rubber and even antibiotics. Here: 'January 22, 1710. An earthquake last night, fierce as the wrath of God, has sealed the entrance to the sulfur tunnel and shaken our island to its core. The chest, with its bounty, is now entombed within, perhaps forever hidden from greedy hands. The abbey stands, but my heart feels the tremor of discovery. The pirate's shadow looms larger in my restless dreams, and I sense it is time to leave this sanctuary. Alas, I must leave the treasure in its security, but I will take pieces with me to promise me an advantageous future. Tomorrow, I embark once more into the unknown, carrying with me the indelible mark of monastic peace, yet driven by the unresolved echoes of my past life.'"

Unresolved echoes. Yeah, she could relate to that.

Ethan closed the book. "It's still in the sulfur mines."

"It says the entrance was destroyed by the earthquake. And that was three hundred plus years ago. No way are we going to find it—"

"O ye of little faith." He reached for his phone and took a picture of the page. Then the previous one. "Let me take care of that." He stood up and put the book back onto the shelf. Shut the glass and turned to her.

"I keep my promises, Tia. If I find this treasure and it's on Hope House land, it's partly yours."

Oh. And the way his pale blue eyes landed on her, the smile—she wanted to believe him. She held out her hand. "Partners."

He took it, his hand enveloping hers. "Partners. Now, why don't you show me that medical clinic, and we'll see what we can do to get you back up and running."

She closed the library, Ethan walking out ahead of her, and she couldn't help but spot Doyle, down in the yard. He was seated on the fountain, Jamal standing in front of him, and for a second, she was in the truck with him, holding on as they sped away from Sebold and the camp.

Yeah, she could have gotten them killed.

And Doyle had somehow yanked her out of disaster again. And then they'd gotten out of the truck, her job—her future—vanishing at the sight of Declan talking to the police, and he'd somehow kept her from unraveling. His blue eyes on hers, camaraderie in his gaze. *"Just take a breath. Everything is going to be fine."*

Below, he held up his fist and Jamal bumped it. Then he reached out, and Jamal went into his arms, a quick hug.

"You coming, partner?"

She looked up. *Oh,* Ethan stood at the stairs. *Right.*

But as she followed him, she couldn't dodge the strangest sense that somehow, she'd betrayed her real partner.

FIVE

TIA WAS UP TO SOMETHING, AND HE DIDN'T like it.

Aw, loosen up, Doyle. He sat on a bench of the dive boat, near the front, trying not to shoot his gaze to the rear of the boat where Tia sat with blond Indiana Jones. Early forties, maybe, Indy wore a wet suit, unzipped to his waist, showing off a tan and buff body, pointing out something on the island of Mariposa.

The boat channeled through the waves, north along the shoreline. The reef and the sunken wreck hung just offshore, maybe a quarter mile from the harbor.

Tia wore a blue one-piece dive skin, also unzipped, with a halter top underneath, listening to Ethan Pine (yes, Doyle had asked Stein the man's name), as if hanging on his words and *aw* . . .

Doyle didn't care.

Did. not. care.

But something had lodged in his craw the minute she'd walked away with the man after this morning's post-drama powwow.

Yeah, she had an agenda talking to Mr. Archaeology, and—

Wait—

"You good, bro?"

He looked over to see Austen step up, hanging on to the overhead bars. She'd braided her hair and held it back in a diving scarf, wore sunglasses and a thin pair of diving pants. Under it, she wore a green one-piece with long arms.

Water splashed, spraying them as the driver cut through a wave, and the boat jerked. Across from him, Heather let out a playful scream, and Dr. Scott put his arm around her. They seemed to be having a good time.

As did Elise and Hunter Jameson, who sat in the back of the boat, holding hands. They'd asked him about Jamal this afternoon as he helped people assemble their dive gear. He hadn't mentioned the kidnapping.

Jamal seemed to have bounced back. But Doyle recognized a kid trying to hide his emotions, having looked in the mirror one or a thousand times.

So as Doyle looked up at his sister, he weighed his answer, then smiled, nodded. "I'm okay."

She narrowed her eyes at him, then sat on the bench beside him. "I see you keep glancing over at Tia. You two—"

"Codirectors."

"That's what Declan said. How's that working out?" She grinned at him.

"Why?"

"You don't 'co' anything." She finger quoted the word.

"I can be a team player."

"Only if you get to call the plays." She nudged him with her shoulder. "And Tia seems the same way. Declan said she used to run the Pepper family charity, EmPowerPlay."

"She's smart, that's for sure. And determined." And maybe didn't have a good picture of her own limitations. But he clamped down on those words.

"And pretty." Austen winked at him.

"Yes. Whatever. We *work* together, Austen."

She sighed as the boat began to slow. "I know. Can't blame a sister for wanting her brother to find a happily ever after."

"I'm fine. I had my chance at happily ever after."

"Wait—what? You get one chance and that's it?"

The boat settled in the water. To the east, Cumbre de Luz rose, lush and peaked, encompassing most of the tiny island. The port was situated at the bottom, a sea of red-roofed homes, whitewashed and scattered along the harbor. Palm trees dotted the boardwalk along the black-sand beach like truffula trees. Around the boat, the deep azure blue of the ocean stretched over a shallow reef, fish teeming in the translucent water.

"Listen. I had a plan for my life. And then I didn't. Now I don't know what the destination is, and frankly, I'm not sure I want one. I'm no longer a candidate for 'happily ever after.'" He finger quoted his repeated words. "To be honest, I'm not sure I'll ever be ready for . . . Well, what Juliet and I had can't be duplicated. And I'm not even going to try."

"It's been five years, Doyle. And just because the plan changed doesn't mean God doesn't have a new one."

He glanced at her. "Maybe I don't want a new one."

He stood up and reached for his tanks. He'd already attached his rig to the oxygen and now opened the valve, tested the air.

Austen stood up too, considered him for a moment. Looked at Tia, back at him. "Whatever you say."

Then she walked over to her rig.

He couldn't stop himself from glancing at Tia as the boat came to a stop. She sat on the bench, working on her dive vest, having zipped up her wet suit. She too wore a headscarf, and now pulled her dive mask over her eyes, held her fins in her hand, and approached the end of the boat.

"Pool's open!" the captain said, and Austen did a scissor jump into the water.

Ethan went in behind her.

Declan and Stein had also kitted up, and Stein checked the Jamesons' gear before he sent them on their way.

H eather opted to stay in the boat, but Dr. Scott, in a shortie suit, his fins on, waddled to the stern and rolled in, back first.

Declan bobbed in the water, giving an okay signal to the captain. Then he grabbed his fins, now wearing his BDC, pulled down his goggles, put in his regulator, and headed to the back.

"The wreck is about sixty feet down, just beyond the ledge. You'll have to swim to it because I can't anchor on the reef," said the captain—Ignatius, if Doyle remembered right. "Good luck." He grinned, his mirrored sunglasses sporting a shot of Doyle and his unshaven mug.

Doyle scissored in, slipped on his fins, and then shot an okay to Austen, their official guide for the tour.

She sent them down, and the noise of the world evaporated.

He loved diving. Austen had first taught him three years ago, when she'd yanked him away from the family's inn during their shoulder month—March. He'd spent three glorious weeks in the Keys, on her boat, getting certified, then diving every day to see the wrecks along the treasure coast. She'd shown him the few gold pieces she'd found littered among the reefs, and he'd gotten a tan, grown a beard, and generally found pieces of himself, like gold, in the crystalline waters.

Now, the old feeling of flying swept over him as he sank, the world turning a kaleidoscope of colors as he descended into the colony of coral that stretched along the shore. They'd anchored to a mooring ball positioned at the edge of the coral bed, the gnarled polyps held together by calcium carbonate. Austen hovered over the coral, pointing to a giant orange barrel sponge, then another, this one red.

Green and red parrotfish nibbled at the algae that adorned the staghorn and elkhorn coral that protruded like tiny trees from the rugged surface, and small, bright-orange clownfish skittered around flowing anemones. *Just keep swimming . . .*

The memory of the animated show rose inside—one of Juliet's favorites.

And see, now she would lodge in his head for the rest of the day.

Austen pointed to an overhang, and he followed her direction and spotted a coiled green eel, asleep in the crevice. A giant lobster stared out at him, its antennae like spears in the water.

A turtle edged out of a crack in the coral and headed away from the cluster of divers.

Doyle took a second to count the crew—yes, everyone was with them—and he gave an okay signal to the Jamesons, who seemed comfortable in the water.

Austen and Ethan had swum farther down the coral, now disappearing behind the shelf, toward where the ocean floor dropped fast into darkness.

The wreck.

Austen and he had already planned the dive—and now he stayed with the Jamesons and Greg Scott on the reef while she headed to the wreck, another thirty feet down.

Declan followed her, as did Stein, but Doyle stayed shallow, pointing out a large grouper and even a reef shark nesting in a nearby lava tube interspersed with the coral. The tubes collected the darkness, and he followed Dr. Scott as the man swam through tunnels, making sure he didn't get caught on the jagged black edges. The Jamesons followed him, and a stingray lifted from the shadows, floating away on angel wings.

Juliet would have loved this.

"Just because the plan changed doesn't mean God doesn't have a new one."

Austen's words thrummed in the silence. He sometimes felt like maybe he didn't want to know what the new plan was.

He'd like his old one back.

Still, yes, *five years.* The sharpness didn't take him down quite so often anymore; the grief was not as suffocating when it swept over him. Yes, he missed her, but the ache had become something deep inside that he had gotten used to living with.

A tapping caught his attention.

He looked around to find the source and spotted Hunter Jameson indicating to him with the tapper affixed to his tank. He pointed to his wife, who'd started for the surface.

Doyle signaled to Dr. Scott, and they headed over, then rose to the surface.

The wind had turned the waves choppy. He spat out his regulator. "You okay?"

Elise nodded. "My mask fogged up and I couldn't clear it. And I'm nearly out of air."

Huh. Doyle checked his pressure. Only half down. Maybe she had a faulty tank. "Okay, let's head back to the boat."

He searched for the vessel and spotted it bobbing in the water farther away than he'd hoped. They'd swum too far. "Let's inflate our swim sausages." Crazy name for the tall inflatable signaling tubes, but they worked. Hopefully the boat would pick them up.

Elise and Hunter deployed their tubes.

"I want to keep diving," Dr. Scott said. "I'm not done."

"We need to stick together. And we have a second dive, so let's regroup, then we'll go down—"

Greg disappeared under the water. *What the—*

"Go," said Hunter. "I'll stay with Elise."

Doyle popped in his regulator and headed down.

Greg had returned to the lava tunnel, scattering angelfish and tang in his swim to the bottom.

He was after something.

Doyle kicked hard to catch up.

In the tunnel, Greg turned on his light, stopped, shone it on the bottom, then up to the ceiling.

Doyle caught up, indicated that they should ascend, but Scott shook his head. He pointed the light at the ground again.

Brilliance sparkling against the glow.

Greg dove and Doyle followed.

The man picked up what looked like a sand-worn gold figurine, barnacle and algae free. Clearly the shadowed tunnel had protected it. Scott held it up, gave a thumbs-up.

He didn't have the heart to tell him that it looked like a souvenir of the bell tower from Esperanza, something a tourist had probably thrown in for fun.

Doyle's attention fixed on the tunnel. And how light poured through an opening at the top, near shore. He kicked away from Scott toward the light.

Surfaced slowly.

The opening seemed to be a deformation in the tunnel, maybe broken up by hurricanes or waves. Beyond it, the tunnel mouth enlarged and led toward the volcano. On the other side of the watery channel rose a small island made from lava debris.

He hadn't realized they'd dived so close to shore. He made out Hope House on the cliffside in the distance. The black beach spanned out to the water below the cliff, maybe also the remnant of this lava tube.

And then . . . *Wait.*

He sank back below the surface and spotted Dr. Scott, still searching the tunnel. Whatever had destroyed the lava tube had also dug an alleyway of sorts between the coral and the dark bottom.

At low tide, the right boat could maneuver through this alleyway and offload cargo to the tube . . .

Cargo like medical equipment.

And it wouldn't even have to go through the harbor control, right? Maybe.

He'd have to talk to the police, get a permit. And perhaps test his theory, but . . .

But it could be a way to avoid Sebold and his tyranny.

He checked his air gauge—nearly at the warning line—then swam back to Greg. He tapped two fingers on his hand, and Greg checked his air supply. His wide eyes showed what Doyle knew—they needed to ascend.

Doyle thumbed up and they started to rise. He identified the boat's hull in the water and surfaced twenty feet away. The captain had turned off the prop and bobbed in the water.

Elise and Hunter sat on the boat, wrapped in towels. Heather sat, eyes closed to the sun.

Greg surfaced next to him, spat out his regulator. "Did you see what I found?" He held it out to Doyle.

"Next time, you listen to me," Doyle said. "The last thing we need is you getting lost or stuck. The lava tubes are fun, but they can be dangerous too."

Scott's eyes narrowed, but Doyle didn't care how much money he might have lost for Hope House. The guy was reckless.

Reckless divers were dead divers.

He waited until Greg climbed out of the water, then took off his fins, threw them onboard, and climbed up the ladder. "That's a trinket from one of the souvenir shops." He gestured to the figurine. Grabbed a towel to wipe his face.

Greg made a sound and pitched the fake treasure back into the sea.

"Wait—aw." More litter in the ocean.

"We're going back to pick up the others," said Ignatius.

Doyle studied the rock formation as they motored away. Yes, a small boat, even a fishing trawler, might anchor at the mouth of the tunnel.

But the plan depended on where the tunnel led. He'd have to do some scouting.

Captain Ignatius consulted his GPS screen as he positioned them over the wreck not far away and turned off the engine.

Doyle checked his watch. The others had the same air as he did, but deeper down, the divers would expend more air.

They should be up by now.

He searched the water. Spotted Declan holding an orange deployed sausage. And with him, Ethan Pine.

But Austen, Stein, and Tia were nowhere to be seen.

Doyle pulled off his BCD, a fist in his gut as Declan swam over. He had already changed tanks by the time his boss pulled up to the ladder.

"Where are they?" Doyle said, affixing his vest back on.

"Tia got caught in a web of old fishing net coming out of a porthole. They're cutting her out."

Doyle put in his regulator, held on to his mask, and jumped into the water.

And this was how she would die. Caught in a fishing net sixty feet below the surface of the water, the light rays unable to pierce the darkness, slowly suffocating.

Don't panic. She read the look in Stein's eyes as he sawed away at the fishing net that she'd swum right into.

Because she'd panicked.

Stupid!

She'd spotted a shark snoozing on the sand beneath one of the barnacle-encrusted cannons of the *Trident,* fallen into a coral corridor. The shark stirred and she bolted. *Sort of* bolted, because she was swimming. But it *felt* like bolting as she turned and headed for the first ray of light through a snarl of coral.

She'd scraped her tank on the coral, and maybe that's why she hadn't seen the fishing net caught on the spires and jagged edges of the opening. *Like swimming through a spiderweb* . . . The tiny holes clipped onto her BCD, her tank valve, then the buckles of her fins, and even snagged on her wet suit.

Her thrashing hadn't helped.

She'd probably set herself up for disaster when she'd first thought she'd be creative and search amidst the deeper coral and lava formations for wreckage that might have floated from the main site with the current. The debris field spread over a hundred-yard area along the bottom, but some of the wreckage had fallen into the crannies of coral on the way to the ocean floor. Ethan had pointed out remains too—not just a cannon, but an anchor and timbers and even the rotted mainsail.

Other debris sifted in the sand, but most of it was gobbled into the bottom, probably under layers of four or five feet of silt.

Given the tugging behind her, Stein had ripped free one of her fins. He went to work on her tank. Austen had sawed on the netting stuck to Tia's octopus, the extra breathing supply that dangled off her BCD.

Austen tapped her hand with two fingers.

Right. Oxygen check. The needle had already dipped into the warning zone, and she showed Austen where it cut into the red.

Don't panic.

But they couldn't possibly get her free before her air ran out. And they'd come down with her, so certainly they had to be down to dangerous levels also.

Austen ripped Tia's octo free, but the netting had wrapped Tia up in the water too. Austen tried to get her finger in between the net and the wet suit, but it wouldn't budge. Tia's O2 gauge had detached from her BCD, and Austen grabbed it, took a look, then reached for her secondary and gave it to Tia.

She spat out her regulator, blew out the water in Austen's secondary reg, and took a fresh breath. But a glance at Austen's O2 gauge said they didn't have a lot of reserve.

And they'd gone so far down, they would need a five-minute decompression stop fifteen feet from the surface.

She couldn't even see the boat above, nor the mooring-ball line that connected the surface to the dive site.

Stein was now cutting at the connection to the coral. If she could break free, maybe she could kick like a mermaid to the top.

Suddenly he stopped, and a beeping sounded in the depths. He grabbed Austen and ran his hand across his throat, pointed at her.

Oh. Austen was on her last minutes of air.

He unhooked his secondary hose and shoved it at Tia.

She grabbed it, released Austen's regulator, cleared the secondary, and breathed.

He ripped off a small emergency tank on the side of his rig and shoved it at Austen. She shook her head, and he gestured up, desperation in his eyes.

Austen inserted the canister's reg into her mouth and let out her BCD air, rising.

Then the man took Tia's face in his hands, his blue eyes on hers. Nodded.

So, they were apparently in this to the end. Her eyes started to fill as he turned back to the netting.

No. She couldn't let him die here on the bottom with her. She hadn't gotten a look at his O2, but it couldn't be far behind hers.

He sawed at the netting, and it started to release.

She tried to pry the web from her leg. *C'mon—please, God—*

And it had been so long since she'd called out, but once upon a time, she'd believed. Called out and God had answered—

Beeping.

She looked up, but Stein kept cutting the line.

She ran her hand across her throat, but he ignored her. All she had to do was take out the regulator. He'd have enough at least for a straight emergency ascent—

Tapping. It echoed against the darkness, and now Stein looked up, around. Reached back and tapped his knife on his tank.

More tapping, and out of the blue, a diver appeared, kicking hard. He swam up to them, glanced at her, then Stein, and then grabbed his secondary octo. He shoved it into her mouth.

She cleared, breathed fresh air.

Then he took out his own reg and handed it to Stein. Stein took a breath, nodded, and handed it back to—

Doyle. *Of course* it was Doyle. He met her eyes with that same crazy, determined, fierce look he'd given her at the camp. And at the medical clinic, and even at the harbor, and *shoot*—he just kept *showing up*.

Stein turned back to his work, bubbles releasing from his mouth, and cut another chunk free. Doyle fed him air again, and then Stein finally broke her free, the netting still tangled around her legs.

Doyle took a breath, handed his reg to Stein, and then faced her as he grabbed her arms and kicked, dragging her toward the downline.

Stein kept up, feeding him the reg for a breath, and then himself, bubbles rising. They reached the downline, and as Doyle held on to her, he and Stein pulled themselves up the line, kicking, sharing the breath of life.

They stopped fifteen feet from the bottom for their safety stop, still trading, and Stein's watch counted down the required five minutes as they hung in the water, the current stirring them. Doyle handed Stein the reg and then looked at her, smiled, winked, and gave her the okay sign before taking it back.

Who was this man? *"I was called to be a missionary. Being a doctor was how I was going to get there."*

He wasn't a doctor, but he did seem to qualify for the other. Brave, creative, a healer.

Dangerous. Terribly, perfectly treacherous for her heart.

She had not come to Mariposa to fall in love. And she certainly couldn't do it with someone who was already taken—she'd already made that mistake.

She spotted the boat, bobbing some thirty feet away.

A splash, and suddenly Austen was in the water, swimming fast. She wore a fresh tank and handed Stein her secondary.

Doyle grabbed his air back, and when Stein's watch beeped, Doyle pulled Tia to himself and kicked to the surface.

Stein and Austen surfaced too.

Tia made to spit out her reg, but Doyle shook his head, and Austen kept her air in too as she grabbed Tia's BCD and helped Doyle haul her to the boat. Stein had gone ahead, taken off his tank and vest and handed it up to Declan. Then he climbed the ladder, turned, and sat, holding out his arms for their rescue package.

A.k.a., Tia.

She removed her regulator, her arms over Stein's knees as Doyle and Austen submerged, cut away the last of the netting, and removed her fins. Then they threw the fins onto the boat and handed up the netting.

Stein unbuckled her BCD, and Tia shrugged it off. He handed her rig up to Declan.

She didn't know what to say as Doyle and Austen surfaced, removed their air.

"You all right?" Doyle asked, breathing hard.

Don't cry. Don't—

Aw. Her eyes welled up and she nodded. Then Stein let her go.

"Hold on to the ladder."

She did, her entire body trembling as he climbed up, then reached down and grabbed her hands. The man pulled her out of the water, then her feet found the deck, and Stein moved her to a bench. Knelt in front of her, checking her over, his hands on her legs.

He thought he'd cut her.

Austen handed up her fins to Declan and then climbed up, ripping off her mask, unzipping her BCD. "Are you okay?"

Tia nodded, and *oh no,* tears burned her eyes. "I'm fine. I can't believe you did that—Austen, you could have *died.*"

Doyle had followed them and stood behind Stein, dripping, shaking a little. He looked at Tia, then Austen. "You good?"

Austen nodded. And then Doyle pulled her into a hug, so much relief in his gesture it turned Tia's heart. Now that was love, the real kind, no lying.

Sheesh, she should have realized a guy like Doyle would be taken. Not that it mattered.

It didn't matter—

"You should have seen your brother when he came up and found out you three were still down there," Declan said, coming over to hand Doyle and Austen towels. "By the time I was on the boat, Doyle was back in the water. I don't think he'd even buckled his BCD before he went down."

Brother?

Stein grabbed a towel, ran it over his hair, then scrubbed his face. "Yeah, good thing because I was almost out of air too."

"And I just barely made it through my deco stop with the bottle Stein gave me." Austen glanced at him.

Doyle had pressed the towel over his face too. Held it there. Maybe a little longer than normal. Now he lowered it, nodded. "I figured you guys would have more air, given your experience—and especially Stein—but . . . Anyway, thank the Lord we're alive."

He looked at Tia then, met her eyes with such directness, she felt it like heat through her entire shivering body.

Oh. She swallowed, nodded. *Yes. Thank You, God.*

So maybe she wasn't an afterthought to the Almighty after all.

"Good thing I taught him how to dive." Austen slung an arm over his shoulder. "I told him that rescue-diver cert would come in handy." She winked.

Doyle still seemed shaken, but now he grabbed on to the bar that ran the top of the roof. "What happened?"

All eyes turned to Tia, including Elise and Hunter Jamesons', who sat quiet, stricken on the other bench, and even Dr. Scott and Heather, who sat in the bow, Dr. Scott draped in a towel.

Declan's mouth tightened.

"I saw . . ."

"She saw a shark." Ethan had been standing near the freshwater supply tank and now came over, sat next to her. "Big one. I saw him too, from above—probably eight feet long. I think she just—"

"I panicked." There, she said it. "I . . . I just . . ." Listened to fear shouting in her head. "Didn't think. I swam for the first escape, and of course, right into a net. And the more I struggled, the more it caught me. If it hadn't been for Austen spotting me . . . I'm so stupid for panicking."

"If it hadn't been for Doyle panicking . . ." Stein said and clapped a hand on Doyle's shoulder. "Good instincts, bro."

"Thanks." Austen patted his cheek. "I take back all those times I called you the family drama king."

Doyle gave her a look, and she laughed and high-fived Stein. And somehow, more laughter infected the group, and Tia could breathe.

Full, easy, normal breaths.

"I guess we'll all be hungry for dinner tonight," Declan said. He went to stand next to Austen.

At the front, the captain started the engine.

Ethan looked at Tia, nudging her. "So, did you see any treasure down there?"

Doyle raised an eyebrow, then glanced at Ethan and shook his head.

Wait—

He turned and headed up to the helm.

"No," she said, glancing at Doyle's back, the way he braced

himself against the edge of the boat, looking at the horizon, the low-hanging sun skimming gold across the surface of the ocean.

And she couldn't escape the sense that whatever treasure she was looking for, she might have already found.

SIX

CLEARLY, HE'D BEEN MORE SHAKEN BY THE near diving death than Tia had been, because she presented the needs at Hope House like a pro. Not a hint of wavering in her voice, the woman had boardroom poise, despite the trauma six hours before.

They hosted the formal event in the dining room of Declan's magnificent home, and Doyle watched the entire thing sort of stunned.

And sure, Declan had a pad that seemed straight out of a magazine for the rich and famous, with white travertine flooring, beautiful walnut cabinetry, a sunken living room with an aquarium center table, a theater, and some twenty bedrooms scattered about the mansion, but really . . .

Doyle only had eyes for Tia, beautiful in a floral summer dress.

And then she walked over to Ethan after the event, and all he could think was . . . *oh no.*

She was up to something. And he'd lay bets it had to do with Ethan's quest for the pirate gold.

Oh, Tia. Please no. But he couldn't exactly confront her in front of a roomful of guests.

Now, she held a glass of vinho verde that seemed untouched and mingled with the guests on Declan's expansive veranda that overlooked the town of Esperanza.

In the distance, Hope House sat on a cliff above the town, soft lights glowing thanks to the twinkle lights the children begged them not to remove from the yard. They did cast an ethereal glow upon the place.

Moving here had been an escape, a desperate act, but it had brought a surprising balm to his soul.

"Bro. You good?" Stein had come up to him, holding a glass of ice water with lemon. He'd parked himself not far from Declan all day. Even now, the billionaire stood not far away, wearing linen pants and flip-flops, a white linen shirt. He stood with his hands in his pockets as he talked with a couple donors.

Stein wore a pair of dress pants, a short-sleeve shirt, and running shoes, ready, clearly, for anything.

"Yeah. Just . . ." Doyle blew out a breath. "Close call today. Thanks for saving Tia's life. You nearly died doing it."

The entire thing had his heart fisting, hammering, his mouth a little dry.

Stein clamped a hand on his shoulder. "You were there. I wasn't worried." He winked.

Whatever. Doyle took a sip of his lemonade. "Declan's estate seems like something out of a Bond movie. Except Declan is the good guy."

"Yeah, it's nice," Stein said, glancing past him, his eyes on the horizon, the crowd. "Lots to cover."

Right. Stein saw the dangers, not the opulence.

The three-story estate sprawled across a hillside, with a patio that jutted out over the side of the hill, bordered with glass railings, a pool set in the middle, now bright with firelight on the glassy water. Above them extended another patio, just enough to offer a covered seating area below, with two long sofas and a low granite fire table between them. The tile extended over the entire ground-level patio, and palm trees in planters sat in the corners, rustling in the breeze.

The second story looked just as fantastic, with floor-to-ceiling windows for a panoramic view. And he guessed another patio might be on the top of the building, given the rooftop walkway.

Elegant. Expensive. Yet Declan seemed a man easy with himself, not pretentious.

Doyle spotted Austen in the group talking with Declan. The red highlights in her auburn hair gleamed in the flicker of the tiki torches around the pool.

She'd nearly drowned today, and that thought punched a hole through him. If he hadn't surfaced when he did—and if he hadn't had that shallow dive—he wouldn't have been ready to dive again. His gear would have been stripped off, his BCD hanging on an empty tank.

Timing. His words before the dive about God's will issued back to him. *"Now I don't know what the destination is, and frankly, I'm not sure I want one."*

Maybe it wasn't so much not wanting one but putting his heart into something only to see it shattered in a moment.

As he watched, Austen smiled up at Declan, a laugh in her eyes. "Is there something going on between Declan and Austen?"

Stein glanced at Declan, frowned. "Don't think so. They met at Boo's wedding, and he invited her to guide. That's all."

Breathe.

"Listen, Doyle. We lived, and it's a gorgeous evening. Enjoy." Stein winked and followed Declan as the man moved away.

Gorgeous was right. Not a cloud to mar the overhead sprinkle of stars, the breeze warm off the ocean, and the smell of Wagyu-beef shish kebabs sizzling on the grill. An armada of chefs cooked the accompanying seafood paella, saffron spicing the air, prawns and clams simmering in the juices. Glistening plantain fried in another pot.

"Shrimp?"

Doyle's attention jolted to a server holding a tray of hors d'oeuvres. He helped himself to a grilled shrimp in some tangy sauce on a cucumber.

Fancy.

"That was amazing today," said a female voice, and he turned to see Elise Jameson standing there, her dark hair down, pushed back with a floral headband, wearing a pink dress and fancy sandals. "Such quick thinking."

Her husband came up behind her, extended a hand. "Indeed. I've never seen someone change out a tank so fast."

"We got . . ." Not lucky—he knew that, deep in his soul. "Blessed. There's no doubt that the timing was right, and I'm just thankful I was able to be in the right place at the right time."

"We call that God's providence," Hunter said. "There's no such thing as a coincidence."

Doyle lifted his glass. "Right."

"People often ask why bad things happen," Hunter said, looking past him, his gaze landing on something, then back at Doyle. "But I always wonder about the tragedies that miss us. What we've been protected from."

"And why God chooses to let some things through." Doyle took a drink. "My sister says He has a plan. I just don't always know what it is."

Hunter gave a warm chuckle. "What if it's not a destination but a position of the heart?" He put his hand on his wife's shoulder. "Looks like dinner is nearly ready. But we did want to talk to you about Jamal."

"And Kemar," added Elise.

"Kemar. I'm not sure—"

"We're not either." Hunter gave him a grim look. "We already love Jamal. And we . . . we don't want to split up a family. But Kemar seems . . . a handful."

"When authorities found Kemar, he was living in their abandoned home, taking care of Jamal on his own. He was eleven, and Jamal was three. He's always been very protective of him."

"We don't like separating families. But we're not sure Kemar . . . We don't want to get in over our heads." Hunter's mouth made a grim line. "But we need to think about this."

"Right." Doyle sighed. "I understand." He didn't want to mention that Kemar might not be returning to the orphanage. Not when he still had hope that the kid would come to his senses.

"But we will provide support for both of them, and all of their education costs."

That was something. "Thank you."

"Especially knowing they're in such good hands," said Elise, and squeezed his arm.

They were. Especially with Tia at the helm.

After the near accident, he'd gone back to Hope House and sat on his bed shaking, realizing—

He liked Tia more than he should.

Even now, as Declan stepped up and announced that the food was ready for consumption, his gaze found his codirector.

She wore her brown hair down and an orange-and-teal-patterned dress that tied around the neck, with a gathered waistline and a drop to her ankles. Firelight flickered against her arms, tanned and muscular (although she wore a gauze bandage over yesterday's burn), and the wind played with her hair. A different fire flickered in those hazel-green eyes, and had she not been standing next to—of course—Ethan Pine, Doyle might have walked over to her, drawn her away from the crowd and . . .

What? Kissed her? No, but maybe pulled her against him and let the rest of the pooled adrenaline from today's near tragedy flush out.

Codirectors. Partners. He needed to keep that forefront in his mind, *thank you.*

The guests loaded up plates, then sat at the round tables, the tablecloths rippling just slightly with the breeze. He found a chair at the table of Dr. Greg and Heather Scott. Greg couldn't stop talking about his son, playing hockey in the juniors, and how he was heading off to hockey camp in Minnesota because "King Con, center for the Minnesota Blue Ox" was teaching this year.

Doyle refrained from mentioning that he, *uh*, knew him. However, "I've heard Conrad is an amazing coach." His brother had spent too many years avoiding one of his greatest callings. Nice to see that he'd stepped out of his past too.

Too? Maybe. Save for the recent memory, Doyle hadn't dreamed of Juliet in weeks, and even his daytime thoughts didn't land on her quite as often as they used to.

He wasn't forgetting, just . . . taking a new path.

"Are these fried bananas?" Heather turned over the plantains glistening with butter on her plate.

"Plantains. You'll love them," Doyle said. Across the patio, he saw Tia, still with Ethan, frown, shake her head, and get up from the table. Ethan turned to catch her, but she walked away.

Doyle recognized Angry Tia when he saw her. And he must have turned into some kind of emotional support dog, because he couldn't stop himself.

She had gone around the side of the patio, toward the stairs that led down to the parking area, and stood in the shadows, staring out at Hope House, the wind playing with her hair.

"Tia?"

She startled, then looked over at him. "Oh, it's you."

That hurt. "Yes. Are you okay?"

She nodded. "I just . . . I might have gotten in over my head." Deep sigh. "Again."

He stood beside her. A slight fragrance of citrus drifted from her, probably shampoo. He didn't hate it.

"Okay." She looked up at him. "Truth is, Ethan Pine asked me to help him look for the lost *Trident* treasure. He thinks it's in a sulfur tunnel on or near Hope House property. And he wants us to go hunting for it."

"I figured."

"You did?"

Now *he* sighed. "Why is . . . why are you doing this?"

"So I can have leverage over Sebold. So he'll give us Kemar and the equipment back—"

"No. It's more than that, Tia."

The words just issued out of him, more impulse than fact. But it stripped a layer of confidence from her face. And then she winced and turned away.

"I'm—" he started.

"Right."

Oh.

She sighed. "Okay, so, yes, I know I'm stubborn. And I know this is pride, and maybe even fury, but . . . I just can't let Sebold win." Her voice dropped. "I can't let fear win. Again."

"Again?"

She gripped the railing, and he squelched the terrible urge to cover her hand with his.

"Fear has . . . it's made too many decisions for me."

He stayed silent.

"Fear made me say yes to my fiancé, and even got him killed."

What? The words landed, took root. Did she say *fiancé*?

"My fiancé was murdered three years ago." She turned to Doyle, arms folded across her body. "I only found out recently, although, to be honest, I had a gut feeling about it, even though I didn't tell anyone."

"How—"

"He was in a house fire. But he was dead before the fire. Shot. Which was frankly a relief because the idea of him dying in a house fire . . ." She swallowed, shook her head. Then, "Anyway, he was killed because of something I advised him to do. Because I was afraid that he'd fail and . . . I just couldn't let that happen."

He stuck his hands in his pockets, mostly for his own protection against the urge to take her into his arms.

So easily give away his heart.

"Edward had created this AI program that allowed cars to self-drive, along with other applications that could be applied to drones and a host of military innovations, and he wanted to sell it. So I sent him to my father, who was on the board of a tech company. My father said no—and Edward went to his competitor. What I didn't know was that conversation was overheard by someone who had invested heavily in my father's tech company . . . and he murdered Edward so that he could keep Edward's program from the competition."

Wow. "Is this what your sister's podcast was about?"

She nodded.

"I haven't listened to it, but, Tia—that doesn't sound like your fault."

"If I hadn't sent him to my father—"

"Seriously. You can't cause and effect everything that happens. It completely takes out the God factor—"

"Are you saying God's *plan* was for Edward to be *murdered*?"

He looked at her, suddenly unable to speak. "No. God never causes evil. That happens because we live in a fallen world. But He did . . . He did know."

And that meant He also knew that Juliet would careen off the road on the morning of their wedding. . . .

Doyle hung his hand on the back of his neck. "We can't control everything that happens to us. At some point, I think we just have to figure out how to move forward. And most of all, we can't look back to our choices and let them hold us hostage." From the patio, music began to play. "What did you mean back when you told Jamal that you'd believed something about yourself that wasn't true?"

She stared at him, then gritted her jaw and turned away.

"Tia—"

"That I matter."

He blinked, trying to let the words land.

She sighed. "The fact is, I think I was trying to make Edward love me. I mean, he loved me, but he loved my sister more. And I thought, if we could be partners, if I could help him get his program off the ground . . . Silly, I know. But I just couldn't admit that I'd said yes to marrying a man just because I didn't want to be the forgotten older sister."

"The forgotten—"

"Never mind." She turned to face him. "I realized tonight that I was doing it again. Getting in over my head. Maybe I was just numb after today's . . . well, after today. But it hit me, sitting at dinner, when Ethan suggested we go into the mines that . . . I *don't* want to find gold and face Sebold and . . ." Her expression broke. "I don't want to put anyone else's life in danger because I'm listening to my fears and trying to be in charge."

"You are sort of in charge. I was impressed with your presentation."

She touched his chest, let the silence of the night slip between them. "Thank you for saving me today."

Oh. And suddenly her hand on his chest heated through him, and she lifted her face to meet his.

His gaze fell on her lips, slightly parted, a question in her eyes.

The rush of desire crested over him, the night stirring the breezes, the shadows luring him to—

He put his hand over hers and blew out a breath. *Coworkers.* And there was too much riding on this job for her for something to go south between them.

Maybe too much for him too, if he was honest. So he slid her hand off, then squeezed and let go. "Please stop trying so hard, Tia. It'll all work out."

She gave him a tight smile, but the warmth in her gaze, the question, was replaced by something he couldn't name. *Sadness? Relief?*

"So, that was your sister today? Our scuba guide?"

He frowned at her question. "Yeah. She's a professional guide in Key West. I think Declan met her at my sister's wedding. Why?"

She shook her head, wearing a sort of wry smile. "No reason."

Hmm. Then, *speaking of diving*—"What if we were able to get shipments in without Sebold knowing?"

Life sparked in her expression. "Really?"

"I found something today that might work. I'm going to hike the mountain tomorrow and see if I can find some answers."

Music spilled out nearby, dinner clearly over, and this time oldies floating in the breeze. Dean Martin, "You're nobody 'til somebody loves you . . ." The lyrics reached out, tugged at him, and maybe her too, because she smiled. Nodded. "Okay, partner. I'm in."

And as he followed her back to the patio, all he heard were his words to Austen. *"I'm not a good candidate for happily ever after."*

Maybe not. But somewhere deep inside him nudged the forbidden desire to try.

Why was this man always a problem? Everywhere Emberly

went lately—okay, just three times now, but seriously—Steinbeck Kingston haunted her.

Like a ghost. Or like an old injury that refused to heal.

An old injury that seemed more handsome every time she saw him—*sheesh,* that tan against his dark hair, those blue eyes—

Stop.

But what kind of crazy bad luck was it that of all the close-body protection in all the world, the one man who could muck this up was the only man Declan trusted?

Fate. It drove her crazy with it's terrible retribution.

She smiled, held out her tray of shrimp on cucumbers to another guest, her face turned away from Stein, who stood not far from Declan, looking too spiffed up in his dark suit and sunglasses.

The man didn't have a hope of blending into the crowd. Not with those shoulders, his somber demeanor, even when he stopped to talk to his brother. And sister.

She remembered them from the wedding. What a small world to see them all here. Not that they'd remember a redheaded server from their youngest sister's prewedding dinner. Or the woman who'd danced with Stein—yeah, that was a moment she would never forget—at the reception.

It seemed that Stein hadn't seen her. Because if he had, he'd what—chase her down, demand answers?

Maybe. Or perhaps he'd be trickier, wait until he could get her alone.

What if he'd simply forgotten about her? It could be that she'd never been more than a blip on his radar, a person he'd met during an op that went bad.

So terribly bad it had derailed his entire career. Yeah, trauma might have wiped her right out of his brain. And she needed to keep it that way.

It helped that she'd added contacts and a dark long-haired wig, but frankly, every time her gaze landed on Stein, then moved away, her skin prickled.

She couldn't see those blue eyes through the shades, but in her heart, her soul, even, she just knew he could see right through her.

On the other hand, everyone else simply didn't see her, the way they didn't see the other waitstaff.

She lifted the tray for another person to grab their treat, then moved to the next group. Sometimes this part felt too easy.

She eased away from the door, then set down her tray of grilled-shrimp appetizers and hustled across the living room to the back stairs.

A week of surveillance, including drone coverage and a hunt through the building plans down at Mariposa town hall (no online files for them), had netted her a floor plan and a fairly accurate time-stamped grid of Declan's security force. Five guys, including Stein. They all lived in a wing of the main floor, in staff quarters, along with a number of housekeepers, local chefs, and a valet. Not a small entourage to keep the place running.

Large enough that she wouldn't be noticed if they suddenly added to the staff, *thank you*.

She'd already hacked into the visual-security feed and replaced the shots with still coverage—okay, not her, but—

"You should be near the back elevator, if you sent me the right specs." Nim, her sister, waiting patiently in her earpiece.

"Mm-hmm," Emberly hummed just above a whisper.

"Let me know if the key card doesn't work."

Footsteps sounded on the travertine, and she slipped into a nearby bathroom. A chandelier dripped from the ceiling, and a marble countertop held a raised bowl. But it was the image in the mirror that caught her attention.

She looked gaunt. The two-plus months since the accident in Barcelona, the lack of sleep, still weighed in her face. And despite her ten days on the island, she hadn't seen much of the sun, most of her surveillance happening at night.

More, she still favored her arm, holding it close to her body even now. And if she looked closely, the scrape still showed in the tender skin on her chin.

Nim's voice interrupted: "You okay?"

"In the bathroom." She opened the door, peeked out. *No one.* "Here goes nothing." Walking up to the elevator, she pulled out the key card she'd stolen via RFID from Declan on the boat. That had been a risk—valeting the scuba equipment to the boat to get close to Declan. Stein had been carrying his own gear and hadn't even noticed the blonde with the long hair in a baseball cap and sunglasses, wearing the Outriggers Dive Shop T-shirt. She hadn't stayed long enough for him to put it together, however.

Nim had programmed the chip, and Emberly produced the card, and *please, please—*

The lift arrived and the doors opened.

She got in, hit the button for the bottom floor, and stripped off the server's dress. Underneath she wore a pair of shorts and a short-sleeve dive shirt, along with a small thigh pack. This shouldn't take long. She just needed a shot of the keypad, the bio-lock technology. If she was right, it wouldn't be too different from the secure digital vault in Montelena. That technology used a retinal-identification scanner as well as a thumbprint and the bio code, so this would simply need the current eight-digit code along with the bio key and—mission accomplished. She'd get in, download the AI program that Declan had developed—Axiom—and deliver it to the people who could put the kibosh on his Evil Plans to Destroy the World.

Okay, that might be overstating it, but—

Silence on the other end. As she descended, the walls thickened, and maybe cell phone reception could be affected. "Nim, you still with me?"

"Stop shouting. Yes."

She let out a breath. "They must have an extender down here. Cut the feed." A moment later, the doors opened to a bare room lined with concrete, with reinforced steel walls, a metal door facing the elevator.

Beneath this platform, water ran through an underground cavern, one that led all the way to the sea. And at any attempt to breach the vault, the outside channel door would close and she'd be trapped.

But if she did her work right today, it would be her escape.

She waited a moment.

"Confirmed."

She stepped out, glancing at the cameras mounted on all four corners and above the door.

"Just get the specs and leave," said Nim. "I don't like this."

Emberly stepped up to the pad and pulled out her camera. "He's here at the party."

"No, really?"

"Yes. I thought it might be him the other night when he stepped onto the patio, but I wasn't sure—too dark. But it's definitely him."

"Did he recognize you?"

"I'm here, right? My guess is that if he recognized Phoenix, I'd be in cuffs, maybe in a locked room answering questions, or at least—"

"He would not hurt you."

She sent the pictures to Nim. "Coming your way. And maybe, maybe not. Depends on what he remembers."

"Like the kiss?"

She opened up her scanner app and ran it around the edges of the door, searching for motion detection or infrared tripwires. Nothing. "I was thinking more about what happened after that—as in the explosion."

"That wasn't on you."

"The part where I took his asset and left him is."

"You had a job to do. Still do. And it's just as important as his—more, now. You're not protecting a terrorist inventor trying to destroy the world."

"No radio frequency here." She pulled out a waterproof cellphone case. "Frankly, seeing Declan over the past few days . . . I don't know, Nim. He seems . . . not like the guy the Swans say he is."

"That's not your job. *Oh no.* They found my hack. You need to exfil, right now."

"How much time?" She glanced at the lift. The light had dinged—someone calling it up.

"One minute—go. Call me when you're out." Nim clicked off.

Emberly sealed the case and shoved the phone into the thigh pocket of her swim shorts and pulled out a small tank the size of an energy drink can, fitted with an oxygen mouthpiece.

Then she walked over to the elevator and lowered herself into the open space of the lift chamber. The level below opened right above the mechanicals on the floor of the lift. The right turn of the right key in the lift panel would move the lift to this lower escape chamber.

Declan Stone wasn't the only millionaire to have installed a secret getaway chamber in his house.

The right conversation with the designer over vermouth and patatas bravas in Barcelona had given her the specs she needed.

She landed on the passageway below, the shadows beyond dark. She knelt for a moment, then pulled out a dive light and flashed it on the secure door.

"Can you open the door with the key card?" She'd leaned over her drink, turning the stir stick, listening to the older man. A week of surveillance and he'd shown up, an easy mark in comparison to Declan.

"Oh no. If the electricity is cut, we need to go old school. Just a key."

"A key. What kind of key?"

"A simple skeleton key."

"So, it's a warded lock?"

He'd seemed pleased with her knowledge. But she'd been filing down the wards in the lock in her mind.

"Yes. But don't forget the false wards. Or the secondary locks." He'd winked.

She'd bring her lock kit. And maybe, pray.

Not that she expected any help.

Now, she pulled out a slim, metallic key and worked it into the lock, feeling for the telltale give of the wards aligning, the tumblers falling into place. Behind her, the lift motor hummed.

Faster.

Don't look.

Down here, the ocean thundered against the cavern walls.

The lock clicked and she heaved open the door. It groaned on its unused hinges. Oops. She'd have to move fast.

Her light cast down steps hewn into the rock and leading down to a cavern, clammy and scented with brine and age.

She closed the door—*too hard*—and it slammed. Again, *oops.* But she started down the stairs, pulling out the pin in her oxygen tank.

A half-mile swim to the entrance. She'd already mapped it, already discovered the spillway. Already swum the length of it, all the way to the door, just to make sure it could be navigated.

Did Declan even know that he'd built his house on an ancient smugglers' river, carved out by the lava tubes that perforated this island?

Probably.

The river fed deeper into the mountain, the darkness consuming. Her mag light brightened the edge of the water, and she affixed the mag onto a Velcro pocket in her shirt.

Above her, the door heaved. *What—*

She turned.

No.

In the gap stood a man, dark suit, staring down into the abyss. He had no flashlight.

She put a hand over hers, cutting off the light.

"I know you're down there!"

She slipped into the water and doused her light.

Then she took a breath, stuck the mouthpiece in, and sank into the dark. Wan light fell from the opening above, just a dent in the shadow, but as she kicked away, a hand on the lava wall, she spotted him standing on the water's edge.

Staring down into the darkness.

Her heart thundered, her breath tight as she hugged the wall.

She couldn't see his face, just his outline, the way his shoulders rose and fell. But she could imagine the tight fists, the clench of his jaw, the fierceness of his blue eyes dissecting the shadows.

And deep in her memory, she heard his voice: *"What are you doing to me, Phoenix?"*

Oh no. Because in her heart, she knew.

Steinbeck Kingston hadn't forgotten her. Not at all.

She'd put way too much hope in Doyle's idea.

Or maybe Tia had simply put way too much hope in Doyle. Not that he didn't deserve it.

No, if anyone deserved for her to throw her trust, her hope, directly into his arms, it was Doyle Kingston, who just couldn't help but show up.

And look good doing it.

He wore a pair of cargo shorts, hiking boots, and a short-sleeve t-shirt with the words *Iron Will* on it, some dogsledding race he'd attended in Minnesota.

Sometimes she forgot he lived in the same state, probably less than sixty miles from her. Funny that they'd had to travel a thousand miles into the depths of the Caribbean to meet.

Although, she might have never fully appreciated his quick thinking and optimistic demeanor if they hadn't been here, facing off with trouble. The man had a quiet determination about him, even as he led the way along a trail into the jungle that wound around the base of the volcano. He kept looking back at her, checking on her, but she'd recovered better than she'd expected to from her near-death dive.

In fact, last night, for the first time in a long time, she'd slept without dreaming. No nightmares of Edward or even the ones that lingered, deeper, from further back. Probably because she'd gone to bed thinking of the way Doyle pulled her into his arms on the dance-floor-slash-patio of Declan's estate during a Dean Martin song. *"You're nobody 'til somebody loves you . . ."* Just one song, but the man had moves.

The kind of moves that had made her put her arms around his neck and, for just a second, wish that he'd act on the look in his eyes.

Unless she'd imagined it.

The dance had ended too soon, and then he'd danced with his sister and some of the other female guests, and maybe he'd smiled at everyone like they were someone special.

The bright sunlight and the early-morning air had put reality back in its place. They were here to do a job, and Doyle had met her in the kitchen with a backpack and a water bottle, along with a map.

They'd headed up along the back of the property to an old hiking trail that should lead them on a short trek around the mountain to where he'd marked an *X* on the map. Apparently his best guess at the location of the tunnel he'd seen.

Now, ten minutes up the trail, he turned and looked back, huffing a little at the steep climb. "Gorgeous."

The town of Esperanza lay in a pocket, the houses scattered along the hillside, dropping into the valley, the sea a deep variegated blue stretching out under a gorgeous sky tufted with cotton. The jungle rose around them, dense with coconut palms and royal poinciana with their big red blossoms, and thick mahogany, and fragrant cedar trees, with wild orchids, and hibiscus, and aloe vera plants stirring up a sweet haze of scents. Humidity clung to the air, settled on her bare arms and legs.

But somehow, up here, she could breathe.

Even if a sweat had started to trickle down her spine.

Her gaze went to Hope House, to where the stone monastery sat on the hill, with the old clay-tile roof, the gardens, the wall around the grounds. It looked like something out of a Spanish tour book, with the bell tower rising from the front entrance, the arched doorways in the back leading to the refectory turned medical clinic. Sunlight shone against the rose window in the church that Doyle had repaired and turned into an art gallery.

"There's so much potential there," he said quietly. "If we can just figure out how to keep it safe." He looked at her then, those blue eyes on hers, and she wondered if maybe he meant something else.

"I think this trail leads to the old airport, but the sulfur mine is on the way." He kept walking.

"I didn't know there was an airport on this island."

"Back when it was an enclave for the wealthy. On the other side of the island—near Sebold's resort—is a village of abandoned, destroyed homes. It took the hit from the hurricane that simply ravaged the town. That's where most of our kids are from. A few of the wealthier homes also got destroyed."

His footfalls landed softly on the loamy soil. "My guess is that without the community to support them and with the infrastructure destroyed, the wealthy on the island cut their losses and moved to St. Kitts, just down the sea, so to speak."

"My family has a home on St. Kitts," she said, not sure why.

He looked over at her. "Really?"

"Yeah. We don't visit it often."

He nodded.

"I know you're thinking, What is a rich girl like me doing on this island, scrubbing for cash? And the answer is, I would have preferred if you didn't know I came with money."

He glanced back at her, eyebrow up. "Why?"

"Because it complicates things. I thought Edward was the only guy who saw me for me because he grew up with our family. Now, I'm not sure, but . . . it's just hard for me to trust people when I know they know. . . . Anyway, apparently you knew all along."

"I did," he said. "Although when you first showed up, that was the last thing on my mind."

"What was the first thing?"

He said nothing.

"Doyle."

"I don't want to say."

Oh. "Because you thought I was bossy."

Another beat.

"No. Because I thought you were pretty."

Oh, and her heart thumped.

"*And* bossy."

She laughed. "I might have thought I could whip this place into shape. But it's starting to feel like it's trying to whip me into shape."

They came around a curve in the trail and looked over a cliff, the ocean spitting against the rock, creating thunder, spray.

"Is the tunnel down there?"

"Somewhere, yes. Maybe."

"What's your big plan, then? We import our supplies to the tunnel and bring them through the cave?"

"I know it sounds crazy, but yes. Although right now, I don't see the lava tube."

"It could be under water. Tide is high. Let's keep going."

The wind stirred the ocean breezes, lifted the heat from the morning. The trail widened, the jungle dropping away, giving over to flatter, more rocky land.

"So, this Edward," Doyle said suddenly. "He was a childhood friend?"

"His mother was our chef. My dad took an interest in him, put him through college. He was at MIT when I was."

"You were at MIT? Studying what?"

"Economics. I wanted to be a financial adviser and take over my father's investments."

"Hence the charity work." He stopped. They'd come to a rocky hillside, the area cleaned off, the rocks whitened. She turned and spotted Hope House less than a half mile away, down the mountain.

When she turned back, he had pulled binoculars from his pack.

"What are you doing?"

He scanned the horizon, then the cliffs. "I think the opening is below us. But there's a fire on the other side of the island." He pointed to a tuft of white-gray smoke curling in the distance. He handed her the binoculars. "It's near the airport, but a little farther on. Looks like they're doing construction."

She found the activity, made out an excavator and a truck.

"It's not Sebold's camp—he's on the east side of the island."

"I'll ask Declan about it. Maybe some organization has come in to rebuild the village. There's our sulfur cave, by the way." He pointed to a yawning mouth up the hill. A dirt road, now crumbled and jutted with weeds, led to the opening of the cave.

Her gut tightened as they walked up to it. *Calm down*. But if this worked, she could tell Ethan that no, she wasn't going to damage the monastery for the sake of the gold. Their conversation from last night stirred inside her. Ethan's proposal—*"I have new technology that can send a laser into the rock and crumble it. We can break through the cave-in and . . ."*

And that's when she'd held up her hand, suddenly seeing the destruction of their entire refuge. *"You can't be serious. You don't know what unsettling that rock could do—"*

"Some things are more important—"

And right then, she'd gotten up, unable to listen to more.

Seeing her own desperate actions in his words.

Now, as she came up to the cave entrance, the stench of rotten egg seeped out from the dark opening. "You want to go in there?"

Doyle pulled off his backpack and opened it. Handed her a headlamp and took one for himself. "We'll be fine."

She fitted on the headlamp. "I don't love small places." In fact, her heart had lodged in her throat. She could do this. Really.

"If my guess is correct, they've widened this enough for workers and even a car to pass through."

Indeed, as she neared, the opening seemed wide enough for their Ford, and as they ventured into the mine—*he might have thought to bring nose plugs*—the space turned cavernous. They walked into a large area carved out, maybe for delivery purposes, and from it led five different tunnels.

"Which one, Magellan?"

He glanced at her, grinned, gave a small chuckle.

It thrummed under her skin, into her bones. *Okay, calm down.* She was in good hands.

"I think this one feels most logical." He pointed to the tunnel nearest the ocean and held out his hand.

Oh. Okay then. She grabbed it and let him lead her down the tunnel, the ground uneven beneath her KEENs. Crystalline sulfur, bright yellow under her beam, covered the ground. The toxic rotten-egg smell seemed to grow thicker, and she put her hand to her nose.

"I know. Usually miners wore masks. And most of this was chipped out by hand."

"You're a sulfur-mine expert?"

"Did some late-night reading." Their headlamps hit on the walls, which were wet and bleeding with amber. They passed an old, rusty metal mine cart set into an alcove.

"This mine was owned by the largest landowner and merchant on the island—way back in 1865. There are actually three mines in this mountain, and a pit nearly a thousand feet deep in which they found sulfur."

"Please let this tunnel not end at that pit."

He laughed. "I think, given my study of the map, the pit is farther north. But there are miles and miles of tunnels, some of them natural, others man-made. It was mined for nearly a hundred years. The mine rights were separated and passed down to family members over the years and finally were sold to the city of Esperanza in 1964. It's been virtually abandoned since then. There, look—stairs."

His light fell on a set of steps cut into the rock. She turned, looked back, but couldn't see the great room. *Breathe. You're fine.*

She braced her hand on the wall as they descended, her other hand on his shoulder.

"Smell that? It's the ocean."

Indeed, the sulfur scent seemed to dissipate, and they finally landed on even ground. Here the tunnel had closed in, but they could still stand, the walls eight feet wide, maybe ten feet tall. And light emerged from up ahead.

Still, she gripped Doyle's hand as they ventured toward the light. The mouth of the tunnel opened to a view of the sea. She stepped up to the edge.

It dropped some fifty feet down to a ledge that protruded into the water.

"It's the tunnel," Doyle said, pointing to the lava rock. "I'd hoped that it connected to the mountain. But it does look like they used this for offloading sulfur." He pointed to a cable that extended to the bottom. "Maybe this was a lift of sorts."

"The tide has gone down—you can see the tide line." She pointed to a protruding rock thirty feet from the cliff. "When the tide was in, ships could reach the top of the tunnel and pick up the sulfur supply."

"Easier than hiking it down to the village."

"Maybe, but it seems this way is harder. And that cable looks early 1900s." Rusty and fraying, part of it grew into the rock, secured by vines and brush.

He sighed. "So maybe this won't work."

There was so much disappointment on his face, she wanted to disagree. In fact, "What if this isn't the only outlet? We haven't checked the other tunnels." *Aw,* why did she say that? Because now he smiled, and *shoot,* she'd sealed her fate.

He took her hand again until they got to the stairs, then they climbed back up, out to the cavern area. He gestured to the next tunnel. "What do you think?"

"I think someone's following us." She pointed into the yellow mist. Tire tracks—bicycle tracks. They led to the tunnel near the entrance . . .

Maybe leading back to Hope House.

Wait . . .

"I'll bet it's Ethan. He's found the sulfur mine and is trying to find the gold."

Doyle looked down at her, frowning. "What?"

"Long story. C'mon."

She headed toward the opening, her gut roiling. "He wanted to blast open the cave-in under the monastery, where he thinks the treasure is buried. I told him no—"

"Good for you."

"Except, clearly he's found another way in." She ducked, this tunnel not as developed but still carved out, the walls six feet wide, and under her feet, tire marks.

It twisted south, descending gradually, the walls weeping, the darkness fighting the light.

"You think this tunnel goes all the way back to Hope House?" Doyle walked behind her, ducking now and again. The sulfur smell thickened, and she tucked her nose into the top of her shirt.

"I'm not sure this is safe," said Doyle. "Sulfur is toxic—I didn't realize how thick it would be until now. I think we need masks. And there are probably still pockets of gases. It could be flammable—"

A rumble deep inside the body of the volcano, as if it might be snoring, or rousing from slumber. The walls shivered, and amber dust fell, sifting into the air.

Doyle reached out and grabbed her, pulled her back, leaning over her as if protecting her from the falling dust.

In a moment, it subsided, and he let her go. But he turned her, shaking his head. "This is dangerous."

"We need to stop him—"

"Yes. But not by being buried with him."

Yes, Doyle was right. She nodded.

Then the mountain shook again, this time with a grumble that echoed through the chambers.

Doyle grabbed her hand and shouted, "Run!"

SEVEN

SO THE IDEA OF SETTING UP A ROGUE SHIPping port through the sulfur mines could officially be categorized in the Bad Idea file.

Four hours later, and despite a shower, Doyle still harbored the rank odor of rotten egg as he sweated on the soccer field. He couldn't believe he'd nearly gotten Tia killed. They'd practically dived out of the tunnel and into fresh air. He'd stood at the maw of the rock, hands on his knees, just shaking.

Worst-nightmare alert: being buried alive.

Maybe for Tia also, because she'd stared over at him with wide, terrified eyes.

They'd said nothing as they hiked down the hill, back to the monastery. Probably her deciding that she'd had enough of the near-death dates with Doyle.

He didn't know how it ended up that way every time—but he'd never been so far from himself and what he'd expected of this mission than in the last few days.

He far preferred to play soccer with his kids—yes, *his*, because weirdly, as Lionel and Aliyah and Jamal spent time with their possible new families today, he couldn't help but hang around, listen to their conversations, even want to join in as Jamal kicked a soccer ball with Hunter Jameson.

The boy's laughter had found his soul, stirred it with a strange feeling.

Please, God, protect him. Let this be the right choice.

Now, as Doyle ran down the edge of the field, the coach of the blue team, shouting encouragement to the Hope House against Hope House players, today's near cave-in seemed a thousand years away.

Especially since Taj had recruited Tia to help him coach the other team. Doyle kept glancing at her, with her dark hair back in a ponytail, wearing a pair of white shorts—wow, she had nice legs—and a red T-shirt. She seemed to have dived full-in with cheering on her team.

And he'd thought she didn't even like soccer.

"C'mon, Gabriella, don't let Jimmie get around you!" He cupped his hands around his mouth, hoping to deliver the message as the ball shot past her, only to have thirteen-year-old Jimmie Costas pick it up.

He kicked and the ball went wide of the goal, and good thing because Rohan had already let three goals shoot past him.

Doyle thought of Kemar and the many times he'd played goalkeeper. For a second, the memory of the boy's broken expression as he pleaded for his brother tore through him.

Please, God, watch over him.

He'd been praying more lately, probably thanks to Tia and her Great Escapades, but . . .

He couldn't seem to purge from his brain his words to her what felt like a century ago—but was actually only three days—about being called to be a missionary.

It was true, but the old calling felt dusty and stale. At least, until he'd heard himself speaking it aloud. Now he couldn't seem to set it away again.

"Out!" Anita shouted, ruling for his team.

He called time-out and ran in, gathering the kids on the pitch.

"Okay, listen—" He put his hand on Rohan's shoulder. The kid wore grass stains on his hands and knees, and a little blood where he'd scraped his chin. "You're doing great out there. It's a new position—"

"I stink at this!" Rohan shook off his hand. "Put me back in at center, Mr. D. Let Elias play goalie."

"He's our best striker," Doyle said, glancing at Elias, whose sweat drenched his shirt. "But . . . if you want to try—"

"No. I gotta look good." Elias gestured to the donors, some seated on a bench, others on folding chairs. "Just in case they want me."

And right there, Doyle's heart opened up and bled. None of the potential parents had spoken up for Elias. Or Rohan. Considered the kids too old, maybe, but teenagers longed for parents too.

Doyle barely refrained from reaching out to pull the kid into his embrace. *Not here.* He needed to tame his emotions. They got him into trouble.

What if the Jamesons and even the Marquezes and the Tuckers didn't want the kids they'd made relationships with? Lionel had already started to pray for his "new mom and dad." Doyle had set them all up for heartache.

"We can't let the red team win," Gabriella said. "I'll be goalie."

Oh. Last time he'd let her play that position, she'd gotten hit, smack in the face, nearly broken her nose. "Are you sure?"

"I don't have anyone here cheering for me," she said with a shrug. "I don't have to be a star."

"I'm cheering for you," he said quietly, "and you're a star to me."

She looked away, her jaw suddenly tight.

Aw. Okay. He looked at the team, so many sweet, eager faces, big eyes, staring at him, and the moment just fell upon him.

Maybe he wasn't so far from the guy he wanted to be. The guy Juliet had seen in him. The missionary calling he'd tried to forget.

"Okay, Lucia, you throw it in to Rohan, and, buddy, you bring it down, shoot it to Elias. We're two goals down, and it's time we showed everyone what you can do." He put his hand in the center, a fist. "Blue on three!"

The team offered the cheer and ran out onto the field. Lucia ran to the corner, where Taj handed her the ball.

Doyle stepped back onto the sidelines and felt a gaze burning the back of his neck. That's when he spotted Tia standing on the opposite side, arms akimbo and staring hard at him.

He lifted a hand in a wave and she nodded. Turned away.

But not before giving him the smallest of smiles.

And he was right back on the dance floor last night, his hand on the curve of her back, moving with the music, her arm around his shoulder. And she was staring up at him with those beautiful hazel-green eyes. Gold gathered near the irises, adding a spark of hidden treasure into her gaze, and with the citrus scent of her hair twining around him, it was all he could do not to fall right into her smile.

To pull her back into the shadows, maybe surrender to the spark, the what-if between them.

Or maybe he was the only one feeling it, but she *had* held on to him today, just as hard as he'd held on to her.

So, yes, *partners.*

But what if . . .

The day had turned gorgeous, with the blue of the ocean translucent and stretching into the horizon under an unblemished sky. A mountain breeze tumbled down, reaped the lush redolence of the jungle, and stirred it into the valley. He wore a baseball hat, sunglasses, a sleeveless shirt, and shorts and longed for a dip in the ocean.

Rosa had planned a cookout on the beach for tonight, and maybe, if the mood was right, he'd ask Tia for a walk through the salty waves. Take her hand.

And then what? They ran the orphanage together, the lives of these children between them, more than a job.

The sense of it thickened his throat, and his cheer hiccupped a second when, indeed, Elias kicked it in for a goal.

Bam!

Doyle looked over and noticed the Scotts cheering on Lucia, and *huh,* he hadn't realized they were interested in adopting.

Or maybe hope had just taken hold of him.

Jaden kicked the ball out of the goal, and Jamal picked it up. The Jamesons hit their feet, and even Doyle recognized the effect it had on him. Jamal raced down the field, dodged Lucia and Elias, and kicked.

Gabriella caught it and fist-pumped, and Jamal's shoulders slumped.

"It's okay, son!" Hunter Jameson yelled. "You'll get the next one."

Son? Oh boy. He'd better tell Hunter to slow his roll. Still, maybe it boded well.

Gabriella kicked the ball out, and the game turned into a track meet, the two teams chasing each other down the field. When Rohan scored, the sun heavy on the horizon, even Doyle wanted to collapse on the grass.

A tie. The teams high-fived each other as the donors descended on the field.

From across the field, Stein stood with Declan, and his brother gave him a thumbs-up. Heat stirred in him, maybe because out of all his siblings, Stein had seen him before and during, and knew what it took to come back from devastation.

Rohan jogged over to him, tossed him the ball. "Thanks, Mr. D."

Doyle high-fived him as the teen ran by, probably on his way to grab water, but the sight of Ethan Pine walking up to Tia caught his eye. He wore a pair of cargo pants, a linen shirt, a baseball hat, something determined in his eye.

Ethan spoke to her, and she shook her head, then started to walk away.

When Ethan grabbed her arm, Doyle couldn't stop himself. He strode across the field, on his way to intercept.

She yanked her arm out of Ethan's grip and rounded on him, so *uh,* maybe she didn't need him. Still, he came up to them quickly enough to catch—

"You trying to bring the mountain down on us?"

Ethan held up his hands. "Don't overreact there, sweetheart. It was just a test to see if I could move the rock. And I could. I know the treasure is just beyond the cave-in—you need to trust me."

"Are you serious? Ethan, the entire mine shook," Doyle said sharply.

Ethan cocked his head. "Wait—were you up there?"

Tia's mouth tightened.

Attagirl—

"I thought you said you wanted no part of this," Ethan snapped. "What, are you going behind my back? Trying to find the treasure for yourself?"

She lifted her hands, a sort of surrender. "No. Of course not."

"Listen, Miss Pepper, I know you think you own the place—"

"I don't think anything of the sort. We have enough problems without you trying to get us all killed!"

Silence fell over the field and everyone turned.

Now Ethan's expression hardened. "Just stay out of my way and out of my tunnel."

"You should probably remember that this is Hope House land, sir," she said, her voice low. "And the city owns the mine, so my guess is the police might have some thoughts on you being up there shaking Mr. Cumbre de Luz."

"We'll see about that." He strode away.

Doyle watched him go, squelching the urge to high-five her.

"There goes the hope of the X-ray machine," she said quietly.

What? "Tia. You're right. He could get people hurt. I don't think the entire mountain would come down, but those sulfur mines have turned the rock into Swiss cheese. The wrong tunnel collapses, and . . ." He glanced at Ethan, back at her. "Maybe it *is* time to pull the plug, at least until we can assess the danger."

Stein had walked up to him. "Pull the plug on what?"

"Ethan is a treasure hunter, and he's looking for pirate gold in the sulfur mines."

"Hey, coach!" This from Elias, who'd come up behind him. "Taj says he can score on you."

Doyle looked at Taj, standing with the ball at the goal. "Does he now?"

"Go play with the kids," Tia said. "I'll get dinner figured out with Rosa." She gave him a tight smile.

And he couldn't stop himself. "It's going to be okay, Tia. We'll figure it out."

Her gaze stayed on him, as if letting his words sink in. "Thanks. Codirector." And then she gave him a real smile. "See you at the beach."

As she walked away, all he thought was . . . maybe he could resurrect this day after all.

She should stop trying so hard.

Doyle's words from last night kept circling Tia's head as she watched Rosa serve up the pig that had been buried and roasted in the sand. A delicacy even for the native islanders.

Tia chopped lemons for the infused-water containers, and behind her, Anita and Raj set the long rough-hewn tables with plates and cups. An island feast, with orchids and passionflowers as centerpieces, the fragrance of the beach, the hush of waves in the background, and the glorious sunset for entertainment. The perfect, right ending to this fundraiser week.

Despite all the chaos.

And despite the altercation with Ethan today. There went that donation. But maybe they didn't need him. With the Scotts' and the Tuckers' promises, as well as a few others, they just might have enough to replace their equipment. And Declan's private security team had arrived this afternoon, right after the game—three men who seemed like the types who could protect the clinic. At least until Sebold and his ilk were stopped.

Which apparently Declan was also working on, hopefully with the local police force. She'd heard a little of the conversation between Stein and Declan and the three security guys from an outfit in Minnesota. The very plain Jones, Inc. security team, according to their T-shirts.

So, yes, maybe she could calm down. Stop trying to fix all the problems herself. Work with her, *ahem,* codirector.

She looked at him now, talking with the Jamesons, smiling, nodding. Maybe *his* brilliant idea had worked out, at least for a few of the kids so far. They would still have to have meetings with their Hope House social worker and confirm the home studies done on the families. And then meet before a judge in Mariposa.

But perhaps these children really could find homes.

She wanted to hug Doyle for that.

Okay, more than hug, probably. Because ever since he'd pulled her out of that cave, her heart pounding through her chest, she'd wanted to throw herself into his arms and . . .

Oh boy.

But Penny's story about Doyle's dead fiancée had sort of snuck inside that thought, and having her own dead sort-of fiancé, it felt a little too much like maybe she might tread on sacred ground.

Tia had broken up with her fiancé, Edward, before his murder, but Doyle had lost his on the morning of their happy ever after.

No, Tia couldn't step into the shadow of what could have been and compete with a ghost.

So just partners, then. She would have to be okay with that.

Yep.

Uh-huh.

Doyle walked away from the Jamesons and ran to retrieve a soccer ball that went into the surf after a hard kick from one of the Parnell twins, Royce and Remy, who laughed as Jane and Perez Marquez played with them.

Lucia had made friends with the Scotts, who built a sandcastle with her. And Aliyah had found a friend in Jacey Tucker and her husband.

Doyle splashed back, having gotten his shorts wet as he retrieved the ball. He tossed the ball to Remy, who headed it and fell onto the sand, laughing.

Such a sweet sound, and along with the smells of barbecue pork and campfire, and the wash of the waves on the shore, the sun turning the foamy tops to fire, this was a beautiful evening.

"It'll all work out."

She didn't know how, but she ached to believe Doyle's words.

As if he knew her thoughts, Doyle walked up to her. "Beautiful night."

She nodded.

"Dinner smells amazing. Was the pig your idea?"

She glanced up at him. "I watched it done at a resort our family stayed at and always wanted to do it. Rosa said she knew how, so . . . I said, let's roast a pig."

"Brilliant," he said softly.

Here went nothing—"You were right about my trying so hard,

Doyle. I just . . . I just really wanted to know that I could do this without the safety net of the Pepper purse, so to speak." She sighed.

"I think you did *exactly* that. Your presentation last night hit all the right notes, and frankly, the ask was perfect. Hopefully you raised enough for operating expenses for the entire year, plus new equipment for the clinic, even if Ethan doesn't donate." He reached for a glass of lemonade. "One thing I learned when I was planning to be a missionary—there are people who go and people who send. And they send because they want to invest in something they can't do themselves. Or aren't called to do. You gave these donors an opportunity to be more than they are, do more than they could do. It's a gift to them. And if the Pepper family—or Declan—had come to the rescue, then they would have missed out on that." He put a hand on her shoulder. A warm, albeit a little roughened, hand. "I'm privileged to work with you."

His touch shot warmth all the way through her body, to her painted toes. She met his eyes, and his gaze found hers, lingered.

Her heart thundered.

"I'm glad to see you two getting along, finally." Declan and Austen had come up behind them. He wore a pair of jeans and a short-sleeve shirt, flip-flops.

Doyle's gorgeous sister had braided her hair into a fat, loose weave, wore a flowing linen dress, and was also in flip-flops. She leaned on Doyle's shoulder.

He broke Tia's gaze and put his arm around his sister.

Declan picked up a lemonade. "I know I sort of pulled a fast one on you, and that wasn't my intent. Thank you for working it out."

Austen stepped away from Doyle. "When you're ready to teach these kids how to dive, call me."

"You leaving?"

"Tomorrow." Funny, but she looked at Declan when she said it, then away, to the ocean. "I have sharks who need me."

Tia laughed, but Doyle turned to her. "She's serious. She keeps track of the shark population in the Keys. She's like . . . the shark whisperer."

"I'm not, actually—"

"She is," Stein said, joining them. "She looks right at them, and then when they come close she just guides them away, like they're dogs coming to play."

"They are like dogs. They're curious, not vicious. Except they use their mouths to investigate—instead of their noses."

"And leave people without arms as they discover we're not seals," Stein said with a shiver.

"But, you *are* a SEAL," Austen said, winking.

"Oh, you're cute." He shook his head. "And I'm not anymore."

"Once a SEAL, always a SEAL, Stein." The voice came from outside their conversation.

Tia looked over as one of the Jones, Inc. guys walked up. Short brown hair, built, he wore a gun on his hip, a knife on his leg, and *oh boy.*

"I don't love the kids seeing you carrying a gun," Tia said. "It could remind them too much of Sebold."

He nodded. "I understand, ma'am. I'll try and keep it hidden." Then he turned to Doyle. "You're Stein's kid brother?"

Doyle nodded.

"North Gunderson. Your cousin Ranger is on our team. He's working with the local police on a strategy to apprehend the Sebold crew."

"Ranger is here?"

North nodded. "Says he'll stop in tonight." He turned back to Tia. "I came to tell you that we've finished installing the cameras around the perimeter and are working on the door sensors. If anyone enters the clinic or the compound, an alarm will sound."

"Thank you, North," she said, her gaze on his gun, back on him.

He crossed his hands in front of him. Looked at Declan. "I'd like to bring some grub up to Skeet and West if that's okay."

"Absolutely. We're about ready to eat," Declan said. "I think that's what Rosa's wild gesturing is all about."

Tia turned and spotted Rosa, indeed calling everyone in. She dropped the last of the lemons into the water and capped the container. Then she headed over to the group.

Declan stepped forward. "I want to thank you all for coming to Mariposa for this amazing event. And thank you for your generosity to Hope House. I know the children as well as the staff and I join you in our gratitude and appreciation. I'd like to say a prayer for the dinner."

He bowed his head, and his prayer seemed genuine and heartfelt.

"It'll all work out."

Yes, Doyle. I believe you.

The kids filled their plates and sat down between the adults at the long table. Most of them used their manners, although Tia did have to give a couple of the younger kids a long look for eating with their fingers. As she sat at the table, the sun sent a golden trail over the water, its last wink before darkness.

After dinner, Taj got out his guitar and started to sing, the kids hunkering down around a beach fire, the stars blinking as if in audience. Doyle slipped up behind Tia. "Care to walk?"

She turned and he looked perfectly dangerous, with the wind tousling his hair, his eyes shiny against the flames, smelling of the surf and the night.

"Mm-hmm," she said and walked after him, barefoot on the smooth, wave-swept sand.

"I think it's only fair that I tell you about Juliet."

She nearly stopped. But she took a breath. "Juliet?"

"My fiancée."

Right. "You don't have to, Doyle. It's none of my business."

He'd folded his arms and now bumped against her, maybe intentionally, as he said softly, "I want to. I think it's . . . important for you to know."

Huh.

Their feet indented the soft, cool sand as the ocean waves brushed the shoreline.

"We were high-school sweethearts. Met in the sixth grade. Her family were missionaries in the Philippines, and they decided to move home so their daughter could attend the upper grades in the States. We had an instant . . . something. I don't know—she was pretty and laughed easily. I used to draw pictures—funny ones of the kids in our class—and she said they were brilliant." His voice softened then. "Doesn't hurt for a pretty girl to call you brilliant as a twelve-year-old. I lost my heart then. We wrote notes to each other and sometimes waited for each other in the lunchroom, but her parents—and mine—wouldn't let us date until we were sixteen. Even that might have been too young, because I wanted to propose on our second date. We managed to make it to eighteen without getting in over our heads, and I proposed the day after graduation. With a ring."

"Wow."

"She turned me down."

Tia glanced at him. "No."

"She cried the entire time. Her father had somehow convinced her that she should wait until she went to college, to date other men. I wanted to murder him. We broke up for the summer, and I was angry. I went to college ready to forget her."

"But you can't forget your true love."

"Not a chance." He'd loosed his arms and now walked easily. The waves curled over their feet, foamy and cool. "She started dating a guy, however, and I nearly lost my mind. Good thing we were at different schools. I doubled up my classes, and with the extra credits I got in high school, I graduated in two years. Immediately took my MCATs and got into the University of Minnesota's school of medicine."

"So you could be a doctor."

"No. So I could win her back. See, I knew she wanted to be a missionary, and she said that she wanted to go back as a nurse, and I thought . . ."

"It was a beautiful plan."

He stopped. "It worked too. She came home over Christmas, called me, and told me she'd broken it off with the other guy. We were back together by New Year's. And I had life planned out. I proposed the minute I graduated from undergrad, and she pushed off the wedding until after she graduated too. And then until I finished my internship. Longest three years of my life. I passed my initial exam for my medical license and had gotten an offer to start residency that summer at the University of Minnesota. So we scheduled the wedding for Thanksgiving."

He'd parked himself facing the ocean, staring out at the night, his hands in his pockets, the wind pressing his shirt against his body. Something in his gaze seemed to search the horizon. "It was perfect. Everything. My life . . . planned out all the way to the happy ending. And then . . ." He sighed, ran his hand across his mouth. "She didn't show up for the wedding."

Tia had stopped too, of course, and now stood a little away, watching him in the glow of the moonlight. He swallowed, his Adam's apple bobbing, then took a breath. His voice softened.

"I stood there at the front of the church, waiting. Feeling like an idiot. And fearing that she'd changed her mind, and all the time, something gnawed inside me like . . . something wasn't right. It just kept growing, even as I stood there." He sighed. "I should have listened to my gut. I even called her, but it went to voice mail. I thought, I hoped she was just running late. Twenty minutes went by, and I wasn't the only one worried. I went looking for her. Stein went with me, and we drove out to her house. It had snowed the night before. The roads were glass. We found the accident on a country road. A truck had hit the limo head-on. The limo went off an embankment and was half submerged in a lake. The limo driver was dead, and she and her dad were trapped—their doors locked from the front. Her dad had a severe head injury and was in shock. She told me to get him out first."

He looked over at Tia. "I did. Stein and I pulled him out, and by then, EMS was arriving and I went back for Juliet. We'd jostled the car enough that it started to settle in the water, and it was almost completely submerged by the time I got there. That's when I realized that she'd been caught by a piece of the door, speared into her back. She couldn't get free—the car pulling her under." He took a breath. "If I got her free, she'd bleed out—and if I didn't, she'd drown."

Tia wanted to reach out, to touch him, but he had closed his eyes as if replaying it, and she couldn't intrude. Her throat burned, her eyes hot.

"I didn't know what to do. And then the car went under and I just . . . I just panicked. I yanked her free and she went limp. I got her out, but the dress—it dragged us both under. If it hadn't been for Stein . . ." He opened his eyes, glanced at her, then away, shaking his head. "I nearly drowned too. By the time we got her to shore, we had to do CPR. But . . . she'd already bled out so much . . . She died in the snow."

He wiped a finger across his cheek. "The last thing she said to me was to keep following the call." He lifted a shoulder. "Hard to do when your entire life has been shattered."

And now Tia did touch him, just lightly, on his arm. "I'm so sorry."

He nodded, shrugged. "Five years. Seems like I should be over it by now."

"Over losing your true love? Please. You don't get over grief. You might learn to get back up faster after it hits you, but you don't get over losing someone. You just bear it better."

He nodded. "It took me the better part of a year to even get back up. And maybe I am bearing it better." He met her eyes then. "I came here to . . . to start over. Maybe try to hear that calling again."

The waves lapped between them, his gaze again in hers.

"I came here to start over too," she said. "Maybe stop listening to my fears."

He took a step toward her, lifted his hand, ran his fingertips across her face, then pushed her hair behind her ears. He smelled of sand and surf and coconut oil and maybe exotic, impulsive fresh starts. "Juliet will always be with me. But . . . maybe this is a good place to start over." He ran his hand behind her neck, and her skin tingled under his touch. "Sunshine, beach, ocean, a little near-terror every day?"

She laughed then, and one side of his mouth hitched up. *Oh,* he was a beautiful man, with an early-evening scrub of whiskers, those eyes, now a dark blue, hued with something . . .

Oh. He took a step closer, caught her face with his other hand.

Well, then. She put a yes into her eyes, her expression, then touched the hollow of his neck. "Maybe we try to cut down on the terror."

"Mm-hmm," he said, and lowered his head.

Her lips parted.

"Mr. D!"

He jerked up at the voice, took a breath, then turned.

A couple boys ran up the beach toward them in the darkness. Elias and Jamal, out of breathing hard.

"What's going on?"

"I tried to stop them—" This from Jamal, who seemed almost in tears. "But they went anyway."

Doyle put his hands on Jamal's shoulders. "Slow down. What are you talking about?"

"It's Rohan. And Gabriella and Jaden—they went looking for the treasure."

He stilled, and Tia caught her breath. Then she bent and met Jamal's eyes. "Where did they go?"

He turned, pointed back toward the monastery, up the mountain. "The caves."

"What do you mean, *the caves*?" Doyle said, reaching out. He grabbed her hand, like . . . like they might be a team.

"They heard that man talking today at the game, about the treasure being in the cave," Elias said. "They snuck out at dinner . . ." He swallowed, put his arms around himself. "There are ghosts in those caves."

Tia wanted to roll her eyes.

"You can smell them—the dead bodies," said Elias, his eyes wide.

Dead bodies?

"Okay, we'll find them, Elias," she said, pulling him into a side hug. Then she looked at Doyle.

He nodded. "Yes. Yes we will."

If he were planning a heist, tonight would be the night.

And of course, Stein couldn't get that out of his head as he stood at the perimeter of the tented eating area, watching his boss mingle with the donors. He had no appetite, despite the aroma of roasted pork that seasoned the air.

A gorgeous night for a picnic, and frankly, he didn't hate watching his brother Doyle play soccer on the beach with the kids. Doyle was smiling again, as if he'd finally shaken free of the grief.

Sorrow had a stranglehold on his brother, and maybe all this sunshine and sand and—okay, Tia, probably—had helped him breathe again.

Doyle had walked away with her after dinner, and it seemed

the two were having a serious chat, given the way his little brother stood with his arms akimbo, watching the ocean.

Good.

He sort of wished he'd found the same full breath, but ever since he'd discovered the underground channel—and the fact that someone had broken into the vault—a terrible darkness had filled his chest.

Phoenix had found them.

He hadn't seen anyone in the darkness of the cavern, but he'd felt eyes on him, just like he had nights ago on the balcony.

She was here, casing Declan's place. He knew it in his bones.

"Are you going to eat?" This from North, one of the Jones, Inc. guys Declan had hired after Stein made a couple calls. Nice guy, former quiet professional who'd parlayed his years in the military into a private security gig. He'd brought food up to his cohorts watching the orphanage and returned to the beach. "I'll keep an eye on your man."

Stein shook his head. "Not hungry."

North nodded, paused. "You were in the Krakow ambush. We heard about that—good to see you landed back on your feet."

Sorta. "Thanks." Stein watched as Declan moved around the tented area, talking to donors.

"Decided to leave the teams, though," North said. "That's a tough decision."

Stein lifted a shoulder. "Medical separation." He could finally say it without a trench digging through him. "Knees."

"Right. Sweet gig you landed, working for Declan. Good guy," said North. "Seems to really care about these kids."

"He's the real deal," Stein said, lifting his chin to Declan as the man looked over at him. *All good, sir.*

"Not a lot of those left," North said. "How long you been working for him?"

"A few months," Stein answered. "Before that I was a dive instructor in St. Kitts."

"That's a hard gig, for sure. I can see why you gave it up." He winked.

Stein grinned. "Reasons."

North nodded. "If you ever want to join a team again, Hamilton Jones could probably find a place for you on Jones, Inc."

Stein glanced at North, then past him to the shore, where the kids now hung out around a bonfire. A family memory nudged him, the many bonfires his dad had made on the beach back at the King's Inn in Minnesota every summer. He missed those.

"Maybe. For now, I'm into this with Declan."

Speaking of, the man walked over to them. Greeted North with a handshake. "Thanks for heading down to the islands."

"Anything to get a tan, sir," North said, and moved away to stand on the beach.

Declan turned to Stein. "You all right? The dive accident still wired up inside you?"

Stein shook his head. "Thinking about the break-in during the dinner."

"You still think someone cased my vault? There was nothing on the video screen."

"No. But we'd definitely been hacked. And someone opened the door to the smugglers' tunnel." He kept his voice low. "I think it's the same woman who stole your blood samples in Barcelona."

Declan shoved his hands into his pockets. "Avery."

"Not her real name, but yes."

Declan eyed him. "You know her?"

Stein's jaw tightened. He probably should have mentioned this before, but—"I think so."

Declan's eyebrow rose.

"I think she was . . . I think we met in Poland."

"Where you got injured?"

"Yes. It was . . . It's a long story."

Declan said nothing, watching the kids throw sticks into the bonfire, the breeze lifting his dark hair.

Okay then. "We were there to exfil a Ukrainian asset who had developed a cyber-encryption program," Stein said. "The Ukrainian embassy had been taken by the Russians and we'd infiltrated, but our team got separated. I was pinned down with the target, and suddenly this woman appeared. She'd been sent in by her organization to do the same thing."

"Her organization?"

"It's called the Black Swans. Female-only operative group that specializes in undercover work and information heists. International, but mostly working in Europe. They were created by a former CIA agent, designed to fight terrorism before it birthed onto the world stage. I don't know what she wanted with our target, but she'd been hiding inside the embassy for a couple days and learned their internal escape system."

"Internal—"

"The passages behind the walls, sir. Not unlike your secret, um, smugglers' route."

Declan nodded.

"We worked together to get out, and she got us to their safe house. The Russian COBRA team, who'd taken the embassy, was searching the city for us."

"COBRA?"

"Like our CIA Special Operations Group. Affiliated with the FSB, they do intelligence-gathering missions behind enemy lines."

"And they needed this guy for their communications."

"Yes. So Phoenix—at least, that's what she called herself—and I had to work together trying to figure out how to get Luis to safety." He didn't let himself linger there—but wow, had she played him. "We finally got ahold of my team and set up a meet. She agreed to hand off Luis." He folded his arms. "I bought it. But what she'd done was set us up. We walked into an ambush. A backpack bomb went off in the café."

"Casualties?"

"Yes. I was . . ."

"Seriously injured."

"My knees were shattered—had to get them replaced, learn to walk again." His mouth pinched. "For a long time, I thought she'd died in the blast. But . . . that was her, in Barcelona."

"You're sure?"

He drew in a breath. Sometimes he could still hear her laughter, taste her kiss on his lips, the tug on his heart to believe. *Yeah, so well played.* "Yes, sir."

"And she staged the accident in Barcelona?"

"Seems like her MO."

He nodded. "To get my blood. To get into my vault."

"That's my theory."

"And now she's followed us here?"

"I think she broke into the vault area and escaped into the tunnel."

Declan's mouth made a grim line.

"What is she after, sir?"

"I don't know." Declan glanced up at the house.

And Stein read his mind. "If I were going to try to rob you, it would be tonight, when everyone is away."

"Zeus and the team are there."

"They don't know about the smugglers' tunnel," he said. "Or do they?"

"Zeus does, but the rest are locals. He decided to keep them need-to-know."

Stein held up his hand. "I get it." He directed his attention to Declan's house too, the lights glowing around the perimeter, a beacon on the hill. "Maybe . . ."

"Yes. Go."

He turned to Declan. "But, sir—"

"I'm fine here, Stein. We have the Jones, Inc. guys, and if you're right, she's not after me but my program."

His gut said the same thing. "Leave it with me, sir. Enjoy your evening."

Declan nodded. "Thank you, Stein."

Stein headed for the four-wheeler on the beach. *This time, Phoenix, I'm onto your game.*

Except, even as he drove, she walked into his memory and tugged him back to the safe house three years ago in Poland. To the night pressing into the windows. She came into the office, her gaze on the screens attached to the office wall, having just checked on Luis.

Stein had been trying to contact his team, to no avail.

"We can't stay here." She'd set a container of ramen noodles on the desk. "I made us dinner. I'd prefer some fresh pierogies, but I don't want to go back out." She'd taken off her tactical gear, wearing only a tank and a pair of camo pants.

He spotted the poached egg, the cheese and milk. "You doctored it."

"Black Swan special. I stocked the fridge two days ago." She sat in the other chair, blowing on her noodles.

"So that's your organization. The Black Swans."

She lifted the bowl. "You'd have figured it out once you got back to command. Our directors run in intersecting circles."

"Not enough to heads-me-up on your gig." He tasted the ramen. *Good.* He made an appreciative sound. She smiled, and maybe he was tired, his guard down, but it hit him, a full-on punch: She was really pretty. Short dark hair, big green eyes. Petite but sturdy.

"Your accent—"

"Midwestern." She watched the screens. "It's quiet. I'll take first watch. You get some shut-eye."

Huh. Right.

"I need to figure out our next move."

"Not without me." He put down the noodles. "That's my asset."

She raised a dark eyebrow, a smile playing at the edges of her mouth. "We'll see, there, Frogman."

Frogman.

It was the way she said it then, and later, that stayed with him, etched inside.

"The name is Steinbeck," he'd said, getting up.

"East of Eden."

"Yes."

"The story of the fight between good and evil." She set down her soup bowl, now empty. "And the idea that maybe it's not quite so black and white." She cocked her head and met his gaze. Smiled.

And that's when he began to wonder.

Yeah, so played.

Now he motored up to Declan's estate and pressed in the code. The gate opened and he pulled in, parked the four-wheeler, and headed inside to the security office, nodding to Ryland on the way in.

Zeus stood arms akimbo as Stein walked into the dark room. The man chewed on a toothpick. Dark-skinned and built like a tank, Zeus ran the small security crew with a tight fist. Former SBS in Great Britian, he'd set up the security system for Declan when he'd first built the fortress.

"Any movement in the vault?"

Zeus glanced over at him. "No. Why?"

"A feeling." He leaned toward the vault picture. The feed indicated it was live.

"No attempts to hack it?"

"We found the code, set up an alert." Zeus glanced at him. "Milton set it up."

Milton, the white-hat hacker imported from Germany who'd

spotted the hack. Too late, but soon enough for them to shut down anything that Phoenix might have tried to take.

Maybe it was a one-and-done attempt.

No. His gut still said she'd try again. Because he knew her.

Knew the lengths she'd go to in order to complete her mission.

And now acid pooled in his chest.

He braced a hand on the screen, still staring, something feeling not . . . *Wait*—"See this light?" He pointed to the bottom of the screen, the slightest hue. It disappeared after a second.

Zeus leaned in. "I don't know—"

"Watch."

It appeared again, almost a flash, before vanishing. "That's the lift opening a second before the feed is replaced."

Zeus picked up his walkie. "Milton. I need you in the control room."

Static.

He tried again.

Nothing.

"I'm going down there," Stein said. "You should be able to see me."

Zeus nodded, and Stein exited the office, striding across the wing to the main lodging. He ran his card—with the new code—over the elevator pad and called it. It arrived . . . from below.

Aw . . .

He stepped into the opening and thumbed the button for the lower floor, hit it again and a third time, just . . . because.

And also just because, he took his gun from its shoulder holster. *Please, please let her not be there—*

The lift opened.

Empty. He walked out into the room, looked at the security pad. The lights glowed green, the locks secure.

"Let me know when you arrive." Zeus, through the walkie.

Oh no. He turned and looked at the cameras. Keyed the mic. "You don't see me?"

"Negative."

His heart sank as he stalked back to the lift. "We're too late," he said. "She was already here."

EIGHT

THIS MIGHT BE A SINGULARLY BAD IDEA.

Doyle, following his gut, again, listening to his impulses instead of taking a breath, stepping back, waiting for an organized rescue team.

But waiting could get people killed, *thank you.*

He and Tia had climbed the trail to the cave under the light of the moon, his Maglite illuminating the path. Now they stood at the opening, the darkness inside thick and brooding.

"There are ghosts in those caves."

Elias's words rose inside him, and maybe he wasn't wrong.

A chilly, ghoulish breath filtered out of the space.

"What were they thinking?" This from Tia. She'd changed out of that pretty sundress into a pair of hiking pants, boots, and a long-sleeve shirt, and pulled her hair back.

Still so pretty, and he had to shake away the memory of a different impulse, the one he'd followed at the beach . . .

Nope. Maybe he should thank Jamal and Elias for stopping him from getting in over his head.

He and Tia were simply two broken hearts on a rebound, colliding into each other.

"They're kids. Who knows what they're thinking?" Doyle pulled off his backpack and dug through it, finding the headlamp. He'd retrieved it from the construction gear he'd accumulated, using it in the chapel overhaul. Now, he handed it to Tia who fitted it on and turned on the light.

It illuminated the opening of the cave, the beam falling on the amber walls, the debris that scattered outside the opening from today's earlier shake.

"I hope they didn't get far," Tia said as she stepped into the dark yawn of the cave.

He followed, with a final glance at the stars, the moon, maybe heaven. He shone his Maglite onto the walls, across the handful of openings that led off the main vault. "Which tunnel?" He started toward the tunnel they'd taken earlier, the one that supposedly led to the monastery.

Tia stopped him with a hand to his arm. "Listen."

Voices. They echoed deep within the mountain, lifting into the cavern. He stilled, pointing his flashlight down one of the other nearby tunnels. "It doesn't sound like it's coming from the tunnel we took earlier—the one that contained Ethan's equipment."

"If that was even the right tunnel. Who knows which one leads to the monastery?"

Right.

She turned toward a different tunnel, one with a narrower opening, and stepped toward the darkness. "I can't believe they had the courage to go down here." She blew out a breath and headed inside, ducking her head a little.

What she said. His gut tightened, and her words from earlier echoed through his brain as he followed her. *"We'll find them."*

He turned off his flashlight and slipped it into his pack to save the batteries. Her light splashed over the amber rock, the tunnel tight, dust layering the floor. "Footprints?"

"It seems like it . . ." She pointed to the clutter of stamped earth. "But look." Ahead, the walls tightened, and farther, rock blocked the path.

Still, the murmur of voices lifted as if they might be beyond the debris.

"Maybe there's another way in?"

She nodded, and they turned around.

"You lead the way," he said, and she slipped past him in the narrow cave, heading back out to the entrance.

"It just seems so crazy to me that they'd go hunting for the treasure," she said as they worked their way back out.

"Teenagers. I get it. I could see them being lured into the idea of an adventure and riches."

"They're almost old enough to leave the orphanage according to Mariposa law. It could be scary, looking out into the future and seeing nothing." Her footfalls thumped against the rock.

Huh. "Yes." And he didn't want to admit how her words settled in him, suddenly felt raw and too real. His life after Juliet died had been so dark, and frankly, he still couldn't see the future.

She reached the main opening and stood in the center, her light brightening the cave, her hands on her hips, fierce, determined.

Or maybe . . . maybe he was starting to see it . . .

"I think the voices are coming from this tunnel." She pointed to another opening, near the back of the cave. This mouth seemed larger, and as she stared at the ground, he too spotted the footprints in the dust.

So many choices. *Please, God,* help them find the right one.

"We should have brought reinforcements. Like some of those Jones, Inc. guys, or even your brother."

"I looked for Stein—he'd gone back to Declan's place. And the security team needs to stay at the monastery." He followed her again into the maw. "Jack should be here—he's the brother who knows how to find the lost."

"Really?"

"Yeah. He's a rewardist—finds people for the reward money."

"That feels a little opportunistic."

"Not for the people who've lost someone. It's comforting to have someone invested in helping you through your nightmare."

She glanced at him, then nodded. "Yeah, I guess so."

He frowned as she continued down the tunnel. This one had been hollowed out to fit a small truck, perhaps, because the ceiling rose ten feet above them, the walls wider. Off the main tunnel shot smaller tunnels that spiderwebbed back into the darkness.

"You guess so?"

She kept walking. "My sister, Penny, was like a bulldog investigating Edward's case. It wouldn't have been solved if it weren't for her, but along the way, a few people got murdered and . . . of course, that wasn't her fault—and she nearly died, too—but it felt invasive. Like having her look into his death would also uncover the truth about our engagement."

"The truth?"

"That we weren't right for each other. That I was the second choice."

She said it without emotion, without a hitch in her voice, but the statement still landed in his chest, a deep ache for her.

And then he remembered her words from their conversation at the dinner at Declan's house. *"I just couldn't admit that I'd said yes to marrying a man just because I didn't want to be the forgotten older sister."*

Forgotten older sister?

"Tia . . . why did you think you were forgotten?"

She frowned at him.

"You said you were the forgotten older sister. The second choice."

She braced her hand on the wall as the tunnel pitched downward. "I was the second choice. Penny was his true love. Edward loved her from the day he rescued her from being kidnapped."

"What?"

Pulling her hand from the wall, she brushed off the dust, then stared down into the darkness. "Do you still hear the voices?"

Actually, they'd quieted, fallen to nothing. "No."

She turned, put her hands on her hips. "Maybe we should double back, keep listening."

He nodded and she brushed past him. But he couldn't help himself... "Kidnapped?"

She sighed. "Yes. It's a long story, but the short of it was that she was kidnapped by our nanny, and Edward, the son of our housekeeper, found her. He hid her until my parents could rescue her—but that bond between them was forever cemented. Except Edward was the chef's son and four years older than her, and he never... he could never breach that. At least, until he went to MIT and met me, and I don't know. I am sure he loved me... just not like he loved Pen."

She started back up the tunnel. "It was glaringly clear to me, especially after we graduated and moved back to Minneapolis. He just... he looked at her the way I hope some man will someday look at me."

"How's that?"

She stood slightly above him and turned. "As if I am the part of himself that was always missing. 'The One.'" She finger quoted the words, then gave him a sad smile. "Probably like how you looked at Juliet."

Then she kept moving, and he stood, frozen.

Yes. Maybe he *had* looked at Juliet that way. Or maybe he'd just seen Juliet as an extension of himself. Not completing him, but belonging with him. Which, at the time, felt perfectly right.

Still did, maybe.

Because, yes, he'd always thought she was *the One.*

Tia had moved up the tunnel, back to flatter ground, a wider space, and stopped.

"What—"

She held up a hand. Listened. Then looked at him and crooked her finger.

He climbed up next to her, stilled.

Voices. They were low, and yet that sounded like a kid's voice.

She pointed down a nearby passageway, smaller but still big enough for a trolley car. She shot him a look. "I'm going to strangle those kids with my bare hands."

He smiled, gave a huff. "Only if you find them first."

She smiled then too and took a step toward the tunnel.

The mountain seemed to shake awake, as if stirring after a long sleep. The ground trembled, and amber dust shifted off the walls into the air.

"Not again! I thought we told Ethan to leave it alone!" Tia had frozen.

He put his hand on her arm. "We're not going in there—"

"Doyle!"

The mountain shook again, this time with more oomph, and she met his eyes, hers widening.

"We can't help them if we're trapped," he said.

"We can't leave them!"

But everything inside him told him to run. And Doyle was a man who listened to his instincts. "C'mon!"

He turned her, pushed her ahead of him, his hands on her hips. She fought him for a second, but the rock continued to shake.

She took off toward the opening—

Dust clogged the air, rocks shaking free now, pebbles scattering at their feet.

"Run!" He put his hand to her back, but he didn't need to.

She broke out into a semi-sprint on the uneven ground, her light spraying across the darkness. There—ahead—the exit—

He burst out after her, into the open area, heading for the entrance—

Rocks spilled down the entrance, careening off the mountain, bouncing into the vault, and he grabbed her around the waist and yanked her away just as boulders rolled in.

"Not that way!"

The landslide thundered across the open space, and he pushed her back, into another tunnel, his arm still hooked around her waist.

Behind them, the entire mountain seemed to break apart, roaring now as they stumbled into the darkness, her light ripping across the jagged, broken tunnel.

"There!" He spotted an alcove, and in it, an old metal cart.

In one swift move, he swept her up and deposited her inside it.

Dust thundered into the tunnel. He held his breath, then followed her into the cart.

He knelt in front of her, his knees on either side of her legs, his arms braced over her, hands hanging onto the edge of the cart. "Cover your mouth!" He hated to think of the sulfur they might be ingesting.

He ducked his mouth into his shirt, his body over hers, listening to the chaos of the mountain—rocks falling, and all around them, amber and blood-red dust so thick he had to close his eyes.

Which led him to the only thing he could do when he made singularly impulsive decisions—

Hang on and pray.

"You need to get out of there."

The last words Nim said to her before Emberly stepped inside

Declan's vault for the second time, this time to secure the AI program.

A plan that seemed to go without a hitch, her downloading the program, sealing the hard drive into a waterproof bag, and packing it into her shorts pocket. Then the lift on the other side of the chamber started to move, and she had nowhere else to go but . . . inside.

The vault . . .

As in *trapped.*

At least she had extra oxygen with her, along with her headlamp, which illuminated the walk-in vault. But she'd had to hunker down while security searched the place.

And pray, really, that no one opened the safe.

Emberly glanced at her watch. Three hours since she'd locked herself inside. The vault had a safety release for just these moments—she'd at least checked before she sealed herself in. But much longer and she'd run out of air.

She'd be forced to leave. And then—what? Walk right into Stein's grip?

Well, she'd been there before, hadn't she?

The memory forced its way in before she could swipe it away, and *gosh*—she had nothing else to do but revisit Poland.

Revisit the early-morning hours when Stein had relieved her from her night watch. He'd come into the room, revived after four hours of sleep, looking every inch the warrior she expected. Lean, built, a haze of whiskers across his jaw, his dark-blond hair askew, and of course pierced her with those blue eyes that could stop her thoughts cold.

She should not have been locked up in the same space with this man. Because the idea of disabling him and leaving him behind, scooting out with Luis, had turned her gut.

That was a big fat N.O. to her boss's great suggestion. Unlike the military, she had the right to improvise.

There had to be another way to disentangle Luis from this man and leave him breathing. But first, she had to get him to trust her.

So she'd gotten up from her chair, let him take the seat, then walked into the kitchen and made him some coffee.

Delivered it with an arm over his shoulder, a whisper in his ear. "Keep us safe, Frogman."

Then she'd patted his shoulder and headed to the sofa.

Maybe she shouldn't have disabled his walkie. Desperate move to control the situation.

She didn't know when she'd fallen asleep—maybe she trusted him too much—but she woke four hours later covered in a blanket, the sun streaming into the tall windows of the main room.

Aw.

The smell of breakfast cooking in the kitchen made her rouse.

She discovered Luis seated at the table, Stein at the stove, scrambling eggs.

"What's going on?"

"Coffee?" He set a cup in front of her, returning her earlier favor.

"Thanks."

He met her gaze, and maybe he had a game of his own, because his eyes had turned a deep, husky blue. And maybe she was tired too, because his smile reached in like the morning sun and hit places inside that weren't ready for light.

She didn't need caring for. Protection. Help.

She lifted the coffee, sipped, and glanced at Luis. "You all right?"

He was early thirties, a few years older than her. And he seemed rattled, holding his coffee cup with both hands.

Stein handed him a plate of eggs. "Eat. You'll feel better." Then he gestured to Emberly to follow him to the next room.

"What?" She kept her voice at a whisper.

"My walkie isn't working. And my burner is dead. I need to get a charger and connect with them."

"Fine—"

He cocked his head. "I'm not leaving him here with you."

"Thanks for the trust." She took a sip of coffee, winked.

His mouth opened.

"Just kidding. I wouldn't trust me either, Frogman. So, what's the plan?"

"We need to take him with us."

"Shopping?"

"We'll make it look like we're tourists. Out for a stroll on the square. I found clothes in the closets."

"Convenient." But she sighed. "Fine. But he's not going with us. Go find something to wear. Add a hat. I'll take care of Luis. I'll lock him in his room. He's not going anywhere. We go out, we come back, no detours."

"You're so much fun." He smirked.

She pressed past him into the kitchen.

And that's when things had started to careen off the rails—

Now she sat up. Outside the vault, in the main area the elevator moved—the sound of the motors whirring against the concrete chamber, like a hum.

Emberly got to her feet. She had to leave *now.* Whether up or down, the lift was in motion, which meant it was between floors.

She'd already secured the hard drive into the sealed pouch in her wet-suit pants, still soggy but drying. As was her dive shirt. She'd left her fins, her mask, and her tank in the chamber below.

Swimming in through the smugglers' river had been too easy. Clearly Stein and his security team needed to up their game.

The manual override key hung in a panel near the door, and she turned it. The electrical panel died and disengaged the lock. Pulling the lever on the door, she pushed.

The heavy metal door moved, and she stepped out into the space. Barren, just her light flickering on the cement floor.

And there, in the space, the cables moved, lowering the box.

Never mind closing the vault, she dove for the opening, sliding into the space. She landed on the mechanism at the bottom, eyed the opening to the tunnel. What if the lift was headed all the way to the bottom?

Flattening herself against the floor, she braced herself. Being trapped under a lift didn't seem any better than being trapped in a vault, and what came down had to go up—

Except the box stopped at the floor above. And as she leaped for the dark opening to the cavern, a word of discovery sounded from above her.

Yeah, sorry to leave such a mess.

She rolled onto the floor, then headed for the door. So much for their lock change—she'd brought in her own lock-picking device, a.k.a., a small detasheet she'd used to destroy the lock on the metal door. Now the door hung half open, darkness beyond, outside the glow of her headlamp.

Behind her, the lift hummed, churning to life.

She scampered down the stairs, her feet slick on the steps. Last thing she needed was to land on her backside and roll her way to the bottom.

Not when she was so very, very close to freedom.

"Hey!"

The lift must have landed. She hit the cavern floor, grabbed her mask, and threw her inflated BCD in the water. No time to turn off her headlamp—*shoot!*

She swiped up her fins.

"Phoenix!"

The name stopped her, jarring through her.

She'd liked that code name. Liked who she'd been, with him back in Krakow.

What if—

No.

Footsteps barreled down the steps. "Stop!"

She slipped on her mask and slid into the water, holding her fins. Took a breath, sank, and slipped on one fin, then the next.

Surfaced.

And he was right there, in the full beam of her light.

Frogman.

Mr. East of Eden, standing on the side of good, drawing a line, his hand on his hips, his blue eyes fierce.

Still possessing the same stun power he had back in Krakow when—

No. He was the enemy. Or had to be, today. Especially now that he worked for Declan Stone.

"Phoenix!"

She turned away, searching for her BCD. *Just get under the water—*

It floated a few lengths away. She lunged for it.

A splash hit the water, and just as she grabbed her vest, he reached for her.

She turned, slammed the heel of her hand into his face.

He grabbed her mask, pushed it askew.

She hit him again, kicking hard—

Then the mountain trembled.

He had her by her dive jacket now, his grip a vice. Her other hand clung to the floating BCD attached to her tank.

The cave shuddered, then rocks began to fall.

What—

He pulled her toward the edge. More rocks falling, this time from the top of the stairs. She thrashed in the water, kicking away, and they went under.

Then the entire cave seemed to convulse, and suddenly, he was no longer fighting her.

He was pulling her up, kicking to survive.

She surfaced, rocks spilling down around them.

"Get to the side!" He pushed her away from the tunnel, toward the other edge where her light illuminated a small landing, probably carved out for the smugglers' boats.

She turned, gripped the ledge, her hand on the body strap of her floating BCD.

And then Stein braced his body around hers, gripping the edges of the lip of the rock with his hands, his breath in her ear. "Stay afloat."

Right.

She held on as the mountain seemed to collapse around them, as the world shivered, as Stein's body trapped her against the rocky edge.

And despite the terror, despite the darkness and the world crumbling around her, she was right back on the cobbled streets of Krakow, Stein's arms around her as he hid them from local police.

In an alleyway.

Probably kissing him hadn't been necessary. But she'd needed to disable that cell phone he'd just purchased, which meant creating a diversion to pickpocket him and . . .

And maybe she'd gotten too into that role. Because as he protected her in the tunnel, her stupid thoughts went to the way he'd reacted when she kissed him.

Surprised.

Then, of course, being the made-for-action guy that he was, he'd gone all in, kissing her back, surrendering to the look she'd seen in his eyes.

Yes, she'd felt the spark too, the lines blurring between them for a moment as she lifted the cell from his pocket and dropped it into her own.

He'd tasted sweet, smelled of the shower he'd taken while she slept, and for the briefest of moments, she'd let herself sink into his arms.

Not that she'd stayed there. But the what-ifs had tiptoed into her head the moment he'd appeared in street clothes, an everyday, not-so-everyday guy in a pair of jeans, boots, a T-shirt, and a baseball hat.

He'd made borrowed clothes look like they'd been made just for him. She'd changed into jeans and a blouse, knotting it at the waist, rolling up the sleeves.

Just a couple of tourists out to buy a cell phone. And when he'd taken her hand . . .

Yeah, kissing him had felt like a moment out of time, a fairytale snapshot. Created a sense that someday, maybe . . .

And it all came back to her as the world collapsed around her. What did that say about her life flashing before her eyes? Apparently, the only memories she wanted were the lies she told herself.

So she hung on, kicking to stay afloat, not fighting him.

For now.

Then the cavern seemed to take a breath, and she lifted her head. Light from her lamp revealed debris on the surface of the ledge.

Stein's breaths came hard behind her. Then, "I knew you were alive."

"Really? Now? You're doing this *now*? The entire cave collapsed around us, and all you care about is—"

"That's not all I care about," Stein growled. "What are you doing here?" But he did loosen his hold on the ledge, moving his hand to her collar, gripping it.

"Seriously. I'm not going anywhere."

"She lies. Again."

"That hurts." She turned then, to face him. Her headlamp hit him in the face, and he moved his other hand to adjust it.

Sank.

And if she wanted to, yes, she could probably push him away, grab her tank, and—

And that's what she *should* have done. Except those mesmerizing blue eyes, and the memory of her sins—no gray area there—made her reach down and pull him up.

He shook off the water, reached for the ledge. Looked at her. Smiled.

Aw. "Stop. Where am I going to go? Look." She pointed up the stairs toward the door. Rocks littered the floor, and the door had shut. "My guess is that we're locked in."

Stein kept one hand on her collar as he turned. "What just happened?"

"It think it's clear," she said, her hand reaching for the knife on her thigh. "The universe moves when you and I are together."

He turned, his gaze on hers, shocked.

Then he caught her wrist as she brought up the knife, squeezing.

"You're hurting me."

"Not as much as you hurt me, sweetie." His eyes narrowed.

Oh. Now he was baiting her. "Please."

His pressure made her release the knife to the depths. *No.* "We might have needed that."

"I'll take my chances."

She sighed. "What are you doing here, Frogman? I thought our dance was over."

Memory flickered in his eyes, sparked to the surface. "That was you, in Minnesota."

"You have moves."

His gaze stayed on hers. He swallowed.

She knew that look.

"Stop," he said softly. "I'm not falling for your games, Phoenix. Or *Avery*."

Right. From Barcelona.

"I didn't think you recognized me."

"Oh, you mean as the lying thief you are?"

She looked away, not sure why that hurt.

He sighed. "I think the earthquake is over. Let's get out of here."

Her eyes burned. *Whatever.*

He still had her by the collar and now tugged her over to the other side. "Let's see if we can move that door."

"We could just swim out." She pointed down the channel.

He glanced into the darkness. Looked back at her.

"Trust me."

He gave a harsh laugh. "Last time you said that, I ended up with two broken knees in the middle of a blast zone." He pushed her out of the water, then rolled up beside her and hauled in her BCD.

And that's when she spotted it. Deep into the tunnel, her escape route, what looked like half the tunnel had caved in. *Blocked.*

He saw it too, perhaps, because he took a breath. "Oh goody. We're trapped together. Again." He turned to her then, his smile gone, water dripping down his face onto his white shirt, plastered to his still-toned body. "Which means we have plenty of time for you to tell me exactly what is going on."

Stop shaking.

Tia wasn't sure whether she was talking to the mountain or herself as she hung on to Doyle's shirt, curled under him, her eyes closed, listening to the screaming in her head.

Please, God, let them not be entombed in the mountain.

Her headlamp had dislodged from her head when Doyle plunked her into the metal cart, and it now lay beneath her, gouging into her hip, the glow extinguished. Maybe broken.

She didn't know whether her eyes were open or closed, really, but they filled with gritty tears—brimming with terror, dust, even relief that she wasn't alone.

Over her, like Captain America, Doyle still braced himself, as if fearing the alcove might collapse, and given the roar of the mountain, that was not impossible.

She shouldn't have been so brazen when she'd told Elias she'd find the kids.

"You okay?"

Doyle's voice rumbled into her thoughts, and even against the sound of debris pebbling into the tunnel, it stirred inside her, broke her free of her internal scream.

"Tia?"

"Yeah," she said, her breaths quick. And she was suddenly very, very aware of the fact that she gripped his shirt with a vice hold, her forehead pressed into the well of his chest.

"I think the worst is over." He let go of the edge of the cart, curling his arm around her back and pulling her against him. He eased back onto his knees, and she went with him, unable to let go.

He held her for a moment, his arms solid around her, said nothing, his heartbeat hammering against her ear.

So, he might be freaking out a little too.

He'd put his other arm around her to secure her, and now he loosed his hold and found her face, cupping it with his hands. His forehead touched hers, his voice soft. "You sure you're not hurt?"

"I'm okay," she whispered. "Thanks to you. I would have run right out into that landslide."

She lifted her head, wishing she could see him, but the pitch darkness gave nothing away.

His breath puffed against her cheek. "It was all just . . . I don't know. Instinct, maybe." He pulled her again to himself, and she imagined him closing his beautiful eyes, possibly reliving that moment.

"Good thing you listen to your gut," she said and sort of expected a chuckle or something.

Nothing.

And then—"Doyle, are you hurt?"

"I think I cut my leg getting into the cart, because it burns, but it's probably not a big deal." He pushed her away. "The bigger issue is . . . how are we going to get out of here?"

He pulled the backpack off and dug around, and in a moment, light flickered on. His Maglite. It illuminated the alcove, the cart, and the debris in the tunnel. It had sounded worse than it was, at least at first glance.

When he pointed the light toward where they'd come in, however, she saw the entrance filled with a cascade of rocks.

So, "Not that way," she said.

"Right."

"But isn't this the cart we saw this morning, when we searched the tunnel?"

He stared at her, and a smile edged his mouth. "Yeah, I think it is."

She met his eyes, and an emotion flickered in them—maybe hope, maybe respect.

Maybe something more, because suddenly she saw herself in his gaze, disheveled, dirty, even scared, but . . . not alone.

Not forgotten. And she blamed that—along with the fear, the panic, even the relief—for the fact that she grabbed his shirt and pulled him down to herself, for the fact that she leaned up and kissed him.

He didn't move at first, and she didn't care. She held on to him and the kiss and—

And then he broke free of his shock and came alive to her touch. He wrapped one strong hand around her neck, held her there, and kissed her back. He seemed urgent, and perhaps also full of fear and relief and panic. And there was a hunger in his touch as if . . .

As if he'd discovered that he, too, wasn't alone.

He tasted of heat and sweat and even strength, a surety she wanted to cling to, and she softened her mouth, closed her eyes, and let him take over.

Let him taste her desperation, her fear, her relief too.

Could be this was a panic kiss, the kind of kiss that told them they would survive. That they were in this together.

Partners.

She wasn't a fool, though, and even as she wanted to give way to the crazy impulse that surged inside her—the one that said *maybe*—she remembered his words on the beach. *"Juliet will always be with me."*

Right.

And then her own words in the tunnel—*"Probably like how you looked at Juliet."*

She was kidding herself to think that she could replace his true love. And she wouldn't be the second choice. Not again. Even to a memory.

She wanted to be the One.

But for now, right now, she had him, so she kissed him with the same ardor that he kissed her with, needing whatever piece of him that he could give her.

He finally lifted his head, breathing hard, and met her eyes. She held his gaze and offered a tiny smile. "Okay then."

He raised an eyebrow.

"Ready to get out of here?"

He nodded, backed away, his gaze still on her.

Aw, and now she had to fix it. "Thank you for saving me."

He swallowed, frowned.

"Doyle. Don't let your brain get tangled up with this. I just . . . panicked. Maybe got carried away. But I'm good now. You?"

He seemed to sigh then, relieved perhaps, and he nodded. "Right. Yeah." And then he smiled and winked, and why had she said that?

It didn't matter. He found his footing and climbed out of the cart, extending his hand to help her out.

She managed on her own but grabbed on to his arm to steady herself. Dust still clogged the air. "I hope . . . the kids . . ."

"Let's get out of here, and then we'll figure out how to circle back and locate them," Doyle said, and yes, that made sense.

He took her hand, squeezing, and she squeezed back as they headed down the tunnel toward the opening to the sea. *Please let it not be blocked . . .*

But the farther they ventured into the passageway, the more the dust cleared. The smell seemed to dissipate too, the scent of the brine and sea filtering into the darkness. The rhythmic thunder of waves hitting the cliff wall beat into the night, louder as they walked.

"What do you think happened?" she said.

He still held her hand, the other steadying the flashlight. "I think Ethan got greedy and activated his stupid laser machine—"

"And brought down the entire mountain? C'mon—"

He stopped then and stared at her, his jaw tight against the dim light, his eyes sparking. "Small things make big impact. We don't know the fragile points in this mountain or how his laser machine might have broken them. It feels like an impossibility, but our choices matter even if they feel small. So yes, it's entirely possible that Ethan brought down the mountain." He turned, kept walking. "At the end of the day, however, it's not Ethan's hand but God's that directs the way of the world, so . . ."

Was he saying that it was God's fault? She had nothing to say to that as she followed him.

Except, a question dogged her. "If it is God's hand that brought down the mountain . . . I mean, how can we trust a God who brings disaster?"

He glanced over at her. Stopped again. "We see God in the here and now and judge his actions against our perspective. It's like us walking into the middle of surgery and calling the doctor barbaric. We can't possibly see the entire picture. So we either turn away, angry and confused . . . or we trust and wait." He swallowed, his gaze almost fierce in hers. "We believe that God is good, and that He has a plan."

The words sank into her, found her bones.

"That's what you've been doing," she said quietly. "Trusting and waiting."

He drew in a long breath. "And holding on." He gave her a grim smile. "Because I believe in hope and truth and love. Even when it feels impossible."

And *oh,* she wanted to kiss him again, to bring those words, that perspective, into her life, her heart. To hold on and believe, too, that God was good.

That he hadn't forgotten her.

But before she could step up, give in to the urge, Doyle added, "And I'm sort of waiting for a little clarity on what to do next."

She refused to let the answers in her heart find root as he turned and continued to lead them out of the darkness.

But she hung on, all the same.

The tunnel turned and descended, and she braced her hands on his shoulders, walking behind him as they worked their way down the passageway. The thunder hammered against the bowels of the cave.

"The tide must be up," he said as the ground leveled out, and ahead, just like before, the cave opened to the edge of the cliff. Light broke the darkness at the edge of the rock, and she joined him, staring out into the night.

Stars drifted over the ocean, pinpricks against waves, and it seemed the wind had picked up, because the waves dashed themselves against the rocks with violence.

"The water is up over the tunnel." He'd flashed the light below, into the swirl of rock. Then across to the jutting of more rock barely protruding from the water.

"What now?"

He let go of her hand and scanned the water.

As she stood next to him, the scent of the ocean cleared away the last of the sulfur stench.

After a bit, he leaned out and grabbed the metal line that ran from the entrance down to the top of the tunnel. Rusty and fraying, it seemed almost melted into the rock. "If they used this to lower goods down, they probably had a box or chest to carry everything."

"And a pulley to move it up and down?" She pointed to a tumble of rock that half buried a small alcove. He moved his light to it. Rusted machinery, a broken hoist, in parts under the rubble.

"Now we know why they stopped using it," Doyle said. He leaned over the edge. "That's rough water down there."

"But it's only about sixty feet down. If we wait until the tide goes out, it's a much higher fall."

"Who's falling?" He pulled off his pack and set it on the ground next to the Maglite. Then he pulled out a first aid kit.

So that's what he'd been doing while she changed clothes back at the monastery. He'd also changed clothes but had been waiting with the pack and headlamp when she met him at the base of the trail. Now, he pulled out gauze and an ACE bandage and scissors from the kit. He cut the bandage in half. "Hold out your hands."

Huh? But she did as she was told, and he wrapped the cloth around one hand, then the other, cutting and tying it. "For a while, after Juliet died, I volunteered with Beacon of Compassion International, an organization that helps after hurricanes and tornadoes and other disasters. I wasn't a doctor, but they let me assist, and I learned a few foxhole tricks." He then took out the gauze rolls and did the same with his hands. She helped tie the ends together.

He picked up his pack—a heavy pack, canvas with leather straps, the kind a Sherpa might use—and stretched the straps out to their full length. Then he unclipped them from their O-rings and crossed them.

"Stand up."

"Bossy."

"Brace yourself, honey. I'm just getting started."

Oh.

He didn't look like he was kidding, and her eyes widened as he turned her, then pulled her against him, the pack in front of her. He held out the straps and climbed in behind her, the straps crossing behind him.

"It's, um, a little snug in here, Doyle." Indeed, the pack squished her against his back, his body pinned to hers.

"This way you don't fall."

"What? You said, 'Who's falling?' I heard you."

"Not you. Not today. Listen, we're climbing down this cable. I just need you to hold your weight against the wall. I'll do the work. Have you ever been climbing?"

"No! Doyle, I can't—"

"Trust me." His voice fell into her ear, soft, calm. "I'll be right here."

Yeah, because he was *strapped* onto her. "I'm going to fall and kill you."

He chuckled then, his body rumbling against hers. "No, you won't."

"Are you sure you're not a SEAL?"

"I'm better than a SEAL. One of my hobbies in college was rock climbing."

"Are you lying to me?"

"You'll just have to believe me." He had tucked the Maglite into the pack, zipping it into the front pocket, the face shining out. "I'm going to reach out and grab the cord. You do the same. Then we'll step out onto the rock. I want you to flatten your feet against the rock wall, stick your backside out, and if you have to, sit on my lap. Then we'll move together down the cliff."

"What about the waves? They'll kill us!"

"No. Even in the few minutes I watched, the tide was going out.

By the time we get down there, the water will be down to the top of the tunnel. Even if it's not, it will only be a few feet deep. Then we'll swim to the beach and walk back to town."

"Just like that." Oh, she wished she could see if he was smiling.

"Or we could stay here, build a nice vacation home."

"What about daylight? I like daylight."

He said nothing as his chest rose and fell. "Yes. But the longer we wait, the more Rohan, Gabriella, and Jaden risk being burned alive."

"What?"

"The sulfur in here doesn't just smell bad—it's flammable and could ignite with heat. If the laser heated the air, it could have ignited, which would mean that deep inside the mountain, there is fire burning. If the sulfur dust accumulates, it can create an explosion. More, the gas can also ignite. So, if they aren't already . . . Well, we're running out of time."

She'd gone cold at his words. "Okay. Yes. Let's do this."

NINE

DOYLE DIDN'T KNOW WHAT WAS RISKIER—HIS crazy plan, or the impulse to simply drop into the ocean and swim for their lives.

The waves still threw themselves, foamy and furious, against the rocks, and he couldn't exactly look down to see if his prediction about the tide proved right.

Please, God.

The night arched overhead, a million stars watching the folly playing out on the cliffside.

He couldn't let his brain circle back to his words about the fire in the mountain.

Nope.

His grip burned against the metal cable, the frayed, rusty edges ripping at the flimsy gauze he'd tied around his hands. But Tia fought to do her part and hold herself up as he worked them down the edge of the cliff.

One terrifying step at a time.

In his arms, Tia also trembled, but she hadn't cried, hadn't gotten angry—

He should also get out of his head the impulsive kiss she'd given him. *"Don't let your brain get tangled up with this. I just . . . panicked."*

He could get behind panic if that was how she handled it. Because for that moment, everything in his head had shut down—yes, panic, but also fear and maybe anger and even grief—and he'd simply kissed her back.

No, it had been more than a kiss. A surrender, perhaps, to the what-ifs. To hope and trust and the fresh start that suddenly felt so tangible that it swept him up like the waves below and carried him away.

Too late. His brain was way tangled up.

"How much farther?" Tia asked, and he glanced down.

The light illuminated the cliffside, and from his guess, they'd traveled almost thirty agonizing feet. "About halfway."

She turned to look and her foot slipped. "Oh—"

Thankfully, it caught on his, and she moved it back to the rock face.

But she'd nearly dislodged his stance, and the very last thing he needed was to lose his footing and have to carry their entire weight by his hands. The slick, rusty rope would slice through his grip and—

Yeah, they'd end up in the ocean. Then the waves would carry them inland to smash them against the rocks.

He stilled, his arms around hers, his stance tight. "You good?"

"Sorry."

"Slowly."

"Mm-hmm."

He moved his foot down, then his grip on the cable, then his other foot, and she moved with him, almost like a dance.

"You really used to rock climb?"

"I took it up the summer Juliet broke up with me. A buddy of mine was headed out west to climb, so I went with him and took some classes in the Tetons, spent about a month climbing every day. Practiced at a few climbing gyms in Minneapolis and then at Taylors Falls and even Palisade Head in northern Minnesota."

He moved again after she'd settled herself, and she followed.

"I've been up there. Beautiful."

"Yeah. You start by rappelling down the cliff face, then climb back up. There's no room for failure. After Juliet and I got back together, we worked with a youth camp that took kids up there, climbing. I once held a girl on belay for two hours as she tried to conquer the cliff."

Tia seemed to relax into his movements. He let go of the cable, stretched one hand, switched and stretched the other.

The waves sounded less ominous.

"Juliet liked kids?"

"Wanted a big family. And she wanted to adopt. She was . . ."

"A good person."

He made a sound deep in his chest. "Kind. Soft-spoken. Sweet. And yes, she wanted to be a mom of many. Probably the perfect missionary."

Tia had also relieved the tension in her hands, regripped the cable. "So, completely different than me."

He stilled, not sure what to say. "Um—"

She stiffened. "Please forget I said that."

"Tia—"

"For the love, Doyle! Just . . . Let's get off this cliff. The fumes have gone to my head."

Right. His too, because the answer stirring in his head was . . . *Not different at all. And yet yes, completely different too.*

Tia was bold and outspoken and determined and a visionary.

But, just like Juliet, beautiful and brave.

"Forgotten."

He eased them down another step, not sure why that word

landed in his head. Except—"Why did you say you were the forgotten sister?" His question seemed lost in the breeze.

Or not.

"I told you—I was the second choice."

"That's not the same as forgotten."

She moved her hands down the cable. "Yeah. Um. Okay. It feels like the same thing. After my sister was rescued, my parents . . . they were overwhelmed with relief and . . . anyway—"

"You felt forgotten." He glanced down. Twenty feet, perhaps.

"She slept in their room for about three months. And I would lie in my bed, terrified that I'd be kidnapped next, and I . . . Anyway, it was a long time ago."

And in his mind, he saw a terrified young girl, wide-eyed in the darkness. "No wonder you refuse to be afraid."

She let out a laugh, bold against the darkness. "I'm plenty terrified now, Spider-Man, so let's get moving."

The urge to kiss her again shook through him.

Later.

Maybe.

For now, his descent plan was working, because his next step hit slick and wettened rock where the tide had crested earlier. Except his foot slipped and his knee slammed into the rock.

He held in a grunt, even as Tia yelped, stiffening to help him get his footing.

Then his other foot slicked off, and his weight slammed them into the rock face.

Her legs gave out.

And then they were sliding, The cable shredded the gauze as he tried to kick out from the rock, to slow their ascent, to stop them from—

Tia screamed, and they dropped into the churning ocean with a deafening splash.

Cold. Stinging. Chaos.

They'd landed in the well of a wave, and it caught him up, Tia struggling against him.

The wave slammed them into the rocks. He took the hit on his shoulder, his arms around Tia, fighting to protect her.

Then the current pulled them back out.

He had to set her free because kicking together would only drown them. Even now, her boots landed in his shins, and despite her paddling, they sank in the water.

And then his feet touched rock. Approximately six feet down—his boots scraped the top of the lava tunnel.

He wrapped his arms around her at the rush of another wave. "Big breath!"

Then he ducked them under the cresting water, kicking hard.

They came up behind the surge into the next roll, and he reached down, fumbling with the backpack strap. The swell caught them up, and again—"Under!"

He ducked with her, found purchase on the tunnel roof, and pushed to the surface. She sputtered, coughing as he released the strap.

She wiggled free, but he caught her hand as the water rose under them again.

"Down!" He took a breath and, next to him, felt her follow. This time, they came up farther from the cliff. He tore off the pack and shoved it at her. "Put this on!"

"I can swim!"

"It'll let me hold on to you!"

She splashed, then shouted, "Duck!"

He took a breath, and this time she pulled him under. The wave caught them, tumbled her, but he grabbed hold and pulled her to himself, again launching himself from the lava base.

They surfaced.

"Listen! It'll just get me tangled up. Let's swim!"

But then he'd lose her in the darkness. "No—we have to stay together!"

She blinked at him, treading water.

"Okay." She grabbed the pack, pulled it over her head and shoulder.

He grabbed the trailing strap. "Stay with me!"

"Go deeper!"

Good idea. Deeper, the current would be less furious. He took a breath and plunged into the water, sinking into the depths.

She swam beside him, using breaststrokes, and he sensed the waves rolling over them.

He surfaced after a minute and found her treading next to him. They'd swum away from shore, out of the breaking waves. "Turn onto your side and do a sidestroke."

"Why?" But she turned over.

"You can save energy that way. SEAL trick that Stein taught me. But first—lose the boots."

"I like these boots."

"You like to breathe too, right?" He'd already started to unlace his boots, sliding out of them, the water chilly against his bare feet.

She did the same, and then she started to twist in the water.

"What are you doing?"

"I'm losing these heavy pants, too."

He'd worn his lightweight Gore-Tex pants over a pair of snug trunks, so he'd keep his on.

Then she rolled over, facing the shore and starting to swim. He swam behind her, the waves carrying them up and down in the water.

He still held the unhooked strap.

The mountain rose dark and forbidding over the island, and he couldn't make out any fires.

"There's the beach," Tia said, stopping and treading as she pointed to an indentation in the shoreline.

"We could keep swimming, all the way to town."

She turned in the water, met his gaze. "That's a half mile away."

Right.

"If we get tired, we'll let the waves carry us in. We can do this, Tia."

She tightened her jaw but nodded. "Don't let go of me."

Never. The word pulsed inside him, jolting him. *What—?*

They kept swimming parallel to shore, slowly, sidestroke, riding the waves, the shoreline glistening under the moonlight. The water had turned cold in the night, and he shivered, but here in the Caribbean, he wouldn't get hypothermia, at least, not unless he got pulled farther out to sea.

"Should we be worried about sharks?"

"Great whites? No, the water is too warm. If we were swimming up the eastern coast of Florida, perhaps, but not out here."

Probably.

In fact, swimming out here, the waves moving them through the water, felt almost . . . peaceful.

All he had to do was breathe and stay afloat and ride the current as it took them toward Esperanza. And, of course, hang on to Tia.

No problem.

No problem at all.

The moon had started to fall, and dawn crested against the far horizon. He spotted tiny lights dotting the pocket of the mountain where Esperanza sat crowded against the harbor.

"I see the town," she said.

Yeah. And along with it—

Fishing boats. The motors rose across the surface of the water, buzzing against the waves and . . .

No one would see them in the water.

He tugged on her strap. "Tia, come here."

She righted herself in the water, and he pulled her in, put an arm around her. "I can hear a fishing boat."

Lifting her arm, she started to wave and shout. "We're here!"

Aw. They didn't have a hope of hearing her over the motor. And then he spotted it. A blue-and-white boat headed out to sea for the predawn morning catch.

Headed straight for them.

"Tia—"

"Here! We're here!"

The boat motored toward them, throttle high, splashing through the waves.

"Tia—"

"They're not slowing!"

Nope. He grabbed her pack. "Big breath!"

"What—?"

He glimpsed the boat plowing toward them just as he pulled her down into the water, kicking hard toward the bottom.

She must have caught on, because she followed him down. Overhead, the motor churned up the water.

His lungs burned, but he didn't want to surface into the path of another boat.

She, however, tugged at him, and he followed her up.

He surfaced just as a wave thundered over him.

"Doyle!"

Her shout cut out as the water yanked his hand from the strap and pummeled him against the rocky bottom. His shoulder scuffed against the rock, then his feet scraped, and suddenly the current had him.

He tumbled over and over, the waves pushing him down, his lungs burning as he lost his bearing in the darkness.

And for a second, he was back in a frozen lake, fighting his way out of a sunken car—

Hands. They grabbed him, dragged him up, and he came back to himself. His feet hit rock and he planted them.

Surfaced. And of course, Tia was right there, standing in water up to her chin. "Gotcha," she said.

He stared at her, gasping, and ran his hands over his face. Then he reached out and pulled her to himself, shaking. "You all right?"

"I would like to leave the ocean now."

He closed his eyes and let out a laugh. "Let's go to shore."

She stepped away from him, met his gaze, and then hers moved off him, toward town. The light flickered in her eyes even as her mouth opened.

"What—?"

He turned, and his chest hollowed out, his hand finding hers and tightening.

The town of Esperanza was on fire.

"At least you have pants."

She got a smile from Doyle as they walked, soaked through and barefoot, down the boardwalk, having dragged themselves out of the ocean.

Tia might, just a smidgen, regret shucking off her canvas pants in the dark depths of the sea, but maybe that had kept her from drowning, so . . .

Now she walked down the street in a sopping-wet black T-shirt and matching underwear, and set against the chaos around her, it might not be a big deal.

Still.

With dawn spilling over the city, the smoke had lifted, revealing the still-smoldering fires of a couple buildings along the boardwalk.

The bank. And a local restaurant, which had probably been the source of the blaze.

No, the source of the blaze was the landslide from Cumbre de Luz, a tumble of black lava rock, trees, and dirt that skidded down the mountain, impossibly avoiding the monastery and cascading in a lethal strip right into Esperanza and all the way to the ocean.

It had somehow missed an apartment building, taken out a couple homes, obliterated the buildings at the boardwalk, and plunged into the ocean.

Locals fought the fires with water and foam, a motley volunteer fire department spraying ocean water onto the blaze. Soot and smoke tinged Tia's skin, adding to her sense of griminess.

Or could be that was a byproduct of the tragedy that maybe, just maybe, she'd been a part of creating. "What happened here?"

She shouldn't have bought into Ethan's crazy treasure-hunting story.

"Stop trying so hard."

Yes, but if she didn't try, who would?

"Earthquake," said Doyle, and took off his shirt, a long-sleeve, wringing out the lightweight nylon. Of course, that left him bare-chested, and who knew Mr. Humanitarian Aid had washboard abs? She should have guessed that, however, given the time she'd spent leaning against him as they climbed out of the mountain, into the water.

She could still feel his breath on her neck, hear the tiny grunts as he lowered them down. Quiet, strong, reliable.

And she'd nearly lost him to the waves.

"Just wrap it around your waist," Doyle said, pulling her away from the terrible moment when he'd gone under and let go of the tether between them.

She took the shirt and tied the arms around her waist, and at least now she had a back bumper.

No one would notice her anyway with the sirens sounding, the crowds watching the fires burn, and a makeshift field hospital setting up on the beach. It seemed the entire town had emptied out and gathered in the harbor, emerging from the rubble to assess their trauma.

An ambulance sat at the curb, lights flashing, and she spotted Dr. Greg Scott, along with a few of Declan's American guests, helping people sitting with gauze held to various body parts—foreheads, arms, legs.

She shot another glance up the mountain to the orphanage. "I can't believe the mountain came down." Smoke filtered through the air, and she coughed, her lungs burning. "We should get up to the clinic."

"I'll try to find us a ride," said Doyle, lifting his hand to someone.

She followed his gaze and spotted Declan jogging over to them through the sand. He wore a white button-down, grimy now and rolled up at the sleeves, a pair of shorts, and dock shoes. Smoke and grime layered his face, his jaw hard, his eyes reddened.

Behind him, Austen looked up from where she crouched next to a mother with a young child, holding his arm as if it might be broken.

Doyle veered off the boardwalk, onto the beach. "Declan." He held out his hand, and Declan grasped it, added a slap on his arm.

"We've all been crazy worried." He glanced back, and Austen had gotten up to join them.

"Long story. We were in the mountain when it exploded. Spent the night at sea, so that was fun. Austen." He hugged his sister, and Declan turned to Tia, put a hand on her shoulder.

"You probably need to get checked out, make sure you don't have any effects from being down so long with reduced air."

"I'm fine," she said, and of course punctuated that with a cough. *Still.* "Have the kids shown up?"

He shook his head. "Not that I know of. I was able to get ahold of the security team—they say all the kids on campus are safe. And Anita just got here to help and confirmed."

"What happened?" This from Doyle.

"Dunno. We were headed back to the house when we heard the thunder. The slide barely missed us." He turned to the mountain. "Seismic activity? We're lucky it didn't collapse more of the mountain. As it is, there are still people missing from the higher neighborhoods. I reached out to a Red Cross SAR team from the States that does some international work—they're on their way. Let's get you two checked out."

Declan motioned to a tent set up on the beach, and Tia noticed Dr. Julia moving between a couple cots along with Anita, her dark hair held back in a scarf. She kneeled in front of a child, examining a scrape across his chin.

"Where did all this medical equipment come from?"

"I had it brought over from St. Kitts," Declan said.

"We'll see what we can do," said Doyle. "In the meantime, the US team can bring in a couple handheld units. When are they due to arrive?"

"Later today," Declan said and gestured to a cot.

"Tia first," said Doyle.

Um, she'd seen his hands now that they'd emerged from the ocean. Deep wounds, the skin scraped clean, raw. "No—"

"Yes," Doyle said. "I need to find Stein and see what we can do to form a search for the kids." He raised an eyebrow and pointed to the cot.

"Fine. But you have to also find me some pants."

He offered a slim smile, nodded.

She sat, and perhaps she did need help because another cough wracked her lungs.

Dr. Julia came over, stethoscope in hand. "What's going on?"

"She spent the night in the ocean after escaping the mountain. Check for sulfur poisoning." This from Doyle.

Dr. Julia's eyes widened, and she crouched next to Tia. "Let's take a listen."

As she pressed the stethoscope to Tia's chest, Austen stepped up to Doyle.

Despite her low tone, Tia heard her words.

"Stein is missing."

Tia glanced over at Doyle, who took the news with a frown.

"He went back to Declan's house last night, but when the landslide happened, he wasn't in his room. Or even, as far as we can tell, on the premises. Zeus said Stein went to check a possible security breach but he just . . . vanished."

Doyle stared at her, as if trying to assimilate the information. "Did you try calling him?"

"Cell towers are down, and he's not answering any calls out on the walkies."

He hung a hand around his neck, glanced at Tia.

"Cough for me," Dr. Julia said.

Tia coughed, her gaze still on Doyle.

"I'm sure he's okay, sis," he finally said. Sighed. "But we need to regroup and find the kids."

Austen nodded. "I might have an idea for that—"

"Lie down, Tia. I'd like to see if you have any internal bleeding."

Tia obliged, watching Doyle follow Austen across the medical tent, then out into the crowd.

Shoot—"I'm fine."

"You're not fine," said Dr. Julia. "Any nausea?"

"I spent the night in the ocean. Plenty of nausea."

Dr. Julia pulled up Tia's shirt, prodded her stomach. "Pain?"

"Hunger."

She smiled and pulled out a penlight. "Dizziness?" The light flickered in Tia's eyes.

Just when she remembered the way Doyle had pulled her up against him after she dragged him from the current. Yeah, she'd been plenty dizzy seeing the look in his eyes.

"Not . . . No."

"Okay, you definitely have something going on in your lungs." Dr. Julia motioned to someone—*oh, Anita.* The RA came over.

"Miss Tia—we were so worried!" She took Tia's hand, crouched next to the bed.

"Let's get some oxygen on her," said Dr. Julia.

"I'm fine!" And then to prove it, she doubled over, coughing. *Nice.* Anita urged her back onto the cot.

"And a couple pillows to prop her up," Dr. Julia added and looped the stethoscope around her neck.

Anita got up and disappeared, and Dr. Julia stood above Tia. "Getting some clean O2 into your lungs might clear them out, ease the irritation. Give it an hour, and I'll come back to check on you."

"I don't have an hour. Kids are missing." Tia made to sit up, but Dr. Julia put a hand on her shoulder.

"You have an hour if it means saving your life."

Her eyes widened, and Anita showed up with the pillow and a portable oxygen tank. Tia took the pillow, then lay back down, and Anita fitted the mask over her mouth and nose as Dr. Julia moved on to the next patient.

Then the RA took Tia's hand and knelt by the cot.

Wait—was she—

"Dear Lord, thank you for bringing Miss Tia back to us. Please heal her from her trauma."

Yes, yes she was.

Tia closed her eyes.

"And please be with Jaden, Gabriella, and Rohan, wherever they are. Help us all not to be afraid. You tell us not to fear, Lord, for You are with us. Give us that grace to believe today. And help us find them. You are a God of hope, and we need that now. In Jesus' name."

A God of hope.

And somehow, Doyle's words came back to her, sifted into her heart even as the oxygen filled her lungs.

"I believe in hope and truth and love. Even when it feels impossible."

Anita let go of her hand, but Tia kept her eyes closed, just breathing. Just hoping.

She didn't mean to sleep. It simply caught her up, the exhaustion folding over her, the oxygen slowing her heartbeat, loosening her muscles, drawing her into shadow . . .

Maybe it was the breeze or a car horn or even the sound of rain on the tent, but she woke with a start, opened her eyes, tried to—

Oh. The medical clinic. She still lay on the cot, but night had swept in around her, a light rain turning the sky pewter gray and shivering the palm trees.

She too shivered, and realized then that someone had put a blanket over her.

Aw, she'd slept through the tragedy that she should be solving. She pulled the oxygen mask off her nose, sat up.

The makeshift clinic had calmed, only a few of the dozen or more cots still holding patients, and a handful of people in green hiking pants and white jackets held coffee, huddling in the middle of the area next to a bank of equipment. A couple portable X-ray machines, EEG machines, a defibrillator, infusion pumps, and oxygen canisters. Just like he'd promised, Declan had brought in supplies and people, and as she sat up, Tia noticed a pair of drawstring pants and a shirt folded at the end of her bed.

She got up, pulled on the pants, kept on her now-dry shirt, and headed over to two woman standing together.

"Hey," she said. "Where's Dr. Julia?"

Tia addressed her question to a woman with blonde hair pulled back in a ponytail, wearing a T-shirt with a Red Cross emblem under her jacket. "She went up to the clinic on the hill." She pointed to the monastery. "But you should lie down."

"I'm done lying down," Tia said. "And I'm the director of that clinic on the hill."

"Oh. Jess Brooks." The woman held out her hand. "Red Cross.

My husband Pete is up there too, working with a team that's going in to look for some kids."

"Yeah. My kids." She didn't mean to be so sharp-edged. "Sorry." She looked around. "How bad is this?"

"Two fatalities so far, the rest are broken bones. We off-lifted a number of the injured to St. Kitts because we don't have a trauma center on the island." This from the other woman, petite, dark hair. "Dr. Aria Silver," she said, holding out her hand. "I came in with the Jones, Inc. Aid team."

"The security team?"

"They do international SAR also. We came in to help the Red Cross group. It's a joint operation, thanks to Declan."

Of course.

"Have you seen a guy named Doyle Kingston?"

"Yeah," said Aria. "I met him earlier. He's Ranger's cousin, right?"

"Yes. But he's also my codirector—"

"Right," said Jess. "Yes. I think he's heading into the mountain with the team."

She stilled. *What?* "Not without me, he's not."

Jess's eyes widened.

"Where's Declan? No, wait—up on the hill."

Jess shrugged.

"Fine." Tia turned and headed out of the tent onto the boardwalk, the drizzle turning her skin to gooseflesh. She didn't care. Shadows hovered over the shattered town, outlining the burnt husk of the bank, the neighboring restaurant, and it looked like the slide had taken out the bike shop as well. Steam still rose from the charred timbers. The rest of the rubble littered the beach—wood, mud, rock—the debris from the homes it had destroyed.

On the hill, both at Declan's home—which seemed untouched—and the monastery, lights flickered like eyes overlooking the town.

She needed to get up there.

"Ma'am?"

She turned and spotted a man standing on the sidewalk, tall, blond, wide-shouldered, soaked to the skin in his long-sleeve T-shirt, boots, and lightweight field pants.

"Are you Tia Pepper?"

She frowned, nodded.

"Hamilton Jones." He held out his hand. "I run Jones, Inc. Jess said that you might need a ride?"

Another man stood with him, dark hair, a grim set to his jaw. He held the same military bearing as Jones.

"This is Ranger Kingston. He's been coordinating efforts to secure your compound. And now he's working on a rescue plan. We're headed back up to the monastery."

"Perfect. I'll take that ride."

Hamilton gestured to a nearby four-wheeler, and she followed the men, climbing into the passenger seat in front.

Hamilton raised an eyebrow, but Ranger got in behind her.

She buckled in. "What's the status on the search?"

Hamilton motored away from the beach, toward the side streets, clearly already aware of a route up the mountain. She couldn't bear the sight of the destroyed homes, but couldn't tear her gaze away either.

How could Ethan have caused all of this?

"We were able to obtain a TRIS unit, and it's mapping the mountain—"

"A TRIS unit?"

He glanced at her, then back to where his lights carved out the road that led up to Hope House. "It's a thermal and acoustic imaging scanner that uses AI to map hot spots and match them with the acoustic signature of humans. Ethan Pine was able to integrate data from satellite observations to enhance the scanning abilities. We've been able to adjust it to detect recent environmental changes—"

"Like a landslide."

"And cave-ins."

Right.

Wait—"Ethan is helping?"

"He was the first to contact Declan, who called us and asked us to retrieve the device. We arrived a couple hours ago."

"We?"

"The Jones, Inc. Aid team, along with the Red Cross team we partner with sometimes."

The monastery came into view, and she saw more four-wheelers and the flatbed Ford sitting outside the entrance.

A man—she recognized him as North from the security team—stood watching.

He nodded as they drove up.

She unbuckled and slid out of the vehicle, followed Hamilton and Ranger into the compound.

They headed straight for the dining hall. The room had been converted to a staging area of sorts, with a handful of men along with Austen Kingston studying a topographical map spread out over two tables pushed together. A tablet lay on the table, and Tia caught sight of Ethan Pine bending over it, moving an image around the display with two fingers. The smells of coffee and baking bread drifted from the nearby kitchen, the patter of rain on the roof, a chill embedding the stone wall and floor.

And, perhaps, her heart. Because as her gaze ran over the group . . . Doyle wasn't to be found.

The conversation stopped as the door closed behind her, and Declan looked up. "Tia. What are you doing here?"

Her eyebrow rose. "Seriously?"

He came over to her, glanced at the team. "Right. Sorry. Are you okay?"

She shrugged away his hands reaching for her and headed to

the table, moving in beside Ethan. "I thought you were in the mountain."

He drew in a breath. "I already told Doyle that no, I had nothing to do with this."

Doyle?

Ethan's mouth tightened. Clearly something had gone down between them.

"There's not a chance my machine would cause this to happen," he added. "This was . . . much bigger . . . could be even seismic, although satellite data has ruled out any shifts in the tectonic plates."

"Then what happened?"

"We're not sure. But there was an explosion deep in the mountain, to the north." He'd leaned over his tablet now, zooming out to a satellite view of the volcano. "It's possible this mining camp had something to do with it." He pointed to a worksite—the same one she'd seen with Doyle. "We're still trying to contact them."

"In the meantime, what about the kids?" Tia asked, looking up at the group. She recognized the two other Jones, Inc. security guys.

Silence.

"What's going on?"

"We're not sure," Declan said and bent over the map. "The TRIS unit, along with Ethan's report, shows a viable heat source here." He pointed to a tunnel leading off one they'd accessed yesterday. "Only problem is, there's a cave-in at the entrance."

"The drone found another access point, however," Hamilton said. He pointed to an area west of the tunnel, past the cliffside exit. "They left a couple hours ago to find their way in."

They. She looked at Declan. "Doyle."

"Yes, he's with them."

Her mouth tightened, but she nodded.

Of course he was, and she fought the terrible fist in her heart. *Breathe.*

But it was Edward all over again, someone she loved getting into a mess that might cost his life—

Wait—what? She didn't *love* Doyle.

Oh. She drew in a long breath. Maybe she did. Or was starting to. And he'd left without . . .

Now her eyes burned.

Only then did she feel the silence. A few men shifted around the table. "You're not telling me something."

Declan moved his hand behind his neck, squeezed. "There was another tremor. This time near the north, near their position."

She stepped back from the table, her hands around her waist, holding on.

"And we've lost contact with the team."

Of course they had.

"It could simply be interference," said Hamilton. "But we're assembling another team to find them."

Perfect. She nodded. "I'm going."

Declan gave her a hard look.

"I'm going!"

"No," Hamilton said, blue eyes hard on hers. "You're not."

She stared at him. His gaze seemed not angry but deathly calm, and unmoving and . . .

"Find them," she whispered. "Please."

"Yes, ma'am."

Then she turned and headed outside, into the courtyard, into the crying night, and stared up at the dark hulk of mountain. And all she had was Anita's prayer stirring inside her. *"You are a God of hope, and we need that now."*

"I don't know who is crazier—you with your conspiracy theory about Declan, or me for listening to it." Stein smacked the residue from his hands, a byproduct of another go at moving the steel door.

It wouldn't budge, and his best guess was that debris had fallen into the chamber beyond.

"I'm just telling you what my boss told me. And I've seen the proof." She sat on a boulder near the channel, now illuminated by his headlamp.

Phoenix. He still couldn't believe she was here, in the flesh. And how he hadn't recognized her before—

His brain simply hadn't wanted to believe what his gut was screaming.

She looked good too—her red hair cut short—still a little Mighty Mouse, fierce and currently smug as she folded her arms. Or perhaps angry that he didn't believe her tall tale about Declan. She wore dive pants with pockets, and a neoprene shirt, an underwater thief.

Stein climbed his way down the rocks. He probably shouldn't have left her sitting at the edge of the tunnel, but if she decided to slip into the water and disappear, where exactly would she go? He'd already searched the rubble for a way through, but it choked the exit, and who knew how far the debris went?

The other route, the one that snaked deeper into the mountain, however, did seem open.

Nope.

He landed next to her on the edge of the water. Everything beyond his puddle of luminance sucked away any light. It felt like being in the belly of a fish.

He shivered and sank down on a boulder. "Listen. I did my own homework on Declan before I hopped on his train. Funny, the wiki about my boss being a terrorist threat didn't show up on my search. Declan the philanthropist, Declan the billionaire inventor, Declan the keen businessman and head of his own tech company, all yes. And he likes to sail, is interested in the space program, and enjoys quiet walks in the park."

"All while playing real-life Risk with the world stage."

"Declan is *not a terrorist*."

"Okay, listen. I'll spell it out for you."

He pulled off the headlamp. Set it between them. "I'm all ears."

"It all started when a guy named Edward Hudson created an AI program called Axiom. He owned a company by the same name."

"The AI program that Declan owns. This is not a secret. It's the hallmark of his company Quantex."

"Yes. Since acquiring Axiom, Declan has developed the program for other applications. You heard him speak in Barcelona. He can add human personalities to the program, make it adapt like a human might. This is at least how he's selling it to the Department of Defense to make it seem more like a soldier on the field, able to figure out right from wrong. Although, by whose standards is the question."

Stein frowned. "I talked with Declan. He hasn't sold it to the US military. Just a tech group that's using it for automation."

"Yet. But that's only because he's playing the bidding game."

"The what?"

"The US military isn't the only organization that is trying to get their hands on his program. China, Russia, even Korea wants to see how they can use it for their defense. But it could also be used for its offensive capabilities. Drones, missiles . . . And that's what makes it so dangerous. And that's why we can't allow Declan to sell it."

She leaned back, and by the look on her face, she believed her own words.

He didn't want to see her fatigue. Or to dwell on how, even in the dim light of the cave, and even a little waterlogged, she still possessed an exotic element, her red hair against creamy white skin, those green eyes that appeared almost haunted.

Do not be played, Stein. He sighed. "What proof do you have of this?"

"Back in Barcelona, did you happen to run into your cousin Colt?"

He frowned. "Yes."

"Colt works for the Caleb Group, a US organization that partners with the Black Swans. They were there to keep tabs on a man named Tomas Petrov."

Silence. "I have no idea who that is."

"For a long time we thought Tomas Petrov might be just a guy who'd been coerced into helping his branch of the Bratva with their money laundering. Just recently we found out that he was the head of a rogue arm of the Bratva operating out of Europe. It's a long story, but he was able to access money that the Swans had captured. We think he liberated it . . . to buy land."

He raised an eyebrow.

"In Mariposa."

What?

"From Declan."

"Declan would *not* sell land to the Russian mob. Why?"

"Maybe he didn't know it was the mob. But you need to ask yourself, why did he buy this island, anyway? Out of all the islands . . . Four years ago, with the island still recovering after a terrible hurricane, Declan Stone buys the entire island, including a destroyed village on the northwest side. Why?"

"Because it was for sale? He likes to scuba dive? It's a nesting ground for turtles?"

She rolled her eyes. "Or how about this—and you'll need to put your STEM hat on."

"My what?"

"Mariposa is lousy with a mineral called obsidite. It's a rare crystalline mineral that is sometimes found in ancient volcanic soil. It looks like dark obsidian, with a sort of blue hue, and contains a blend of lithium, scandium, and etherium, which is known for its high conductivity and energy-amplification properties. Obsidite conducts electricity ten times more efficiently than copper, and the atoms naturally amplify any electrical signal passing through, meaning that it dramatically enhances the performance and efficiency of electronic components. It's also heat resistant and extremely durable."

"What are you getting at?"

She took a breath. "Obsidite is used in the production of AI chips, the kind that are used in AI soldiers."

"Like the Terminator?" He grinned.

She didn't. "Like the Terminator."

"That's . . . No. That's—"

"Welcome to the future. The chips can process vast amounts of data in milliseconds. And with the enhanced applications of the program Declan developed, the soldiers can make real-time strategic decisions in combat scenarios."

He had nothing. More, he'd heard Declan's presentation about Axiom months ago in Spain, and even then Stein had come up with nefarious ways someone might use AI. It had sent eerie chills through him, his brain imagining the exact scenario Phoenix had just drawn.

"And here's the rub," Phoenix continued. "Like I said, obsidite is really rare. Which makes this mine a strategic asset. Declan is fielding offers to sell it—to the Germans, to the Chinese, and even to the Russian mob. That, in my book, makes him a terrorist."

"That's a big leap." But even as he said it, in his memory he stood on a hotel rooftop in Barcelona, watching his boss talk with a German researcher—in German. And that in itself wasn't proof, because plenty of other international scientists had glad-handed him during the conference.

Meanwhile, Stein had been catching up with Colt.

Oh no. Colt's words slammed into his memory. *"The DOD has used it with some of their cybersoldiers—"*

In fact, Colt had been the first to use the word *Terminator. Aw . . .*

Declan had either lied to him or didn't know about the dangers . . .

"That kind of leap keeps the world safe," Phoenix said.

He stared at her. "No. He's not that guy." But to his own ears, he sounded like he was trying to make himself believe it.

"Even Hitler had friends."

"Really?" He narrowed his eyes at her. Found some footing. "I've spent time with this guy. He's generous and yes, smart, but genuine and . . . I'm sorry. He's just not the monster you say."

She held up her hands. "I hope not. But he won't get a chance to be without his program."

Another beat.

She smiled, closemouthed as if in victory.

"You got into the vault."

She shrugged but held his gaze. "Swans don't fail."

He stilled, and then memory clicked into her eyes. She looked away.

Yep, they were right back at the café before the bomb, weren't they?

"Wow."

She closed her eyes briefly, as if in pain. Then she turned back to him, her jaw hard. Her expression, however, suggested something else. "I never meant for you to get hurt. You weren't supposed to be there—"

"I saw the backpack, and I thought you were inside. I went back to *save* you."

She shook her head. "It wasn't supposed to go down like that—I didn't even know what the plan was, Stein. They just told me to be there and then when to evacuate."

"You had to know they'd set off a—"

"Diversion! I had no idea that included a bomb! And—if you'd stuck to the plan—"

"*Your* plan still would have killed people!"

"No, it wouldn't have. I'd already pulled the fire alarm, already gotten people out—"

"Not me." He didn't mean to snap, but—*fine.* "Okay, I know you said to leave but . . ." He held up his hands. "It doesn't matter."

She drew in a breath, her mouth tight. "For the record, I didn't want to leave you. I called the police—got you help as soon as I could."

"For the record, *I thought you were dead.*"

She flinched. Nodded.

Okay, perhaps that had come out a little stronger than he'd wanted. He schooled his voice. "What happened to Luis?"

A beat. Then, "He lives in Portugal. Does some work for us occasionally."

And right then, an odor hit Stein's nose.

Smoke.

He stood up. A glow came from the edge of the door, a strip of light. "Something's on fire."

"It's all concrete in there. How—" And then she got up, put her hand to her nose. "Oh no. Don't breathe in."

He looked at her.

"The lift—I'll bet it had a lithium backup battery. It could have overheated, especially if it was damaged in the earthquake. It must have ignited."

It made sense—especially since he started to cough—

"Don't breathe in!"

And then she tackled him into the water.

What—?

He surfaced, the water hitting his bones, turning them to ice.

Her eyes shone just above the surface. She swam over to the edge, grabbed her face mask, her fins, and then pulled the BCD and oxygen tank into the water. Handed him the regulator. "Breathe."

He took a breath, handed it back to her. She took a breath.

"Are you saying the air is *poisonous*?"

"Yes. And the smoke is going to seep in here and poison this entire tunnel." She pulled out the secondary line of oxygen and handed it to him. "Smoke rises—we're probably safe right now. But lithium smoke is lethal. It won't be long before this entire chamber is filled with gas. We need to get out of here."

"How?"

She stuck her reg back in her mouth. Turned and stared into the darkness. He shone his light into the mountain.

"No."

She pulled out the reg. "Yes."

"Sorry, but getting lost in the labyrinth of a volcano seems like a dumb way to die. I can't think of a worse idea."

She pulled on her face mask.

"What are you doing?"

She turned back. "I've been here for the better part of two weeks trying to figure out how to get into this fortress. I found this smugglers' river on a map in the city archives. This tunnel goes all the way through the mountain."

"No."

"Yes. I swam this tunnel—went farther to see if I could get out."

"And?"

She swallowed. "I . . . It's a web. But I have a GPS. And an extra flashlight in my pack." She dug into her pack, found a wrist GPS, and put it on. "And I loaded the map into it, just in case."

"In case what?"

"Just in case you . . . were on to me."

His mouth tightened. "You knew I was here."

"I've been watching you for days."

Of course she had. He shook his head.

"So, just . . . get past that and listen. We can do this."

"These tunnels are miles long! We could get lost down here forever. It's like getting lost in the catacombs under Paris."

"Is that a thing?"

"Yeah, it is. There are catacomb monsters who steal your lights and your maps and leave you to die."

"Now you're just trying to scare me."

"Good. Are you scared?"

Her mouth made a tight bud, maybe holding in fury. Or laughter.

He suddenly, terribly wanted laughter.

What—? He hadn't *missed* her. He'd known her for all of two days.

Two explosive, interesting, intense days.

"Why, every time I see you, does it involve running and near death? And bat-crazy ideas."

"I'm just that much fun."

She glanced at the headlamp.

He reached for it, pulled it on.

"C'mon—"

"I have the light, you have the O2."

"You still don't trust me."

He cocked his head. "I never should have."

She flinched.

And shoot, that was a lie, wasn't it?

Then her mouth tightened. "Right."

He looked past her into the dark water. "I'm going to regret this."

She smiled. Then, "C'mon, Frogman. The only easy day was yesterday, right?"

"Don't do that." He leaned down to pull off his shoes. Threw them onto the rocky ledge. He liked them—he'd purchased them in Catalonia.

"Do what?" She treaded water, snapping on her BCD.

"Give me SEAL quotes."

"Aw. Get comfortable being uncomfortable."

"For the love." He settled in the water, reached out, and hooked his hand into one of her straps. Tugged her body closer to him. His secondary oxygen line only stretched so far.

"Slow is smooth, and smooth is fast."

"That is actually a good one. It's about doing things right so you save time—"

"I prefer 'Come with me if you want to live.'" She'd lowered her voice, turned it mechanical.

"That's not funny."

"It's a little funny." She met his eyes, smiled, then popped in her reg. Sank into the water.

He yanked off his jacket, left it floating.

And the one SEAL saying that settled into his brain and seeped through him as they started into the darkness, his light bright against the dark lava tunnel, was: No plan survives first contact with the enemy.

Hopefully it would survive the second.

TEN

IF ANYTHING FELT LIKE THE BOWELS OF HELL, IT was the tunnels under Cumbre de Luz. Maybe the heat from the lava still simmering deep inside the giant, because sweat poured down Doyle's face, around his face-mask-slash-ventilator. Dust still clogged the tunnels, a blood-red haze against the headlamps of the SAR crew.

The most recent vibration hadn't helped either. Just a rumble deep inside the volcano, but it had shaken loose more of the dust and frankly, a little of Doyle's courage.

Please, God, don't let him be buried alive.

Doyle should have agreed with Pete Brooks, the head of the Red Cross SAR team Declan had brought in, and stayed behind. But no, Doyle knew the mine.

He might be as recklessly stubborn as Tia. Whom he'd left sleeping in the cot back at the medical tent so many hours ago. He'd wanted to wake her, but he'd foreseen a small, *okay, epic,* scuffle and . . .

Perhaps that hadn't been fair, but daylight had been burning, and in his brain, all he'd seen were the kids suffocating under the toxic sulfur dust.

So yes, he'd left her behind, armed himself with gloves and protective gear and a gas mask, climbed up the mountain despite his fatigue, and lowered himself into the belly of the beast, again.

"Anything?" said a man named Jake, who'd arrived just a couple hours ago with a team of specialized SAR techs on a plane from the States, bringing medical equipment. He'd also brought his physician wife, Aria. A big man, he possessed the same military aura as Doyle's brother Stein.

Who was missing.

But Doyle couldn't go there. *Kids first.*

It hadn't taken Ethan and Declan long to boot up their fancy tech and identify an approximate location for the kids. Jake's boss, a guy named Hamilton, and Pete had huddled up and deployed their recon crew with an urgency Doyle respected.

He hadn't even asked about Stein as he grabbed gear and suited up. Pete had driven them on the four-wheeler up to the base of the cave-in, and after a quick assessment, kept going on the trail, around the mountain to another entrance.

That information about the other entrance might have been useful before his survival swim in the ocean, *thank you.*

Now, Doyle ran on adrenaline and hope as he turned to Pete to hear his answer to Jake's question.

"Nothing. Radio cut out." Pete wore a cap over his short blond hair. He tucked the radio away. "We're probably too deep. Doyle, you recognize anything?"

They'd trekked down a long tunnel and emerged into the entrance chamber, debris spilling into the vault. "Yes. We tried that tunnel before, but it had been blocked off." He pointed to the tunnel where they'd followed Ethan's footprints.

And maybe he shouldn't have been quite so, *ahem,* he'd call it *committed* with Ethan about his suspicion that Ethan had caused this mess. His brain had simply been on overdrive, given the fun in the ocean and Tia receiving oxygen in the tent and the missing kids and Ethan on his cell phone—

Good thing Declan had stepped between them.

"How about that one?" Pete walked over to the tunnel they'd taken before, when Doyle and Tia heard voices. "I see footprints."

"That's where we last heard them," Doyle said, and Pete turned, his headlamp lighting up the craggy tunnel.

"Let's go," he said.

Pete held a GPS with the map of the mountain loaded in and now oriented himself in the tunnel. "According to this, this tunnel leads to the monastery."

So, Ethan had been wrong.

Another reason not to blame him for this disaster. Still, it was Ethan's big mouth that had enticed the kids to hunt for the stupid treasure.

Later. Doyle followed Pete and Jake down the tunnel.

"Ethan thinks the kids are located in a parallel tunnel," said Doyle. "He followed this one, but it's blocked off from a previous tremor. He thinks they took one of these rabbit holes." He indicated a tunnel that jutted off from the main vein.

Pete had stopped, red dust stirring up around his boots. Moved his GPS unit, then—"That one." He walked over, crouched, and stared into the gap. "Can anyone hear me?" His voice echoed in the shaft.

Nothing.

Please, God, don't let them be dead—

"We're here! We're here!"

A male voice. It sounded lower than Rohan's or Jaden's, but that could be the echo, or the dust. Pete turned and pulled off his pack, then eased out a large Maglite. He set it up at the edge of the tunnel, shining it inside.

"Let's see if we can get to them before we call it in. Doyle, you stay here."

Doyle's jaw flexed. "I know these kids."

"I know you do. That's why we need you here, in case . . ." His mouth made a grim line.

Still. "They'll be scared. Let me go."

Pete considered him for a moment, then looked at Jake, who nodded.

"On me," Pete said and turned down the corridor, ducking a little, then crawling as the space tightened.

Doyle followed him, his helmet scraping the top of the tunnel.

"This was probably a connecting tunnel, not mined but just a passageway. That's why it's so small," Pete said. "We see these a lot in coal and silver mines."

"You've done a lot of rescues in mines?"

"A few. Old mines that kids explore and get themselves lost in. A couple deep caves where people were stuck."

"And international rescues?"

"Some. Mostly training exercises. But I know Ham, and he knows Declan, and we're glad to help. I see the blockage."

Doyle looked past him to an opening blocked by a tumble of rocks. It hadn't completely closed, however, and a dark face, grimy with dirt, peered at them through the tunnel. A kid. Doyle couldn't make out whether it was Jaden or Rohan.

"You guys okay?"

"Yeah," the boy said, and the voice nudged deep inside him. "But I'm stuck."

"We'll get you out. Hang tight." Pete pulled a pry bar off his pack. Worked it between the rocks. "Doyle, give me a hand."

Doyle gripped the bar alongside Pete, and they dislodged one boulder, then another. The rocks spilled down, and Doyle pushed them out of the way.

The opening was now big enough to pull a body through. Pete pushed his arm into it. "Can you move?"

"Yeah," said the boy, and again, the voice—

Oh. Wait—

"Me first," said another voice, also male.

No. Doyle knew that voice, that accent, that tone—

"Pete—"

But Pete had already grabbed the man's hand, and the pebbles broke free as the man scrabbled into the opening, wrestling himself out of the hole.

Doyle leaned away, his chest tight as realization slid over him, took his breath.

Sebold fell onto the tunnel floor covered in red dust, coughed, and then coughed out blood-red spittle.

What—?

"Head up the tunnel toward the next opening," said Pete to the man. "There's an SAR tech there with a mask."

Sebold pushed to his hands and knees, heading toward Jake, and Doyle *simply. couldn't. move.*

Pete reached for the next person, another man, this one covered in dried blood, a wound on his scalp. Doyle helped him climb free and caught his breath.

"Keon?"

The man looked up at Doyle, frowned. Maybe the former security guard didn't recognize Doyle under his helmet and ventilator mask,

"Get out," Doyle said and watched him crawl away, the truth pitching his gut.

"Here's a kid," Pete said, and Doyle turned as Pete helped someone out of the hole. What if their kids had run into Sebold and . . .

No. As the boy rolled out of the hole and sat up, as Doyle stared at his tear-streaked face, he didn't know whether to retch or reach out for him and pull him into a desperate embrace.

Kemar.

He leaned against the cave wall, breathing hard, staring at Pete, then Doyle.

Doyle pulled off his mask. Kemar's eyes widened and he took a shaky breath.

"It's okay, kid." He crawled over to him and put the mask on him. "You're going to be okay."

"Doyle—" Pete started, but Doyle glanced at him, shook his head. Pete's mouth pursed, and Doyle turned back to Kemar.

"You hurt?"

"No." He hauled in breaths, however, as if he was terrified. Doyle set his hand on Kemar's shoulder, gave a squeeze.

"It's going to be okay. What were you doing in here?"

"I told Sebold about the treasure and what that guy said, and he wanted to find it. He saw him coming out of the cave yesterday, and . . ." Kemar was crying now, his nose running and gooing up the mask.

"Shh. Everything will be fine. We're going to get you out of here." He winced then, hoping. "Did you see Rohan or Jaden or Gabriella?"

Kemar's eyes widened and he shook his head.

Doyle ran his hand around the back of Kemar's neck, squeezed, and met his eyes. "Calm down. Let's get out of here. It'll be okay."

Oh, he wanted to believe his own words.

He pushed the boy toward the entrance. Pete handed him a neck gaiter, and he pulled it on, then up over his mouth, and followed.

Pete came behind them.

Where were the Hope House kids? The question hammered in Doyle's head, his chest.

Worse, he'd just risked his life for *Sebold*.

And Kemar. Hello.

His headlamp illuminated the entrance.

"Jake?"

No response. Perhaps he was attending to Keon.

Kemar reached the connecting tunnel, stood up. Doyle came out after him, looking for Jake.

"Jake!"

Pete's voice made Doyle turn.

In the glow of Doyle's light, Jake was stumbling toward them down the passageway. Blood drenched his uniform, a slice across his chest, and one hand pressed on the wound, the other holding his backpack.

"What happened?" Pete said, meeting him and taking the pack from him.

"That guy came out foot first. Kicked me in the face, broke the vent, stole my headlamp." He sank to a crouch. "He got the pack and took off. I followed. He ambushed me." He released his hand. Bloody. "Slowed me down a little."

Pete had pulled off his pack, dug out a kit, found a gauze pad. "Just a little?"

"I got the pack back, didn't I?"

Doyle dug into it and found two ventilators. He pulled one out and went over to Keon. Crouched in front of him. "This is for you." He shoved it over his head, affixed it on his face.

Keon grabbed his wrist. "It's not what it looks like."

Doyle's eyes narrowed. "What it looks like is that you betrayed Hope House."

"I had to—"

Doyle yanked his hand from Keon's grip and turned to Kemar.

Pete held out the ventilator to Doyle.

"It's for Jake. You and I can trade off."

Pete hesitated a moment, then gave it to Jake.

Good. Doyle took a breath from Pete's vent, then turned to Kemar, who sat against the dusty walls, his legs pulled up, his arms locked around them. Dust covered his worn tennis shoes, and he trembled.

Doyle pulled off his overshirt and wrapped it around Kemar,

buttoning it up. Then he put an arm around the kid and helped him to his feet. "Ready to go home? Your brother is waiting."

Kemar's eyes filled, but he nodded.

Pete had grabbed up Keon, Jake struggling behind him.

"Let's get out of here," Doyle said and walked through the blood-red dust.

"They found Doyle and the team." The male voice carried across the mostly empty dining hall. The words weren't directed at her, but Tia still heard them from the dark place she'd gone in her mind, her head on her folded arms as she sat at a long table, fatigue trying to pull her away from the search conversation.

As it was, she'd downed three cups of coffee and a hot currant roll that Rosa brought from the kitchen. They'd fed the children earlier, the rain and darkness pressing against the windows, turning the night somber. Lucia and Aliyah had held hands and cried, and Jamal had stirred his rice and beans around in his bowl before setting it away.

A few of the American donors had shown up, and Jane and Perez Marquez had carried Royce and Remy to their dorm, read the other children stories. The Jamesons had arrived as well and played a game of Chutes and Ladders with Jamal.

Sweet people really. Doyle had done the right thing trying to create families.

And of course, that only made her think of her conversation with Doyle, his words about Juliet . . . *"Kind. Soft-spoken. Sweet. And yes, she wanted to be a mom of many. Probably the perfect missionary."*

Then she'd made that stupid, *stupid* joke—*"so, completely different than me"*—and instantly wanted to take the words back.

But it was probably true. She'd never thought of herself as a mother. Never as a missionary.

Frankly, she didn't know what she dreamed of—

"Ham called and said they have people with them." Again, the male voice.

Tia lifted her head and found the source—Ranger Kingston, who had manned the comms since Declan, Hamilton, and one of the two Jones, Inc. security guys left.

Ranger wore glasses as he scanned the map. "They're on their way back." Water dripped from a rain slicker hanging on a hook by the door. Could be he'd been outside, where reception was probably better. He stood next to Austen, his cousin, so clearly there were Kingstons everywhere, and pointed at the map.

Tia stood up, and the movement of her bench made Austen look over at her, give her a tight smile. Tia climbed over the bench and walked to them.

"People? Not kids?"

Ranger met her eyes, took off his glasses. "I dunno. He said they were on their way back, one injured."

She stilled. "Doyle?"

"I don't know." Austen touched her arm. "You all right?"

Tia nodded. "Tired."

"It's been a wild week," Austen said. "And now this horrible tragedy." She appeared drawn too, a little grime on her face, her shirt dirty. She gave Tia a tight smile. "Doyle is lucky to have found you."

Tia frowned. "Um . . ."

"Please. I know my brother. He's been . . . very dark, and lost, for a long time. But he's different. I noticed it the minute I arrived. He looks at you and something sparks in his eye—"

"Annoyance." Except, that wasn't fair. Maybe once upon a time, but . . .

Although, she did seem to keep getting him in over his head.

What if she'd dreamed up . . . well, not the kiss. Because that had definitely happened, *hello.*

But perhaps the meaning of it.

It was probably just a panic kiss. The kind of kiss people shared when they were trying not to give up.

Austen laughed. "Intrigue. Maybe even challenge. And that's good. Doyle always reminded me a little of MacGyver, the guy on television who could fix anything. Quick thinking, and . . ."

"Smart. Brave."

Austen smiled. "Handsome."

Tia blinked away the image of Doyle handing her his shirt. "Mm-hmm."

"The thing is, I know he loved Juliet with everything inside him, but she was larger than life in his head. When they got back together, he was so in love with her that I'm not sure he ever really fought with her. Stood up to her."

Tia sat on the table, folded her hands.

"Don't get me wrong. Doyle is a good man. A godly man. And he's not weak. It's just . . . it's good to see him working alongside you . . . you're his equal, his partner."

"And Juliet wasn't?"

"You know how sometimes it feels like one person in a relationship loves more than the other? Like it's a little lopsided?"

Um, yes. Tia swallowed.

"Doyle definitely loved Juliet more."

"Isn't that a good thing?"

Austen lowered her voice. "Don't ever tell him this, but I think he made Juliet into a little bit of an idol. She was everything to him, and when she died, he fell into a hole, completely lost."

"What do you mean, an *idol*?"

"He worshipped her. And yes, Juliet surely loved Jesus—but she also loved having a man who would do anything for her. And that's not healthy. Every woman needs a man who can stand up to her." She winked. "Because we're not always right—even if it feels like it."

"Why, why, why are you so intent on getting yourself killed?" Doyle's words speared into Tia's head.

"No, we're not," she said quietly.

Austen smiled, then reached out and touched Tia's hand. "I like seeing my brother smile again. Laugh again. And act like the guy I used to know."

"Ornery and bullheaded and impulsive and—"

"Yep, that guy." She grinned.

Tia laughed, and . . . *okay, yes*. She liked the idea of putting spark back into Doyle's life. So . . . maybe . . .

The doors to the dining hall opened, and the rain washed in along with big Hamilton Jones, Declan, and another guy, blond, helping a man with a head wound—

"Keon?"

He limped over to a bench and sat down. Blood saturated his shirt. Gauze wrapped around his head, taped, bloody. The amber dust had soaked into his dark skin, turned to rust with the rain, and he looked stripped.

What on earth?

"Let's get you to the clinic," she said, reaching for him. He stood, and she steadied him, turning.

And stilled.

Doyle stood at the door, his hands on the shoulders of . . . Kemar? He'd been crying and appeared injured as a welt rose on his cheek.

But the look in Doyle's eyes gutted her and . . . she got it.

"You didn't find them," she said quietly.

He walked in, and a second later, Jamal shouted, running across the room. She watched the reunion, the way Kemar swept him up, then began to cry, and felt . . .

Angry.

"What happened?"

"The . . . hot spot . . . The images weren't . . ." Doyle looked at Keon, then back at Tia. "We need to get him to the clinic in town." He walked over to Keon.

She stepped in front of Doyle, her hands out. "Doyle. What is going on?"

He took her by the elbows. "We need to talk. But not here."

She stilled and the room went quiet. He grabbed her hand, his grip tight, and pulled her through the room to the kitchen, then along the corridor inside the building.

"Where are we going?"

"Someplace quiet."

"You're scaring me."

He said nothing, and she wanted to yank her hand away, but her feet simply kept moving.

They stopped at the chapel door and he opened it. Held it for her.

She walked inside. Dark, shadowy, lined with the children's drawings, the smell of sawdust lifting from the small room.

He led her to one of the prayer pews.

"Doyle—"

"Sit."

She lowered herself onto the bench.

He sat beside her. "It was Sebold. He was the heat signature."

She blinked at him, trying—"What?"

"He was the voice we heard in the mine yesterday. He was trying to find the treasure. He saw Ethan come out of the mine, and according to Kemar, they went into the tunnel—which I think must have gotten blocked in that first tremor. And then came back out and went in the other way. They got trapped in the quake, or whatever it was."

Sebold. "Where is he now?"

"He ran. He injured Jake. Jake's going to take Keon and go to the medical tent in the village to get stitched up by his wife."

"Sebold attacked one of the rescuers?"

"Yeah. And somehow made it out of the cave. He took Jake's headlamp—ran into Ham and Declan on his way out. Declan didn't recognize him, and Ham didn't know him. They let him go."

She nodded, pressed her hand to her forehead. "But . . . what about the kids?"

He touched her hands then and held them, his gaze on hers. "They're . . ."

"Not there."

He swallowed, drew in a breath. "The TRIS spots heat sources, and with Ethan's satellite and Declan's AI program to decipher them . . ." He sighed. "There are no more heat sources in the mountain, at least none that are human."

"So they're not there—" But she stopped at his grim-mouthed look. "Doyle?"

He said nothing. And then—

She got it. Her voice turned stricken. "You think they're dead."

He nodded, gently, slowly. "Their bodies have stopped giving out heat."

She cocked her head. "No, Doyle. No—no, that's not . . . that's . . ." She got up. Walked away. Rounded back on him. "Those kids are my responsibility, and they—" She pointed at him. "No."

He got up then, walked over to her, but she straight-armed him. "Stay back."

"Tia. You couldn't have—"

"No!" Her eyes burned, and she pressed her hands to her stomach. "No," she whispered. Her back hit the stone wall, and she slid down it into a crouch on the floor.

He knelt in front of her, not reaching out. His own eyes glistened. "I'm sorry. I don't know what else . . . I don't know . . . I mean, we can go back, but those tunnels are . . . Tia . . ."

She put her hands over her face, pressing back the images of Gabriella on the soccer field, laughing, and Jaden and Rohan on the beach and . . . "I was supposed to take care of them . . ."

She felt him move toward her, pulling her to himself.

And she had no bones to resist him, just fell awkwardly against his chest, her jaw tight, her breaths coming fast, hard . . .

He eased her closer, her legs to one side over his so she could lean a shoulder against him, and then, quietly, gently, drew her into the pocket of his embrace.

She could do nothing but cover her face with her hands, and sob.

And maybe she even loved him a little more when he lowered his head to her shoulder and let himself cry too.

No, probably she loved him a lot more. All the way, even.

Outside, rain bulleted the roof, the breath of the dark chapel chilly as she let herself weep. And probably not just for these children, actually, but . . .

For everything.

For the trauma of the last week, for her mistakes, and even for the terrible hope that somehow she might do it *right* this time. That people wouldn't die under her watch. Which of course led her to the memory of Edward. And the fact that she'd wasted so many years trying to be the One. And now she was just pathetic.

Which brought her back to sweet Gabriella, who would never have the chance to fall in love or go to medical school, and Jaden, too young to die, and smart-mouthed, charismatic, and funny Rohan . . .

"I'd hide something in the crypt under the chapel. No one goes there."

She gasped, her breath caught, and she looked at Doyle. "Wait."

He lifted his head too and stared at her. "What?"

She wiped the heat from her face. "Is there a crypt . . . or catacombs or something under the chapel?"

He loosened his grip. "Um, I found a wine cellar behind the altar."

She disentangled herself. "Show me."

He frowned but got up, then walked over to the altar, fished out a headlamp from his thigh pocket, and put it on. He motioned to her.

She followed him and he pushed against the wall behind the cross.

A door opened. The scent of age and dirt rose from the darkness. He pointed his light down the steps. "I found it when I redid the chapel. It just leads to a small room, nothing—"

"C'mon."

"What?"

She pushed past him. "Remember when Ethan was telling his stupid pirate story in the yard that first night of the fundraiser?"

"No."

She had landed at the bottom of the stairs. "Rohan said he heard about bootleggers hiding whiskey in caskets."

"From who?"

"I don't know. But he definitely said he'd hide something in the crypt under the chapel." She looked around the room. Dirt walls, a packed floor, a small tower of wine casks against the wall, and shelving filled with old, dusty bottles. She picked one up, blew on it. "It's full."

"It's probably a hundred years old."

"The air is cool down here."

"What are you getting at?"

"Just thinking." She put the wine back, looked around. "Did Rohan know this was here?"

"I don't think so. Or . . . I don't know. The kids came into the chapel sometimes when I was working, but I don't think . . ."

She turned to him. "Doyle. The chapel would have been in the *church*. The prayer room in the back of the church was a chapel, used for private prayers." She stepped up to him. "I think I know where the kids might be."

He stared at her, his blue eyes sparking, a smile tugging his face. "I like it when you get a really crazy, brilliant idea."

And *oh,* she almost did it. Almost gave in to the impulse. Almost leaned up and kissed him.

Instead, she grabbed his hand. "Let's hope this is just crazy enough to be right."

ELEVEN

HER IDEA DID SOUND CRAZY, BUT DOYLE HAD nothing left but crazy, so . . .

He held Tia's hand and let her pull him up the stairs, out of the remodeled chapel, and through the corridor back to the dining hall.

A few of the team had left—Jake, along with Pete Brooks and Keon—but Declan and Austen remained, sipping coffee, standing over the table and map while Ethan and Ham stared at a tablet, searching for a fresh heat source.

"You're looking in the wrong place."

Of course that's what Tia led with, always jumping right to the sharp point, but maybe that's what he liked about her. That and so many other things, like her courage, and her dedication to the things she believed in. So yes, in that way, she was like Juliet.

And yet he could hardly call Tia soft-spoken or sweet.

He was done with soft-spoken and sweet. He rather liked spirited and bold.

She burst into the room like lightning, sparking life in the darkness. "I think I know where they are."

Declan leaned up from the table. "Where?"

"Ethan, remember when you were telling the pirate story at the fundraiser? One of our kids—Rohan—said that he'd hide the treasure in the crypt."

Ethan nodded, frowned.

"I told you that the storage areas had been redone. But maybe that's not what Henry van der Meer meant when he said 'storage.'" She finger quoted the last word. "Back in medieval times, they often stored valuables—like art or church treasure or even people—in crypts. We assumed he meant the food storage areas, but . . ."

"Yes," Ethan said. "Brilliant. Does the church have a crypt?"

"Rosa would know," Doyle said, and Tia looked at him, nodded.

"C'mon." She headed to the kitchen, but it had been cleaned and secured for the night, the lights off. "She might be sleeping."

He ignored the word, just in case his body decided to remember that he hadn't slept for way, way too long. Right now it simply buzzed, part fatigue, part what-if.

She headed up the stairs off the kitchen to the apartment, stood in the shadowed alcove, and knocked.

Nothing.

"Rosa? It's Tia. I think I know where the kids—"

The door opened. Rosa stood in the frame, her dark hair down, wearing a housecoat, a pair of worn slippers. She seemed remarkably young, or perhaps he simply spotted the youth in her expression. "You found them?"

"Does the church have a crypt?"

Rosa frowned, a beat passing, and then, "Yes, of course. It's an ancient church, and the crypt runs all the way under the courtyard, the refectory, and even past the gardens." She cinched her belt tighter. "But the crypt entrance was sealed years ago. It used to be under the sacristy."

"Is there another entrance, somewhere the kids might be able to access?" Doyle asked, because suddenly, in his head, he heard Jamal's words, *"You can smell them—the dead bodies."*

What if he hadn't been talking about the sulfur mine but . . . "Caves. Jamal said caves."

Rosa frowned, shook her head. "I don't know about any other entrance."

"Let's find Jamal," said Tia.

"I saw him with Kemar and the Jamesons in the hall before I retired," said Rosa and closed the door behind her as she followed Tia down the stairs. Doyle landed in the kitchen and headed out to the hall.

Elise and Hunter Jameson sat across from Kemar and Jamal at a table. Kemar scooped up beans and rice, shoveling them into his mouth.

They wore concern on their faces as Doyle walked up to them.

"Jamal," Doyle said, "when you said that Gabriella and Rohan and Jaden went into the caves, did you mean the sulfur mine?"

He frowned, then shook his head. "They went into the caves by the soccer field."

By the . . . soccer field?

"Doyle, Ethan found an old document with the original monastery blueprint," Declan said. He stood with Ethan, looking over his shoulder, and Doyle headed over to them.

Ethan showed him his tablet. "I pulled this from Esperanza records during my initial search of the building." He pointed to the church, then the sacristy. "There were stairs here, going down under the church. But in a later drawing, there is a map of the burial plots of various family members. The crypt is under the entire monastery."

Just like Rosa said.

"Jamal mentioned caves," said Doyle.

Ethan set the tablet down, shrank the drawing. "I don't see—"

Doyle pointed to an area east of the monastery. "How about

over here, past the gardens? Near the edge of the soccer field. There's an area that I think used to be a grotto—"

"I know where you're talking about," said Tia.

"The statues are gone, but the floor is stone, and it has a small bench . . ."

Jamal had gotten up, walked over. "I told you—it smells like dead people."

Doyle turned to him, crouched in front of him. "Yes, you did, Jamal." He glanced past him at Kemar. If he hadn't misunderstood Jamal and gone to the caves in the mountain, Kemar wouldn't be reunited with his brother.

Huh.

Tia was already fumbling through a nearby pack. She unearthed a flashlight.

Outside, the rain had turned into a miserable, chilly drizzle.

She grabbed a drying slicker hanging on a hook near the door. Doyle picked up his jacket, still covered in amber dust, and pulled up the hood. He grabbed one of the SAR packs that had been left behind on the bench.

Ethan had put down the tablet, turned up his collar. Declan set down his coffee. Austen went to stand with Rosa, whose expression had turned stricken. "You think they're down there, with the dead?" Rosa said.

Tia flicked on her light. "If they are, I'm going to find them." Then she drew in a breath and looked at Doyle, her eyes landing on his, so much hope in them that he wanted to reach out and . . .

What? Kiss her? Another panic kiss?

No. Not panic. Hope. Maybe even . . . Well, as he headed out into the murky darkness, forgotten feelings stirred inside him, feelings that included belonging and camaraderie and even, *okay,* desire.

She pushed out into the night, and something about following her and her light as it parted the darkness felt perfectly right.

He turned on his own headlamp, adding to the glow, and strode through the courtyard to open the gate for her. Light shone on the slick grass, haze showing in the puddle of light. An alarm sounded, and *oops,* he'd forgotten that they'd added a security system.

Around the corner appeared a man—one of the Jones, Inc. guys, in a black rain jacket, armed and striding toward them.

"It's us," said a voice behind him—Declan—and the man nodded and punched in a code to silence the alarm.

"We'll be back soon," Declan said.

"I'll disable the alarm and leave it unlocked for when you return." He lifted a hand and walked away.

Tia had taken off at a jog across the wet earth, her light bobbing against the tall grasses and rock. The smoke and mist and the eerie night swept over Doyle, prickled his skin.

Please let us be right.

They crossed the soccer field, and it occurred to Doyle that once upon a time, these had been gardens. Then they headed down stone steps overgrown with weeds and dirt, and he found himself in the grotto. A circular, stacked-stone area with an empty arch where once probably fitted a statuette of the Virgin Mary.

And built into the stone beside it stood a rusty iron door. Except, stones had broken free of the wall, cascaded in front of it, blocking the entrance.

Could be a result of the landslide.

"Help me move these," Doyle said, and Declan and Ethan helped unbury the door, Tia shining light on their work.

They cleared a path, and the hinges creaked as Doyle grabbed the door handle. He pulled off his pack and found the crowbar that Pete had used to move the rocks earlier. He shoved it into the space.

The door looked damaged and had been wedged shut by the rocks, but now he levered it open and found steps leading into darkness. Must and a feral scent swilled through the open door.

Dead people.

Hopefully not children.

Tia stepped past him into the darkness, heading down the stairs, and Doyle took a last gulp of fresh air and followed.

Footsteps behind him suggested Declan and Ethan followed too.

Tia stepped down onto a stone floor and splashed her light around the room. A tunnel, narrow, stone walls, low ceiling, with vaults built into the sides. Most of them remained empty, but a few held burial urns and other trinkets. The place harbored a chill different from the soggy air outside. It swept into Doyle's bones, his cells.

"This is creepy," he said.

"Yeah," Tia whispered and glanced back at him.

"You really think the kids would come down here?" Declan said behind him.

A few burned-out wax candles sat in sconces affixed to the walls. And as they ventured deeper, crucifixes hung on the stone caskets sealed into the walls.

"My sister used to hang out in our cellar—our cook stored apples down there, and she'd sneak in and eat them," Tia said. "I realize it's not the same as a crypt, but maybe the kids thought it would be an adventure."

"The monks must have kept the place up while they lived here," said Ethan. "It's in better shape than some of the crypts I've seen in Europe. No skulls or bones."

"That's a cheerful thought, Pine," Declan said.

"Where are the kids?" Tia said. "I would have expected them near the entrance—"

"Unless they gave up trying to move the door and went searching for a way out." Doyle put a hand on her shoulder. "Look at the ground."

She pointed her light down to see footprints in the dust. Her glance back at him held hope.

"Gabriella! Rohan! Jaden!" Her voice lifted, but the catacombs devoured it.

"Keep moving," Ethan said. "Usually the tunnels lead to a main chamber under the church. It's possible the kids made it there and are trying to get out via the sacristy."

Tia pushed away an ancient, low-hanging curtain of dust, and Doyle put a hand over his nose. More vaults, these sealed with coffins bearing inscriptions. Late eighteen hundreds, but as they walked, he found the dates receding in time.

"Early eighteen hundreds, and this name reads *Esperanza*, so it could be one of the early mayors of the town." This from Ethan, who ran his flashlight across the tombs. "We're getting closer to the time of Henry van der Meer."

"We're not here for the treasure," Tia snapped.

They had turned south, down another corridor, and in his thoughts, Doyle mapped out their location. He guessed they were under the courtyard.

"I see a light—Gabriella! Rohan!" Tia's voice echoed down the tunnel. Dust shifted off the ceiling, and Doyle looked back to see Declan ducking.

Hard to be the tallest guy in the room.

And it made him suddenly wonder if anyone had heard from Stein. Austen hadn't seemed worried, but . . .

"Here!" A voice emerged from the distance. "Here!"

"Gabriella!" Tia took off jogging, and Doyle kept up. The light bounced off more vaults along the tunnel and then burst into a large chamber.

Gabriella stood, her arms around herself, her face reddened, clearly from tears. She launched herself at Tia, sobbing.

Rohan pushed himself up from where he'd been sitting on the ground, his eyes reddened. Jaden wiped his hands down his face, leaving grimy streaks.

"Hey, guys," Doyle said. "Anybody hurt?"

Jaden shook his head, and Doyle walked over to Rohan, put his hand behind his neck, met his eyes. "You're going to be okay."

"I'm sorry, Mr. D," Rohan said. "This was my idea." He ran his hand across his face. "*Stupid.* And then we got in and our flashlight died, and when we found our way back, the door was locked . . ."

"We thought we were going to die down here," Gabriella said, her voice broken.

"Shh," Tia said, putting down her flashlight and holding Gabriella's face. "You're found. You're safe."

Gabriella nodded, and Tia pulled her tight again, her eyes closed, her cheek against Gabriella's head.

Doyle looked up, his headlamp flashing light around the chamber. "Are we under the sacristy?"

Rohan nodded. "I think so. But the door is sealed." He pointed to ornate metal stairs that curled down from the ceiling.

Declan had stepped into the chamber and stood with his hands on his hips. "You okay, kids?"

Doyle didn't hear their answer as he moved the light around the room, across the various nooks and arches that held artifacts—statues of the Virgin Mary, crucifixes. A bench sat in the middle of the room. "I think this was used as a prayer room."

"And for storage," said Ethan, who'd walked over to an arched doorway and stepped inside. "I think this is the tunnel entrance."

Doyle pressed his light into the space. A tunnel, and at the end, a blockade of rubble.

Ethan stared at it. Sighed. He turned and headed back to the chamber.

Well, that ends that, thank you. Doyle stepped out and watched as Declan climbed the stairs. He held the light steady as Declan reached the top and pushed against an iron door at the top.

It creaked, and Declan glanced at Doyle. "I think we can move it."

Ethan lifted his flashlight as Doyle climbed the stairs and perched next to Declan.

Declan stepped up, put his shoulder against it, braced his hands on the door. "On three."

Doyle braced his hands on it too, and on the count, pushed.

The metal door groaned, fought them, and Declan let out a grunt.

But it moved. Pebbles and broken stone rained down over them.

"I think it's just rusty," said Declan. "Let's go again."

Doyle readjusted, and this time when Declan pushed, he added his own grunt—

With a terrible shriek, the door broke free. Dust clouded Doyle's hair as cool air rushed into the dark space. Declan climbed up. "It's the sacristy. There's a rug over the door."

Doyle stuck his head up into the small room, dark, night pressing through the tall stained-glass window.

He looked down at Tia, and she grinned up at him, so much light and triumph in her beautiful eyes, her arms around Gabriella. And it swept through him then—the sense that this, right here, was what he'd been looking for, waiting for, even perhaps hoping, without knowing the answer.

He'd always felt a little less-than with Juliet.

Tia made him feel bigger than himself. Made him feel part of something that could change if not the world then the lives that he'd been granted stewardship of.

"Let's get out of here," said Rohan, and climbed the stairs. Doyle moved aside and helped Declan lift Rohan to freedom.

Jaden followed, climbing up on his own. Except he gave Declan a hug as he jumped out. "Thank you, sir. Thank you."

Tia had released her hold on Gabriella, and the girl ran up the steps. Declan and Doyle lifted her into the church. She hugged Declan too.

Doyle turned back to Tia. "Let's go."

But Tia was looking back down the tunnel and now receded into the darkness. "Ethan?"

Doyle headed down the stairs. "Tia—what's—"

Oh.

Ethan stood in front of one of the vaults, his light shining on a plaque.

Tia had walked over to him. "What does it say?"

Doyle stepped into the tunnel, close enough to hear his reply.

"This is the tomb of Henry van der Meer." He turned to Tia, then Doyle, and smiled. "And I'll bet inside is the treasure of the lost ship *Trident*."

And that was just *enough* of this stupid nearly-lethal treasure hunt.

"No," Tia snapped. "We are not breaking open a crypt! Seriously." Tia stepped in front of the tomb, blocking it with her body as she faced Ethan. "Have you lost your mind?"

She glanced at Doyle like *Back me up here*, but a weird deer-in-the-headlights expression cast over his face.

He didn't *believe* Ethan, did he?

Although, he'd believed her crazy brilliant idea about the catacombs, so . . .

Maybe it was a night for out-of-the-box ideas.

"We should quit while we're ahead." She stepped up to Doyle, cut her voice low. "Let's get out of here. The kids are okay, and that's all that matters."

He seemed to come back to himself, put his hands on her arms, nodded. "Yes." He turned to Ethan. "She's right. We're not breaking—Ethan!"

Ethan had picked up the crowbar Doyle had used to open the door and advanced on the stone.

And the nightmare in her mind showed him opening the resting place of who knew who, really, spilling bones and a skull and whatever final peace the monk had onto the ground.

"Stop!"

Ethan glanced at her. "This is not a coffin, Tia. My guess is that the monks found the treasure and hid it from Henry. They might have even rocked up the entrance and called it a cave-in. And then they sealed it inside an unmarked grave, at least until he decided to leave. I promise you that Henry van der Meer's body is not in this tomb."

"Then why didn't they sell the treasure?" She put a hand on his arm. "Stop."

He lowered the crowbar. "Because of the pirate."

"The . . . Wait—*what*?"

"Raging Rodrigo did not die in that shipwreck. And Rodrigo wasn't his last name—it was his *first*. I found records on the island that he lived, or I think so. I found a death certificate from the late seventeen hundreds of a Rodrigo Sebold. He fathered a number of children, all of whom claimed the treasure belonged to them. You met one of them."

She stilled. "Sebold."

"Mm-hmm," Ethan said. "You want to stop Sebold from looking for the treasure and end his terror? Then *we* find the treasure."

"And what—pay him off?"

"Of course not. We take our cut, hand it over to authorities, and let them deal with him."

And for a second—a terrible, long, silent second—it made sense. Find the treasure. Take their cut, and she gets back her medical equipment and Sebold leaves them alone.

Maybe they'd even have enough money to update the medical center and start a college fund for the kids who weren't adopted and—

Except—*hello,* wasn't grave-digging a *crime*?

Ethan wedged the crowbar into the wall.

"No—stop. We need to at least ask Declan. He owns the property—"

"Declan left us in charge." The quiet voice beside her sent a chill through her body. She turned.

Doyle stood there, his light shining on the crypt, eyes earnest in hers. "Ethan's right, Tia. We find this treasure and we have the upper hand. Sebold has to play to our rules. We have the power. And as for Declan—my guess is that he's going to want to seal this place off to keep the kids from ever getting lost here again. So it's now or never."

Never.

Except he stepped up next to Ethan, put his hands on the crowbar.

"Doyle!"

He looked at her. "This is the right thing to do. Please, trust me."

She blinked at him, swallowed, and *oh no,* she *did* trust him. With every cell in her body.

"Oh, I hope we don't burn in hell for this."

Doyle raised an eyebrow.

"Or break some ancient Mariposa law. Am I going to have to learn how to say 'pass the bread and water' in Spanish?"

"I think it's Dutch," Ethan said, and then he and Doyle heaved against the stone.

It broke, chipping off a large section of what looked like plaster, and the piece thudded on the floor at their feet.

Doyle leaned in, his light exposing decaying wood. "It's just plaster over a wooden crate."

"Like a *coffin.*" She folded her arms.

"No," Ethan said. "If it were a coffin, it would be actual stone." He wedged the pry bar against the wood and plaster, and again Doyle added oomph.

The next section broke off, revealing the end of the crate. "That's not a treasure chest."

"It's a shipping crate." Ethan lifted the flashlight. "Oak, and look at these dovetail joints." He pointed to the corners of the box, then dusted off the front. A faint stamp had been burned into the front.

"WIC," Ethan read. "Vereenigde West-Indische Compagnie."

"What does that mean?" Doyle asked.

"It translates to 'United West Indies Company,' which was active in the Atlantic trade, including the Caribbean." He palmed the edge of the box. "This is it. The treasure of the *Trident*."

She stilled, looked at Doyle, who met her gaze with a hint of a smile, a nod.

And then Ethan slammed the end of the pry bar into the box.

"Ethan!"

It broke, enough for him to open a hole with his next strike.

He stuck his hand inside, and for a second, she imagined one of those river-monster shows—

He pulled out a fist. Opened it.

A gold ingot roughly the size of an old school eraser, with rough-hewn edges. He held it under Doyle's light.

An eagle stamped in the center with a bear beside it, a number and a mysterious symbol at the end, along with a date.

1697.

Ethan handed it to Tia. She took it, the weight surprising, at least a couple pounds.

"What are these symbols?" She handed it back.

He studied it. "The eagle is Prussian, so the ingot probably belonged to Duchess Eleanora Maria of Valmont, and the bear signifies royalty, so that fits. The number signifies the purity, and this is the assayer's mark, along with the date." He seemed to debate for a moment, and then Doyle reached out and took the ingot from him, put it back into the crate.

"We need to get one of the guards down here," Doyle said.

"You said it—it's now or never." Ethan made a move for the crate.

Doyle stepped in front of him. "Ethan, we need help getting this out of here. It's late, and if this is as big of a find as you think, we need documentation and pictures and yes, Declan's permission to retrieve this."

Ethan's mouth tightened, and after a moment, he nodded. "Of course. You're right."

Tia eyed Doyle, who seemed to study the man. He held out his hand. "Give me the crowbar."

And if Ethan wanted to do something sinister, like overpower Doyle and grab the treasure and make off into the night, it was now—

Silly. Her brain had clearly taken a walk into trauma land, expecting the worst, because Ethan handed over the pike. "You'll put a guard on the door?"

"On both of them. We can trust Jones and his team."

Ethan exhaled, then turned to Tia and winked. "We make a good team."

But her gaze fixed on Doyle, who looked at her, a soft smile on his face, his eyes warm.

Yes, yes they did.

She followed Ethan up the stairs to find Declan returning from bringing the children to the dining hall.

Ethan was telling him about the treasure as she emerged, Declan's hand in hers, pulling her out.

"Ethan, I never know what to think about your stories." Declan shook his hand. "Well done." He looked at Tia. "Both of you."

Doyle came out, then turned and closed the door. "We need to lock this room, set a guard outside the door and another one at the grotto."

"I'll talk to Ham," Declan said, moving the carpet back into place. He stood, glanced at Ethan, who stared at the carpet as if wistful. "How much do you think is in there?"

"According to ships' records, about a hundred thirty thousand pounds, or, if you do the math, about two hundred thousand dollars."

"In 1702," Tia said.

"Mm-hmm."

"And today?" Declan asked.

"With the current price of gold? Sixty million and change."

Silence.

"Yes," Declan said. "We'll get security on this." He looked at Doyle. "Stay here? I'll send North or Skeet over to babysit the, um, carpet."

Doyle smiled.

Declan opened the door for Ethan. Gestured to usher him out.

Ethan sighed and exited, and Declan closed the door behind him.

Tia walked over and locked it. Turned to Doyle, her back to the door. Her entire body tingled, and maybe not from fatigue.

"Sixty."

"Million," Doyle said. "And change."

She pressed her hand to her head. "Even for me, that's . . . that's a lot."

He laughed and stepped over to her. Took off his backpack and let it drop to the ground. Propped his hand above her head on the door, those blue eyes on hers.

She put her hands on his chest, smoothing it. He still wore a little grime on his whiskered chin, a dampness to his jacket, but as he smiled down at her, everything inside her heated, her bones turning to fire inside her.

"You trusted me," he said softly, his gaze roaming her face.

"I mean . . ."

"You trusted me." He touched her cheek with his fingertips, ran his hand under her chin.

"Of course I did," she said. "You're my partner."

He smiled then, shook his head. "Codirector."

"Whatever."

Then he leaned down and kissed her. Softly. Perfectly. His mouth gentle, exploring.

But she didn't want exploring. Not now. She wrapped her arms around his neck and pulled him against her.

And kissed him. Really kissed him, with a sort of abandon and freedom and joy and hope that maybe she'd never had with Edward—no, for *sure* had never had with her former fiancé. Instead, she'd always reserved a little piece of her heart to hang on to, just in case—

But Doyle, he was . . . he was nothing like Edward. Impulsive and fierce, and charming and annoying and devastatingly handsome and capable and . . .

And hers. *Please,* hers.

He groaned deep inside and stepped her back, her body against the door, his against hers, both hands moving to hold her neck, his thumbs caressing her face, angling it up so he could deepen his kiss.

Yes, hers.

He tasted of safety and home and the future and that fresh start that he'd talked about, smelled of adventure and tomorrows, and in his kiss, something unlatched inside her.

Fear, maybe.

And peace washed through her. Or joy. Or perhaps just that sense that here, right here, her what-ifs had vanished.

Replaced by *yes, yes,* and again, *yes.*

Doyle.

Oh, she loved this man. And that thought didn't even scare her. Because he loved her back. She felt it, knew it in her soul.

He lifted his head, touched her forehead with his. "See? I told you everything was going to be okay."

"You did? I don't remember that part."

"I did." He smiled. "On the cliff. Or could have been in the ocean."

"I just remember a lot of 'Stop talking' and 'Keep swimming' and—"

"What if I just thought it?"

She laughed. "Thought it—when?"

"The first day I met you, when you showed up in the four-wheeler, your hair pulled back, all ready to take over the world, or at least Mariposa."

"You did *not* think that."

"I did. I thought, *This woman is going to drive me crazy. And it's going to be okay.*"

She laughed then. He didn't.

"You're so beautiful, Juliet."

He stilled, his eyes wide, his breath caught.

It was a punch right to her chest, resounding through her entire body, shattering the moment into a thousand jagged-edged shards. "What?"

"Tia. I meant—" His eyes widened. "It was a—oh, Tia. That's not—"

She held up her hands, her heart slamming into her throat. "No, right, it's . . . it's fine." She turned, unlocked the door to the sanctuary.

"Tia!"

She opened the door and couldn't stop. And yes, she knew—in the front of her brain where her common sense still survived—that he hadn't meant it.

But she was there, wasn't she? Juliet. His true love.

And she'd always be there, in his heart, between them, and

maybe Tia could learn to live with that—perhaps it wasn't even fair that she wanted more but . . . *No.*

"Tia!"

She fled through the church, across the sanctuary and the nave, then out the back, nearly running smack into one of the Jones, Inc. guys.

"Ma'am—you okay?"

She nodded, her throat too tight for words, and launched out into the dark, gloomy night still heavy with fog and chill and drizzle, and that seemed exactly right. She didn't even realize she'd been crying until she reached her room, tried not to slam her door—she didn't want to wake the entire compound—and locked it.

She shucked out of the slicker, toed off her shoes, and climbed onto the bed fully clothed, the blanket around her.

Then she lay in a ball, tears burning her cheeks as she listened to the darkness echo in her heart.

TWELVE

P*LEASE*—THAT DID *NOT* JUST HAPPEN.

Where had his brain been? Clearly on autopilot.

Doyle watched her go—the impulse to run after her nearly moving his legs but . . .

The stupid treasure sat beneath his feet and he couldn't leave. Not with sixty million—the number still made him stagger—at stake and . . .

Run. After her.

He put his hands to his face, unable to dislodge his words from his brain.

"You're so beautiful, Juliet."

C'mon, dude!

Because not once, not even for a millionth of a millisecond, had he thought of Juliet when he was kissing Tia.

No, he knew very well who he'd kissed, the taste of her cresting over him, through him, igniting his hunger for this woman who intrigued him, challenged him, kept him running and thinking, his partner in every way—

Tia.

In her kiss, she tasted like everything he'd forgotten, and more—acceptance and trust, and maybe also respect, and even surprise, which he hoped meant that he'd wowed her a little.

No, a lot.

He'd never been kissed the way Tia kissed him. With spark and challenge and boldness that he'd never gotten from . . .

She Who Must Not Be Named. Although that wasn't fair. Juliet deserved a place in his heart. Just not first place. Or even second place. Not anymore.

A door slammed, echoing through the church. Then footsteps—*please, please be Tia*—returning to him.

"Everything okay?" North opened the door, stuck his head in. "I saw Tia bolt out of here."

"Fine," Doyle said. "You here to relieve me?"

"Ham asked me to guard this room. Not sure why—"

"Lock the door behind me," Doyle said and took off into the sanctuary.

The night had swallowed her up, and he took off across the monastery courtyard, but he didn't see her.

Could be she'd gone . . . to talk to Rosa?

He stood in the yard, the rain hard upon him, staring up at her room.

Knock on her door.

The impulse thumped inside him.

Fix this.

"Doyle?"

The voice jarred him out of his panic—*yep,* that was the name for the thundering of his heart, the clogging of his throat—and he turned to see Austen, wearing a rain slicker, coming out of the dining hall. "Declan and I are headed back to his place. You good?"

Doyle hadn't put his hood back up, so water trickled from his hair, around his ears, into the neck of his jacket, down his back, chilly. His entire body buzzed, exhaustion a relentless master, and he sighed.

"I called Tia . . . Juliet."

He didn't know why he said that, but Austen . . . she would understand.

"Aw, Doyle." She stepped up to him. Touched his arm. "She'll understand."

He tightened his mouth, gave a grim shake of his head. "I don't . . ."

She raised an eyebrow.

"I had just kissed her."

"Bro."

He held up a hand. "Never mind. Any word from Stein?"

"No. My guess is that he's helping out somewhere. But you—listen. Are you falling for Tia?"

He looked back to her room on the second floor, then to Austen.

"It's me, little bro. I covered for you that time you snuck out in eighth grade to go stargazing with Juliet on the dock."

"It was ten o'clock at night, and I think Mom and Dad saw us."

"Shouldn't have sneaked out your second-story window, then. Still, I didn't rat you out. Nor did I tell anyone how you curled up with a bottle of chilled chardonnay down in Key West one night."

"Yeah, first and last time for that option. I still can't drink the stuff."

She smiled at him, stepped up. "Do you love Tia?"

He drew in a breath and then, "Yes. I think . . . Yes. But it's different than Juliet. With Juliet it felt almost like . . . okay, I guess *panic* is the right word. Or even like someday it was all going to blow up in my face. I loved her so much that . . ."

"You lost yourself."

He frowned.

"First love can do that. It takes over and you suddenly can't see beyond right now."

"We had a future planned. And then I had nothing. There was no future without Juliet."

"But see, there was. There *is*. And that's what's been so hard to get into your head. You don't want to imagine a future without her."

He stared at her. *Maybe.*

"And that's why you've been stuck."

"I've been waiting for God to show up, tell me what to do. And for a short bit there, I thought . . . I thought Tia might be the answer."

"Tia might be part of your future, but she is not the answer to God's will for your life, Doyle. Peace is God's will for your life. Joy is God's will for your life. Love is God's will for your life."

She grabbed his hand, held it. "God might have changed the plan, according to your vision, but he never changed his will. He wills that you find joy in your every day, despite sorrow, and that you know his deep and abiding love for you, even in grief. And that comes only from a yes to God's invitation to follow Him, even if you don't know where you'll end up. Or with whom. You do have a future. You just have to have the courage to hold on to God and let Him show it to you."

She stepped up, kissed his cheek, put her arms around him. "Tia is not the replacement for God's will. But she might be a byproduct of it. Your heart is making room for someone new."

She let him go. "'The steadfast love of the Lord never ceases; his mercies never come to an end; they are new every morning.' Go to bed, Doyle. Tomorrow is a fresh start."

Declan had come out into the courtyard wearing a raincoat, holding keys to one of the vehicles. "Hamilton has set up watches with his guys. Everything is secure. Ready, Austen?"

And again, the warmth in the way Declan looked at Austen, put his hand out as if to settle it on the small of her back . . .

"Something going on between you two?"

Austen raised an eyebrow. Declan dropped his hand. "No." He patted Doyle on the shoulder. "You're the right guy for this job, Doyle. Thanks." He winked and headed out, holding the door open for Austen.

So maybe he was just a gentleman.

Doyle headed upstairs to the balcony, and then he couldn't stop himself from walking down to Tia's room.

He stood in front of her door, his fists tight. He should knock. Apologize. Because the idea of waiting until tomorrow knotted his gut.

"Tomorrow is a fresh start."

Yes it was. And frankly, if Tia did open the door, did invite him in, did accept his apology . . .

He was tired and maybe a little broken, and he saw himself kissing her again, and . . .

Okay then. He walked to his room, went inside, pulled off his rain gear, and headed to a hot shower.

He fell like a rock into bed, closed his eyes, and sleep took him, despite Tia's horrified gaze in his head.

Sorry, Tia.

But maybe, terribly, Juliet did own a part of his brain, because even as he slept, she walked into his dreams and sat down on the bed.

He was sleeping, right?

"Hey there, DK." She wore her blonde hair down, a tan on her skin, her green eyes luminescent. He put his hand over hers on his chest, warm and real. *"I miss you."*

He couldn't speak and his throat burned.

"You miss me too, right?"

He nodded, his hand hard on hers.

She stared at him, searching, but his body had turned to stone. Then she let go, got up.

Juliet!

No words from his mouth. She stood at the door, smiled at him.

He was choking, his breath gone. *Juliet.*

And then, just like that, she disappeared.

He gasped and opened his eyes, and dawn streamed into his room, the rain gone, sunlight skimming the wood floor. He sat up, his feet on the cold, his heart hammering, and clung to the side of the bed, his gaze out the window.

Cumbre de Luz still rose in the distance, but a great swath had furrowed a deep scar in her face. Still, the light landed on the rainforest, turning it a rich emerald, and the dawn swept lavender and marigold across the sky.

"His mercies are new every morning."

Doyle closed his eyes, savored the moment, took in a deep breath. *God, I don't want to walk in yesterday. And I don't want to be stuck. Help me see Your goodness in the land of the living, find that joy of following You even if I don't know where I'm going.*

He looked up, and suddenly . . . *yeah,* he knew exactly where he was going. Pulling on fresh jeans and a T-shirt, he slipped on flip-flops, brushed his teeth, tunneled a hand through his hair, and headed down to Tia's room.

So it was early. This apology was long overdue. He knocked.

The door creaked, eased open. He pressed it wider.

Her bed lay mussed, her slicker on the floor. And his gaze fell on her tennis shoes, toed off at an angle next to it.

Huh. He turned and looked out over the courtyard. The fountain had filled almost to overflowing with yesterday's rain, and a few pigeons pecked in the yard. In the distance, a rooster crowed. Maybe she'd gotten up early?

Except a stone sat in his gut, and then he remembered . . .

Last night when Declan left, Doyle hadn't heard the alarm beep.

Either to arm it or in alert. And then he heard the security guy's voice: *"I'll disable the alarm and leave it unlocked for when you return."*

He headed downstairs and into the dining hall.

North sat at a table, drinking coffee, texting. He looked up at Doyle. "You good?"

"Have you seen Tia?"

He shook his head. "I just got up. Heading out for my shift at the church—"

"What about the grotto?"

"Ham pulled Skeet off the main entrance and sent him there last night. Glad I wasn't pulling that duty." He set down the phone. "I think Ham relieved him this morning. Skeet was asleep in his cot when I got up."

"And West?"

"My guess is at the chapel."

"Who was . . . Was anyone watching the gate?"

"The gate is secure. Alarm set." He picked up his phone, swiped open the app.

Doyle read it on his expression. "It's not armed, is it?"

North got up, his eyes on the screen, his mouth a grim line. "It says it's been disarmed for twelve hours."

"Is there a video feed?"

North clearly had already opened it, because he was thumbing through it, his gaze on his phone.

He groaned and shook his head, looked away.

And Doyle knew it—he just *knew* it—

"Looks like Tia left around six this morning."

"What?"

"And she wasn't alone." He held up the video. "You know this guy?"

Doyle went hollow, his hand braced on the table as he took

North's phone, watching Tia as she walked through the gate, a man holding her arm. He paused the video. Turned it to North.

It took a long second for him to find his voice, to pry it free from the terrible knot in his chest. "That look like a gun to you?"

North leaned in. Took the phone. "Who is he?"

"His name is Keon. Used to work for us. Now works for Sebold Grimes. Local pirate. And I'll bet he found out that we have his gold."

North frowned, pocketed the phone. "Gold?"

Doyle stood up. "If my gut is right, we're in for big trouble."

Emberly had turned the headlamp onto the lowest setting to save battery, but even with that, the light had dimmed to nearly nothing. A dent against the darkness.

Stein walked behind her, footfalls, a breath, his presence enough to keep her from spiraling out into panic.

Breathe.

Maybe this hadn't been such a brilliant idea. But Emberly refused to say that, despite the hours and hours of swimming and now hiking through the bowels of the mountain.

Wetness seeped from the walls, and she didn't want to imagine what kind of crawlies might be embedding into her grimy skin.

"Your GPS still working?"

"It's not getting a signal if that's what you mean, but it has been keeping track of our movements." She pressed the button on the side of her wrist unit, and the tiny map illuminated the darkness.

Stein stepped up to her, looked over her shoulder, his body against hers.

Weird how just having him around felt . . .

Safe. Like if she were to fall, he might catch her.

"You still don't trust me."

"I never should have."

That had been a spear to her soul. But frankly, he was a smart man. She had a mission to finish.

"According to your map, it seems like we're under the western edge of the mountain." He reached out and grabbed her arm. "This looks like a large opening—" He pointed to a circular depression at the end of a tunnel that angled north. "Maybe that's a way out."

She moved the map. "It looks like the closest exit."

"Let's break out your flashlight." He pulled off the headlamp.

She stifled a shiver. Her wet clothes plastered to her body, her hair damp, even though they'd found an exit from the water over two hours ago.

He opened her pack, pulled out the Maglite, and turned it on. The brilliance against the dark rock had her blinking.

"Sorry." He turned down the brightness. "You're shivering."

"So are you."

His white shirt slicked against his form, and he walked in his stocking feet. She wore her padded dive booties, so she was a little better off, but they couldn't escape this dungeon fast enough.

He stepped up and put his arm around her, pulling her to himself, her back to his chest.

She stiffened. "What are you doing?"

"Trying to warm us up."

She turned her head to look up at him. "Don't get any ideas. This isn't an alleyway in Krakow."

He raised an eyebrow. "You didn't seem to mind."

Whatever. She pushed his arm off her. "I had a mission to complete. Besides, what was I going to do—shove you away and alert the police to some domestic scuffle?"

"Yeah, I'm sure that's why you kissed me back." He flashed the light over her shoulder, down into the tunnel, as she started walking.

"Don't flatter yourself, Frogman. It was just business."

He made a sort of huff.

"At least for me."

That shut him up, but her chest pinched.

She hadn't forgotten the kiss, had she? Sometimes, in lonely moments, she let herself unlock that door, experience again the feel of his arms around her, the moment when it hadn't been a game or a job but a what-if.

Then she locked it up again because the answer was always . . . never.

"What if he's already sold the program?"

She glanced over her shoulder, her hand on the wall as she ducked under a low ceiling. "What?"

"Colt says the DOD is already using his program."

"An older version, maybe. My intel says they don't have the upgrades."

Silence.

"Okay, we have a plan for that too." And Mystique, her boss, would strangle her, but Mystique wasn't here in the darkness with a guy who might actually become an ally.

An informant?

"It's not about stealing the program to stop it from deploying—we know he probably has a number of copies of the master." She came out into a larger area with two more tunnels branching off. Checking her GPS, she pointed to the one on the right. He followed. "It's about creating a defense against it."

He had to duck as they entered the tunnel, his light skimming the jagged rock. "You're sure this is the right way?"

"No."

"I feel so much better. How are you going to create a defense?"

The tunnel opened up a little, the ceiling rising. They stepped into another chamber. She turned to him. "We're going to create a virus. Something we can download into anything that uses the AI program."

He stared down at her, the planes of his face sharp in the shadows. His hair was a mess, late-night—or early-morning—whiskers skimmed his face, and his eyes were bold in hers. Yes, if she were to be trapped in darkness with anyone, it would be this man.

Even if he didn't trust her.

"Luis."

"What?" She checked her GPS.

"Don't dodge me. You're using Luis to create the virus."

She looked up. "I think we're close to that pit."

"That's why you needed him."

Her mouth tightened. "Listen. Yes, he's working for us now. At the time, he'd created a program to decrypt high-level encryption codes. We used that to . . . acquire information."

"Like by breaking into DOD servers?"

"I don't know. But . . ." She sighed. "We did use it to check on you after I saw you in Minnesota, at the wedding. Frankly, I almost didn't recognize you. Not in a suit and tie."

He raised an eyebrow.

"You looked different back then. A beard. Longer hair."

"Blood, grime—"

"Maybe harder." She lifted a shoulder. "When Nim found your medical records . . ." She let out a breath, ignoring the sirens inside. "I never got over leaving you, Steinbeck."

He stopped, his voice soft. "I never got over thinking you'd died and I couldn't save you."

Oh. His blue eyes held hers. *Oh.*

And suddenly, the what-ifs weren't so crazy. What if she could step up to him, grab him by his soggy shirt, and make it real? Or as real as it could be with her living her life out of a backpack.

It was possible he saw that thought in her eyes, the questions, the desire, because his Adam's apple bobbed in his throat, and his gaze roamed her face . . . fell on her lips.

Yes—

Then he shook his head, winced, and held up a hand, stepping back. "Wow, I'm weak. Seriously."

He brushed past her, what seemed like anger steaming off him.

She stood there, heart hammering. *Yeah, well . . .* "Aw, calm down, Frogman. We're just cold and tired, and you started it with the whole *just trying to warm you up* business."

This man. She had to get him out of her brain.

She hurried after him, catching up as he entered another tunnel, his light flashing ahead of him. "We'll be out of here soon, and then I promise, you'll never see me again."

He grunted.

And weirdly, her eyes burned.

Fatigue, probably.

"Who's Nim?"

Right. She'd dropped that name. But he seemed to have calmed down so, "She's—" *What could it hurt?* "My sister. Nimue. She's a computer hacker in the deep web. She lives in Florida."

"Is she a Swan?"

"No." She fell into step behind him. Clearly he'd decided to be in charge. "She just helps me out when I need it."

"How'd you become a Swan?"

Oh. "I got recruited."

"Out of jail?"

"Ha, ha, but . . . let's say that I had a small reputation for . . . my ability to get in and out of locations without being seen."

"Like what, bank vaults?"

"Have you ever heard of the Scepter of Charles V of Spain?"

"I've never even heard of Charles V of Spain. Why?"

"No reason. Just . . ."

He stopped, and she nearly bumped into him as he rounded. "Did you steal it?"

She shrugged. "Sort of. I mean, technically yes, but I was caught. Although not by the police."

"You stole a national treasure? From where?"

"The royal palace in Madrid. But again, they got it back. Sheesh."

"How?"

"Oh, I'll never tell all my secrets." She smiled.

His eyes narrowed.

"Fine. It involved a month of surveillance, a detailed 3D map, Nim's hacking abilities, and a trial run to test their system."

He turned back around and kept moving. "I'm going to need more."

"Fine. But this stays between us."

"What happens in the mines of Moria stays in the mines of Moria."

"Thank you, Gandalf."

He laughed then, and maybe they were okay. She could just forget that she still wanted to reach out, stop him, and—

Nope.

"So, I pulled off the job during the Fiesta de San Isidro. It was chaos in the city, and I knew the palace would be understaffed."

"Smart."

"Thanks. Nim disabled the security, and I jammed the electronic feed from the scepter's display to a separate security sensor. I was in costume, thanks to the fiesta, so I just switched out the scepter with a replica. And then I walked out the staff door, which I'd already stolen the code for. Blended into the crowd. Bam. The hard part wasn't the theft—it was the fence. Is that light ahead?"

He turned off his flashlight. The softest ribbon of light bled into the tunnel. He flicked the flashlight back on. "I have the overwhelming urge to weep."

She laughed.

"How'd you get caught?"

"The fence. He ratted me out—a patriot. But the Swans got to me first. I was in Morocco when Pike picked me up."

"Pike?"

"He's the founder and boss, although he died a few years ago. He, along with a woman named Ziggy, talked me into a life of sanctioned heists and undercover gigs."

"And you said yes, just like that?"

They'd neared the edge of the tunnel, the light spilling into the darkness, cresting over Stein, illuminating his soggy attire, casting his hair a deep bronze. He turned, eyebrow raised.

She met his eyes. "I had my reasons. But the biggest was that I could start over, reinvent myself. Let's get out of here."

"Hence the name Phoenix. What is your real name?"

She stepped out into a space approximately six feet wide, and as she looked up, the height hollowed her out. "It's probably two hundred feet up to the surface." Still, light streamed in, and above that . . . dawn. It bled gold and pink and lavender across the sky.

Now she wanted to weep too.

He touched the edges of the rock. "These are lava blocks. They get ejected from the volcano already formed, and then the lava flows on top of them. They're much harder to cut through than an old lava flow."

"Which means what?"

"Which means that something blasted these out." He searched the rock.

"What are you looking for?"

"Old bolt anchors or pitons that might have held a cable—like this one." He pointed to an anchor protruding from the rock, affixed into the stone at two points, with what looked like a pulley securing them together. "My thought is, we climb up these to the top."

She spotted the next one, about four feet higher. "That's a tough climb. No three-point anchor holds. And one of us isn't eight feet tall."

He glanced over at her, handed her the flashlight.

Then he reached up and grabbed the higher point. Put his stocking foot on the lower anchor and lifted himself up. He grabbed the next higher point, put both hands on the anchor, and walked up the wall, hand over hand, feet bracing on the anchors.

"Okay, Spidey, that works for you. But I can't reach the taller anchor."

He kept moving.

And it occurred to her then that . . . He wouldn't just leave her, would he?

He kept ascending.

She stepped back. "Just for the record, I can't catch you."

"You could if you tried."

For a guy with bad knees, he could scale walls like an Olympic climber. Or perhaps desperation just added a little oomph to his antigravity powers.

He reached the top. And she stepped back, waiting as he disappeared.

A minute. Another. "I hope you have a plan!"

Nothing.

Perfect. She walked to the wall. Jumped. Caught her hand on the anchor a foot above her but now dangled and scrabbled to get her foot on the lower anchor.

She'd have to jump for the next one.

And the next.

And sure, she had climbing abilities, but—

"Rope!"

She looked up in time to see a frayed rope careening down the side of the hole. She hugged the rock.

"I tied a bowline loop for your foot. Climb on and I'll haul you up."

What—? "You sure?"

"No, I thought I'd leave you down there to think about your crimes. Yes, I'm sure, Phoenix. Let's go."

She found the loop and put her foot in. The other she used to push herself away from the wall.

And then, as if *no problem, thanks,* Muscles pulled her up. With her help. *Sorta.*

Whatever. She reached the top and found that he'd looped the rope around a nearby tree, then his waist, and made a pulley of sorts.

Still, sweat poured down his face into his shirt, which was starting to dry in the heat of the day.

Air. Fresh air. It filled her lungs, and she couldn't take enough in.

She climbed out of the hole and fell to her hands and knees, wanting to openly weep at the light and fresh air and freedom.

He collapsed next to her. "Please, let's never do that again."

"My master plan to hike out might not have been the best."

He eyed her. "We're still alive." Then he held out his fist.

Huh. She smacked it with hers. *What*, they were buddies now?

Rolling over, she lay on her back.

They'd emerged onto what looked like a small hill, volcanic boulders the size of her Fiat littering the area, a few scraggly evergreens, and brush fighting to survive. Beyond, the deep blue of the Caribbean Sea stretched out under a glorious dawn-painted blue sky.

He sat, staring out over the ocean. Then, suddenly, he got up. "We need to move."

"Why?" She rolled to her feet.

"Because the people I stole the rope from are coming back." He grabbed her and hauled her behind a boulder. Pointed.

Fifty-some feet away sat a portable drill rig, a truck, and a couple men in work clothes and hard hats, carrying a drum between them, coiling out a line.

"I took the rope off their truck."

"Is that—*wait.* Is that detonation wire?"

He nodded. "They were inside the cave. I think they're on a

mining team." He yanked her back and indicated down the dirt road to the base of the mountain.

What looked like a mining camp was set against a cleared-out portion of rainforest. Modular units circled a central compound, and drilling rigs and an excavator sat in a nearby lot. A satellite dish lifted from one of the units, pointed toward the sky.

A few men moved around the camp in the early morning.

Voices lifted from nearby, and she stilled, listening.

Russian.

A chill ran through her. "We need to get out of here. It looks like they're checking the detonation wires. They're going to blast into the mountain." She pushed away from the rock.

"They'll see us!"

"Better than being blown back into that hole. Move, Frogman."

She edged away from the boulder. Then, as one of the men disappeared behind the truck, she took off.

Boulders and dirt and scrub brush evidenced previous mining efforts, although years had gone by, because trees had found footing in the soil.

A shout lifted behind them, but she ignored it. And then shots. They pinged off the boulders around them, shredded bark—

The shooting stopped, and now a shout lifted. *Ogon'!*

Fire in the hole. She skidded behind a protruding boulder, Stein on her tail. He slid, then caught up to her—

The mountain blew. The explosion rumbled the entire mountain, the hillside shuddering, rock spitting down over them, dust rising from the hole.

"Now we know what caused the earthquake," Stein said, but his voice sounded tight, his breathing fast.

"C'mon!" She grabbed Stein's shirt and hauled him up, but he was already moving. She ran down the hill ahead of him, spotting a dirt road ahead. It led back around the mountain, hopefully toward Esperanza and her boat ride out of here.

And it hit her then—

She'd done it. Gotten her hands on the program, and *hello,* mission accomplished. Sure, Stein might try to grapple the program away from her, but frankly, he could have done that any time during their trek.

Or negotiated for it on the cliffside—her life for the program.

But he seemed rattled by what she'd told him about his boss, so . . .

They reached the road, and she lit out into a run, the dirt and stones of the unpaved road digging into her feet, despite the padding. But she ignored it, kept moving.

This island wasn't so big that she couldn't simply run all the way back to town, her fatigue gone in the rush of adrenaline.

A grunt lifted behind her, and it occurred to her then that Stein hadn't caught up to her. She slowed. Turned.

He went down hard, twenty feet behind her. Rolled onto his back, and now his grunts turned verbal.

What the—"Stein!"

She ran back, her gaze on the mountain. Dust still puffed the air, but it seemed they hadn't alerted anyone. For now.

He lay on the ground, grimacing, holding his torso, and—

Blood soaked his hands, his shirt.

"What happened?" She skidded to a stop, dropped to her knees beside him.

He grimaced. "Sorry."

"Sorry? You're sorry—" She moved his hands away. "Oh—"

Blood spurted from a hole right below one of those perfect pectoral muscles. "You're shot."

"You don't have to sound so disgusted. It wasn't on purpose." He groaned, lay back. "It's getting hard to breathe."

"You could just be out of shape."

He opened one eye.

"Okay, probably not. I don't understand—did the bullet go

through you?" She moved his shoulder up, with his help, and looked for an exit wound. No blood. Which meant the blood was filling his pleural cavity. *Oh no.* "You have a hemothorax. And me without my thoracostomy kit."

"Clearly not a Girl Scout."

"I washed out." She still wore her dive pants with the pockets and now unvelcroed one, tried to still her shaking hands.

"Now I wish I hadn't made you drop your knife."

Breathe. "Me too." She rooted around and pulled out a multi-tool.

"What, you're going to stab me? Just get me up. We can make it to medical help."

Not how he was breathing. All she had to do was relieve the pressure in his chest. Then find transport and then . . .

"Do the next thing." Mystique's words in her head. She picked up his wrist, felt for the pulse.

Fast and weak. *Yep.* She pulled out her small collapsable water bottle filled with potable water.

"You had that all along and didn't tell me?"

"We weren't desperate yet." She ripped open his shirt and poured the water onto the wound, washing it. Then she opened the water bottle and pulled out the attached straw.

"Phoenix." He caught her arm, still enough strength to stop her trembling. "You can't be serious."

Right. What was she *doing*?

She looked up toward the camp. Still no action. She could run. Escape the island. Accomplish her mission.

But more important—"I left you behind once. I'm not doing it again."

His eyes widened. "Actually, I wasn't thinking you'd leave me *behind*." He made to get up and gasped. Breathed out a couple times. "Okay, so that is an option."

"No. It's not." She picked up the multi-tool and flipped to the knife.

"Oh . . ." He bit down on whatever word might have wanted to emerge.

"You're just going to have to trust me."

He closed his eyes. "God, please save me from this woman."

She pressed on his ribs, Mystique's training in her head, found the fifth intercostal space along the side of his body—*the midaxillary line, where the arm meets the torso.*

Yes. She took a breath. "This will hurt."

He opened his eyes and met her gaze. "I know."

And then she lifted a small prayer—*Please, God, save him from my mistakes*—as she tried to save his life.

THIRTEEN

IT JUST COULDN'T GET ANY WORSE.

Tia sat on the floor of a hurricane-ravaged hotel room, the paint peeling from the walls, the wind shifting through a ragged curtain, the bed soiled and sheetless, her mouth taped, her hands zip-tied behind her back.

She just wanted to go home.

Adventure, fresh start, whatever this was . . . *over.* She was tapping out.

If she survived.

She didn't know who to trust, really. Not after, at zero dark thirty, she'd answered a knock on her door only to find Keon—seriously, Keon—standing in the shadows, holding a gun.

He'd slammed his big hand to her mouth, shoved her back into the room and against the wall, and said, "Don't scream."

Yeah, whatever. She still might have if he hadn't added, "Or Kemar dies."

So there was that.

Although she hadn't seen Kemar, even after Keon led her

through the compound, his gun to her back. And maybe she'd thought—

No, *definitely* she'd thought that this might be one of those times when Doyle showed up, the superhero he was with his cape and quick thinking, to save her.

But nope.

Keon had loaded her into his Jeep, strapped her in, and driven her—*yep.* To Sebold's resort. *Look who's back.*

And when she'd made a break for it the minute Keon pulled up to the outside entrance, he'd tackled her, hauled her up, and told her not to fight him.

Whatever.

He hadn't hit her, however, when she did exactly that, just grabbed her by the arms and twisted them behind her back and marched her into the compound by dawn's early light.

She didn't see Sebold on the way to her new accommodations.

"Why are you doing this?" Her words to Keon as he'd tied her up, then forced her to sit on the floor. She'd shouted at him on his way out the door.

Whoops. Apparently not the right move, because he'd returned holding duct tape, which he'd pasted over her mouth.

She'd wanted to quip something about the hospitality at this place. The words kept replaying in her head. She was probably losing her mind.

Now, her arms ached and her backside hurt. She'd been able to loosen, just a little, the tape from her mouth. Outside, the sun rose and baked the room, the ocean culling the shore.

And all she could think was . . .

Doyle wouldn't know what happened to her. He'd think she'd left him, maybe.

Or not. Could be he wouldn't notice.

"You're so beautiful, Juliet."

She might have overreacted to that just a smidgen. Or a lot.

Because it had been a long night and he'd been tired, and the names of people we love get stuck in our heads and maybe it had just been a reflex . . .

"Tia!"

He'd tried to run after her. That much she could admit. Although he hadn't chased her to her room, hadn't knocked on her door, so what did that mean?

She'd probably talked herself into the meaning behind that kiss. Because she definitely remembered his words—clearly spoken about her. *"I thought, This woman is going to drive me crazy."*

So, yeah, probably he wouldn't miss her at all.

The door opened, and she looked over. Stilled.

Sebold walked into the room. He wore a pair of jeans, slides, a sleeveless T-shirt, and chewed on a toothpick. He took a straight chair with the wicker back kicked through and set it down near her. Straddled it, leaning on the back. Took out the toothpick and smiled. "You're back."

She might have responded, but she had this duct tape, see . . .

So she tried to communicate with her eyes something that might turn him to a pile of ash.

He grinned, then looked over at the door. "Good job, Keon."

Her gut clenched. Keon leaned on the frame, gave a nod.

Sebold turned back to her. "See, I knew you'd find my treasure."

She stared at him.

"You can't hide it from me. I own this island." He got up. "I always have." He leaned into her space. "It's my *birthright*."

Right. Raging Rodrigo Sebold, the pirate. She shook her head.

He walked to the window, moved the curtain. "He should be here soon."

He?

Dropping the curtain, Sebold turned back to her. Glanced at Keon. "He thinks we should trade you. But I think you're more valuable than that." He walked over to her, lifted her chin. "I did some homework. Daddy might pay a high price to get his little girl back."

She yanked her chin from his grip.

"Let's get her ready."

Ready? Ready for what?

Sebold walked out, past Keon, who didn't leave.

Instead, he shut the door.

She scooted away from him as he came over and crouched in front of her. Lowered his voice. "I'm sorry, Miss Tia."

She kicked at him.

He held up his hands. "I know you're angry. But everything is going to be okay."

She stilled. *In what world?*

"Mr. D is on his way with the gold, and then it will all be over. You need to trust me."

Except everything inside her had frozen.

Doyle was on his way? With the gold?

Oh no. She shook her head. *Please don't let him—*

Except *of course* he was on his way. And had a trick up his sleeve. *Okay, yes . . .* She nodded.

"Just . . . do whatever Sebold says." Keon reached for her arm and pulled her up. "I promise, it's all going to work out."

Yeah, it would. Because Doyle would figure it out. She knew it in her soul.

Keon walked her through the house, down the stairs, and out through the lounge area, where a few men sat, some eating, others smoking cigarettes. Most of them young, skinny. They watched her with dark eyes.

A couple bony dogs got up and barked at her.

Keon led her out to the sunshine, and she stood in the yard next to the pool, the algae in the green water rising to poison the air. Patio furniture had been shoved around a firepit, the ash spilled out onto the broken tile.

Sebold leaned against a gate, threw down his cigarette, and stood up.

Beyond the gate, she spotted the old green Ford.

No.

But what else was he supposed to do?

She swallowed, watching Doyle pull up. Two men sat in the back—

North and Skeet. The security guys from Jones, Inc. Yes, there was certainly a plan here. She glanced at Sebold, twisted her hands against the straps.

"Stay calm," Keon whispered.

She wanted to kick him.

Doyle got out and put up his hands. He wore dirt on his shirt, his hands, his jeans. And fury in his blue eyes.

That was new.

"Walk her out here," he said, looking at Sebold, then at Tia, hard emotion in his eyes.

Keon pushed her forward.

Sebold put up his hand. "Not yet."

Doyle took a step forward. Pitched his voice low. "I have sixty million dollars' worth of gold sitting in a bag in the back of my truck. If you want to have any hope of seeing that, you let her walk out here."

Sebold pulled a gun from under his shirt, and she didn't know guns, but it seemed lethal enough when he pointed it at her.

"Show me the gold."

A muscle moved in Doyle's jaw. "Or we can put you down right here. Right now, I have a sniper aimed at your head. I raise my hand, you die—"

Sebold turned the gun on Doyle, marched out to him. "Give me my gold."

Keon's hold on her arm tightened. "Not yet."

What—?

Doyle didn't move. "Go ahead. You shoot me, they drop you right here."

And that's when North and Skeet each dropped a duffel bag on the ground in front of them.

Sebold looked at them, then Doyle.

Looked back at Keon and nodded.

Keon walked her outside the gate. She looked at Doyle, but he'd motioned to the guys to bring the bags in.

They set them inside the gate, went to retrieve more.

Doyle pushed the gun aside. "Step back and you'll get your treasure, Rodrigo."

Sebold held up his hands and watched as the men delivered two more bags. He glanced at Keon. "Open them."

Keon let her go but leaned into her ear. "Go to Doyle."

What?

But as soon as he released her, she took off.

Maybe it was her imagination, but it seemed as if Keon stepped between her and Sebold.

She tucked herself behind Doyle.

He moved back, his hand reaching for her arm, gripping it. Then he backed her up to the truck. "Get in."

She slid into the front seat.

"Get down."

See? This was when he would do something amazing. One of the bags would explode, sending ink or even sand everywhere, and then they'd make their mad escape.

Or maybe Skeet and North would simply turn on Sebold, take him down while Doyle whisked her away—

"Look at this, boss," Keon said, lifting two of the gold bars. Smiling. "We got it."

No. That wasn't—

Doyle couldn't possibly have just given away sixty million dollars' worth of gold to a pirate . . .

Skeet and North delivered the last of the bags and jumped in the back of the truck.

Doyle got in. Glanced at her. "You okay?"

She nodded, and he put the truck in reverse.

And backed out.

What? That was it?

She fought her ties, her gag, and he glanced at her. "Hang tight."

Really?

He drove them away from the resort, turned onto the highway, then pulled over and reached for her. "Let's get that tape off you." He eased it off her mouth, his expression wrecked, swallowing hard.

"Doyle—"

"It's going to be okay."

Someone had thumped on the roof, and he turned and opened the window to the back end. North handed him a knife, and he turned her, cut the plastic ties. Handed the knife back to North.

She rubbed her wrists as he put the truck into Drive.

And lumbered down the road.

"Wait—what—you're not . . . Where's your trick? Your sexy MacGyver move that saves the day."

Doyle glanced at her, frowned. "There is no sexy move. You were the priority, Tia. Getting you back. That's all that mattered."

At least he hadn't called her Juliet, but—"No. Doyle. What? You just gave away *sixty million dollars* in gold."

He nodded, his eyes on the road, drew in a long breath. "You're going to need to trust me."

"I'm tired of people saying that! No—I don't want to trust you. I don't want to trust anybody. I want . . ." Her eyes filled. "I want this to be over. I want it all to be over. I want to stop turning around to find the world exploding and kids missing and bad guys showing up and—and life imploding around me and I can't do anything about it!"

"Of course you can't!" He glanced at her, his jaw tight. "We can't control anything that happens, Tia. That's the point. It's not what happens to us—but how we deal with it."

"It just feels like . . ." She shook her head. "It feels like nothing I do is ever enough."

"Enough for what?"

She looked away. Her voice dropped. "Maybe . . . enough to matter to God."

"Get in line," he said.

She stared at him. "What?"

He glanced at her. "My fiancée died on our wedding day. And I was going to be a missionary. So what does that say about mattering to God? Clearly, not much."

It took a minute. "You believe that?"

"Not for a minute."

Oh.

"But I did. Or I wanted to." He sighed. "But the truth is that bad things happen to good people. To God's people. And it's not because he doesn't love us or we don't matter to him."

She wiped her face. "Feels like it."

He glanced at her, then, "Yep."

Oh. She'd sort of hoped . . .

"That is exactly what evil wants us to believe. That somehow God doesn't care and we're better off without Him."

She looked out the window.

"But the truth is, I'm not. I desperately need God's grace to carry me because I can't do it on my own. Even though I've spent years trying."

She nodded.

"And God does care. He says, 'My grace is sufficient for you, for my power is made perfect in weakness.' Sufficient strength, sufficient hope. *Sufficient.* So, somehow, when I wake up to a new morning, God's grace is just enough to carry me through. I just have to hold on. At least . . . that's my new game plan."

They'd reached the road to Esperanza, and he hit the brakes.

Skeet and North piled out and joined their other security guy, along with Hamilton and Ranger. She spotted a number of Jeeps and cars on the side of the road.

"What's going on?"

Doyle put the truck back into Drive and left them there.

"Doyle."

He bumped up the road toward Hope House. "When I woke up and found you missing . . ." He glanced at her. "*You*, not Juliet, I . . . I lost it. I couldn't believe Sebold had won. After everything, evil won."

"Evil did win."

"The Jamesons showed up about then. They wanted to talk to me about Kemar and how they wanted to adopt him, but I was . . . I was frantic. Rosa found a note in the kitchen that said they'd trade the treasure for you, and of course . . . Yes."

She shook her head, her mouth tight. *But what could he have done?*

He pulled into Hope House and put the truck into Park. Turned to her, his voice low. "You remember Hunter Jameson?"

"Of course."

"Do you know what he used to do for a living?"

"No."

"He was a JSOC tactical operator."

"I don't even know what that is."

"He planned and executed secret missions for the military. He did his twenty and is now retired. After that first night, he found out about Sebold's attack on the medical clinic and reached out to the local police. They've been trying to figure out how to arrest Sebold for years. They never had any hard proof, anyone who would agree to testify against him. They had even sent in a man to join his crew, hoping they might be able to catch him in something. Then last night, we found the gold."

"And?"

"Ethan. He went back to Declan's place, angry, drinking, and told Hunter everything."

"Seriously?"

"Don't be too hard on him. Hunter went to his contact at the police and put together a plan. Called their inside man and set up the kidnapping."

She blinked at him. "I was kidnapped on *purpose*?"

His mouth tightened. "According to Hunter, that wasn't part of his plan. He was supposed to take the gold. But it was guarded so . . ."

She wanted to be ill. "Keon had a *gun*, Doyle."

He nodded.

"And all I could think of was—"

"Your sister. And how she'd been kidnapped, and how afraid you'd always been that it would happen to you."

Her eyes rounded.

"I have been paying attention. To you." He touched her hand. She looked at it. Then drew it away.

"What was the big plan?"

"To give the fortune to Sebold."

"Brilliant. That's awesome. Just think of all the ways a man like Sebold might spend sixty mil."

"Except, it doesn't belong to him, does it? According to Ethan—and Declan's lawyers, and the Treasure Hunters' Rights and Compensation Act—Mariposa owns fifty percent of the treasure. Which means . . . he has now stolen from the city."

It took a second. "And they can arrest him?"

"For grand theft. And since he used a gun against the deputized agents of Mariposa, that's armed robbery."

"That group back there was the local police?"

"On their way to arrest Raging Rodrigo Jr."

Huh.

"God works in mysterious ways." He reached for her hand again.

She shook her head.

"Right. Tia. Please forgive me—I didn't mean to—"

"I know." She held up her hand. "I really do know. It was a mistake—you were tired. *We* were tired. And who doesn't occasionally call someone by the wrong name?"

"Yes—"

"So of course—I forgive you. But that's not the real problem."

He stilled.

"You still have half your heart in Minnesota."

He opened his mouth. "I don't—"

"And I don't mean with Juliet. I mean with the man you were going to be. The doctor who wanted to be a missionary."

"I don't . . . That's not—"

She touched his chest, his heart thundering under her fingers. "But it is, Doyle. I don't know what Juliet saw, but I know what I see. I see a man who broke in half when his fiancée died. You left part of yourself in the lake that night, and you've never dealt with losing that."

"Yes—"

"Let me finish. Your future, your vision, your calling—it all died with Julia and left a hole inside you, and until you deal with that, you won't have anything to give to . . ." She sighed. "Anyone else."

His mouth opened. Closed. "Tia—"

"Listen." She pulled her hand away. "I can see when a man is searching for something. And when he tries to tell himself it's me. But it's not, Doyle." Her throat burned. "This has been . . . Well, you have been more than I imagined. But maybe that's all this was. A jumpstart—a reminder that there is more. Like you said, the fresh start. It just . . . it just isn't the happy ending." Her eyes filled. "I don't want to be the Band-Aid or the rebound. I want to be the One. The someone you've been waiting for all your life."

He didn't move, his expression stricken.

Oh, Doyle. "You taught me how to ask for help, Doyle. And that a little fear is okay because it's the perfect time for me to watch God show up." She wiped the tears off her cheek. "But I probably need to learn what it means for God to be sufficient too."

She reached for the door handle.

"Tia—wait—"

"Doyle!"

His name lifted from a voice at the gate, and she looked up to see Declan running toward the truck. He stopped at the open window. Glanced at Tia. "Thank God."

Then, "Doyle, I just got a call from the hospital. Stein is there—and he's been shot. We need to go."

She touched Doyle's hand. "Thanks for not forgetting me." His eyes widened as she got out. "Go find your brother."

And then she walked away and didn't look back.

Stein felt like he had a hot poker shoved through his body.

Which was why he gasped as he opened his eyes. Cool oxygen poured through his mouth and nose, a strap securing him at the shoulders to a gurney.

Overhead, the sky arched a dark blue.

What—?

He looked over and spotted, *wait*—"Doyle?" His brother wore a grimy shirt, his beard thick, concern in his blue eyes. "What's going on?"

Doyle held up a hand and the gurney slowed, and Stein watched as a nurse handed Doyle a bag of IV fluid. She patted Steinbeck on the shoulder. "You'll be okay."

Probably not, considering he didn't have a clue how—*wait.* "Where's Phoenix?"

Doyle bent over him. "You're going to be okay, bro. Nearly lost you there, but they stopped the bleeding. Declan called in a chopper. We're just waiting for Jake and Aria to join us. Then we're scooting you over to St. Kitts for surgery."

"Who's Jake?"

"One of the rescuers. He got stabbed during the rescue—"

"*What rescue?*"

"The kids—never mind. It's a long story."

Now Stein made out the scent of oil on a tarmac. "Are we at Declan's helipad?"

Doyle nodded.

But—"Where. is. *Phoenix*?"

"Who?" Doyle shook his head. "What happened to you, anyway? Were you caught in the landslide?"

Landslide? Stein closed his eyes, trying to roll back the film.

He'd been on the side of a mountain, his chest tight, unable to breathe, and then—

Yeah, she'd stabbed him. He remembered nearly ejecting out of his body. Then the tube went in and—

And he could breathe. But things got shadowy after that. A bumpy ride on a four-wheeler, he thought. And then voices—he didn't recognize any of them.

Or, wait.

"Don't say I never did nothin' for you."

He licked his lips. Felt like . . . No, just a scant memory. But in his mind, she was bending over him, her green eyes holding his. *"Stay alive."*

Yeah, she'd definitely kissed him. Sweet, almost gentle.

He thought he remembered reaching out to her, grabbing only thin air.

A ghost.

He groaned, the pain meds not quite taking the edge off.

Doyle looked up. "They're here." And then a woman leaned over him. Dark hair held back with a handkerchief. She wore a T-shirt and had a stethoscope around her neck.

"So, you're Steinbeck. I've heard of you from your cousin Ranger." She patted his arm. "We're going to get you home."

But wait—"I need to talk to Declan."

Doyle nodded. "Don't worry, bro. He set this up. I think you're approved for medical PTO."

No, that wasn't—"Where is Declan?" He grabbed Doyle's arm.

Doyle put his hand over Stein's, his mouth tight. "Declan is helping out in town. I promise, everything is okay. Everything is *going to be okay*." He seemed to say that last part to himself and looked past Stein.

As if into the horizon.

And then the gurney was moving toward the chopper.

Stein closed his eyes. *No, no,* this was not how this was supposed to go down. "She has the program—she's . . ." Of course no one was listening. But what if Phoenix was right? *Please let her be wrong*. Please let him not have been protecting a *terrorist* for the past few months.

And if she was wrong? She'd be helping America's enemies devise a way to dismantle their defenses.

Although, the idea of the kind of AI defenses that Phoenix had described . . . even he wasn't sure. . . . Maybe she was right to shut down Declan's program—what she called Skynet—before it began.

They brought him to the chopper, and then hands lifted him off the gurney, bringing the backboard into the belly.

He was in Krakow all over again, on his way to Landstuhl, his career over.

Not this time.

Doyle sat down in a seat beside him.

"What are you doing?"

Doyle strapped in. "Taking you home."

Stein stared at him, then reached up and pulled his mask aside. "You can't go home. You have work to do here. What about Hope House? And Tia—"

"Hope House is fine—"

"And Sebold—"

"Dealt with. Put your mask back on."

"What about Tia—"

Doyle moved the mask for him. "She's . . . I don't know." His mouth tightened and he looked out the window.

Oh no. "What happened?"

Doyle leaned back and pulled on headphones. Someone added earmuffs to Stein, and the chopper fired up.

Across from him, Dr. Aria and another guy, moving a little slowly, strapped themselves in. The guy leaned over to Stein. "We got you, brother. Hooyah." He gave him a tight smile.

Oh, a former teams guy.

The door closed and the chopper lifted off.

Stein closed his eyes. And all he could hear was, *"I left you behind once. I'm not doing it again."*

Yeah, well, right back atcha, Phoenix.

FOURTEEN

TWO WEEKS PUTTERING AROUND THE KING'S Inn grounds, getting ready for the summer season, and Doyle still couldn't get Tia's words out of his head.

"I can see when a man is searching for something."

He sank his axe into the log, his body shuddering with the blow. The wood split in half, fell on each side of the block.

He picked up the pieces and parked them on the growing woodpile.

Maybe he shouldn't be doing his brother Jack's job, but he needed to sweat, to burn off the ache inside him.

Right. Wow, he missed Tia. As if he were missing a lung, every breath sharp. How she'd gotten so far inside so quickly, he didn't know, but . . .

The early June air whisked off the deep blue lake, holding summer in its breath. Leaves on the poplar and birch trees rustled around him, and the scent of freshly mowed grass turned the inn's grounds into a summer escape. Geraniums bloomed in pots seated on the steps of the main building, a vintage white-painted

Victorian built in the early twentieth century, during America's Gilded Age.

His brother Jack, now their maintenance guy, had applied a fresh coat of white paint to the Welcome to King's Inn sign affixed to the main entrance, along with the pillars of the apron porch, now festooned with hanging floral baskets.

Frankly, it looked like the prodigal son was doing a better job at upkeep than Doyle had. Although, Jack seemed to be itching to leave, given the work he'd accomplished on his mint 1973 GMC forty-five-foot passenger-transit bus, turning it into a someday home for himself and future wife—hopefully—Harper Malone.

Who knew that the One for Jack had been next door all his life?

Doyle picked up another log. He could probably stop anytime, but the King's Inn hosted a bonfire on the beach every Friday and Saturday night during the summer, so having an ample supply of firewood wouldn't hurt.

He set it up, stood back. Sent the axe down. The crack split the morning air, reverberated in his soul, and raked up Tia's words, again.

"Your future, your vision, your calling—it all died that night and left a hole inside you, and until you deal with that, you won't have anything to give . . ."

He picked up the pieces, set them together on the rack. They still fit together, even after they'd been torn asunder.

"This place never looked better. I like having my sons around."

Doyle turned and found his father carrying an old green thermos under his arm, a couple plastic cups, and two muffins wrapped in napkins. He set the thermos on the back wheel rim of a nearby four-wheeler and handed Doyle a muffin. "Your mother worries. Says you're too skinny."

Doyle laughed and opened the muffin. "Raspberry?"

"With white chocolate. She's trying a new recipe. Don't argue."

Doyle sat on the chopping log. "Nope." He bit into the muffin. "It's good."

"Leave some of this chopping for your old man; otherwise, I'm going to get fat." He winked and sat on the seat of the four-wheeler. "So, you ready to talk about it?"

Doyle looked up, then at the lake.

"Stein told us a little. Said that it was the first time since your life imploded that he'd seen the old Doyle. Or maybe a new Doyle—you tell me."

"I dunno, Dad." He picked at the muffin. "I went to Mariposa because I thought it was time to get moving, find a fresh start."

His dad was soft-spoken and wise, a man who listened, and always reminded Doyle a little of an older Russell Crowe—sturdy, salt-and-pepper hair. Now, he set down his muffin and poured Doyle a cup of coffee. Handed it over.

Doyle took it. "The problem is that . . ." He sighed. "I guess I always saw myself doing something . . . big for God. And now I'm just . . . chopping wood."

"You and Juliet had a big future planned."

"Yeah. By the way, how'd Conrad's game go yesterday? The Blue Ox still in the playoffs?"

"Yep. And he scored a goal. Top of his game this year." His father took a sip of coffee. "So—you didn't find your big life in Mariposa?"

"I don't know."

"Stein mentioned a woman. Tia?"

Doyle's mouth tightened, and he sighed.

"Oh, I see. Juliet get in the way?"

His expression must have betrayed him.

His father nodded. "She'll always be a part of you, son. Your first love. Any good woman will understand that."

"I think she does. But that's not why . . ." Why she'd pushed him away. *Sheesh,* he should just accept that.

Tia didn't want him. And of course her words raked through his head. *"You have been more than I imagined. But maybe that's all this was. A jumpstart—a reminder that there is more. Like you said, the fresh start. It just isn't the happy ending."*

"Why . . . ?"

He looked at his father. "Right. So, she told me that I'd left a part of myself in that lake—"

His father frowned.

"Not Juliet—but maybe my calling. My future."

His father took another sip of coffee. "Death does that—it cuts off our vision. I remember when your grandmother died. Your grandfather was absolutely lost. I'd find him standing in his bathrobe on the front lawn, just staring out at the lake. It took a while for him to figure out who he was without her." He finished off his muffin. "I don't think he ever really did—although it helped when he realized he could pour himself into you kids."

"I thought I could pour myself into Hope House. I just felt so . . . Well, I'm grateful for my time here, but I wanted to start moving forward again. And I thought . . ." He too finished off his muffin and picked up his coffee.

"You thought Hope House was the answer. Your big mission."

No, he'd thought Tia was the answer. But he nodded. Took a sip of coffee. "Being a missionary felt so right with Juliet. It was direction and purpose and . . ."

"A big life."

"Yeah."

"So when she died, you thought the vision died too."

He nodded.

"But I submit to you that you answered the call to Hope House because it's *not* dead. You just can't see it clearly."

"That's the thing. I wish God would tell me what to do. I feel like ever since Juliet died, He's gone silent. I don't know. Austen says God's will for me is joy. And love . . ."

"It is. That's the result of the salvation of your soul."

"I met this guy who said that God's will is just a state of being, not a direction."

"I think it's both. Consider what Proverbs says: 'Trust in the Lord with all your heart, and do not lean on your own understanding. In all your ways acknowledge him, and he will make straight your paths.' It's relationship, trust, and then following." He took a sip of coffee. "Consider Peter. Jesus said, 'Follow me,' and Peter obeyed. But he didn't realize that he had to hold on to Jesus, keep looking at Jesus, to stay afloat. And then, in his deepest grief, Peter just went back to fishing. Jesus had to call him out again and send him on his way."

"Are you saying that Jesus is calling me out again?"

"I don't know, Doyle. I do know there is a time to grieve. But we're not supposed to stay in that forever. Paul talks about pressing on, moving ahead into the abundance God has for you. That's my paraphrase of Philippians 3:14, by the way." He winked.

Abundance. Doyle's own words stirred inside him: *God is sufficient. "Sufficient strength, sufficient hope. Sufficient."*

No, more than sufficient. But abundant?

"I don't know, Dad. I went to Mariposa hoping for some clarity on my future. All I got was . . . confusion."

"That's because you're asking for the wrong thing, Doyle. What your heart needs isn't clarity . . . It's trust. That's what was shattered when Juliet died. If we had clarity on God's big plans, we might never follow. But He gives us direction for the next step and asks us to trust Him. That's where you need to start."

His dad drew in a breath, nodded, gave Doyle a tight-lipped smile. "God isn't done with you yet, son. You'll always miss Juliet. But your future didn't have to die with her. Tia is right—pull yourself out of the lake, come to shore, and let the Savior continue His good work in you."

He stood up. "I meant to tell you, Dave Birch asked that you stop by. He saw you in town and mentioned it at church on Sunday."

"Great."

"You saved his life. Don't forget that." He poured out the last of his coffee and picked up the thermos. "Oh, and bring some firewood to the bonfire pit. Your mother wants a cookout tonight. Con and Penny are coming over."

Super. So he could be haunted by the ghost of Tia. "Thanks for the muffin."

His father headed to the house as Doyle loaded up the wheelbarrow. He dumped the wood near the bonfire circle on the sandy shore of the resort beach, then headed into the house to change.

Abundance. The word felt almost cruel against his grief.

An hour later, he found himself pulling up to the Birches' ranch house. The hosta had exploded around the front walk, and the big pine in the front yard towered above the house.

He spotted the wooden swing hanging from the oak on the side yard, and a memory tried to nudge in.

Nope. He took a breath, climbed out of the King's Inn truck, and headed up to the house. Stood on the stoop—

The door opened. Misty Birch stood in the frame, wearing a pair of shorts and a pink shirt, her glasses shoved up into her whitened hair. "Doyle? Oh, it's been . . . too long."

Then she stepped out and pulled him into a hug. She'd lost weight, for sure, but didn't seem frail. When she let him go, she held on to his arms, smiled up at him.

Juliet's eyes.

"Dave is out back."

"I'll go around the house."

She let him go and he nearly—admittedly—made a dash for his truck. Instead, he forced himself around the end of the house—no glance at the swing—and spotted Dave holding a hose to a raised garden bed. Tiny sprouts pushed from the earth.

The man seemed thinner too, wore a baseball hat over his whitened hair and the scar underneath, a pair of shorts, and a T-shirt.

Doyle cleared his throat.

Dave turned, and for a second, his jaw dropped. Then, "Doyle." He let go of the sprayer, left it in the garden, walked over with an outstretched hand. "Son."

Son.

Doyle met his handshake. "How are you?"

"Oh, you know Misty—always a list to work through."

Silence dropped between them.

"My father said—"

"Yep. I have something I've been meaning to give you. Stay put." He turned to go inside.

Misty stood at the door, holding an envelope. She handed it to her husband, then looked at Doyle, smiled.

Her eyes glistened.

Dave came back to him, holding the envelope. He tapped it on his leg, then looked up at Doyle. Wetness rimmed his eyes. "This belongs to you."

He held out the envelope.

Doyle frowned, took it and eased it open. "Oh, no . . . No, sir—" He shoved it back to Dave.

"That ring belongs in your family, Doyle. I know it was your grandmother's. We shouldn't have hung on to it for so long, but . . . I had some trouble letting go."

Yeah, he got that. Doyle pulled out the ring, his throat thickening. A vintage band with a small diamond in the center. "This should be with Juliet."

"Juliet is with the Lord. She has everything she needs or wants."

Yes, she did. He stared at the ring.

"How are you doing, Doyle?"

He looked up. Away. Until this moment, just fine . . . Well, not really, but—

"I heard you went on another mission trip. Beacon of Compassion International? I know you've been involved in some relief efforts."

Oh, right. "No. This was with an orphanage in the Caribbean."

"Medical work?"

"Not . . . No. Just helping out."

Dave put a hand on his shoulder. "That's one thing Juliet loved about you—your heart for helping others. I remember the first time she told me that she was going to marry you. She was fourteen."

"What?"

"It was right after that missions conference at church. Some guy from some crazy band, with long hair and dreadlocks, showed up and told our youth that they could make a difference." He smiled when he said it, light shining in his eyes. "I watched Juliet go forward and make a commitment to God. And you, son, were right there. You went to the altar first. I very much believe that Juliet followed you up there."

His entire body tingled with fire and . . . truth. *Yes.* "I remember that."

"Whatever drove you to the altar is still inside you, son. You care—you cared about your parents' inn after Juliet died—and don't tell me that you didn't stick around to keep an eye on Misty and me too."

Doyle glanced at the door. Misty stood inside the screen, her arms around herself.

"And then you started volunteering for disaster teams. And cleaned up after tornadoes and hurricanes and floods . . . and finally, you left." He looked at the ring in Doyle's hand. "I want you to go, Doyle. With Juliet's blessing. With our blessing. Into the future God has *always* planned for you."

He put his hand on Doyle's shoulder, then pulled him to himself, spoke softly in his ear. "And it's okay to let yourself love again too."

He released Doyle. Walked back to the hose, picked it up, and returned to his garden spraying. The mist rose, catching the light of heaven.

Doyle pocketed the ring and walked away.

But hours later, as he sat at the bonfire, the sparks popping into the darkness, the fire inside hadn't died. *"I want you to go."*

Conrad had driven out from the city, his hair long, a middle-of-the-playoffs beard on his chin. He was laughing at his girlfriend Penny's second burnt marshmallow. "You need to give it time to cook." He took the roasting stick from her and blew on the blackness, then shook the mess into the fire.

"I wasn't born with the patience gene," Penny said, grabbing a fresh marshmallow from the bag his mother passed to her.

Harper sat next to Jack, trying to harness the melting goo of her s'more. Jack had gotten up to stir the glowing embers. He seemed more content than Doyle had ever seen him, really, the prodigal erased from his countenance. It seemed that, even with the bus project, Jack might be sticking around. He wore a green shirt, jeans, a baseball cap backward on his head, and set the poker down, sitting next to Stein.

Stein stared into the flames. Two weeks of healing had him up and walking around, but his brooding reminded Doyle of the Stein that had arrived home three years ago, broken, angry and trying to figure out his life.

They'd been a pair.

But not today. "You guys remember when David Pierce came to our church and told us about his crazy rock band for Jesus and how he'd started a missionary school in Amsterdam?"

Stein shook his head.

"Sorry, no," Jack said.

"I do," his mother said. She wore a pair of jeans, an old flannel shirt, her hair back in a bandanna. She met his eyes. Smiled. "You came home and said you wanted to be a missionary."

He smiled back. "I did."

She nodded.

He drew in a breath. "I think . . . maybe my time in Mariposa wasn't so much about starting something new . . . but a restart."

"Are you going back to med school?" His father came over with a couple loaded pie irons for roasting and handed one to his mother. "Blueberry."

"I'm not sure. I do know that it's time I return to myself. Or to a better version of that guy. Hopefully wiser."

Silence, and Jack looked over, smiling. Conrad ran a hand over his mouth, nodding.

Stein stared at him, hard. "A stronger version."

"Even if you don't exactly know where God is going to take you," Harper said, glanced at Jack. He winked at her.

"And maybe that journey won't be alone." Penny pulled her marshmallow stick from the fire. The marshmallow had started a nice brown edge. She put it back over the coals. "Tia is back."

He looked at her. "Really?"

"Yeah. Home, but not out of the game. She's working on something new for Declan."

"Declan is back too?" Stein asked, a sharpness in his voice.

"I don't know. But I do know that Tia's up to something. She's been holed up in her home office ever since she came home about a week ago. You know her—she always has a plan."

Doyle sat up.

And just like that, in the glow of the fire, he saw it.

Them, together, building something new. Where, he didn't know, but . . . yes. The sense of it filled him up, settled into his soul.

Beyond the fire, in the darkness, waves washed the shore, and overhead, the summer night stirred the leaves.

Do you love me, Doyle?

He drew in a breath.

Across the bonfire, Penny's marshmallow lit.

I do, Lord.

Then feed my sheep.

He was back on the soccer field with Jamal and Rohan and Kemar and Gabriella, laughing.

Feed my sheep.

He was on the beach, walking hand in hand with Tia, the wind in her hair, her green eyes on his, her smile lighting him up.

Feed my sheep.

He was sitting with Jamal, telling him he was loved, no matter what happened with the Jamesons.

Go, make disciples.

Doyle pressed a hand to his chest.

"You okay, son?" His father's voice lifted from across the flames. Doyle looked up, met his gaze.

"Yes. Yes, sir, I am good."

Overhead, sparks winked out into the night, the stars watching.

And for the first time since longer than he could remember . . . he was very, very good.

"You'll be brilliant. I have no doubt. You always seem to figure it out."

Tia looked up to see her mother standing in the kitchen doorway, pausing a moment before she came into the room. She wore a tennis dress, diamond earrings, her dark hair back in a sleek ponytail.

"What?"

Her mother came over and sat down in the chair opposite where Tia sat at the table, her laptop open, scrolling through her slides. She'd put the presentation together herself, not sure anyone else could capture the essence of Hope House and the need for a proper, rebuilt hospital.

Especially since the treasure money would be held up for years in the war between Mariposa and the Netherlands over who was the rightful owner. Ethan was beside himself—but he'd been generous enough to call some friends and set up today's presentation.

"You have that look on your face, your thinking look."

"My . . . *thinking* look?"

Her mother nodded. "Reminds me of your father."

Huh. Maybe. "I'm trying to secure funding for the hospital. An MRI machine."

And a project kept her mind away from . . .

Yeah. Him.

Whatever.

"What time is the presentation?" Her mother draped a gold bracelet around her wrist, trying to latch it.

"In a couple hours. I'm meeting Penny for lunch, then it's after that." She got up to help her mother. Took the bracelet. "You off to a game?"

"Oh no—lessons. I just can't get my serve right. Thanks." Her mother shook her arm to where the bracelet fell to her wrist. "Tell your sister that if she misses another family dinner, I'll send the dogs after her."

"That dog?" She pointed to her mother's basset hound, who'd come in and flopped on the floor. Sighed. "Yeah, he's terrifying."

"It's okay, Rochester. You can be scary when you want to be."

He blinked at them, heavy brows, sad eyes.

Tia crouched and petted Rochester. "I think Penny was at Conrad's game. Besides, Mother . . . you might need to loosen up on the mandatory family dinner. Or even, dare I say, Penny's security detail. It's a little creepy."

Her mother gaped. "Her podcast gets her into trouble—"

"I don't have a security detail. Never did." She stood up.

Her mother swallowed. "You didn't . . . You weren't—"

"Kidnapped? Funny you should say that . . ." But no, maybe her mother didn't need an update. "Truth is, I lived with the fear of being kidnapped all my life."

"You did?"

She cocked her head at her mother. "Yes. Of course I did." Tia dropped into the chair.

"For the record, we did have security for you—"

"Mom. I don't care about the security anymore."

"I'm sorry, honey. We did have security, for both you girls, but yes, we gave Penny extra because we felt she needed it for her emotional state. But frankly, you never acted like you needed it. You were always so brave and calm and put together."

Tia stared at her. "I didn't feel like that."

"It seemed you were born that way. You stopped nursing at four months, learned how to walk at nine months. I thought I was raising a small adult rather than a little girl." She laughed.

Tia didn't. "I . . ."

Her mother reached out and touched her hand. "I'm very proud of you, Tia. Please don't hear anything but that."

Oh.

"And I'm so sorry that you came home with a broken heart."

Tia's breath caught. "What?"

"Oh, honey. I know you. You're always so . . . I don't know. Full of life and passion and determination. You have a strategy for everything. Except . . . Listen, I'm not sure you even showered that first week. Started to get a little rank."

"What? I showered!"

Her mother smiled. "Haven't you finish the entire twelve seasons of *Bones* in a month?"

"I have a little crush on Seeley Booth."

"Don't we all." Her mother got up, went to one of the cabinets. "Where does Annette keep the insulated water bottles?"

Tia got up and pulled out a drawer. Handed her a pink bottle. "Okay, yes, I might have . . . met someone in Mariposa."

Her mother took the water bottle. "And falling for him wasn't part of the plan."

"I didn't fall—"

"Please." She came over and leaned against the counter. "You broke up with Edward and two days later you went to a fundraiser that he was attending, and you acted as if . . . I just didn't see you spend a couple weeks in your pajamas after Edward. I think he was the easy answer."

Tia stared at her mother. "The *easy* answer? I loved him, Mother."

"Oh, I'm sure you did. A love that fit into your neat box, with all the right conditions and parameters. A love that felt safe and controlled and—"

"I *did* break up with him—because he loved someone else. I wasn't exactly in charge of his heart—"

"But you also asked him out first. And who wouldn't be wowed by you, Tia? You're a force of nature—a woman who knows her mind, who isn't afraid of anything."

"Oh, I'm plenty afraid, Mother."

She couldn't believe she'd said that, but—probably it was time to admit it aloud.

"I know you are, honey. That's why you always make a plan. And that makes you feel safe, and in control, and that's why whatever happened—*whoever* happened—in Mariposa totally shook you." She leaned in. "What, did he sweep you off your feet?"

Tia gaped at her. Then, "Maybe. Mostly he just . . . he just showed up. Whenever I needed him, Doyle was there. And even when I didn't need him. And he was . . . so impulsive. Just over-the-top. You have no idea."

"I think I do," her mother said quietly, winked. "That's the smile I've always wanted to see, the one you never had with Edward."

Tia shook her head, looked away. "It doesn't matter. He lost his true love on their wedding day, so—"

"Are you talking about Doyle Kingston?"

She looked at her mother and must have worn a look of surprise, because her mother leaned back, nodded. "I see."

"What do you see?"

"I met Doyle a couple years ago, at a fundraising event for Beacon of Compassion International. He was one of the team leaders for disaster relief. We sat at the same table. Such a nice man, but sort of quiet. Distant. I felt like he had a lot behind that smile. I asked later and heard about his fiancée dying. And then, of course, I met Conrad, and small world. This Doyle is the same man who swept you off your feet?"

"Stop saying that."

"It feels right."

"Mom."

She held up a hand. "I find it interesting that you both lost intendeds. It seems that you might understand each other better than most."

Tia closed her computer. "Except Juliet was his true love."

"You loved Edward. Maybe not the same way, but you lost a future too." Her mother stood up. "I am proud of you for saying no and waiting for your true love as you and your sister used to say."

"I don't think I'm Doyle's '*true love*,' Mom." She finger quoted the words. "Juliet was perfect for him. I'm . . . bossy and stubborn and—I just got him into trouble."

Her mother raised an eyebrow.

"Trust me, I drove the man crazy."

"You?"

"Mom."

"I'm just saying, I know you're perfectly capable of taking care of yourself, but maybe it's okay to find someone who steps between you and your desire to save yourself."

She had nothing, except for Doyle's voice in her head. *"Why, why, why are you so intent on getting yourself killed?"*

Oh, he was handsome when he was standing in her way.

Her mother's voice softened. "Darling. I loved Edward. But we both know that he didn't make your heart sing. He wasn't your One. You need someone who sees you the way God does—for the passionate, brave, determined woman you are—who stands up to you, and who makes you feel safe and cherished."

"Please, trust me."

Ugh, now he'd sat down in her brain. After she'd worked so hard to forget him.

Right.

"Has it occurred to you that God made you two for each other, knowing you'd need each other?"

She met her mother's gaze. "No, it hasn't."

A beat.

"Because?"

"Because God doesn't . . . He doesn't really . . . I mean, I'm not important to Him. He doesn't . . ."

"Oh, I see. You think because God rescued Penny, He's forgotten you?"

She lifted a shoulder.

"Darling. If you were the one sheep lost, He'd leave the rest to find you. He has not forgotten you."

"I just haven't ever, you know, wanted to need God. I just figured He wouldn't hear me even if I called out to Him."

"You really believe that?"

"I don't know."

"Interesting. Or maybe you just don't recognize when you have needed Him. Or called out to Him." She folded her arms. "God knows what you need even before you ask. We ask because that puts us in a place of surrender, even expectancy, watching for Him to show up. But He goes before us every single day, saving us from things we have no idea about. Because that's what love does."

Tia looked out the window. "And when He doesn't?"

"Then He's giving us the opportunity to need Him a different way. If you never have problems, you miss the grace of God showing up." She leaned back. "None of us want to be in the place where we are over our heads, when all we have is God, but frankly, it's the safest place to be."

She stood up. "If you really want to trust God, let Him be in charge of your heart. Love isn't safe. It's terrifying and freeing and—what was it?—oh. It sweeps you off your feet."

"Seriously." But Tia grinned.

Her mother winked. "I'm off to learn how to serve, again. Good luck on your presentation."

Her presentation. She checked her watch. *Oops.*

Forty minutes later, when Tia pulled up, Penny was waiting outside the café, dressed in a summer dress and sandals, wearing a jean jacket, texting. She looked up and grinned, her dark hair in a braid down her back. She looked tanned despite her too-many hours in an ice arena.

She gave Tia a hug.

"I've never been here," Tia said as Penny opened the door. Twinkle lights and café tables and a shelf of used books. The scent of baked cookies filled the room.

"Ironclad Desserts."

"I thought we were having lunch."

"We're having *inspiration.*" Penny walked to the counter, spoke to the server. "Hey, Marcie, I need a Peanut Butter Panache and a Twilight Temptation. As Conrad would put it—

stat."

The server laughed. "Coming right up, Penny."

Penny walked them over to a couple empty leather chairs by the window. "You can have a salad for dinner."

Tia sat down. "What's a Twilight Temptation?"

"Dark chocolate, espresso, black cocoa, raspberry ganache. I promise you, you'll be awake for your presentation. You ready?"

"I think so. Beacon of Compassion International is known for its big donations—"

"How big?"

"If I can get Dad to match it, maybe ten million?"

"Is that enough to build your medical clinic?"

"I think so. The one we currently have, attached to Hope House, isn't big enough, so we need to expand the one in Esperanza. I originally wanted three million, but after the landslide, we realized we needed to upgrade the trauma center and add a pediatric wing to the hospital . . . it's all in the proposal."

"And what comes next—you heading back to Mariposa?"

Marcie arrived with the cookies, warm and gooey, along with silverware. "Coffee?"

Penny nodded while Tia looked at the mound of chocolate. "I'll be awake for a week."

"Splitsies." Penny cut her peanut butter cookie in half.

They traded plates.

"Oh, no, this is . . . this is too good," Tia said.

"Right? Conrad likes to come here after games. When they win." Penny took a bite of the peanut butter. "Okay, and when they lose."

Tia laughed.

"So—are you heading back?"

Marcie delivered their coffee, and Tia picked up her cup. Sipped. "The coffee on the island is so strong that Rosa has to put sweetened condensed milk in it. It's amazing."

"I'm going to say that's a yes."

Tia shrugged. "I keep thinking about Gabriella, this amazing teenager who just needs someone to believe in her. And the Parnell twins, who I hope will be adopted—"

"And Doyle?"

She sighed. "I think Doyle . . ."

"Misses you too."

She met Penny's gaze. "I don't—"

"He's going back."

"What?"

"I was at Conrad's game a few days ago and heard that Doyle's talked to Declan about doing his residency in Mariposa."

Tia had nothing.

Especially when Penny stood up. "Don't kill me."

She walked away.

What—? Tia turned—

And there he was.

"Doyle?"

He wore a jean jacket, an oxford shirt, and . . . *a tie?* He'd shaved, his hair shorter than on the island yet still windblown, and wore a pair of aviator sunglasses that he took off and set on the table. Tanned, strong, those blue eyes on her and . . .

And if she'd ever wondered if she loved him . . . Her heart just exploded, right there, a mess of unruly, clumsy, inconvenient emotions.

Her true and perfect love.

She got up. And . . . managed to spill her gooey cookie plate right down the leg of her white linen pants.

"Oh no!"

He grabbed her shoulders. "Don't. move."

He bent down—*oh boy,* he smelled good, the kind of good that spoke of hot summer air and stirred up memories of his hand in her hair, his kiss on her skin—

"Okay, I think I got this. Very carefully, step away from the cookie."

He'd taken a knife and a napkin and plopped the cookie back

onto the plate. Then he held the hem of her pants and lifted the melted chocolate away.

"I think it's going to pull through." He set the plate on the table.

"The cookie?"

"Oh, no." He made a face. "I think that's done for. I was thinking of the pants. Unless you want to go No Pants to the presentation."

And just like that, the memory rose of her walking through Esperanza without pants. She started to laugh.

He grinned. "I'm thinking that isn't a bad idea. You do have excellent legs."

"Stop. I'm wearing pants." She leaned down and rolled up the cuffs. "I think I'll just have to improvise."

"Attagirl," he said.

And then silence dropped between them.

"How are—"

"Me first." He sighed. Nodded. Swallowed, then, "You were right, Tia. I did lose myself. And I was searching. And I thought you could fill that empty place. Instead, you helped me find myself again. Helped me see the man I thought I'd lost."

"That's great, Doyle."

He drew in a breath. "Tia, being with you showed me that I can trust God again. That there's more out there . . . for me." He swallowed. "For us."

Us?

Oh, Doyle—

She picked up her satchel. "I gotta go. I'm giving a presentation in about"—she checked her watch—"twenty minutes. It was nice to see—"

"I know about the presentation. Declan called me."

A beat.

She stared at him. *Wait . . .*

He raised an eyebrow. "Oh no. It looks like he didn't call you. Aw . . ."

"What? Are you—"

"I'm your copresenter. For the new Esperanza trauma center?"

She closed her eyes, looked away. "Of course you are."

"Listen." He took a step toward her.

Up close, his presence simply washed over her. She looked at him.

"We got this," he said, his blue eyes shining. Stupidly mesmerizing. "I'll tell a couple stories; you wow them with whatever slick PowerPoint you've come up with." He held up a fist.

Her heart had woken up, and suddenly everything spilled over, heat and hope and the sense that . . .

No, no . . . She shook her head. "I . . . I can't do this again. I can't fall into your world, let you sweep me away, Doyle. I can't be—"

"The One?" His grin had vanished, leaving only his gaze on hers.

She couldn't move. Except, softly, "What?"

"You're the One, Tia."

She drew in a breath, shook her head. "Doyle—"

"Hear me out." He reached out to touch her, then pulled back, his gaze earnest. "See—what I forgot is that God had a future for me already written out. He knew Juliet was going to die, and He knew I'd need someone who was . . . who is completely different from her, who could meet me where I'm at, who could push me and challenge me and make feel like I just might be enough for her too."

She opened her mouth. Closed it. Took a breath.

He lowered his voice, but she felt it rumble through her entire body. "I'm in love with you, Tia. So in love with you, and . . . please, just . . . take my hand. Let's go do this thing. And then do the next thing and . . . live happily ever after?"

His gaze reached out for hers, so much in it that she could nothing but—

Nod.

Oh no. Oh yes. She nodded.

The truth in her heart had just . . . taken over. It was impulsive. And yet perfect and right, and she had the sense then of . . . not being forgotten. Not being second place.

Being the One.

"Yes?" he said. He held out his hand.

"Yes," she said, and smiled. "Because I'm in love with you too, Doyle. And it scares me—"

"Because it wasn't planned."

"It's completely crazy."

He stepped up to her. "And yet entirely right."

She nodded again, and he was so close she could just lean . . . in . . .

"Attagirl," he whispered. Then he grabbed her hand, and she held on as he pulled her out of the Ironclad.

"What are you doing?" she said as he parked her under the awning next to the shop, in the shadows of the summer afternoon.

"This is a pre-presentation pep talk."

Oh?

And then he leaned in and kissed her. Sweetly, his hand around her neck, his thumb caressing her face, not rushed, not urgent, gentle and perfect and exactly the inspiration she needed.

He was impulse and safety and the future she hadn't known she needed until he'd shown up, and kept showing up, whether she asked him to or not.

Because that's what love did.

He lifted his head, his eyes meeting hers. "You are so beautiful, *Tia.* Just so we're clear."

She laughed. "We're clear."

"Good." He pulled away from her. "Presentation time. Let's do this, boss."

She laughed. "Codirector."

Meet Austen, a shark specialist who finds adventure, danger, and romance on the high seas...

Book 4 in the Minnesota Kingston series by USA Today bestselling author Susan May Warren.

His secrets could get them killed...

Austen Kingston isn't impressed with Mr. Billionaire, Declan Stone. Sure, he's handsome, and has a generous heart, but she is happy with her life as a treasure hunter-slash shark diver. Besides, she's seen what wealth can do to someone...no thank you.

Except, a routine dive turns treacherous, and she finds herself in need of rescue...

Billionaire Declan Stone can't stop thinking about the beautiful woman who led his dive team, and frankly, she seems just the kind of woman who isn't afraid of danger (hello, shark diver!) The last thing he expects is to find her adrift in the middle of the Caribbean...

What she doesn't know that while Declan appears to be just another wealthy philanthropist, he's also living a double life...one that could cost him everything. And the last thing he needs is the woman he's come to care for in the middle of the crosshairs...

But what's he going to do—leave her adrift at sea?

More...when Austen discovers who he really is, can she fall for a guy whose life means danger?

When his shell game against the Russians backfires, Austen and Declan must survive being lost at sea, dodge international hitmen, and expose a deadly conspiracy.

With time running out and enemies closing in, can they trust each other enough to survive? Or will the secrets they keep drag them both into the depths of betrayal?

Dive into this closed-door, survival, forced proximity romantic suspense, perfect for readers who love their romance with a side of heart-stopping action.

SNEAK PEEK

RULE NUMBER ONE: DON'T RUN AWAY FROM the shark.

Of course, when Austen said exactly that to her two dive clients, they stared at her as if she'd told them to stand in front of a moving freight train.

"Listen. You panic, you start splashing and swimming away--you become prey." She'd been checking their tank connections and opening the air valves as she said it.

Elise Jameson sat on the seat of the dive boat, holding on as the private charter banged through the waves. Spray coated the deck, but it landed warm, refreshing, the sun high as it baked the cloudless day.

It would be a perfect day to dive the *USNS Vandenberg,* seven miles off the coast of Key West. The waters glistened a deep blue, and the sun's rays just might reach all the way to the massive sunken ship, some ten stories tall, over five hundred feet long, and settled into the sandy bottom at one hundred forty-five feet.

The artificial coral-reef habitat of moray eels, green turtles, stingrays, barracuda, and, of course . . . sharks.

Mostly nurse sharks and nonaggressive reef sharks, but okay, occasionally Austen had seen a tiger shark snoozing in the shadows of the upper decks.

Hence the warning.

"I heard you should just hit them on the nose." This from Hunter Jameson, Elise's husband and a seasoned diver, so yeah, Austen might have guessed he'd heard that.

She pulled on her BCD and tank, strapping them on and reaching for her mask. "If they get that close, it might be too late."

The boat slowed, and she reached out to steady herself, glancing back at Hawkeye, who stood at the center console, under the Bimini, his hat on backward, wearing aviator sunglasses, sporting a tan against his white Ocean Adventure Divers swim shirt.

He pointed, and she followed his gaze to the dive buoy, an orange floating ball onto which Hawk would moor his forty-foot dive skiff. The divers would follow the line down, sink into the quiet, and . . .

And she'd be flying. It happened every time she dove. As she descended, the ocean turned into the sky, and even as she swam through schools of fish, somehow the world dropped away into peace, only her heartbeat and her rhythmic, slow breathing tethering her to reality.

For those brief moments, she was free.

She turned to Hunter. "Just follow me, and should we startle anything down there, remember these rules: Don't panic, maintain eye contact, and back away slowly. Feel free to shout through your regulator, to blow out bubbles, but don't thrash. Even better—tuck your hands under your armpits. Your gloves can reflect light and look like fish so—"

She stopped talking at Elise's wide-eyed look. She held up her hands. "Listen. This is a great dive. The ship is covered in barnacles and green and yellow algae, with coral already growing in areas. It'll be inhabited by all sorts of fish. We might even see a goliath grouper, and definitely parrotfish and angelfish, lionfish, maybe silvery tarpons, and hopefully, Millie our resident loggerhead." She pulled on her mask. "Just stay with me. I promise—I'll keep you safe."

Then she sat on the edge of the boat and backrolled into the water.

Promises, promises.

She'd seen Hunter and Elise dive before—they knew how to handle themselves in the water. And Hunter had been in the military, so he didn't seem like a guy prone to panic.

They descended the line, no problem, and Austen had called it—the light pierced the depths even this far, although she needed her dive light to illuminate the inner passageways of the ship.

The first time Austen dove the former transport ship, the length had shaken her. The second largest intentionally sunken dive ship in the world, it stood ten stories tall, with nooks and crannies and stairwells and compartments. But she'd dived the wreck for the better part of the last four years, so she easily guided them along the upper deck, then down a stairwell to the mess hall, where a bright green eel emerged from the empty burners of the large rusty stove.

They watched a parrotfish scrape algae from a bloom on a railing, the crunch echoing in the depths. And Millie rose from one of her favorite spots under an anchor winch on the bow, paddled into the current with her flat oar arms.

Hey, Flash, Austen wanted to say as Millie struck out for the great beyond. *Wait for me.*

Austen checked her time—thirteen minutes down. Four more minutes and they'd head up. Time enough for a quick trip to the satellite dishes.

Rule number two: Keep your eyes on the shark.

It might have helped if she'd seen it lurking, but she'd already swum through the spokes of the satellite array.

Not until she turned did Austen see Elise at the bottom, her tank hooked on the array.

In all her attempts to break free, she'd kicked up dust and splashes and . . . yep, awakened a tiger shark sleeping in one of the superstructure sublevels.

It edged out, curious.

Hunter swam down to help his wife, and the two got jammed up in one of the spokes. Worse, Elise's mask had dislodged and she struggled to clear it.

So she was clearly not watching the predator as he circled.

When the shark darted in and veered off, Austen knew she had to engage. She swam down, outside the satellite, reaching back for her tank tapper, the metal ball strapped on a band that encircled her tank. The tapping might scare him away.

Nope. He circled just below them, then darted in again.

Elise had broken free, her mask on but still half-filled with water, in full-out panic as she swatted and kicked away.

No—stop!

The tiger shark jerked away, but Elise's movement only fueled his curiosity.

Austen grabbed Elise's hands. Shook her head. Glanced at Hunter.

He got it, nodding, and took Elise's hands. She struggled, but Hunter gripped her BCD, stilling her.

Of all the places to have a panic attack, a hundred feet down on the ocean floor might be the worst.

Stay calm. Austen tried to communicate with her eyes while also looking for the tiger.

Go down. She pointed to the upper deck of the structure, flattened her hand, and indicated that they should sink down to the platform.

Sharks typically attacked from behind or below—

Hunter pointed behind her, his eyes wide.

Austen turned, and *yep,* he'd come in for another look-see.

A shout filled her regulator. The sound echoed in her head, but it might startle the shark. Then she blew out hard—bubbles rising around her.

The shark jerked away some six feet from her.

Glancing down, she spotted Hunter and Elise on the platform, also blowing bubbles. Hunter had put himself in front of Elise—*sweet*—and pulled out his dive knife.

Okay, everybody calm down.

Austen sank down to them, held up her hand, shook her head. Indicated that Hunter should put the knife away. But he shook his head and she turned. *Oh no.* The tiger wanted a taste.

Most likely it was just very, very curious about these erratic seals. But she faced him, stayed vertical, and despite the thundering of her heart, she kept her eyes on the animal and Didn't. Move.

At the very least, the tiger wanted a bump, but she put her arm out, kept her elbow stiff, and caught it on the snout.

It had opened its mouth, but she deflected it even as it started to roll.

She pushed with her other hand, moving herself away from the shark.

It darted away, probably a little stunned. Hunter was right about the snout being sensitive, but she hadn't hurt it.

The shark swam around the end of the superstructure as if retreating. Her watch beeped, a tiny shrill in the depths. Austen gestured toward the line leading to the surface, and Hunter grabbed his wife's hand.

Turning her back to them, Austen searched for the shark as she grabbed the thick rope with her glove. Then she let out the air in her BCD and started to ascend. Twenty feet from the ship, a dark shadow still circled the superstructure. She didn't take her gaze from the shark as they rose to their deep deco stop at fifty feet. Her dive watch settled into a three-minute countdown and she searched the water.

So much for flying. She hung here like bait, waiting, the outline of the ship below.

A shadow in her periphery caught her eye and she glanced over. Stilled.

A barracuda. Long and silvery, but not a threat as long as No. One. Panicked.

Her timer beeped, and they ascended up the line to their fifteen-foot safety stop. From here, the white hull of the boat dipped in the water, and Hawkeye had already put down the ladder.

Elise seemed to have calmed, but Austen's gaze swept the depths, her breaths hard. A glance at her O2 levels said her tank had emptied faster than usual. *Well, no duh.*

The alarm dinged and Elise shot to the surface, Hunter behind her. Austen hung on the line, floating up slowly, watching.

Elise pulled off her fins, unsnapped her BCD and let her tank float in the water. From above, Hawkeye fished it out of the drink.

Hunter did the same, disappearing next, and Austen was just reaching for the ladder when she spotted him.

Tiger, back, and maybe angry.

He darted from the depths, hot for the surface, probably attracted by the splashing. She kept her eyes on him, her hand on the ladder, her heartbeat in her throat.

Stay calm.

She put him at a good eight feet, so not the monster great whites she'd seen in Hawaii, but big enough to inflict damage.

She preferred to keep all her appendages.

There was shouting above her, but she sank in the water and put the ladder between her and the tiger.

Then she hung below it, waiting.

He came at her faster than mere curiosity would explain but not in full attack, so maybe intending to bump her again. She hung onto the ladder with one hand and set her other cupped hand on his snout. He reared up, and she rode with him, her elbow stiff.

Her hand dislodged. But she flipped above him, moving over him, and pushed him away. He shook his tail fin and darted away.

She chucked off her fins and dove for the ladder. Scrambled up, still wearing her vest.

Hands grabbed her and hauled her onto the boat, dumping her into the bottom.

A splash and a scream, and she guessed the tiger shark had found a fin still floating in the water. She unsnapped her BCD, then rolled out of it and lay, breathing hard, the sun hot on her dive skin.

"You okay?" Hawkeye stood over her, then picked up her vest and set it in the rack at the back of the boat.

"That just might have been the bravest thing I've ever seen," Hunter said.

She pressed her hands over her face. Closed her eyes.

There was a vast difference between bravery and desperation.

She finally scrubbed away the shaking and sat up against the side of the boat. "Anybody see my fins?"

"Sorry, Austen. I think they're at the bottom." Hawkeye had started the boat, probably not wanting to stick around.

She scooted up to the bench, the adrenaline still ripping through her.

"Wow. That was . . ." Elise wiped her hands across her face, clearing more tears than saltwater. "Thank you."

Austen held up her hand, nodded. "It's my job."

Hunter shook his head. "Declan said that you were some sort of shark expert, but I didn't . . . I guess I thought it was a euphemism."

Declan. The urge to ask about the philanthropist rose inside her. He'd hired her to lead a dive expedition for his big charity event earlier this summer on the island of Mariposa and she'd thought . . .

Well, she'd been a little stupid, really. The man had the body of Henry Cavill, not to mention the jawline, and his dark-gray eyes could turn the ground under a woman to sand. Clearly, all the sunshine and seafood—not to mention how he'd handled unexpected trauma—had gone straight to her sun-bleached head. Plus, the man helped fund an orphanage while managing to run a large tech firm. According to her sister, Boo, he was worth billions.

So there was that, too.

She hadn't heard a word from him since she returned to Key West. Probably because she'd just been the hired help. *Hello.*

Still, if she'd known how uber-wealthy he was, she might have given him the same stiff-arm she'd given the tiger shark.

Austen picked up a towel and started to dry her hair. "I studied shark behavior for two years in Hawaii. I was on a shark preservation and tagging team." Hawkeye had picked up speed and she turned her back to the setting sun. Her stomach growled.

"Dinner is on us," Hunter said. "We have reservations at Latitudes. I'm sure they'll let us add another person."

She held up her hand. "No, I'm good. I'm heading out for a week of vacation tomorrow and I need an early night." In the distance, the city of Key West edged the horizon, the ocean a vivid aquamarine.

"Oh, Declan will be sad to miss you."

Declan?

"He's picking us up on his yacht in a couple days."

The bait just hung there, and she couldn't resist. "Really? Why aren't you flying in? My brother Doyle is on his way back to the orphanage on a seaplane."

"The airfield is still torn up on the island, and Declan's chopper is being used to shuttle supplies back and forth from St. Kitts. And"—Hunter glanced at his wife—"one of us isn't a fan of small planes."

"I've tried the patch. I just can't make it work," Elise said. "We had an ugly incident over Denali once." She made a face. "Thankfully, Dec offered to pick us up."

Huh. Austen shouldn't immediately assume it was because they were massive donors. Declan wasn't like that.

But who was she kidding? He was probably just like every other billionaire. Still, she drew up a knee, wrapped her arms around it. "How is he?"

Elise had grabbed a towel, worked it through her dark hair, turning it curly. Petite and sweet, she and Hunter had been among Declan's guests during the charity-event-turned-earthquake trauma. "Good. He set up the court date for us to adopt Jamal and Kemar from the island, which after the landslide was no small feat. I think he wants to get them out of there and into their new lives as soon as possible. We already had our home study done, so . . ." She reached for Hunter's hand. "We're very excited to bring the boys home."

Austen had met the two boys during her stay. Jamal and his older brother, Kemar. "They're very blessed."

"Oh no. We're the ones who are blessed." Hunter wrapped his arm around Elise. "We've been waiting so long for a family . . . It hardly feels real."

Elise nodded, wrapped her hand into his.

"It's like being set free from a long prison sentence," Hunter said. "I'd sort of given up."

"Not me," Elise said. "I knew God had a family for us. We just needed to wait for it." She turned to Austen. "You know the saying—'a longing fulfilled is a tree of life.'"

Huh. Austen nodded as the boat hit a wave, thanks to a catamaran flying past them, and water sprayed them.

Elise laughed.

So apparently they were over their scare from the depths of the sea.

"Where are you going on your vacation?" Hunter asked as they slowed, moving toward the green buoys.

"Oh. Um . . . I'll be doing some diving off Sosúa, in the Dominican Republic."

"Dominican Republic?" Hunter said. "We dove the *Zingara* wreck there a few years ago."

"That's not the wreck she's diving," said Hawkeye as he cut the motor. They were puttering into the Key West Bight harbor. "She's looking for the *San Miguel,* a Spanish ship that went down in 1551."

She made a face. "No, I'm not looking for the ship."

"Okay, Spanish gold, then." Hawkeye's mouth tightened around the edges.

"What's that face for?"

"It's the middle of pirate country," Hawkeye said as they turned into their canal.. "Right off Haiti."

"Calm down," Austen said. "My boat is hardly a yacht worth attacking. And I'm not looking for Aztec gold." She stood up. "I'm looking for the statue of Santa María de la Paz." She picked up the rope, ready to catch the dock. "It's a sixteenth-century statue of the Black Madonna, about three feet tall, inlaid with pearls and rubies, sent by the King of Spain to a monastery on the island of Hispaniola—a.k.a., DR. It was sculpted by Diego de la Piedra, one of the king's private artists. He died shortly after he sent the statue to Hispaniola, so it's a one of a kind. The *San Miguel* went down on the Silver Bank after breaking up on coral in a storm. A few relics from the wreck have been recovered, but not the statue." She jumped onto the dock and wrapped the mooring rope around a dock post.

"And you hope to be the one to find this statue?" Hunter got up.

Hope might be a strong word.

"It's just a vacation." She jumped back into the boat and headed to the back to unrig the gear.

"Sounds like a job for Ethan Pike." Hunter gathered up their gear. Elise had already climbed out of the boat.

"The treasure hunter? No. I'm not looking to get rich."

She just wanted . . . *Aw, shoot.*

She stood, her gaze landing on a man standing at the end of the pier, long blond hair held back in a bun, wearing shorts and a tank. *Mo.*

And with him . . . *Oh boy.* Built like the ex-SEAL he was, dark blond hair, sunglasses, and not appearing at all like he'd taken a bullet to his chest a couple months ago.

"Is that your brother with Mo Winters?" Hawkeye had hoisted the BCDs onto the dock.

She sighed. "Yes. Yes it is."

So much for escaping town.

"Right. I forgot what the date was," Hawkeye said quietly as he unhooked another BCD from its tank.

Yep.

Mo and Stein headed her direction.

Hunter had gotten out. "Thanks again, Austen. Have fun on your trip. Should I say hi to Declan for you?"

While she debated her answer, her twin brother walked up, took off his sunglasses, held out his hand to Hunter, and said, "No. You most certainly shouldn't."

Then, even as he shook Hunter's hand, he glanced at Austen, his mouth grim, a definite we've-got-trouble expression on his face.

And she had the strangest urge to turn around and run.

Note to Reader

Thanks for diving into Doyle's story! I hope you enjoyed watching our strong-willed rivals find love amidst the chaos of Mariposa as much as I loved writing them.

There's plenty more adventure ahead—two more books to be exact! So stick around for more island intrigue, heart-pounding action, and unforgettable romance.

If Doyle and Tia's journey from enemies to soulmates touched your heart, would you consider leaving a review? Even a quick note helps other readers discover their story (just keep those earthquake surprises under wraps!).

Enormous gratitude to my dream team. To my editor, Anne Horch—your insights make these adventures truly shine.

Special thanks to Rel Mollet—your keen eye for detail and masterful organization keeps our ship running smoothly. You're the anchor that holds everything together, and I'm deeply grateful for your dedication.

Heartfelt thanks to my brainstorming crew, Rachel Hauck and Sarah Erredge, who never fail to help navigate plot challenges.

To my husband, Andrew, my personal consultant on everything from earthquake safety to how to hotwire a car. I choose you for my adventure buddy.

Kudos to Emilie Haney for creating covers as thrilling as the stories within, and to Tari Faris for crafting beautiful interiors.

Thanks, Katie Donovan, for your razor-sharp proofreading, especially during those tight deadlines.

To my wonderful readers—thank you for bringing these adventures into your lives. I hope you find both excitement and inspiration in these pages. Share your thoughts or wishes for future stories at susan@susanmaywarren.com.

For exclusive content, behind-the-scenes peeks, and latest updates, join my newsletter at susanmaywarren.com, or scan the QR code below.

Get ready for the next wave—Austen's adventure is coming soon!

About the Author

With over 100 books published and nearly 2 million books sold, critically acclaimed novelist **Susan May Warren** is the Christy, RITA, and Carol award-winning author of over ninety-five novels with Revell, Tyndale, Barbour, Steeple Hill, and Summerside Press. Known for her compelling plots and unforgettable characters, Susan has written contemporary and historical romances, romantic-suspense, thrillers, rom-com, and Christmas novellas.

With books translated into eight languages, many of her novels have been ECPA and CBA bestsellers, were chosen as Top Picks by Romantic Times, and have won the RWA's Inspirational Reader's Choice contest and the American Christian Fiction Writers Book of the Year award. She's a three-time RITA finalist and an eight-time Christy finalist.

Publishers Weekly has written of her books, "Warren lays bare her characters' human frailties, including fear, grief, and resentment, as openly as she details their virtues of love, devotion, and resiliency. She has crafted an engaging tale of romance, rivalry, and the power of forgiveness." Library Journal adds, "Warren's characters are well-developed and she knows how to create a first rate contemporary romance..."

Susan is also a nationally acclaimed writing coach, teaching at conferences around the nation, and winner of the 2009 American Christian Fiction Writers Mentor of the Year award. She loves to help people launch their writing careers. She is the founder of www.MyBookTherapy.com and www.learnhowtowriteanovel.com, a writing website that helps authors get published and stay published. She is also the author of the popular writing method The Story Equation.

Find excerpts, reviews, and a printable list of her novels at www.susanmaywarren.com and connect with her on social media.

Yeah, those Marshalls...

what have they got themselves into this time?

THE MINNESOTA MARSHALLS

SUSAN MAY WARREN

susanmaywarren.com

Available on Amazon and at susanmaywarrenfiction.myshopify.com!

Susan May WARREN

Over the years, writing has become, for me, a way to praise God and see Him at work in my life. My hope is that readers will be blessed and encouraged by soul-stirring stories of regular people interacting with a God who loves them.

If you're interested, sign up for my newsletter, a weekly sneak peek into my life and upcoming releases! Thank you for your interest and support.

SusanMayWarren

SCAN to sign up for the newsletter!

FOLLOW Susie May on social media!

@susanmaywarren

More Books by Susan May Warren

Most recent to the beginning of the epic lineup, in reading order.

The Minnesota Kingstons

Jack
Conrad
Doyle
Austen
Steinbeck

Alaska Air One Rescue

One Last Shot
One Last Chance
One Last Promise
One Last Stand

The Minnesota Marshalls

Fraser
Jonas
Ned
Iris
Creed

The Epic Story of RJ and York

Out of the Night
I Will Find You
No Matter the Cost

Sky King Ranch

Sunrise
Sunburst
Sundown

Global Search And Rescue

The Way of the Brave
The Heart of a Hero
The Price of Valor

The Montana Marshalls

Knox
Tate
Ford
Wyatt
Ruby Jane

Montana Rescue

If Ever I Would Leave You (novella prequel)
Wild Montana Skies
Rescue Me
A Matter of Trust
Crossfire (novella)
Troubled Waters
Storm Front
Wait for Me

Montana Fire

Where There's Smoke (Summer of Fire)
Playing with Fire (Summer of Fire)
Burnin' For You (Summer of Fire)
Oh, The Weather Outside is Frightful (Christmas novella)
I'll be There (Montana Fire/Deep Haven crossover)
Light My Fire (Summer of the Burning Sky)
The Heat is On (Summer of the Burning Sky)
Some Like it Hot (Summer of the Burning Sky)
You Don't Have to Be a Star (Montana Fire spin-off)

The True Lies of Rembrandt Stone

Cast the First Stone
No Unturned Stone
Sticks and Stone
Set in Stone
Blood from a Stone
Heart of Stone

A complete list of Susan's novels can be found at
susanmaywarren.com/novels/bibliography/.

Made in the USA
Monee, IL
10 June 2025